Tom McMullen reserves all rights to be identified as the author of this work. No copy in any format may be reproduced without prior permission of the author.

Other books by the author:

A Cheyenne Trilogy - Between the Rivers (2015, Amazon)

Only the Earth Shall Last:

The Second Cheyenne Trilogy

By

Tom McMullen

Preface

The Cheyenne were one of the great horsed, fighting tribes on the Great Plains of the United States of America during the nineteenth Century. Never as numerous as the Sioux, they were still held in high regard by other Plains tribes as well as the westward-moving whites who traded and fought with them.

My first book ('A Cheyenne Trilogy; Between the Rivers' – Amazon Kindle Direct Publishing, 2015) followed the fortunes of a small band of *Suhtai* Cheyenne as they struggled against nature, enemies and inescapable white encroachment into their sacred country. It ends after the real Battle of the Solomon Fork in July 1857. This second trilogy takes up the story.

As before, this book has fictional characters set against a real cultural background. Some of the tribal structures and ceremonies are fictional though they are taken from the mould of reality. The events that provide a chronological and historical framework are mainly true and well documented.

I take full responsibility for any mistakes or cultural shortcoming encountered in the story.

Tom McMullen
Cumbria
England
2019

BOOK ONE

*Be brave,
We are but dust.
Only the earth shall last.*

(Warriors' exhortation before battle)

Chapter One

See the Dark took out his left eye and washed it in the river. When he did this, he was always careful not to expose the empty flesh socket to others; the gaping hole in his head was a sign that he was different and, in a silent admission to himself, when the eye was out, he never felt complete as a man.

He called it his 'eye' but, in truth, it was a globe of polished black stone with an etched picture of a deer on it – he always liked the deer to face outwards when the eye was back in his head. Dark liked the weight of the stone in his skull; it gave his face some shape and prevented the muscles on his left cheek from sagging.

The river water ran cloudy here and tasted of soapstone but, in this high summer on the grasslands, the eye needed to be cleaned. He caged the stone globe in his fingers and ran it through the listless stream, brushing off weed fronds as they tried to cling to the bright black surface.

Viajero sat on his pony watching the young Cheyenne's ritual; the boy always turned his back and hid his face at these times. It was a strange habit but one that Viajero respected. He rested his rifle on his thigh and held the reins of his friend's horse as it nibbled the dry grass; he just wished that Dark would finish quickly.

Shapes drifted across the sun, shadows flitting and side-slipping across the ground; Viajero looked up - vultures wheeled in the sky above them and he shifted nervously in the saddle. Birds of prey always gave away positions and the white pony soldiers couldn't be far away.

Dark now put his head closer to the water's edge, scooped some of the cloudy liquid in his palm and splashed it into his eye socket, rinsing out the troublesome grit and small flies that blew in when the wind was in his face. He dried off the empty eyelids with a soft deerskin cloth, overcoming the usual feeling of oddness as his fingertips probed inside his own head. Then, making sure that there was water enough on the stone, he slipped it back into the leathery fissure.

Out of habit, See the Dark checked his appearance in the water, adjusting the eye until the deer shape faced outwards. He nodded in approval.

"You are as vain as a girl!" Viajero called out as the young man walked back to his pony.

"Well, it was a good of you to give me the stone…" said Dark, "…though, it now serves a nobler purpose in the head of a handsome, young Cheyenne warrior rather than being carried around the wrinkled neck of an old man of the N'De."

Viajero's snorted at the boy's impudence – old? Ten or twelve summers older than Dark, perhaps – no more than that. Viajero's knowledge of the Cheyenne tongue was improving but he still had to pause and sort out the alien words in his head before he could understand what was being said.

Dark laughed at the Apache's feigned annoyance as he took the reins and climbed back into the saddle. Then, suddenly sombre, both men got back to their unpleasant task.

The stench hit them first as they nudged their ponies forward, the horses snickering and skittering sideways as the unsettling scent of meat rotting in the midday sun touched their nostrils. There was another smell too – wolves were close.

Dark and Viajero brought their mounts back under control, letting their ponies pick a careful path through the discarded lodge poles and *tipi* skins of the recently abandoned Cheyenne camp.

The younger man felt the prick of tears in his good eye at the disgrace of the sight; almost the entire Cheyenne nation had gathered here in a colourful, noisy mass before going off to meet the threat of the bluecoat column. Now squawking clouds of ravens and vultures rose from the chaos of the deserted camp ground. The place reeked - not just of spoiled food but, also, of defeat.

Two wolves on top of a raised mound were tearing at the carcass of an abandoned colt; they looked up briefly as the two men rode in but continued to rip at the skin and flesh, their grey muzzles red from the unexpected feast. The warriors reined their horses' heads away from the sight to keep them calm.

Dark's pony sneezed in the rising dust; the summer sun had leached all the moisture from the ground and a light breeze blew eddies of soft earth into twirling columns the height of a man. Dark watched them – none of his Cheyenne kin had died at the camp but it was as if ghosts already walked here.

"Our People left in a hurry – the main trail leads south towards the Flint Arrowpoint River– it'll be hard to find our families," he said, leaning down from the saddle and inspecting the churned earth. He rode around the circles of flattened grass and earth where the lodges of his own *Suhtai* band had stood in their allotted tribal place - a couple of stray ponies drank at the river and dogs, left behind in the panic of the move, scoured the remaining meat drying racks, balancing on hind legs to snap at pieces just out of reach.

Viajero hadn't heard him; he'd dismounted and was staring at the dust.

"The trail is over two days old. I'm glad that Bad Elk sent our kin away first but all these later tracks have covered up the ones we want to follow." he said. He looked over his shoulder at Dark. The boy still sat on his pony and seemed to be deep in thought. He knew what the boy was thinking but they needed to get moving.

"Yellow Bear's dreams had great power – he was brave to speak out" said the Apache and stood up.

Dark nodded and reined his pony towards the river; the water wasn't good but horses could drink it. The young warrior dismounted but stayed silent - the feeling of disgrace in his gut wouldn't go away; the Cheyenne war bands had been defeated in battle by the white pony soldiers two days ago and Yellow Bear, the *Suhtai* medicine man, had foretold it.

But this was no time for regrets - See the Dark just shrugged and looked around the campsite. It had lost its meaning as his home; now it was just an opportunity to scavenge to survive – before the whites arrived to burn or spoil it all.

"We'll need food for the journey" he said picking up a couple of *parfleches* of buffalo meat and tying them across his saddle. His pony whickered in complaint at the extra weight of the full rawhide pouches.

Viajero just grunted and sniffed inside an open food bag; packrats had been inside, eaten their fill and scattered their droppings. He would eat almost anything but plenty of food lay around and he went to seek better fare. An abandoned brindled bitch and a new litter of pups followed him hopefully, the young ones yipping and tottering on outsized paws. On a nearby ridge he could see a pack of wolves trotting towards the camp, homing in on the rising scent of the putrefying meat.

"Hoh!"

The shout was a loud one from the far end of the desolate village and it made Viajero and Dark look up in surprise. The two wolves feasting on the colt ran off a short distance but skulked in the sage brush, ready to go back to their meal. The advancing wolf pack stopped some distance off and lay around their panting leader to watch this new threat.

Viajero swung his rifle up into the aim and See the Dark pulled his gun from the saddle bucket; both pointed their weapons in the direction of the noise. They stood behind their ponies, rifles resting on the saddle seats – ready to mount and ride off if danger was close.

Out of the space between those lodges still standing stepped a fully-painted Cheyenne Dog Soldier, his pony walking behind him nuzzling at the poor grazing at the village edge. Dark wondered how long he had been there and was embarrassed at not seeing him arrive. The Dog Soldier stood and stared.

"My brother," he said eventually, looking at See the Dark. "We seem to be doing the same thing."

The Dog Soldier then caught sight of Viajero and hefted his own flintlock pistol out of his belt; the dark-skinned warrior wore no feathers, just a cloth headband, and didn't seem to be Cheyenne though the youth obviously was. The older, darker man seemed to have been wearing war paint and hadn't washed it off properly. He looked fierce and troublesome.

See the Dark walked around his pony and put the rifle back into its rawhide sleeve. The Dog Soldier started in surprise when he saw the black slash of Dark's ornamental eye but, out of politeness, did not mention it. He put his pistol back into his belt and tried to relax; though, getting a better look at the dark skinned one and the strange medicine of the stone-eyed youth, his relaxation wasn't total.

There was a moment of silence as each side assessed the other; a hawk wheeled in the pure blue sky.

"Were you in the fight with the soldiers up on Turkeys Creek?" asked the Dog Soldier eventually.

Dark nodded but offered no more information.

"And him?" he gestured towards Viajero. "Is he your slave?"

"I am not a slave," growled Viajero "I am a man of the N'De and I understand the Cheyenne tongue." Viajero kept his rifle trained on the painted warrior.

See the Dark smiled as he saw the Dog Soldier nervously reach out and test his saddle; the Dog Man was obviously disturbed by the sight of Viajero and the menace of the aimed gun. The Dog Soldier would probably not have met a man of the N'De before and, despite the need to escape the oncoming whites, Dark sensed an opportunity for some light goading. It would do these smooth, overpainted ones good to show respect to the Suhtai.

"We are just gathering food before we go and find our families," he explained.

"And me," said the Dog Soldier. "But I have just ridden from the north; the bluecoat Indian scouts are not far away, looking for this village."

Neither man mentioned the defeat of their nation two days ago; it was still too raw.

"Thank you for the information," said Dark, "We'll sleep away from here then head south."

The Dog Soldier nodded. "My family has gone back to the Red Shield River so I'll head west then swing north."

See the Dark had an afterthought: "Did you manage to wash in the magic lake before the soldier fight?"

"Yes" replied the Dog Soldier. "It made me feel strong and ready for battle. I wiped some of the water onto my pony so he could be strong too."

"Well, it didn't do us much good," replied Dark rudely, "the whites still whipped us."

Yellow Bear had prophesied that the water of the magic lake would not stop the bullets of the whites and he'd been right.

Viajero hissed through his teeth at the boy's inability to hold his tongue; unaccountably, he felt a twinge of sympathy for the Dog Soldier but kept his rifle barrel trained on him anyway.

The Dog Soldier looked sharply at See the Dark but refrained from an angry outburst – he was a mature warrior and would behave accordingly. So, he turned and took some drying elk meat from the frame outside a well-decorated lodge that was still standing. It was a big tipi – plenty of room for the large family of a wealthy man.

Dark watched him closely. Despite the man's war paint giving him a face that all enemies would fear, the Dog Soldier looked sad. He stroked the hides on the side of the lodge as if remembering something. His hand ran over the painted images of an eagle and a bear, the marks of a powerful owner.

"Was that your tipi?" asked Dark, trying to lessen the effect of his sarcasm.

"My father's" replied the Dog Soldier "My mother would have hated to leave this behind."

Dark nodded in agreement; it was not the right time to boast of Bad Elk's wisdom in getting his own group of families to pack up and leave early. See the Dark's people, at least, had shelter and food – unlike the rest of their kin.

The Dog Soldier put a head noose on an abandoned pony nuzzling at the brown grass and began loading it with meat from the drying racks. He looked across at See the Dark as though he'd remembered something; something he'd just recalled from the stories told at the many campfires of their large village:

"You are from the Suhtai band?"

"Yes" said Dark, a hint of caution in his voice.

"I hear that your women fight alongside you" said the Dog Soldier conversationally as he looked around for some sinew rope to tie the bundles of dried meat together. There was an edge of derision and disbelief to the Dog Soldier's tone and Dark resented it. But now it was his turn to be calm and polite; his moment would come.

"They didn't fight with us against the bluecoats but they have done in the past," said Dark. "They have their own soldier society. They went with us on a raid against the Pawnee last winter …"

The Dog Soldier raised his head and looked at Dark, as if absorbing some important new facts. Even under the Dog Man's mask of battle paint, Dark could see that he had a smirk on his face. He was probing him for a reaction.

See the Dark watched as the stranger slashed and pulled at some lashings on an abandoned pack saddle and then looked at Viajero who tilted his head towards the Dog Soldier, inspiring Dark to embellish the story.

"…our women did well and ran off the horse herd" Dark added with some pride.

He struggled to keep his tone flat but he was proud of the Forked Lightning Women soldiers; more so, as his own woman, White Rain was their leader. He decided to keep this fact to himself. The stranger's tone was irritating and it was annoying to see him still wearing his full paint, as though they had been victorious against the *vehoe*. Now it was time to annoy the Dog Soldier:

"Don't your women ever fill saddles on war ponies?"

The Dog Soldier looked genuinely astonished:

"Never! Our rituals are far too sacred for women to take part." The man's voice rose up a tone and he sounded slightly rattled; Dark was pleased.

"Ah" said Dark. "Ours have their own rituals and helped us kill many Pawnee on our revenge raid; I have often said that we Suhtai are very advanced in our thinking."

He knew that the part about the women killing many Pawnee had not been strictly true, though White Rain Woman herself had killed at least two warriors before being unhorsed in the mad gallop through the Pawnee villages on the Loup River. And, though he would never admit this to the Dog Man, the Forked Lightning Women had since become annoying in giving their unwanted opinions; they now seemed to think that they were free to criticise anything and everything. It was a worrying departure from tradition.

"But what about their bleeding time? We men can be contaminated and our protecting spirits can desert us." The Dog Soldier sounded even more rattled and petulant; women on the battlefield were incomprehensible to him.

"Our women know that" snorted Dark. "We made them promise before the Pawnee fight that if that time came, they would leave us alone."

The Dog Soldier stared; he looked impressed - but only slightly. Dark pressed his advantage:

"We Suhtai, as the original people of the Cheyenne, have always seen ourselves as bold thinkers. That is why we have powerful allies from far away..."

He gestured at Viajero. He omitted to say that the Apache was the *only* ally from far away but the Dog Man didn't need to know that.

The irritated warrior said nothing but shook his head in disbelief. Those Suhtai were always a cocky bunch – for ever laying claim to be the founders of his beloved People. Their harsh accent grated on the ear of other Cheyennes. He tightened the cinch on his saddle, tied down the loose and ragged bundles of dried meat on the spare pony and remounted. He had time for one more insult:

"Your families left the sacred circle early; perhaps it was the disloyalty of the Suhtai and their powerful allies that lost us the battle."

Viajero, who usually got bored with any long conversation in his second language, caught the Dog Soldier's remarks and butted in:

"No. Your magic only covered bullets; the soldiers charged us with their long knives. My own God, *Usen*, had already sent me a sign me that you would lose that day."

The Dog Soldier, flushed and standing in his stirrups, pointed his war hatchet at Viajero and shouted:

"I don't care what your strange God said. *Maheo,* the One True Life Giver to our People said we would win!"

He sliced his hand horizontally above his saddle pommel as his final gesture as Viajero cocked the hammer on his rifle. With a chilly look of farewell to Dark and a curt nod to Viajero, the Dog Soldier kicked his heels into his pony's flanks.

As he rode past, Viajero looked up at him and growled:

"Well, *your* God was wrong."

The Dog Man kicked his pony into a trot to get away from the tension; his pack horse whinnied with the effort. He rode over a low ridge and out of sight. Perching ravens clattered into the sky as he went past and the waiting wolf pack trotted into the shade on the far side of the hill.

See the Dark looked at his friend in exasperation, Viajero was a dangerous man to know, insulting the Cheyenne God could bring retribution on them both. However, a rare spark of maturity in his own brain forced him to admit that sometimes he should just stay silent and not bait others. He breathed out to calm himself and said:

"Are you ready to ride?"

The Apache looked up absent-mindedly and seemed to remember something. He reached down and picked up four gambolling puppies, their heads peeping through his fingers; the small fur bundles yipped in excitement.

See the Dark looked puzzled – he had never seen the Apache show affection for anything except his wife and daughter.

Viajero though, remained true to his nature; he swiftly broke the pups' necks, gutted them and skewered them onto a sharpened stick.

Viajero looked up:

"Food for the journey – I like dog."

---- o o o ----

Chapter Two

Under the morning star, Trooper Cobb experimented with his piss stream. First, he used it to flatten a bunch of grass then, seeing a marching column of ants, scythed it up and down the line making them scurry for cover. He had enough left to splatter his initials in the dust; a perfect finish.

Cobb fastened his pants flap, snorting in disgust at the ragged, stinking state of his uniform; he had been better clad working on his father's farm in Iowa. After eight weeks in the saddle, the leather patches on the inner thighs of his cavalry britches were almost worn through. It had cost him almost a dollar for one of the wives at the fort to sew them on, now they seemed as thin as parchment. Worse, when he bent his legs, both knees showed through the cloth, emerging like pink skulls from blue graves.

He stood up straight and eased the bones in his spine; at twenty-three he was already suffering from the hard campaign. Perhaps, after the 1st Cavalry were done with chasing the Cheyenne, the Army would issue him with new pants. He doubted they could issue a new backbone.

He smiled to himself; those ants had broken and scattered just like those damn Indians two days ago. Though seeing some three hundred screeching heathens in full battle paint riding in a disciplined line towards him along the valley of the Solomon's south fork, the outcome of the fight had seemed much less certain. The yelling warriors had seemed full of confidence.

And they had every right to be confident, in Cobb's opinion; a blind man could see how two months of hard riding had worn down both the cavalry and their mounts.

It didn't improve much as both sides closed with each other on the sloping valley floor of the Solomon Fork, the cavalry had outpaced the infantry and artillery in the column; Cobb would have been a bit more confident himself if the cannon and the long-range rifles of the foot soldiers had had the chance to whittle down some of those Indians.

Billy Cobb walked back to his horse, now silhouetted black against the rising pink dawn. He sat down beside it, held the bridle over his shoulder and waited for Trooper Herschel to return from patrolling the edge of the ridge. Then they could ride back to their camp on the Saline River for some well-earned coffee. Sleep would be a bonus too but Colonel Sumner, their hard ass commander, would want the column on the move just after daybreak. Cobb sighed.

Weary or not, Cobb and the other troopers had chafed at the two-day delay after the battle – those Cheyenne had been given a chance to escape. Two wasted months in the saddle from Leavenworth without seeing a single gut-eater and now the Indians were getting away after a small skirmish.

He had been hot for blood when the Cheyenne line had broken, their surging charge quickly becoming a mass escape from the fight. But the soldiers' pursuit became bogged down in the quicksand lying below the shallows of the river; the Indians avoided them but many of the 1st Cavalry didn't. His own mount had been sucked in up to the stirrups alongside that of his Company officer, Lieutenant Armstrong. Cobb was not a churchgoing man but Armstrong's frustrated curses would have made a whore blush. Of course, Armstrong was an Englishman and those John Bulls had a reputation for extreme profanity.

Now, under the growing grey light, Cobb stretched his legs on the warming earth and stroked the fetlock of the grazing mare; she was in poor condition and could benefit from a day of not being ridden.

He and Herschel had seen nothing on the slow ride round the camp perimeter just before dawn broke. What they could see though was the deep, rutted trail of hundreds of departing Indian ponies pulling laden travois; most were going south towards the Arkansas River. The Cheyenne that they had charged on the Solomon had been well-fed and well-mounted – now they were just paupers. They would be easy to follow and Sumner would have his way; the Cavalry would find the Cheyenne again and deliver the death blow.

Cobb chewed a stem of grass; it was tasteless, with all the nourishment leached out from it as it had dried under the summer sun. Sitting under a tree on his father's farm and eating a juicy apple seemed a long-lost luxury and a lifetime ago. He spat out the shreds of yellow grass stalk. No wonder their horses were getting thinner; they'd been eating this stuff all the way from the South Platte.

He looked up as the sound of dust being ground under boot heels reached his ears; Herschel was coming back. He was about to call out when he saw that the other Trooper was unmounted and leading his horse back at a swift pace, his hand clamped over its muzzle.

Herschel raised his finger to his lips for silence. Cobb stood up and drew his pistol as Herschel reached him:

"Indians" whispered Herschel.

---- 0 0 0 ----

Chapter Three

Lieutenant Henry Armstrong had been surprised to see the wolf skinner. Henry was at the rear of Sumner's southbound column with the mule train; no-one was supposed to be behind him. He had been dozing in the saddle when one of the infantry escorts tugged at his pants leg and pointed behind.

The infantryman had already alerted his comrades and they'd deployed, kneeling in the hot dust, rifles in the aim, to take on this new threat. Henry grunted back to consciousness, unhooked his carbine, sighted along the barrel and took in the approaching apparition. It took a while for a complete picture to emerge, the heat haze bending light and perspective.

It was a man on a horse leading a fully laden mule about a half a mile back. The man was probably white though Henry couldn't be sure. Some Cheyenne could still be around, looking to avenge their defeat on the Solomon; even stealing some stock or killing a couple of straggling soldiers might ease the pain. Though why a Cheyenne would ride out in the open like that was anybody's guess.

He let the rider come into rifle range; the man rode like a white man but oddly, as the sun had already climbed into the sky baking the Plains country again, he saw that the rider was cloaked in fur.

Henry was going to fire a warning shot but decided against it. His carbine was a fairly useless weapon – temperamental and inaccurate. Sometimes the safest place to be was in front of it. Also, if he fired, the infantry detachment would do the same and they were better marksmen than him. The rider could be a messenger from Fort Floyd, their temporary base for the wounded after the Solomon battle.

Henry hailed him instead:

"Are you from the fort?"

The man stopped, took in the array of weapons pointing at him and replied.

"Kinda, yeah."

"Hold your hands straight out and come forward."

The man did as he was told, arms akimbo, nudging his horse forward with his heels. The mule brayed in annoyance at the stop and start motion. She was carrying a heavy load and it jarred if she got out of her stride.

"Jesus!" One of the infantrymen caught the raw stench of furs worn by the man. It became worse as he got closer; it wasn't just the pelts he was wearing but the laden mule's pack saddle was full of them. Most of the top hides were fresh, blood and scraps of flesh still on them. They all seemed to be wolf skins; a horde of black flies followed the mule. Henry gagged as the man drew up alongside him.

"Mornin' Lootenant. Pythagoras Carver - at your service, sir."

Henry laughed despite his uncertainty; whether the wolf skinner was friend or foe he hadn't yet decided but with a name like that he veered towards the former.

"Pythagoras? Were your parents mathematicians, Mr Carver?" asked Henry.

The man looked puzzled.

"No, Lootenant, my Daddy owned but one book when he was trappin' fer beaver in the twenties. I never saw the book or knew what it was about but it had that name in it. My Daddy thought it had class so I got stuck with it."

The exchange in English had taken the tension out of the meeting and Henry motioned the infantry back to their escort duties. The detachment, rifles held across chests, trotted up the trail to catch up the mule train. Dust rose from their boot heels.

Henry urged on his own horse and let Carver ride alongside. The mule brayed again at the change of pace.

"You said you came from the fort Mr Carver?"

"Sort of, Lootenant. I was there for the wolves."

"The wolves?"

"Yep. Wolves know when there's goin' to be pickin's around. After a battle is always a good time."

Henry nodded. He had lain awake that first night after the Solomon fight listening to the howling of hundreds of wolves around the perimeter of the column's camp.

He actually liked the sound; the last wolf in England had been killed way back, well over a century ago. Henry thought it was a pity not to have any large carnivores on his father's estate any more. They would have been a useful deterrent to poachers, preachers and politicians – all categories of human life that were cordially detested by the only son of the Armstrong dynasty.

Occasionally the wolves at the Solomon had found prey – probably some of the spare mounts abandoned by the Cheyenne as they fled back to the Saline. The sound of their teeth tearing into flesh and their growling spats with other pack members kept Henry and many an exhausted trooper free of sleep. Burying their two dead comrades under the Solomon bluffs the next morning, the 1st Cavalry grave diggers made damn sure that wolves would not be able to add white men to their larder.

"Did you see the battle there?"

"Nope. Must've got there the day after."

"How are things at Fort Floyd? Is Lieutenant Stuart recovering?"

Carver looked astonished:

"It's bad enough you calling that sod sheep pen a 'fort' – but you gave it a *name* as well?"

Carver laughed.

"You Army boys have ambition, Lootenant – I'll give you that. And yes, Mister Stuart is making the best of it – he has his own tent outside the walls and he watches the river all day."

Henry smiled. Jeb Stuart had been a good friend, especially as the regiment went into action. Stuart had arranged for Henry to leave the mule train and join G Company in the charge. Still, his moment of glory had been short-lived.

Unlike Henry, Stuart had at least avoided the worst of the quicksand and had been able to close with a Cheyenne warrior who was on foot. At the last moment, the warrior had whirled around and shot Stuart through the chest with an old pepperbox revolver. The young Virginian had survived but was keenly embarrassed about being shot by what looked like a much older man with an ancient weapon. Henry and the other officers had decided *not* to let Stuart forget it.

After the charge, Henry's reversion to commissary officer had now come back into effect; he re-joined the mule train as the column tracked the Cheyenne south. It was bloody depressing.

"Were there any messages from the fort?" he asked.

"No sir, just thought I'd join ye heading south – I need to get to Bent's New Fort on the Arkansas. Travellin' with you Army boys gives me some English-speakin' company."

"Indeed," mused Henry. "Have you seen any Cheyenne around – between us and the fort I mean?"

"I saw a couple of bands of families headin' north from the Saline – not many, just some *Omissis* and Dog Soldiers. They were keepin' well out of your way."

"Do you know the Cheyenne, Mr Carver?"

"Depends what you mean by 'know,' Lootenant. I trade with 'em from time to time; I give them presents of pelts, mainly so's I can keep my hair. I can speak a little of their lingo."

Carver kept quiet about once having a Cheyenne wife; he had courted her when he was younger, thinner and less rancid. She had been a pretty girl, the daughter of an *Omissis* elder. She'd borne him a baby daughter but both had died of some damn fever after visiting a trading post up on the Platte. He had buried them both down in their Smoky Hill country and had never looked back nor sought out her village to tell her father. It had been a long time ago but the loss occasionally still swamped his heart.

He looked up again, the Englishman was speaking…

"…well, if you speak Cheyenne, Mr Carver, we may have some work for you; we captured two Indians after the battle. We'll ride up to Colonel Sumner, tell him you're here and get you to talk to our prisoners."

"Talk – to Injuns?" he snorted, "Huh! It's a waste of time. You can put the pot on to boil Lootenant – just don't expect any coffee."

Henry looked blankly at him but then understood:

"Ah, a genuine piece of frontier folklore no doubt, Mr Carver?"

"Yessir. My Granmaw was keen on wise sayin's"

His Granmaw was obviously an idiot, thought Henry but kept it to himself. Still, his idea of using Carver to talk to the prisoners had merit and he felt a stirring of his native English cunning.

Henry Armstrong, late of Her Majesty's Light Dragoons and of the noble English county of Cumberland, now had a plan that could lead to better things.

First - he could shake off his dull packtrain duty by showing initiative - *he* would make the arrangements to talk to their two Cheyenne captives, recording what they said on paper to present to Sumner. Second - *he* would be the lead man, coaxing information from two savages using Carver as his interpreter. Such intelligence might help Sumner in his campaign and, third - that might lead to more responsibility and a more active role in the expedition. Henry smiled smugly to himself – it may be a wilderness outside his head but the active Armstrong brain seemed to be an inner oasis of cultivation.

Henry's overactive imagination soared…. perhaps he could get command of a troop, then perhaps a full company then…? Well, anything was better than watching mules shit.

---- o o o ----

Chapter Four

See the Dark and Viajero both had headaches and bruised faces as they trotted along, hands tied and roped to the lead mule in the cavalry pack train. Four of the walking soldiers were their escort and the *vehoe* prodded them along occasionally with their rifle muzzles.

Both warriors were profoundly embarrassed by allowing two blundering bluecoats to surprise them in their sleep; they had scarcely struggled awake when they were clubbed into unconsciousness by the carbines of the soldiers.

Now they were common captives of the detested whites. Their ponies were somewhere to the rear, tied to the last mule; their rifles and ammunition had been taken by soldiers and their food thrown away. The two long knives that had caught them had seemed especially disgusted by Viajero's stick of puppies. It had earned the Apache another beating, though only after he had been tied hand and foot. The whites may be brutal but they weren't stupid.

Still, after overcoming their initial fear, they counted themselves lucky that they had not been killed. Perhaps there was something worse ahead – See the Dark had heard of whites hanging men with a rope tied around their necks until life left them. It was not a warrior's death.

He glanced across at Viajero. The Traveller, as Dark sometimes called him in rough translation of his Spanish name, never seemed to let anything worry him; he just trotted along, scuffing dust with his high moccasins. He could hear the Apache singing his walking song under his breath.

"They probably found us because they heard you snoring…" See the Dark said bitterly.

Viajero looked puzzled; not because he agreed with Dark, just that he didn't understand the Cheyenne word for 'snoring'. But he understood that he was getting the blame for the whites taking them. Dark was a fine young warrior and a trustworthy battle companion but he was still young and sometimes petulant.

"…or because you insulted Maheo."

Viajero said nothing; silence was the best way to avoid a quarrel with his friend. Eventually he said:

"The *indaa* were lucky to find us, that's all."

Viajero was more upset about the loss of his beloved rifle. It was a powerful and accurate weapon and had served him well in battle and in the hunt. The linen cartridge cases were hard to come by and, as he'd found out, impossible to make. He had used many of the cartridges in the attack on the Pawnee villages last year. Now his gun was in the saddle bucket of the young *indaa* chief in charge of the mules. No matter - he had killed a white man to get the rifle and he was prepared to kill another to get it back.

"We should escape," whispered Dark.

"Not yet," said the Apache.

Dark was appalled; surely it was better to try and break out and run for it. The soldiers wouldn't find them in the gathering dusk.

"Why not? Being a captive is a disgrace" he hissed.

Viajero clicked his tongue in annoyance. He gathered the Cheyenne words in his head to explain:

"The *indaa* are going south, the same direction that we want to go - towards the Flint Arrowpoint River; no other soldiers will attack us while we are in the column and they feed us once a day. A man of the N'de would think this was an advantage."

"Only you would think being captured was of benefit" snorted Dark. "The men of the N'de are obviously stupid."

Viajero again kept silent. He had killed men for lesser insults but Dark just needed to mature into a responsible adult. His reputation in his own arid country, far to the south west, had allowed him no such luxury as forgiveness. He was known as a powerful and fierce killer of men, women and children, dragging their bodies through clumps of spiny *cholla* cactus then spread-eagling them on the tall, wide-armed *saguaro* as a sign of his power. Even his tribal brothers trod with a light foot around him.

"Just think of it as letting a river take you downstream – it helps you get there" he said.

See the Dark grunted doubtfully.

Up ahead, there was the sound of ordered activity; the pace of the column slowed, orders shouted and the mules began to bray anticipating food and rest. The bluecoats were making camp.

Prairie chickens, disturbed from roosting, flew up from the scrub and clattered back down to earth some distance away. A lone coyote saw them and headed in their direction to try his luck.

In the fading light, See the Dark looked around - they were on the banks of a small creek, the trail of the fleeing Cheyenne bands was still clear and heading south across on the far bank. He had expected the bands to split before now to leave fewer tracks. He hoped that his father and the other Cheyenne warriors had returned safely from the battle

Viajero and Dark's chains were unhooked from the mule harness and they were jostled by anxious young soldiers towards a canvas shelter. A man lit a lantern inside the overhang as twilight deepened; the two warriors were forced to sit down under the light. Dark's mind started to race – perhaps this is when they would be killed?

Two white men appeared out of the dusk and walked towards them; one of them was carrying Viajero's rifle.

---- o o o ----

Chapter Five

The return of the Suhtai warriors from the battlefield was greeted with great joy by Bad Elk's people. But Smoke on the Moon and Broken Knife were more sombre – they praised the courage of their soldier societies but the abject spectacle of the Cheyenne war bands running away would stay with them for life. Neither of the soldier bands had any brave deeds to mark on their war shirts or shields - no scalps, no trophies, no coups counted. There were no paint symbols for defeat.

Smoke on the Moon looked with satisfaction at Bad Elk; his brother's decision to move early and put distance between the pony soldiers and themselves had proved justified. Bad Elk's wisdom continued to grow. Yellow Bear, who had led the early departure from the large Cheyenne encampment, had been proved right about the flawed magic; his power and stature had soared. The small band had suffered no losses in the fight with the bluecoats and only the absence of See the Dark and the Traveller clouded the happy moment.

See the Dark's mother though lost no time in confronting his father:

"Have you seen our son?"

Smoke on the Moon braced himself for criticism but he knew where his responsibilities lay; he had brought back all his Striking Snakes warriors and Broken Knife had successfully led all his Thunder Bears home. It had been their responsibility and they had done it well. Some thirty fighting men had re-joined their kin; this was no small thing in Smoke's opinion. Neither his son nor the Traveller was a member of either soldier band - they had chosen not to be. Son or not, Smoke had no responsibility to bring See the Dark home.

"I only saw him briefly when we started the fight; he was with the Traveller. When we…." Smoke hesitated to use the word 'ran'.

"…when we broke off. They both headed north up the bluffs and probably had to swing east to avoid the pony soldiers then head south back here. They'll be along soon I'm sure."

Badlands Walking Woman gazed at her husband in her usual unsettling way. Smoke looked into her black piercing eyes and flinched slightly; she was a fearsome woman.

"It's been five days now" she said.

"I know" said Smoke through gritted teeth," they will have had to be careful – avoiding the pony soldiers and hiding during daylight. They'll be back soon."

"But many of the People have fled south as we did, their trails will cover ours. How will our son find us?" demanded Badlands.

Smoke sighed; he just wanted to lie down on his bear robe and sleep. He knew his wife well; she was not a Cheyenne woman and she would often ignore traditional polite behaviour to get what she wanted. He hoped she had brought some of his tobacco when she'd packed their lodge. A pipe would soothe his rising temper.

"Well?" Smoke's wife was insistent. "I don't want to stay here with the Snake People for ever."

Smoke looked around the large encampment. The Comanche people had welcomed the refugees and had offered food and shelter to the majority of homeless Cheyenne. But their hospitality wouldn't last indefinitely. Bad Elk's small band of Suhtai still had their own tipis and winter food and clothing. They shared what they could but strictly within the limits for their own survival.

White Rain Woman and Bright Antelope, carrying Viajero's daughter in her arms, joined Badlands and looked anxiously at

Smoke on the Moon. The weary war leader sighed – he was not going to get much rest.

"I'll take some men in a day or two and see if I can pick up their trail."

White Rain offered the services of her Forked Lightning Women to help in scouting for her man and the Traveller. Smoke declined it, fighting back the irritation of unasked for help from the ever-confident woman warrior.

"No. Too many riders will attract the whites again – we can't risk another fight."

White Rain seemed unimpressed but, tactfully, she stayed silent.

Smoke looked at the three pairs of eyes boring into his face and accepted defeat.

"Tomorrow - we'll go tomorrow" he said testily as Badlands led him back to their lodge.

Bright Antelope and White Rain watched him go; they had half-formed, knowing smiles on their lips. Their men may be fierce warriors but they knew where the real power rested. The scorn of Cheyenne women for any hint of cowardly behaviour was well known and feared by most men. Despite their anxiety, they spontaneously giggled.

A woman walked past carrying water in two buffalo stomach pouches. In a shrill voice, she admonished them for their laughter reminding them that their nation had just suffered a great defeat and giggling was unseemly. She seemed very pompous for one so young.

White Rain recognised her; the girl had tried to join her Forked Lightning soldiers two winters ago but had been rejected for her gossiping and untrustworthy nature. She was about to tell her to hold her tongue when the woman turned on Bright Antelope:

"...and you, *notae,* my husband says that it was your man who brought defeat to us. The Traveller refused to bathe in the magic lake before the battle so the spell was not complete. That's why the whites won."

Like Viajero, Bright Antelope was not a Cheyenne and, like her husband, she struggled to cope with an outpouring of rapid, alien words. Being openly called a *notae* or a woman from another tribe was a new and bitter experience for her. It made her remember she was an outsider.

Moments passed until she had made sense of what the arrogant young woman had said. In the stillness, a butterfly danced past the face of her accuser who, distracted by its fluttering, watched it settle on a greasewood clump. That was her mistake.

Bright Antelope handed her daughter to White Rain, took a pace forward and punched the woman hard in the face. The younger one grunted and fell backwards into the greasewood, water pouches exploding on the ground in a fine spray.

Bright Antelope had seen the power of a punch before when her people had been trading with Mexicans. It was not a common method to use in hand-to-hand fighting – her Mescalero Apache kin preferred the knife or club – but it was more severe than a slap, more disabling. A Mexican had punched her brother once and she had seen him go down quickly and remain on the ground. She had not had much cause to use it before but now had seemed the right time – the young fool had deserved it.

White Rain, shocked by the outburst but impressed by the punch, caught Bright Antelope's sleeve and handed the child back. Bright Antelope stood breathing heavily, right fist still clenched waiting for the younger Cheyenne woman to get up and explain herself.

"What did she mean about my husband bringing defeat to the *Tsis-tsis-tas*? He fought alongside your warriors."

White Rain tutted soothingly and tried to pull Bright Antelope away:

"She doesn't know what she is saying. The People are still trying to work out why the magic didn't work. It is easier to blame an outsider like the Traveller for not sticking to our rituals than it is to accept that the *vehoe* were just stronger on the day."

Both women walked back towards the Cheyenne circle of lodges within the camp of the Snake People.

The young woman struggled to her feet behind them wailing about her scratches and spilt water. White Rain took Bright Antelope's elbow and hurried her on but they were still close enough to hear the woman shriek:

"The Traveller is a traitor to the Cheyenne people!"

Bright Antelope, again a few moments behind in understanding the language of the Cheyenne, set her mouth grimly. Such an accusation could not stand without revenge.

Some passing Comanche warriors on fine horses smiled at the women. They couldn't understand what was being said but they knew a women's fight when they saw one; they were sorry they'd missed it. Their Cheyenne guests seemed to be a hot-blooded crowd, just the sort of allies the Comanches liked.

Bright Antelope glared at their smiles and, for now, shook the insult off. A small glimmer of panic about their future with the Suhtai took hold – if what the young woman had said was true, they could be cast out of the tribe. She would talk to her husband when – if - he got back.

She looked down at her right hand – her knuckles were red and swollen but the satisfaction of overcoming an enemy appealed to her basic Mescalero instincts. When the time was right, she would speak to See the Dark's woman and join her Forked Lightning soldiers.

---- o o o ----

Chapter Six

See the Dark watched the grizzled *veho* in the rank wolf skins carefully – the man's hands and nails were still dark with wolf blood. The white man was speaking Cheyenne but it was poor and slow; Dark knew that the Traveller wouldn't mind this, it would make his task of understanding the conversation easier. The pauses gave him time to work out what was being said.

The white soldier chief, still carrying Viajero's beloved rifle, sat on a wooden box opposite them, occasionally asking the older man a question then getting him to translate it for Dark and his friend.

The *veho* soldier looked very young and was very skinny; he was burned red by the sun, scraggy side whiskers grew out of his light hair and his blue clothes were patched and badly sewn. Under a rip in the blue cloth, Dark could see that the young man wore a strip of red cloth around the skin of his upper right arm; perhaps he had been wounded? The veho had taken off his broad brimmed hat and a white area of skin showed below the hairline on his forehead. He had a gold ring on a little finger – Dark thought it would make a good prize when he killed him.

The older white man with the black beard spoke again:

"Did you fight in the battle with the pony soldiers?" he asked.

Dark pondered his answer and decided that being evasive was the best way to handle their impudence. He opened his mouth to speak. The Traveller, however, got in before him:

"Yes of course we fought, we are warriors."

Dark groaned; Viajero had admitted that only a few days before they had been trying to kill these white men. Now they would surely die.

Wolfskin reported this answer to the soldier chief who looked pleased.

"Well Lootenant, they's the enemy all right. This old 'un here..." - he pointed at Viajero - "...ain't no Cheyenne though. He don't look like one and as sure as Hell don't speak like one."

Viajero knew they were discussing him and leant forward towards the two *indaa*. He had a plan forming in his mind.

"Getting closer won't help you to understand the white man's talk" said Dark sarcastically, "They'll kill us now they know who we are."

"Not if we make them think we are important..." whispered Viajero, hoping the *indaa* would not hear them over their own conversation.

"I *am* important," interrupted Dark, his voice bordering on a petulant whine.

Viajero was harsh with his friend:

"No! You are just a warrior like me. You are the one-eyed son of a pipe holder of a small war band in a small tribe. We won't be worth much if they know that."

Dark snarled at the insult; his friend had gone too far.

"What are they talking about Mr Carver?" Henry Armstrong asked, gesturing towards the two Indians.

The wolf skinner looked embarrassed:

"Sorry Lootenant, I was too busy talkin' to you to hear."

Carver looked on as the older Indian held onto his friend's arm as though restraining him. The dark skinned one eventually spoke; he was hesitant and spoke poor Cheyenne in a harsh accent that Carver couldn't place. It took a while and some questions to understand it all. Out of the corner of his eye he could see the Englishman tapping his foot with impatience.

"Well...?" demanded Henry.

"The old 'un says he's an A-Patch, *Sierra Blanca* people, and a war leader to boot..."

"A-Patch?" asked Armstrong puzzled at the slang term unknown to him.

"Apache - White Mountain. He reckons that the Apaches and the Cheyennes are allies now. He says the boy is the son of a great chief..."

"Hold on, Mr Carver, hold on..." Henry took out his journal from inside his tattered shirt and patted his pockets for a pencil.

The leather-bound volume had been given to him by his mother who had obviously expected her only son to faithfully record his adventures when in the wild lands. Sadly, Henry's literary activities had only warranted two entries – one when the 1st Cavalry had set out from Leavenworth and the other when the converging columns met on the South Platte some two months later. Jeb Stuart had said that he had seen more writing on a Mormon's drinks bill. At least, there was plenty of space to record the intelligence from the two Indians...

"Right – 'son of a great chief' – got it" said Henry.

"The Apache says that his people didn't make it to the fight on the Solomon in time but they'd be along anytime soon. They'd be angry with the soldiers when they found out that their war leader was being held as a common captive."

Henry scribbled furiously, delighted to have first knowledge of this alliance and the importance of their prisoners. Colonel Sumner would be pleased. Carver spoke again:

"The A-Patch says his name is Makes the Rivers Red and his people are fierce warriors. But…"

In the darkness, outside the pool of lantern light, Viajero clamped his hand over Dark's mouth to keep him quiet. He had to be careful but the wolf skinner and the young *indaa* chief were busy looking at the snake trail marks that the soldier had made on the paper sheet to pay them any attention. Viajero knew that Dark was struggling with being described as less important than him. No matter, the Apache knew that he had to convince the white soldiers that their lives were worth something. Dark had given him the idea of an alliance when he had been goading the Dog Soldier. The more time he bought, the better they could plan their escape.

"But what?" said Henry, turning over a fresh page and ready for more writing.

"He says that he can stop the bloodshed coming to you if you release him and the boy. He can persuade his warriors off the war trail."

Henry snorted in disbelief. He put his hat back on his head and beckoned the two out of the shadows. Viajero and Dark shuffled forward still roped together at the wrists. Henry, from his perch on a biscuit box, looked at each one in turn, hoping to look authoritative and stern. He turned to Carver:

"What do you think Mr Carver? It seems a bit far-fetched to me."

Carver rubbed his beard and hissed his rank breath out through his teeth:

"Well sir, I don't get paid to think. Far as I can tell, from the markings on his clothes and possibles, the boy is a Suhtai Cheyenne, possibly one of the northern bands and the older one may well be an A-Patch from the south west but it would be a stretch to say that they could ever be allies – too far away from each other, I reckon."

"What about his name and the warriors coming here? Have you ever heard of him?" asked Henry.

"Not too sure about any Apache chiefs, Lootenant. I did all my trappin' and survivin' between the Milk River and the Arkansas. But my understanding is that Apaches are plain against telling folks their given name – so ol' 'Makes the Rivers Red' here bein' so free and easy with *his* makes me ponder some."

Henry was thinking about Carver's explanations when suddenly the young Cheyenne said something to him; Henry's eyes widened at the direct spoken contact though he tried to look nonchalant and turned to the wolf skinner:

"What does the young fella want, Mr Carver?"

"He wants to know your name Lootenant."

"Tell him then."

Carver, instead of saying Henry's surname in English, used Plains hand sign to make the words. Henry was surprised to see the two Indians glance across at him in disbelief and laugh. There was a babble of conversation and more laughter that included Carver but excluded Henry.

"What's the joke Mr Carver?" snapped the annoyed and embarrassed officer.

The wolf skinner looked sheepish:

"Well, I must be rusty on my hand signs Lootenant. These boys reckon your skinny limbs don't suit your name."

"Meaning..?"

"I must've got the signs mixed up. They now know you as Strong Arm."

Henry tutted but was secretly delighted – as mistakes go that wasn't too bad. It made him sound like a strong war chief even if, in reality, he just wrangled stupid mules and kept lists of stores. He would put *that* in his journal; his mother would be pleased.

Carver sensed the young Englishman's pleasure at his mistaken new name and said:

"It ain't a bad name Lootenant – you can be struttin' like a peacock carryin' that."

"Well, Mr Carver…" said Henry, his voice full of false modesty, "…we all know that a peacock is just a big chicken with a fan up its arse."

"That a sayin' from yer Granmaw, Lootenant?" asked the puzzled wolf skinner.

"No Mr Carver, that is a direct quote from Miss Jane Austen's *'Pride and Prejudice'*," lied the Englishman cheerfully.

---- 0 0 0 ----

Chapter Seven

Lieutenant Henry Armstrong and Trooper Billy Cobb both hit the ground at the same time. Cobb, as duty galloper, had ridden to the rear of the column to pass on the message that the packtrain, on orders from the Colonel, was to close up rapidly and get in before darkness fell. He did not have time to pass on Sumner's instructions before the arrows struck.

The Iowa boy, shocked and breathless, lay in the dust and heard the screeching of Indians and shots from the infantry. The arrow had pierced his windpipe and he couldn't suck down any air; he could feel his warm blood leaking down his neck and into the dust. He thought he might be dying.

His eyes watered as he dimly registered the English officer slumped in the dirt beside him, an arrow in his ribcage; Lieutenant Armstrong wasn't moving.

Hoofbeats, muffled by the thick dust, thudded in his ear as mounted men, Indians or soldiers he couldn't tell, rode by. There was a lot of yelling and sporadic rifle shots - he could hear spooked mules crashing off into the scrubland. His mouth drooped open and dust swirled into it.

Cobb's pain suddenly disappeared and, for a second, he thought that he had recovered. But it took him only a heartbeat to realise that the dulling of the pain was just a sign that his life was ending.

He was vaguely disappointed. There was no Corps of Angels, harps in hand, beckoning him to cross a crystal-clear river; no sight of his long dead mother with arms outstretched nor a sign of the True Rapture as he'd been promised by Pastor Dickinson. Sitting under a tree in Iowa eating an apple was the closest to Paradise that he would ever get.

Billy Cobb, born onto a patch of profitless farmland either side of a muddy creek that fed into the Missouri, had thought he was dying that day. And he was right.

---- o o o ----

Chapter Eight

Smoke on the Moon's triumphant return with his son and the Traveller was met with ear-splitting shrieks of delight by his Suhtai family. Smoke, Broken Knife and Dark had galloped into the village circle yelling their victory songs, taking everyone by surprise; Viajero followed behind at a more sedate canter and maintained his usual dignified silence.

Badlands Walking Woman pushed through the gathering crowd and almost dragged Dark off his pony to embrace her son. White Rain, whilst delighted to see her warrior return, stood respectfully aside and let the young man's mother take pride of place in welcoming him home. She needed to remind See the Dark that they should marry soon so she could take her rightful place at his side in future.

Bright Antelope Woman too barged through the well-wishers, Viajero's daughter in her arms, fending off outstretched hands. Welcoming though her Cheyenne neighbours were, no-one got too close to Viajero if they had any sense. He was not interested in emotional outpourings and, as Bright Antelope would admit, neither was she.

The Apache smiled gravely at his wife, swung off the unsaddled pony and took his daughter, cradling her for a few moments before handing her back. The child grizzled and mewled a little:

"Our daughter has still not learned the benefits of following a quiet trail in life," he grumbled.

Boldly, Bright Antelope told him to 'hush' and he looked sharply at her.

"She is just a baby, husband – all that can come later. She is probably just pleased to see her father, even if he is out of temper."

She smiled and put her head on his shoulder. This seemed to soothe him. In truth, he was glad to be back and knew that he was in a sour mood because he hadn't been able to retrieve his rifle from the young veho chief during their escape. No matter - he would thank Usen for his good fortune later.

The Apache looked around uneasily at the Comanche camp - despite fearing nothing that walked or breathed, they were traditional enemies of his people and he would need to be careful - he would avoid contact with them until he and his family moved out with Bad Elk's Suhtai.

Badlands Walking Woman, linking her arms with son and husband, sang a low song of joy in her own tongue as they made their way to their tipi through the smiling crowd. Neither Dark nor Smoke on the Moon could understand the words but Badlands often sang in her own Kiowa-Apache language.

"I hope you are singing of the good food you'll be cooking soon" said Dark. His mother slapped him good naturedly on his shoulder.

"Perhaps White Rain Woman can oblige; you spend a lot of time together."

Smoke grinned and kept out of the banter; Dark had once told him that White Rain's cooking was far inferior to his mother's. Smoke had advised that he should then marry two women – one for cooking and one for coupling. His son had blanched and looked appalled – he admitted that marriage to *any* number of women just hadn't crossed his mind. Smoke had sighed - there were some hard times to come for his boy.

Bad Elk, hurried up behind them; he had been with the Comanche elders when Smoke's party had returned:

"Welcome back nephew, you seem uninjured…" he said but then adopted a more serious tone, "…your experiences among the white soldiers will be interesting for our People to hear."

This was men's talk though; he looked meaningfully at Badlands Walking Woman, silently willing her to leave them alone. Badlands just stared back, her head on one side.

Bad Elk snorted with frustration; the womenfolk in his small Suhtai band seemed stronger-willed and more annoying than the ones in the other Cheyenne family groups. What had he done to deserve this?

Smoke rescued him:

"Wife, go and prepare the welcome feast for our returned son"

Badlands bowed her head in mock obedience, giggled and walked away. Under the dappled shade of a cottonwood tree, she unhooked the cradleboard of her newest son and carried him off to the family lodge, cooing at the boy' grave olive face and quizzical brown eyes. This one would need a name soon; she hoped that he, unlike his brother, would keep both of his eyes throughout his life.

Bad Elk, Smoke and See the Dark sat under the same cottonwood and discussed the young warrior's time in the hands of the whites. Bad Elk pieced together what was said and decided that a village meeting should hear the details; they would gather after the welcoming feast. He would send criers around the camp to announce it. They stood up and Bad Elk put his hands on his nephew's shoulders:

"It is good to have you back safely; your aunt and I were…"

His words were interrupted by a screeching yell, not of joy but of accusation. Smoke watched as the young woman who had been punched by Bright Antelope a couple of days earlier, stood outside Viajero's lodge, pointing with a trembling finger at the Apache.

"You were the cause of our defeat! You didn't bathe in the magic lake. You broke the spell and…"

Viajero, who had much less patience than Bright Antelope, grabbed the girl around the throat, sending the young woman to her knees. She gurgled as he throttled her. He didn't know why she blamed him personally or even how she knew that he had avoided the useless ritual. She had insulted him as a warrior and the killing cloud had come over his eyes and heart. Dark, Smoke and Bad Elk tried to restrain him but they were unable to prise his hands from pressing her windpipe closed.

The Apache was boiling with anger– women had been his victims before; this one would soon join them. He released one hand and clawed at his belt for his knife, but the pony soldiers had disarmed him days ago.

He broke away from those holding him and threw the spluttering girl to the ground. He dived inside his lodge to find a weapon; his wife usually had her hunting knife somewhere. He would gut the arrogant young creature like a gazelle. He re-emerged only to be buried under a press of restraining bodies; he thrashed and shouted in his own tongue. Flecks of foam spat from his mouth and he struggled some more. Reinforcements arrived to calm the demented warrior and eventually Viajero lay limp under the hot pile of flesh.

See the Dark peered into the depths of tangled limbs and caught the Traveller's eye:

"Welcome home, my friend" he said with just the hint of a mocking grin.

Viajero glared and snarled like a cornered bobcat.

---- o o o ----

Chapter Nine

See the Dark looked at the villagers gathering outside his father's lodge to welcome him back. Viajero and Bright Antelope had turned up, though the Apache had not wanted to attend. The homecoming feast, even in the warm twilight, had a chilly edge.

Across the circle of tipis, Bad Elk looked hungrily across at the food and the assembling Cheyenne. He had been delayed. Yellow Bear was already consecrating the small portions of food to Maheo and the Spirit Helpers – the People would eat soon - Bad Elk tutted impatiently.

The husband of the young woman struck by Viajero was with him to demand vengeance for the insult to his wife. Sweet Water, he explained, was now too injured to come to the feast and too insulted to be in the same company as the foreigner who had broken a sacred Cheyenne spell. The husband would fight the Apache in single combat to excise the bad medicine.

Bad Elk shook his head:

"There will be no vengeance fights in our circle – we are a small band. Both you and the Traveller are far too valuable as warriors to let either of you waste a life…"

Bad Elk always spoke in a loud voice; constant explosions from his rifle had made him slightly deaf. The young man was rattled as the details of his personal wishes carried across to his neighbours.

Bad Elk paused to let his words sink in. He knew that the chances of Feathers on His Shield, a well-respected member of Broken Knife's Thunder Bear military society, beating the Apache in a hand-to-hand fight were slim. Instead, he reminded the warrior that their own spirit caller, Yellow Bear, had foreseen the disaster and that several of the scouts, like See the

Dark, his own nephew, had not had the chance to bathe in the sacred waters. Did Feathers blame them too?

The young man looked away sullenly:

"Then I'll need six good ponies from the Traveller to ease my wife's hurt."

Sensing an easing in the young man's complaint, Bad Elk countered his offer:

"We both know that the Traveller has no wealth to speak of – just *two* ponies and your wife must apologise to him for the insult."

Feathers glared at his chief.

"She will not apologise – she is very proud."

"Then take a stick and make her *less* proud; it must be done by tomorrow. We'll be leaving the Snake People soon and this must be resolved."

Bad Elk dismissed the young warrior with a flick of his hand. He was not sure if Viajero would accept his wisdom but now he was hungry. He stood up and strode over to the feast. He sought out Viajero and whispered in his ear.

Bad Elk's return to the campfires prompted a surge in conversation; all his people knew that the dark warrior from the south had been accused of a terrible deed by Sweet Water. But they were reassured when the young woman and her husband eventually joined the outer circle of villagers, sitting in the shadows just out of the firelight. Even they wanted to hear about the whites that the son of Smoke on the Moon and the Traveller had met. Perhaps the quarrel was over - though looking at the Apache as he pointedly stared into the middle distance - perhaps not.

The People relaxed as the evening wore on, food was brought in relays from various fires close to the circle and hands plunged into kettles to retrieve the welcome morsels. Glowing cook fires spread warmth and cheer into the crowd.

Earlier, a wandering dog had been lured into the Suhtai circle, pounced upon by the gathering women and rapidly chopped into portions; everyone knew that the Traveller liked the taste of dog flesh. Many people did – it was a delicacy and Badlands could cook it well. No-one recognised the dog so it probably belonged to the Comanche – Badlands hoped that they wouldn't notice. She had buried the distinctive brown and white pelt under a tree stump.

Talking grew louder and there was some laughter. The Forked Lightning Women sang a newly-composed song about the brave conduct of Dark and the Traveller. Dark glowed with the praise but Viajero, he knew, would never bother to listen to the words.

As one particular verse faded into the night air, Dark sat quickly upright, craned his neck towards the singing group and listened carefully. He was not sure but he thought that there might be implied criticism in the words:

Make sure that tales
Of your courage are true
For if you lie
The Forked Lightning Women
Will eat you

He saw White Rain Woman singing as loudly as anyone else; she avoided his gaze. She was singing about him but wouldn't look at him – what did *that* mean? He shrugged – even the tricky whites were easier to deal with than women.

Smoke nodded benignly to his son, proud that he had not disgraced himself whilst among the hated *vehoe*; even the taciturn Broken Knife seemed satisfied. He nodded to Smoke and, as far as the austere war leader could manage it, smiled.

Broken Knife had been pleased to be part of the rescue - in the end, after many pointed accusations about tribal courage from their screeching women, both war band leaders had decided to go together to find Dark and the Traveller. Success would settle the women and the rest of the camp.

It had worked well – Smoke had killed two white soldiers with his new arrows while Broken Knife cut the prisoners free, counted coup with his bow on the dead bodies and then ran back to the tethered spare ponies and all four galloped off, yelling songs of triumph into the red dawn.

The air at the campfire turned slightly cool, this time because of a breeze rather than the stiff relations between Viajero and Feathers on His Shield – a reminder that the Moon of the Falling Leaves was getting near. The tops of the cottonwoods at the edge of camp, swayed and rustled in the stirring air.

Bad Elk pulled a buffalo robe over his shoulders; the People would need to leave soon and find their way back to their own country. They could only hope that the soldiers had left by the time they got there. He looked across at the Apache and hoped that the incident with Sweet Water would soon be forgotten.

Viajero responded slowly to Bright Antelope's urgings to take an interest in what was going on as he thought about what he would say to Feather's demand for two ponies. He had lost his war pony to the whites and he only had three others – his hunting pony, Bright Antelope's own pinto and a plodding mare that pulled his travois with all their possessions on it. He couldn't afford to part with any one of them. Killing Feathers on His Shield might be cheaper.

Bad Elk shrugged off his robe and stood up, belching slightly after eating too quickly. The voices of the people went silent and faces, warm in the fire glow, turned towards him. Their chief smiled and chatted to them in his natural, if loud, way – he was not a great orator but he spoke with good sense and judgement:

"Friends, seeing your faces tonight, gathered round our fires always reminds me of that other time…"

He paused; his small band of Suhtai knew what 'that other time' meant. It was the time of death and destruction following the crippling Pawnee raid on their village. He continued:

"Tonight though, our bellies are full, all our people are safe and we don't have to build any more lodges from earth and timber..."

Those who had been present during that dying time recalled the burnt tipis after the attack and lack of shelter as winter approached. They had built earthen lodges as temporary homes just as their ancestors had done and lived like badgers during a harsh winter. They laughed politely at his poor joke; those who hadn't been there yipped joyously in their ignorance.

"Our two warriors, See the Dark and the Traveller have returned safely to us and have much to say about their time in captivity with the *vehoe*."

This seemed to come as a surprise to Viajero who shook his head vigorously, refusing to stand and speak however much Bad Elk beckoned him to do so. Dark did not try hard to convince him otherwise; these days his boyhood shyness seemed to have gone and he liked to address the people - he would speak for himself as well as the Apache.

Yellow Bear sat next to Dark and took his ceremonial pipe out of its decorated hide case. He lit the sumac smoking mixture with a twisted grass taper from the fire, sucking in the smoke from the redstone bowl and invoked the Spirits and the Spirit Helpers to make the truth flow. He passed the pipe to Dark who pointed the stem to the four cardinal points to ensure he spoke truly and puffed on it. Viajero watched him, a half-cynical smile on his face – the boy was now much more confident; the Apache put this down to the man-making effect of the black stone eye. He wondered how long it would take the boy to exaggerate their adventures. It wasn't long in coming:

"We were taken in our sleep because of Viajero's snoring…it led the pony soldiers to us"

Viajero still hadn't worked out the Cheyenne word for snoring and was surprised by the shout of laughter from the people. At least Dark had not mentioned the insult to the Cheyenne God during his exchanges with the Dog Soldier. The Apache sat up and paid more attention.

"We were captured by many soldiers…" There was a gasp from the crowd.

Viajero now looked up and chipped in:

"There were only *two* soldiers and they clubbed us back to sleep with their rifles."

Yellow Bear gave a sharp exhalation of breath at the break in custom – the Apache did not have the pipe and shouldn't speak. He shrugged though and realised that changes in the band came from different people living in it. He stayed silent.

The crowd murmured solemnly, the warriors were lucky they hadn't been tortured or killed straight away - which is what they would have done to their own enemies.

Yellow Bear noted the discrepancy in the account of Dark and the Traveller – he nipped Dark's ankle with his fingers and pointed to the sacred pipe. The boy must keep to the truth, jokes or not.

Dark nodded and abandoned his plan to speak of the harsh cruelties that they had suffered - mainly as they only existed in his own imagination and love of storytelling. He re-started his tale, keeping to the facts as Yellow Bear and Viajero nodded in approval. When he had finished, Dark was about to sit down when a thin voice spoke out from the far side of the main campfire:

"What do white men smell like?"

It was unusual to have questions when a warrior was recounting his deeds but it was a habit they had got used to during the dying time when all knowledge became valuable to survival.

"Bad" said Dark to much laughter. But the youngster's question had opened the way to others; they came like a flood down a dry creek. Every subject of interest about the whites came tumbling out and even though both men had been held close to the pack train and hadn't seen much, their opinions were valued. Very few of the People had seen a white man before and even fewer had looked one in the eye.

There was a lull in the happy chatter until Broken Knife asked a question:

"What were the names of their chiefs?"

"We only met one chief; a young man named Strong Arm" said Dark. Broken Knife looked impressed; it was a good name.

"Perhaps we should follow the soldiers and kill him" said Broken Knife.

"No need," said Dark "he is already dead; my father's arrows saw to that. He was the young man you counted coup on who lay dead on the trail."

There was some satisfied nodding around the cookpots. White Rain Woman though thought differently, her future husband couldn't meekly accept capture like that:

"Well someone will need to pay for the disgrace you suffered as captives," she said boldly.

Smoke looked up and across at Dark. What was this woman up to? Yellow Bear seethed – another speaker, and a woman at that, without the spiritual guidance of the pipe.

"The white soldiers took your ponies, your guns and powder, your bows – even the knives from your belts…" White Rain continued.

Viajero looked slightly agitated; he was surprised at the criticism evident in the speech. He rose as if he was about to speak, to silence White Rain – he looked at See the Dark, a question on his lips. The woman soldier leader though, shrugging off any embarrassment, ploughed on:

"You both left here as valued warriors on fat ponies. Now the whites have made you paupers."

Dark had not thought that much about his situation now he was back home – but White Rain was right. Both men needed to feed their families and fight off any enemies. He and Viajero would need to get new ponies and guns - and quickly.

---- 0 0 0 ----

Chapter Ten

It had been another six weeks after Billy Cobb died that the final remnants of First Regiment of Cavalry struggled home. Edwin Vose Sumner had watched them plod into Fort Leavenworth; they had fought no more Indians but the brutal nature of the country, harsh weather and lack of provisions for man and beast did not make for a glittering homecoming. They were a ragged, starving bunch.

Sumner was anxious – the expense of the foray into Cheyenne country was difficult to balance with the poor results. There were not many glorious episodes to include in it. Certainly, the action at the Solomon Fork had been positive though not even Sumner could describe it as a resounding victory - nine dead Indians after a weary three months in the saddle didn't make a compelling story that would ensure promotion.

And now his superiors in Washington had more work for his exhausted troopers. Those shiny-assed, port-swillers wouldn't know a dragoon saddle from a piano stool – hardship for them was missing lunch. Sumner would allow as much recuperation time as he could but sooner or later, he would need to break the bad news to his men.

---- 0 0 0 ----

Henry Armstrong, jolted on the bed of a worn-out wagon, grimaced in pain as the winding down of the expedition went on around him. Horses, at least those that remained upright, were watered and put out to graze onto the blue-stem grass pasture; stores were handed in and accounted for; weapons cleaned and fresh clothing distributed to the ragged troopers. Everyone reeked with the harsh, gut-wrenching stink of living outdoors too long.

Troopers Herschel and Garber helped him out of the wagon and he staggered slightly as his frame took the unaccustomed weight of his body.

The field surgeon out in camp on Walnut Creek had removed the arrow shaft from his ribs, smiling as he did it:

"You know Henry, that this is the stuff of dime novels? Only the life of a true hero is ever saved by a book."

And it was true - the leather-bound journal tucked into his shirt had stopped the Cheyenne arrow, deadening its power and killing capacity. It had still gone through his ribs though and hurt like Hell.

In reply, Henry had made an attempt at a joke saying he wished that he'd been carrying one of those bloody awful Jane Austen novels – they were a lot thicker than his journal. The doctor had tried to throw the blood-caked note-book and the Cheyenne arrowhead away but Henry had stopped him:

"Not just yet Doctor – I need those as proof of my adventures."

The journal and arrowhead had become real-life artefacts of his marches on the Plains. He intended to waft the punctured and bloody tome under his mother's nose if she ever asked about his journalistic endeavours - the arrow point fitted well into the groove it had cut in leather and paper. It was a perfect combination to fascinate young women at dinner parties.

There was also the added benefit of shocking his three vapid and ready-to-faint sisters in Cumberland. They were the very essence of idle English womanhood so beloved of that damned Miss Austen. There would need to be a reckoning for his five childhood years that the sisterhood had kept him in dresses and forced him to put flowers in his hair - the bastards.

The cavalry trio now lurched across the parade ground towards the infirmary; Henry gasped for breath but tried to put on a brave show:

"It's good to see you back, Private Garber – we thought we'd lost you too."

Garber had got lost during the ride south from the Saline. Search parties had been dispatched in various directions but couldn't find him, though they did find his emaciated horse. Colonel Sumner, along with the rest of the column, had assumed that he'd been killed by Indians or had successfully deserted.

Garber looked embarrassed; his seven days of endurance on the Plains had become regimental legend.

"Well sir, I was lucky that the mail coach found me; I think I'd gone kinda crazy with the heat and all. I'm just pleased to be back in blue clothes and gittin' three squares a day."

Herschel butted in:

"You was eatin' grasshoppers in yer underwear when they found you boy – goddamn grasshoppers!"

Garber grinned but said nothing; he gripped Henry tightly under his armpit and speeded up towards the waiting doctor as he held open the door to the post's sick quarters.

"Easy men," the doctor called out," …there still may be a piece of that arrowhead in Mr Armstrong."

The two troopers laid Henry carefully on a stripped-down bed and stood back. Herschel saluted and said:

"Thank you for the words you said when we buried Billy - I mean, Trooper Cobb – out there. It was much appreciated by the men sir."

Henry merely nodded in acknowledgement; he had attended the burial with the broken arrow shaft still pinning the journal to his ribs, despite the protestations of the doctor. He had got out his Bible and read a few chosen words – though not well. Still, the soldiers had noted his determination while he was still in pain. To Henry, it was the least he could do for a young man who had died in his own sweat and urine on a rutted trail in the middle of nowhere.

Herschel stood for a few moments; Garber grabbed his arm and said they ought to go, let Lieutenant Armstrong rest. Herschel brushed his hand away. Henry seemed to know what was coming next – he had heard the rumours at the campfires.

"Billy and me come down from Jefferson Barracks as recruits afore we set out after the Injuns. We was friends for a long time. On that mornin' he got killed, he'd told me that Billy Cobb wasn't his real name – he'd shot someone up in Iowa and skipped town. Joined the Army and changed his name. Dunno why he mentioned it then."

Henry sighed and looked at Herschel. The two men had been close – Cobb, or whatever his name was, had often led the straitlaced Moravian astray. But they had been friends in the bunk room and on the trail. Cobb's deceit must have hit Herschel hard.

"Well Cobb would not be the first or last to join under a false name…" Henry said.

"Yessir, I know but I was the one who burned his name into the cross we made out of biscuit boxes…"

"And?" said Henry.

"Well, I buried my friend under a Christian cross with a lie on it – it just don't sit right with me."

"I know," said Henry soothingly "but you did your best for him. That's all soldiers – friends – can do for one another. Don't feel guilty."

Garber put his arm around Herschel's shoulders and led him out.

Henry lay back on the bed and thought about the grave on the trail. It had been shallow and there weren't enough rocks to keep predators out. Pretty soon the wind would take the cross with the fake name and blow it God-Knows-Where. Wolves would dig up the rotting flesh and scatter the boy's bones in the dust.

Back in England, his father had said that it was the lot of a soldier to take his final rest under foreign soil; Henry had agreed but he'd assumed that his – or any other soldier's – death would be a matter of record with some sort of monument.

Being in America had changed his mind – here in this vast country it was possible to be in your own land but still in a foreign and separate place. The Great American Desert was just as alien to Billy Cobb as the fields of Waterloo were to British infantry over forty years back.

And now, the last remnants of an unknown Iowa farm boy would disappear, unmourned, into the great emptiness of the Plains.

---- 0 0 0 ----

Chapter Eleven

White Rain Woman looked around the semi-circle of her Forked Lightning Women sitting cross-legged in front of her. There were only four of them left now. In the heady days of seeking vengeance on the Pawnee camp of Stone Turtle, she had managed to recruit enough young females to fill eleven war saddles. They had run off the entire Pawnee pony herd up on the Loup River and had killed enemy warriors whenever they could during their wild ride. Their own people, though, seemed to have quickly forgotten their value and, with the loss of that respect and usefulness, several of her soldiers had drifted away to marry - even before the recent battle with the whites.

White Rain didn't stand to speak - it would seem odd with such a small group - and, as they had few formal rituals, there were no prayers or a pipe ceremony. Instead, she held one of her own arrows and drove the point into the earth in front of her. The three young women looked on in silence. White Rain, touching the arrow, spoke slowly and tried to remove the bitterness from her voice:

"Our people don't seem to need us now…"

The trio in front of her nodded in silent agreement.

"Our last worthy task was to guard the families when we left the Great Circle early before the men fought the pony soldiers."

"But that was a great honour wasn't it?" asked Crow Dress Woman, leaning across to touch the arrow.

White Rain looked at Crow Dress - she was a plump and pleasant girl who had never shown any fear during her time with the Forked Lightning Women. Her braided hair glistened with bear grease and the neat lines of elk teeth decorating her deerskin shift stood out well, gleaming as they caught the light.

"Sister, you are young and a good warrior. Our village has moved three times since we left the Comanche. Has Bad Elk ever again trusted us to carry out any more important tasks?" Without waiting for an answer, she went on:

"No, he hasn't. He knows the skill and courage of women like us but now the men have returned he just wants us to revert to the old ways, leave the war trail and bring up children."

Crow Dress again leaned forward and tapped the arrow shaft:

"Most of our soldiers have done that. They have gone back to being good Cheyenne women..."

Crow Dress hesitated: "Except for poor Tall Grass."

The women nodded in sisterly remembrance. Tall Grass had been at the forefront of driving Pawnee ponies along the Loup riverbank, screeching like a demon and deliberately running down anyone who got in the way of the stolen herd. Warriors, women and children had gone under the flailing hooves if they weren't quick enough to move. Back with her own people, she had grieved deeply for Thorn, the Contrary warrior - the only Suhtai death in the Pawnee villages. Tall Grass had gone missing at one camp site; they had found her naked and face down in a river, later stories emerging of her drinking her unused love potion that she had infused with poisonous berries.

White Rain nodded:

"She was a good warrior and war sister. We must make sure that her deeds - and ours - are not like a spring shower that passes and is forgotten."

White Rain watched as Willow touched the arrow next. She was a lanky girl and didn't have to lean too far in to reach the shaft.

Willow spoke with a strange accent as she was from a Hunkpapa Lakota family; she had been taken as a child in the long-ago times when the Cheyenne had fought the Sioux.

"But we are few now - even I am standing under the blanket with a man who is collecting a dowry. And you…"

She pointed her chin at White Rain:

"Your man is a hero and you'll surely marry soon? What are we to do?"

White Rain remained silent on this tricky subject - See the Dark had never mentioned marriage though they had coupled like man and wife since the Pawnee fight. As for being a hero, her man had been lucky not to be killed when the vehoe captured him. Now he was a warrior without a horse, weapons or wealth. Her first husband, killed during the Pawnee raid on the Suhtai village, had, at least, accumulated some fine ponies and iron goods during their marriage. Dark seemed destined to be poor.

Mouse, the quiet one, now leant forward but couldn't reach the arrow. The others helped her, pulling the front of her dress - White Rain pushed the feathered flights closer to the girl's chubby hands. Mouse was the youngest of the group and often shy.

"We have come to a fork in the trail," said Mouse, pushing her hair braids away from her face then using her hands to indicate the left and right fork in the air.

"We all need to choose which trail to take - one way will keep us together as warriors the other will mean the break-up of our group. Either way will mean sacrifice."

White Rain smiled at her; Mouse may be small but she spoke like a true Cheyenne. The sacrifices, Mouse said, came with either fork of the trail that they took - give up being in the Forked Lightning Women meant a settled and routine life, perhaps married with children and foregoing the excitement of the war trail. Staying as a military society may deny them those family ties - White Rain knew many male warriors were convinced that the women soldiers were just going through a waiting time until they found husbands; See the Dark was one of them. She also knew that some men avoided them, unsure if they would have all the qualities of traditional wives.

White Rain pulled the arrow back to the vertical position and sat back:

"I agree with your forked trail picture - fighting the Pawnee made us independent but now we are isolated. We live in our own lodge away from our mothers; we carry weapons instead of awls or hoes and cook only for ourselves and not husbands."

Willow reached forward again:

"Yet we can't be like the Striking Snakes or Thunder Bears - they have tasks to do that are known by the People - tribal discipline, organising the hunt, raids on enemies. We have no such role…"

She hesitated then flicked the arrow with the backs of her fingertips:

"We were only useful once - perhaps our isolation is a sign," she said bitterly. There was a short silence.

Then Crow Dress Woman leaned across, a copper bracelet on her wrist catching in the feathers of the arrow:

"Broken Knife has spoken to me - he says that we can join the Thunder Bears as their ceremony girls. We can lead the dancing, serve food, help at their rituals - other girls do this for the Striking Snakes…"

"No!" shouted the other three in unison and giggled at their own audacity.

White Rain took the arrow from the earth floor as a sign that the communal part of the meeting was at an end. It was time for leadership and she had a plan to announce. They would ride together again soon.

---- 0 0 0 ----

Chapter Twelve

See the Dark handled his new bow with caution; it was well made and handsomely marked but his interest in the traditional Cheyenne weapon was limited. He had never been a good with it and still lacked the accuracy of other youths many years younger.

He had sent a pipe of tobacco to a retired warrior to ask if he would make one for him; the man, Standing Wolf, had called him to his tipi, smoked the proffered pipe and agreed to make the bow. Dark was embarrassed at his own poverty and did not have a gift to give the bow maker so Smoke on the Moon had furnished a good pair of beaded moccasins and a trade blanket as recompense - Standing Wolf seemed satisfied but Dark just felt like a boy again, reliant on his father to pay his debts.

The loss of his rifle to the whites was hard to take; Viajero had also given him the rifle at the same time as his black stone eye. Getting used to the bow again was going to be tiresome. His one eye made it vital to get close enough to game to ensure a killing arrow. This was all very well but did not compare to the sheer joy of watching a distant animal fall to a well-aimed shot with powder and ball. As a hunter and warrior, he needed to overcome his limited sight - his lone right eye was perfectly suited to align the front and rear sights on a rifle barrel. He needed a gun and ammunition - nothing else would do.

Dark kicked his heels into the side of the rough little pony he had borrowed from Bad Elk and caught up with Viajero at the treeline. The Apache was on his hunting horse and it wheezed at the unexpected harshness of the terrain. Normally it could overtake a buffalo at a dead run but those short, joyous bursts of speed were not needed now - just the ability to keep upright and climbing over the rocky forest trail.

In a shallow valley below lay a small Ute camp.

Viajero dismounted and both men tied their ponies inside the forest where they couldn't be seen or smell any Ute horses. Both men blew into the nostrils of their mounts to calm them before making their way to the tree line. Dark and Viajero watched the small camp from behind a screen of fallen spruce.

"How many warriors do you think are there?" asked Dark.

"Not many - only two lodges; maybe four men or less," said Viajero,

"I don't see any dogs," he added.

"You may have to go hungry then" joked the Cheyenne youth.

Viajero said nothing and didn't look at him. He still wasn't sure if he'd forgiven his friend from stopping him killing the arrogant young woman who'd called him a traitor.

"No dogs mean we can approach closer without them giving us away."

See the Dark was about to say "I know" but noted the tension in the air and decided to act as the inexperienced warrior:

"Do you have a plan?" he asked.

"Even four Utes will be a dangerous enemy against only two of us. Especially if I have to rely on you to shoot that," Viajero pointed at Dark's new bow.

Dark grinned; the Apache was regaining his sense of humour - even if it *was* limited to insults about his marksmanship.

"I count four horses on the pasture over there and two tied up - one outside each lodge," said Viajero, "The best ponies will be the tethered ones but also the most difficult to take."

Dark agreed; choice ponies were generally picketed close to the owner. It would be a risk to charge down and run off the grazing horses and find that they had taken the worst ones. Viajero needed two good ones to pay off Feathers on His Shield and both warriors needed a good war pony each. The risks were high but *all* the Ute horses were needed.

Viajero continued with his plan:

"Running off the grazing and tipi ponies is a risk - it will be difficult to get them away through these forests…"

Dark nodded but added his own plan:

"We could wait until they sleep and steal their horses from outside their tipis - we'll gain great glory and good reputations from that…"

"True," said Viajero in an unusual burst of agreement,

"But they may post sentries - it is only a small camp and they are weak."

Dark looked puzzled - no attack on the horse herd, no sneaking into the circle to take the ponies - what was left?

"We'll take our time and kill them all," announced the Apache.

---- 0 0 0 ----

Chapter Thirteen

"Bloody elections?" shouted Henry Armstrong at his Commanding Officer.

"Supervising elections? In Kansas? What sort of soldiering is that Colonel?"

Colonel Sumner watched his young English protégée rant in front of his desk. The boy was naturally upset but his outburst was unseemly - perhaps these things were tolerated in an English regiment. As Henry stomped about on the plank flooring, a trickle of dust fell from the ceiling - Sumner brushed it off his paperwork. He had more bad news for Henry.

Through the open office door, Sumner could see Carver and the Orderly Corporal smirking at the young officer's behaviour. He got up, strode across the room and slammed the door shut; more dust fell from the ceiling. He would need to break the bad news carefully. Settling back in his armchair, he tried a fatherly approach:

"How are things at home Henry?"

"Much improved sir. My wound is healing and my room in the officers' quarters is quite large, airy and..."

"No Lieutenant Armstrong, I meant at *home* - back in England?"

Henry looked puzzled; Fort Leavenworth was his home. What had Cumberland to do with anything?

"Well, I got a letter from my father just yesterday - he's been ill but seems to have recovered. My mother is still alive as are all my sisters. One of 'em even got married a year ago to the Reverend Ainsworth - I think he must be short-sighted - or desperate."

Sumner smiled:

"Good. I'm glad all is well there. Do you ever think of going back? You are still officially on the strength of the British Army - don't you want to re-join your, er..."

Sumner looked at a piece of paper in Henry's file:

"Your Light Dragoons?"

"Christ No!" exploded Henry again. "I only ever assisted the Adjutant - bloody paperwork and messenger duties. It bored me rigid."

Henry had never missed his English regiment and didn't know where in the world it was now. None of his fellow officers had kept in touch. His father had written a couple of years back to say that the Light Dragoons were fighting the Russians in the Crimea. Henry had no idea where the Crimea was and hadn't bothered to ask or look in a book of maps.

Henry had left the Light Dragoons over five years ago on attachment to the American Army. It had been a panicked move back then - his father didn't want the disgrace of acknowledging Henry's woeful lack of judgement in getting young Maisie Bowman pregnant. The old skinflint especially didn't want to *pay* the Bowmans for Henry's misdeeds. So, his father had contacted his kin with influence in America and spirited his errant son across the Atlantic - away from the accusing Bowman relatives.

Henry wasn't even sure if the child was his - Maisie Bowman had a fairly chequered reputation in that regard - though he did remember the occasion of the possible conception; in the butler's pantry after a ball at his family's house. Henry vaguely remembered quickly losing interest in the act of fornication, eating a piece of cheese while the Bowman girl shuddered under him.

No - good luck to the boys in the Light Dragoons, of course - but he was happy in the American cavalry. There was no going back.

Sumner cleared his throat - the boy still misunderstood his future:

"Lieutenant Armstrong, *you* will not be going to Kansas..."

Henry beamed with delight but it was too soon. Sumner continued:

"...because General Harney has insisted that the Kansas elections be policed only by American citizens. He feels that it would be too politically sensitive to have an Englishman - a foreigner, if you will - present if the cavalry has to enforce order against our own people."

Henry thought and then nodded:

"I agree Colonel - I'll be more than happy staying at Leavenworth until my wound fully heals and then resuming my duties..."

"No Henry - it is worse than that. General Harney has applied to end your secondment to my regiment. You'll have to leave the First Cavalry."

Henry went white and grasped the arms of his chair. Leave? What the hell would he do? Where would he go? He considered throwing himself on Sumner's mercy - on his knees if necessary. But his family's stoic breeding saved him from that. Instead he just nodded, stood up and left the room. Carver and the Orderly Corporal looked at the young Englishman's grim, white face and decided not to chance any remark, however innocent.

Outside the Headquarters building, Henry tore off his campaign hat and threw it across the parade square:

"Bollocks!" he yelled at a party of troopers curry combing their horses in the shade of the stables. One of the horses, startled by the noise promptly defecated onto the boots of its groom.

---- o 0 o ----

Chapter Fourteen

Viajero and Dark watched the Ute lodges until the shadows lengthened and wolves began to sing among the high mountain peaks. They had decided to wait until dawn to see the true strength of the two-lodge camp before they embarked on their attack, mainly as Dark had misgivings about their ability to overcome four people in the gathering dusk - especially if they turned out to be four warriors. The Utes may have guns; they often traded down at Bent's Fort on the Flint Arrowpoint River. There was no telling which way the fight might go until it was light enough to see.

Both men chewed on pieces of jerked buffalo meat and drank water from a skin pouch. Viajero was glad that he'd brought his buffalo robe and pulled it round his shoulders. His southern desert country also had chilly nights but these mountains seemed to have their own type of cold - chilling a man's bone-marrow by day as well as by night.

"Are Utes the enemy of your people?" asked the Apache, his voice coming as a surprise out of the gathering dusk.

Dark thought for a moment and said:

"Well, they're not Cheyenne, Arapaho or Lakota so I suppose they are."

In truth he couldn't remember any past wars against the Utes, mainly because the Utes stayed out of the way in the mountains. Still, they had ponies and the two warriors needed them – that would have to be sufficient reason for now.

"You Medicine Arrow folk are strange people," said Viajero.

"This coming from a man whose spirit sign is a lizard and who eats dogs," countered Dark. Both men nodded amiably in the gloom.

"Did your God send any lizards to tell us how our pony raid will go?" asked Dark mischievously.

Viajero narrowed his eyes at the question; the boy mocked him for many things but now he was verging on insulting his deeply held beliefs:

"No," he said evenly, trying to stay calm, "Usen only sends a horned lizard sign at special times – usually when I can't see the right trail to take."

"Ahhh…" said Dark, as though he understood, "…I just wondered why a lizard? They're so…small. Surely it's better to have a powerful animal like a buffalo or a wolf as your sign?"

Viajero snorted in exasperation; he didn't have the words or the patience to explain to Dark his religious beliefs, especially when the young Cheyenne had so few of his own. Instead, he coughed and spat; the conversation was at an end.

See the Dark shrugged deeper into a blanket loaned to him by White Rain Woman. He sighed bitterly at his inability to provide his own but the decision to steal horses from the Utes was, at least, a start in regaining some of his dwindling status in his village circle. His time in captivity with the pony soldiers had given him an aura of being heroic but he was now a warrior afoot. He couldn't always rely on his father to give him things; wealth had to be earned by being successful. Pony raids were much admired amongst the Cheyenne - a man showing dash and courage in carrying these out would always be looked up to. That was all that mattered.

Viajero prodded him out of his thoughts and pointed to the Ute camp. Inside one of the skin lodges, a flame burst into life, probably lit from the central cooking fire. The hide door was flipped back and an old woman, carrying a burning taper of sticks, came out. She went to a pile of lumber between the lodges and set it alight; the flames crackled, spat and then roared into the cold air.

The Apache could see Dark's face in the moonlight - he was smiling and probably had the same thoughts as him. One old crone in front of them now made only three warriors or less to worry about in the two lodges. The horse stealing had suddenly got easier.

In the light from the fire, Dark could see that the two tethered ponies looked to be in good condition - nothing as good as an Appaloosa or a painted stallion but better than nothing. No ribs showed on their bodies and their sleek hides reflected the firelight well. In the background, the four grazing horses moved towards the comforting light; they knew that fire kept away the dangers of a mountain night.

Viajero relaxed more - climbing the rough mountain trail now seemed worthwhile; they could soon go home. He breathed easily as he watched the old woman. They would kill her and remainder of the people in the lodges when the morning star came out and the new day had started.

The pair's smugness though was premature. Out of the second lodge stepped a well-built young man. He was unarmed and unpainted, his long hair hung low to the middle of his back and he was dressed in an unadorned deerskin shirt and leggings. Dark and Viajero watched him intently and, though the young man was some distance away, something about his spare attire and calm manner carried to the two watching warriors. The man sat down in front of the roaring fire; the crone banked up the blaze with logs forming a conical shape so that air could pass through them quickly.

Men of simple habits and dress made See the Dark uneasy. Unlike him, such men turned their backs on ritual decoration like hanging scalps or painted war shirts and often just concentrated on a single thing. Sometimes that single thing, as with Yellow Bear, was a spiritual way of life - a simple existence of prayers, healing and visions; sometimes their skill in painting tipis or making arrows became the focus of their lives but sometimes too they just craved battle for battle's sake.

Dark's own people had their Contraries - men who had taken up the Thunder Bow and did everything back to front; they rode backwards on ponies, washed in sand and said 'Goodbye' when they meant 'Hello'. His own friend Thorn had been one and had become unstable - he had been killed during the battle with the Pawnee, refusing to stick to his war leader's plan. These men were dangerous. This Ute would need to be killed early.

Dark looked across at Viajero. The Apache's face was, as ever, impassive - no hint of emotion or fear evident - just studied concentration on the enemies at the fire. The Apache was looking at the crone's deerskin shift in the firelight - it was painted in strange shapes and patterns - he had never seen a woman's dress like it. Viajero was about to whisper to Dark when the old woman let out a piping wail.

Many Ponies, the young Ute, winced at the sound. His grandmother had great powers but her voice was high and cracked and it set his teeth on edge. Even the advancing ponies from the pasture turned around at the strange noise and trotted off, back into the darkness. The tethered horses whinnied uneasily.

The old woman lit sweet grass bundles and wafted the smoke over his shoulders; she wailed to the spirits in a language that not even he could understand and pointed to the moon, then to his heart, her gnarled fingers urging the power to flow from that faraway spirit place into her grandson.

His grandmother's original name had been Grass Lodge Woman but, after her close interest in torturing and mutilating fallen enemies, she was known by her newer name of Skin Cutter. She was adept at skinning captives and it seemed to have given her a new lease of life. These skin peelings seemed to bring her powers of prophesy and, more importantly, of victory.

Many Ponies remembered their great triumph last summer against a band of the Nez Perces when the Utes had captured a wandering hunter before the raid. His grandmother had carefully removed the skin from the hunter's back, cutting and slicing each section to ensure it came off whole, and then examined the trophy to foretell the outcome of the fight. The hunter, of course, had still been alive - Skin Cutter could not determine any prophesies if her subjects were dead - and he screamed for many hours. His grandmother had been able to tell from the patterns on the man's back skin, draped over a war lance, that victory over the Nez Perces was certain. And it was true - they had trailed their enemies, attacked their camp and Many Ponies found himself famous. His warrior skills had brought him three scalps, four counts of coup and a string of fine horses - many of which he had given away to his people. Perhaps his grandmother was right about his powers, though Many Ponies, a modest young man, just thought he was lucky.

Skin Cutter finished her song and seemed in some sort of trance. She now raised two buffalo hide rattles to the sky and shook them. Her grandson had seen this before but was always amazed at the result.

In the surrounding blackness, Viajero and Dark watched the old woman uneasily. Her singing and incantations had been reason enough to worry but now the rattles compounded some deeper fear.

Each time the crone shook the rattles they glowed with a blue-white light. They were not on fire; both warriors could tell the difference between the warm red and yellow flare of a normal fire and this unearthly white, pulsating gleam that came from within the body of the rattles. There were powers here beyond their understanding.

Dark shifted under his blanket and whispered to the Apache:

"This could be harder than we thought. What do you think of the old woman?"

Viajero knew without question what they had seen.

"She's a witch" he said.

---- 0 0 0 ----

Chapter Fifteen

White Rain Woman and her three women soldiers rode out of Bad Elk's camp shortly after See the Dark and the Traveller had left to raid the Utes for their horses.

White Rain was bitter. Dark had scarcely bothered to bid her farewell, only coming to her lodge to borrow a blanket. They had not spent much time together since the night of the homecoming feast - Dark had seemed uneasy and distant in her presence and they had only lain together once. Perhaps it was her outburst at the feast or the gently mocking songs - she knew See the Dark could take offence easily. She had mentioned her plan to him to take her soldier society to the village of the Omissis band along the Red Shield River and bring her mother back.

Dark seemed about to question the wisdom of this but merely shrugged and said:

"Your mother will be pleased to see you - I'm sure she is tired of life with our Omissis cousins; she has no friends there."

Buffalo Lodge Woman, White Rain's mother, had been a staunch believer in the strength of the magic of the young medicine men before the battle with the white pony soldiers. She had been sure that Maheo would prove to be all powerful and thought that Bad Elk's decision to move his Suhtai families early was cowardly and a sign of bad faith. She had refused to move from the great Cheyenne encampment and, when the defeated warriors came racing back and packed up their families, her daughter and Bad Elk's band were already a day's ride away to the south heading for the safety of the Flint Arrowpoint River.

Her Omissis neighbours in the nearby circle of lodges insisted that she come along with them and Buffalo Lodge, already frightened and cast into gloom over the defeat, was happy to accept. Her husband moved only slowly these days; a withered leg rendered him almost immobile and he found it difficult to even mount a pony without help. She had rushed at the dismantling of their lodge and packing of her rawhide parfleches, standing and breathing heavily whilst leaning against the sagging travois poles. Her husband sat on his pony, gazed with disinterest at her breathlessness and chided her for her poor work:

"Woman, you are run down like an old pony. I may have to take another wife."

Buffalo Lodge had shoved her carving knife into her buckskin belt, silently vowing to disable his other leg if he didn't keep quiet. Glaring at her man, she had pulled the bridles of both ponies and followed the Omissis band west and then north, her footprints mingling with hundreds of other human and animal tracks that marked the abrupt departure of the Cheyenne nation.

White Rain and her women warriors rode along silently at first, enjoying their release from Bad Elk's encampment and the humdrum activity of finding new campsites, fresh game and water. They were all well-armed, had spare food in a deerskin sack and were happy to have something positive to do.

Mouse and Crow Dress Woman did not remember the way to the Red Shield River but White Rain and Willow did. It was only a two-day ride, more than enough time to return with White Rain's parents. The weather was fine and sunny with just enough of a breeze to make the top spindly branches of a live oak clump wave against the blue sky; a dense flock of pigeons were pushed across the wide horizon by the stronger wind higher up.

The going was easy on their ponies and their first day's ride put them within easy reach of where the Omissis were usually to be found. There were bear tracks around but the women shouted and beat branches to scare them off before settling for the night into the trees that lined a small stream.

Setting out next morning, Mouse sang one of the first songs they had ever composed - it told of their heroic deeds against the Pawnee up on the Loup River two snows ago. Their taking of the Pawnee pony herd was still a great victory to them, even if the rest of the Suhtai seemed to have forgotten it. The other three joined in the song and laughed at how lucky they had been to get away from the Pawnee winter camps unscathed.

White Rain remembered when they had first sung the song, sheltering in a stand of snow-bound trees - a pause on the long ride back to their own camp. The captured pony herd had crashed through the underbrush, greedily eating the strips of bark that the Cheyenne boy helpers had cut as forage. The other warriors from the male soldier societies had got annoyed about the amount of noise and complained that women had no idea how to behave on the war trail. It had been Willow, the Hunkpapa girl, who had told them to be glad that their women could carry weapons as well as children.

It had also been the first time that White Rain had coupled with See the Dark. She thought wistfully of their closeness then, lying under a buffalo robe, gasping breath and sweaty limbs as the sound of wolves tearing at an abandoned mare outside the treeline seeped past their low laughter.

All of the four women smiled and chattered loudly as they remembered those exciting times. Going to collect White Rain's mother and father was not a war quest but meant that no male warriors would need to be diverted from more important tasks. It would be a way of recouping some of the pride and independence that they had lost.

The trail now narrowed into a small defile with a rocky outcrop on one side and riverside bushes on the other. The women fell into single file. Mouse, now in full voice on a verse she had just recalled, rode in the lead, arms outstretched to the sky. The verse had been her response to those men who considered that the women on the raid had merely been given easy things to do. Mouse was good at songs. Her piping voice made birds crash out of the box elder bushes on whirring wings and swoop into the more protective thickets of wild rose along the banks of the stream.

Suddenly, Mouse's pony stopped dead and she almost fell forward from the saddle. The others hooted at her for her poor riding but then reined in their own horses.

Out of a rose thicket stepped a bluecoat soldier pointing a rifle at them.

---- o o o ----

Chapter Sixteen

Many Ponies left his lodge as a dawn rain spattered onto the taut hide covering of the tipi. He yawned and looked disgustedly at the sky - the high trail that his grandmother and he would take today would be wet and treacherous now. Still yawning, he urinated into a bush and then walked across to the grazing ponies, beckoning them to him with a soft clicking of his tongue.

Skin Cutter was already up. She sat near the smoking embers of the ritual fire, rummaging in a parfleche for pemmican that they would eat before they set off deeper into the mountains. There were more rituals to perform at a sacred pool she knew about, high in a mountain pass. Many Ponies paused to watch her as he called to the horses again.

Three ponies came up but one, an ugly horse with blotched russet colours on its grey and white hide, stayed back. The young warrior plucked handfuls of grass and fed each one - they had grazed well enough, the pasture here was green and thick - but the ponies liked the ritual of being fed a little by hand. They snorted and barged each other, trying to get more than their share. Their owner gently separated the thrusting muzzles and ensured each one had a taste, chuckling at their greed. He waved some grass at the reluctant ugly pony but it just stared at him. It was an odd creature.

Suddenly, the three ponies shied backwards as strange scents and sounds carried to them. A screech from his grandmother brought Many Ponies out of his confused drowsiness; Skin Cutter had fallen onto her back with what looked like an arrow sticking out of her chest. Out of the drizzle, two mounted warriors charged from the tree line yelling their war cries. The Ute was unarmed and ran back towards his own lodge to grab his weapons; the two enemies saw him and spurred their ponies in his direction.

See the Dark whooped his satisfaction and delight in the charge. His first arrow had killed the old crone - he considered hitting an enemy with *any* of his arrows to be a miracle. He shot off another at the running Ute.

Viajero meanwhile reined his pony towards the grazing horses, shouting in his own language, as Dark headed for the tethered mounts.

Dark's second arrow missed the Ute who dived inside his lodge; the skin covering bulged and swayed as the man frantically sought to arm himself. He fired another arrow through the tipi cover where he thought the young man might be. But it was in vain - as Dark dismounted to untie the horses at the lodge entrance, the Ute ripped open the side skin and clambered out with a hatchet in one hand and a long knife in the other.

Dark slapped both mounts on the rumps and they galloped off, Viajero whirling his pony round to head them off. His hunting pony was badly out of condition after the long climb through the forest the day before and he had to quirt it hard to catch up to the runaways.

The Ute, who had glanced at Viajero running off his horses, now saw Dark and turned on him. The Cheyenne tried to notch another arrow onto his new bow but fumbled it - the Ute was too close and leapt towards him with hatchet raised.

It wasn't a glorious moment in the long history of Cheyenne warfare but Dark stepped back, tripping on his own bow stave and fell onto the crone's tipi. He had the good sense to immediately roll off and onto the ground as the Ute's axe came down towards him.

The hatchet didn't go through the hide covering but hit a springy lodgepole and bounced back, hitting the Ute in the mouth. He grunted, dropped the hatchet and stood still momentarily as blood spurted from his gums. This was Dark's opportunity and with a small hunting knife - his only other weapon - reached up from the ground and slashed the hamstring of the Ute. The man screeched in pain and fell over, clutching his leg.

Dark searched for the dropped axe and found it, standing up to watch the man rolling round on the bloodstained earth. The Ute wasn't a threat now, just a vanquished enemy - Dark would decide when he died.

Viajero rode up; the six captured ponies were now all on headropes, and he watched dispassionately as See the Dark stood over the writhing Ute.

"Finish him, brother" said Viajero.

Dark nodded, breathing more calmly as the surge of battle energy ebbed away. He would scalp the Ute while he was still alive - the man should know he was dealing with superior beings on Maheo's earth. The Ute was in the presence of the fighting Cheyenne - it would be a good image for him to take to the next life.

The Ute still clutched his long knife in his left hand; he was beyond using it for serious retaliation but gripped the bone handle tightly to ease the pain of his slashed leg. He made a feeble attempt to arc the blade into Dark's calf but the young Cheyenne merely stood on the Ute's knife arm, raised the hatchet blade and chopped off the Ute's left hand. Blood coursed out and into the rain-spattered dust though, annoyingly to Dark, the Ute did not cry out in pain. Still, scalping him alive would change that.

Dark knelt down and reached for the man's hairline. Viajero had dismounted and walked over to watch his young friend scalp and kill the troublesome Ute. Even he was surprised at what happened next.

The Ute's hair just slid off in Dark's hand. The Cheyenne found himself holding a full head of hair without a single scalp knife cut. He stood up quickly:

"Hah!" he said, his lip curling in disgust.

Viajero took the hair from him and examined it:

"He has the hair of a pony - this feels like a tail from a mustang."

Dark and Viajero craned over to look at the Ute - the young man's skull, beyond a few tufts of original black hair, was crinkled and red. His head had been obviously been badly burnt in the past. Perhaps the crone had covered his head with the pony hair to disguise his weakness - a man with no hair could not thrive for long. Unaccountably, Viajero felt embarrassed for the young warrior.

The Ute looked at them both and wept; his tears were not of pain or the fact that he had been beaten in a fight - it was just that an enemy had seen him without his head covering. Dark hesitated with the hatchet - he also had a physical weakness that he wouldn't show to others. There was a small, kindred moment - Dark couldn't speak the tongue of the Ute but he tapped his stone eye with the tip of the knife. The Ute swallowed and went silent.

Viajero, upset by the strange event, walked back to his pony. But something else was wrong:

"I thought you killed the old woman," he shouted over his shoulder.

"I did," answered Dark testily walking over to him.

"Where is she then?" said Viajero pointing at the ground

There, in exactly the position the crone had lain, was her empty dress; Dark's arrow still in the centre of it, pinning the material to the ground. There was no blood or signs that the woman had crawled away.

Both men stood puzzled as the Ute began to sing his death song. It was a high keening wail, reminiscent of the old crone. The mountains seemed to close in suddenly; the air was hard to breathe and the earth seemed to rock under their feet - there was too much magic that they didn't understand.

Dark and Viajero set fire to the lodges in a hurry, the flames a welcome burst of heat in the chilly, damp air. Each man gathered three of the roped Ute ponies and prepared to head off down the mountain, leading their spoils slowly across the clearing.

Mounting their horses, both Viajero and Dark decided to leave the Ute to his lingering fate rather than be contaminated by any further contact with him. He would bleed out or a bear would get him.

As they passed the arrow-pinned dress, a large black snake slid out from the folds and undulated away towards the trees. Dark shivered as though he had been dashed with icy water and kicked his pony into a trot.

---- 0 0 0 ----

Chapter Seventeen

Private Donal Mulvenna had been reflecting that he was good at many things - he could hold his drink, sing well, play a reasonable game of poker and fornicate with enthusiasm. Well, he was a little rusty on the latter as there had been few opportunities back at the fort, apart from some ragged squaws owned by the panhandlers. And they cost money - something that Privates in Mulvenna's Army didn't have - or at least, not for long.

What he wasn't good at was being a soldier. No Sir; marching across a parade ground, saluting damnfool drunkards masquerading as officers or eternal guard duty in some Godforsaken shithole was not for him. No, Donal Mulvenna was far too clever for that so he looked on his enlistment into the infantry as just a ticket west to California. The gold fields were still going since the days of the 49'ers and new strikes were happening all the time; that's where a man could make his fame and fortune - just as his mother had predicted as he'd walked away from his family's stone hovel in Cork.

He'd had to be patient of course, enduring the training, the chores and the false camaraderie of the barrack room. These had just been steps on a ladder to get him to where he wanted to go. The call for volunteers to act as escort with an Army survey team planning a road through the Cheyenne country was heaven sent; he had signed up immediately and even got to ride a horse. He wasn't a good horseman but it beat the Hell out of walking.

His eye for fine detail, however, was as poor as it had always been. Mulvenna had failed to register that the survey was through Cheyenne country and by the time he realised the potential danger, it was too late. The young Irishman was not a coward at heart but frontier tales of wild warriors made him determined not to meet one. He had never seen an Indian, apart from the whiskey-begging dregs of humanity at the fort.

The officers in the survey team though had reassured him - the Cheyenne had just been beaten by the 1st Cavalry down on the Solomon Fork only a few months ago. The survey work wouldn't be interrupted by savages.

That had settled it. His desertion from the survey camp, taking his horse, a carbine, pistol and a few rations had been easy - the team had no soldiers to spare to pursue him without leaving them exposed. He had headed into the setting sun, bound for his personal Promised Land.

Since deserting, he had mentally kicked himself for not looking at a map - California was to the west of course, everybody knew that - but once he'd actually set out, it seemed a fair pace off. And, blocking his path, were some high, jagged mountains that never got any nearer however much he rode. He didn't want to winter up there - dying, by starvation, cold or Indians, was not part of Donal Mulvenna's plan - he had to think of a different way and try again in Spring.

Two weeks later found him on the bank of some nameless stream, eating oats meant for his horse, his belly rumbling and his heart beating wildly. For here *were* some Indians - God Knows what tribe they were from - four of them, well mounted and well fed and, the icing on the cake, they were all women. One of them was strikingly pretty but he wouldn't have kicked any of the others out of his bed on a cold night. He stepped out of the bushes - this could be a happy day...

He motioned for them to halt by holding up his left hand, his right hand traversing the carbine barrel across all four riders.

The trail was narrow and all four couldn't get in line - he couldn't see them all at once. He had heard them coming from some distance as they had been loud and laughing - they may even have been singing but it was hard to tell with redskins. In his underused military brain, Mulvenna realised that this was a poor place for stopping four horses but continued to hold up his hand as he approached them.

Mulvenna heard his worn-out horse rustle out of the thicket behind him as he took the bridle of the first Indian pony to bring it forward; his Army mount was always looking for grazing. Instinctively, he looked round to see where it was going.

Despite the fact he was now close to the first two of the young Indian women, Mulvenna only fleetingly noticed that they were armed. Women in his world also carried knives and axes but only to gut fish or chop wood. Irishwomen didn't normally use them as weapons, though their treatment of his cousin in a shebeen in Sligo had probably been a rare exception - and poor old Michael probably didn't need all of his fingers anyway.

Mulvenna's rapid thoughts were rudely interrupted by a hard blow on the side of his head; he collapsed onto his back, his final view before he lost consciousness was of his own horse licking off the oats that he had spilt down his shirt.

Mouse shrieked in victory and put her stone war club back in her belt. Taking her hatchet from the other side, she dismounted and prepared to kill the bluecoat.

White Rain, Willow and Crow Dress Woman also got down and hurried forward, their loose ponies jostling each other as they pushed for space on the narrow trail and caught the scent of the white man's horse in front of them.

Mouse was ablaze with joy; this would be the first white man she had ever killed. Hitting him with the club would certainly count as a first coup and killing him would entitle her to mark her clothes and pony with these war deeds.

White Rain though held her arm, refusing to let Mouse's axe fall. She was leader for a reason - there was a wider benefit for them all. She spoke soothingly to calm her young companion:

"Sister, I ask you not to kill the veho yet..."

Mouse's plump face darkened - she did not like to be disturbed in pursuing her warrior's duty. She wrenched her arm free and glared at White Rain.

"He is an enemy," she spluttered. "The pony soldiers defeated our warriors - we, at least, can win our small battle here…"

White Rain saw that, despite Mouse's anger, her hand with the hatchet now hung at her side. She started again:

"You are right. But if you kill him here - only we four will know of it. It would be better if more of our people knew of your bravery…"

Mouse breathed heavily and cocked her head to one side, waiting to hear of the better trail that her war leader wanted to follow.

"I know what you are thinking," said White Rain. "We could take his scalp, horse, weapons and clothes back to Bad Elk's people. Then, we hope, they would rejoice with us…"

Willow knew what White Rain was getting at but put it more bluntly:

"Our own folk wouldn't believe us. Oh, they might *say* they did but many would doubt us in their hearts - how could a bunch of young women overcome an armed soldier? No, they would just think we had found him and taken his things after someone else had killed him."

Crow Dress Woman though was on Mouse's side:

"Let her kill him! He is an enemy and deserves it. Other people can say what they like."

A groan and sound of retching came from the pony soldier; he was waking up. White Rain looked at Mouse and shrugged. It was Mouse's decision - kill the man here and not be believed back in their own circle or save his life for now and kill him when there were more witnesses.

Mouse's shoulders slumped as she put her hatchet back in her belt. White Rain grinned, patted the younger woman affectionately on the shoulder and ran to get a rope.

The Omissis village would now get to see the power of the Suhtai Forked Lightning Women.

---- 0 0 0 ----

Chapter Eighteen

"That's an ugly horse!"

Bright Antelope Woman spoke for them all. Viajero's share from the pony raid had seemed satisfactory until she had looked closely at the mottled grey. Its bulging eyes followed Viajero everywhere - it was a weird beast.

"It will be one of the two that I owe Feathers on His Shield," said the Apache. His other two ponies were sleek and seemed to have good wind; both were sorrels and he would test them for speed and stamina and see which one would become his new war horse.

He had seriously considered giving Feathers his broken-down hunting pony as well but, deep down, knew that presenting him with both the ugly grey *and* his wheezing hunter would be deemed an insult. So, the remaining sorrel pony would be the last of the hurt price that he would pay to the tetchy Thunder Bears soldier.

Dark showed his own ponies to Smoke on the Moon and his mother. His father was proud and showed it, calling passers-by to come and look at his son's war spoils. Badlands Walking Woman smoothed the hides of the ponies and scrubbed the Ute markings off them with a damp piece of deer hide. They needed her son's war deeds painted on their pelts; they were Cheyenne ponies now.

Bad Elk and Yellow Bear walked over to join the small crowd admiring the horses. They congratulated the warriors on their safe return and successful raid. There were unanswered questions of course - neither Dark nor the Traveller had returned to camp in triumph; they had ridden in casually during the day and it was some time before the village heard that they were back.

It could be, thought Bad Elk, that the warriors were too modest to proclaim their success - though knowing his nephew, he soon discounted that. The Traveller may not be open in his boasting but Dark made up for that. His nephew had spent the intervening time dressing up in his finest clothes and braiding his hair as befitted a returning warrior. Still, he was unusually quiet. Perhaps something had gone wrong on the raid that had robbed them of a complete victory. Neither of them showed any scalps or other captured items like guns or shields - Dark would have been the first to do that. As most warriors knew only too well, such raids were unpredictable - sometimes there was no time to do anything other than just take the horses and run. There was no disgrace in that.

Bad Elk called the men to him; he wanted to know how the raid had gone.

A young boy, bareback astride a bay colt, came past and Dark asked him to guide the new horses to the pony herd grazing not far from the camp. The boy obliged and shrilly mustered the ponies towards the pasture.

Bad Elk beckoned them to his lodge and the small group walked through the busy camp. Many meat racks were now getting empty as the women took the remaining slices and made pemmican, putting the finishing touches to the winter food supplies. Dogs roamed in occasional packs and scavenged morsels from children, tethered ponies skittered out of the way of playing youngsters, old men sat and smoked outside their lodges, backs cradled against sapling rests and women knelt on newer, pegged out hides and fleshed them with bone scrapers.

Bad Elk pointed to the activity -

"We are lucky to have all this - many of our cousins are still sleeping on cold ground without shelter." His companions nodded - they all knew what hardship meant.

Outside his lodge, Bad Elk's wife, Burnt Hair saw her returned nephew and squealed her delight, embracing him as though he was a young boy again. Dark recoiled in horror at the show of emotion but Smoke smiled; Dark had always been a favourite of his brother's wife. Viajero merely stared in another direction until the greetings were done. His N'De people were much less outgoing.

Bad Elk invited all the men to sit inside the lodge whilst they talked. He sat in his usual place, his spruce backrest facing the door and the rest in a semi-circle facing him. Burnt Hair brought him a bowl of soup and his pipe, freshly charged with field tobacco. She retreated, diplomatically, to her outside chores.

Bad Elk lit the pipe, puffed at the stem and came straight to the point:

"So, the raid went well?" he gestured in the vague direction of the pony herd. Dark and Viajero nodded but remained silent.

Bad Elk's eyes narrowed slightly - as camp chief he had to talk to many people on many things - he knew when he wasn't being told the whole truth or when men evaded telling it. He puffed on his pipe and passed it to Dark's father.

"Did you have to kill many Utes?" he said, coming at it from a different direction. He dipped a horn spoon into the soup and slurped the contents with relish.

"Only two," said Dark. Viajero looked at him in surprise; he would never betray his young friend but it couldn't be good to lie in front of your own father and the chief.

Yellow Bear sensed that Dark was hiding something and coughed out loud. It was a polite signal that the boy should think again about his tales. Maheo would not forgive such a deed.

Dark realised his mistake; this was not a childish stretching of the truth for humour or effect - it would not be a noble Cheyenne virtue to lie about what they had seen.

"That was a lie," he said, "We killed no-one."

Bad Elk choked momentarily on his soup; Smoke on the Moon blew out the pipe smoke in disgust; Yellow Bear smiled knowingly and Viajero relaxed. At last they could get to the truth.

See the Dark began:

"There was too much bad medicine - nothing went right…"

It was a strange tale to tell – the witch, the white-fire rattles, the snake – all impossible to understand. At the end of the story of the raid, there was much sympathetic nodding from all in the circle though all were worried that Dark and the Traveller had brought the bad medicine back into camp.

Yellow Bear though had the solution:

"I'll need to search for some special herbs but in a day or two, we'll hold a purifying ceremony. I'm sure I can cast out any bad spirits that you have brought back from the Utes."

Viajero shrugged and said nothing. Maheo couldn't purify *him* - only, Usen, the One God of the White Mountain Apache could do that. The Cheyenne Life Giver probably wouldn't even know who he was.

Yellow Bear spoke again:

"In the meantime, we'll need to cut the Ute horses out of the herd and keep them separate - the bad magic may be in them…"

He looked steadily at Viajero:

"Your new horse is very ugly - it could be in that."

---- o 0 o ----

Chapter Nineteen

White Rain thought that her women warriors made a great display. Riding into the Omissis circle in extended line and singing their war songs, the bluecoat soldier stumbling along roped behind Mouse's pony.

Mouse herself sat bolt upright, the prisoner's rope secured to the saddle cantle, with her captured carbine resting on her hip and the soldier's pistol stuck into her belt. She sang her own victory song. Her companions smiled at the words:

In your world
The mouse will flee
But not me.
Inside I am
A panther

The leader of the Forked Lightning Women had directed the route for their ponies to bring maximum effect to the village. She herself was leading the white man's horse as yet another trophy. Omissis warriors tried to attack the white soldier but she kept them in their place by pointing her hatchet at them and shrilly reminding them that her war sister owned the captive.

Crow Dress and Willow rode in silence but were secretly pleased at the dumbfounded looks on the faces of their tribal cousins. The Omissis gaped at the sight - elders were shocked, male warriors tutted and their own women glowed with envy.

Their arrival was not unexpected - the Forked Lightning Women had come across some Omissis girls washing skins in the river and they had been sent hurrying home to wake up their chief to let him know that the Suhtai women fighters were coming.

Red Backed Bear, the Omissis leader, stumbled from his tipi and blinked in the sunlight. He had heard of them, of course - all Cheyennes had heard of the Forked Lightning Women and their fighting qualities against the Pawnee. He had just never set eyes on them before. He was surprised that they seemed so young and quite pretty. Perhaps he could take one as a wife - his other two were old and wrinkled and complained a lot. His wives didn't do much work and the poor repair of his lodge disgraced the village.

It was then that Red Backed Bear saw the white soldier staggering along behind the ponies. Women warriors were one thing but a captured bluecoat was quite a different and dangerous matter.

"Go away!" he shouted in alarm, "…and take the veho with you."

White Rain looked hard at him and remained on her pony; this was not the welcome they had been expecting. She was about to speak when Mouse butted in:

"What do you mean 'go away'? We bring a prisoner - he is one of the bluecoats who attacked our warriors at Turkeys Creek two moons ago. He should be made to pay for that."

Red Backed Bear strode to Mouse's pony and tried to pull her down; Mouse smacked him on the nose with the iron butt plate of the carbine - blood trickled out and down the man's lip. He sat down in the dust, dazed and shocked.

"Listen to what the chief is saying, you young fool!"

This was from Buffalo Robe Woman who had heard the commotion of her daughter's arrival. She had ridden in from the other side of the tribal circle with her crippled husband in tow and their lodge already packed on a travois behind her horse. She turned to White Rain:

"Daughter, the chief knows that he cannot keep a captured white man in the village - other soldiers will hear of it and come to avenge him. Take him away and kill him - leave no trace of him here!"

Mouse was outraged:

"No! He is my captive and we chose to bring him here to pay for the defeat to the warriors of the People - including those of our Omissis cousins."

Of course, the young Cheyenne woman had no idea if the bluecoat had been part of the attacking pony soldiers at Turkey's Creek but it did no harm to remind the Omissis of the Cheyenne shame that needed to be avenged.

Her face darkened as her temper rose; she stood in her stirrups and with the carbine in one hand, pointed to the assembled villagers, spitting out her words:

"None of you are fit to call yourselves Tsis-tsis-tas! You are all cowards…"

Several of the warriors ran towards her but Mouse would not be silenced. She cocked the carbine and pointed it at them:

"We wanted to bring honour to our cousins' lodges by putting the white man to death here. But you are all…"

She hesitated, looking directly at the startled warriors, snarling and searching for the right word:

"…Women!" she shrieked.

The men burst out laughing, mainly out of relief that the stupid girl was now silent. Their jeering ceased when Mouse pulled the trigger.

The shot jerked Trooper Mulvenna back to reality. He had no idea what the screaming and shouting was about but the way people pointed at him, it probably involved him. He hoped the old man with the bleeding nose would rescue him and talk some sense into the four strange girls that had captured him. But, as he looked round the circle of ragged gut-eaters, they were all the same - just Indians; his life may not last too much longer.

He looked at the ground where the carbine ball had embedded itself deep in the soft earth, a wisp of blue smoke came from the hole and the dry grass round it had briefly burst into flame. The short girl he was tied to was certainly a force to be reckoned with. If he had the time left on earth, he thought he might try and charm her into letting him go.

After shooting, Mouse pushed the carbine barrel into her saddle girth and pulled out the pistol, ready for any other trickery from the disbelieving menfolk of the Omissis. There was none - the surrounding throng was silent with a mixture of embarrassment, fear and anxiety as to what the girl would do next.

Red Backed Bear, holding his crushed nose, gestured to the trail and told them to leave. The women looked at White Rain who eventually nodded and gestured with her head to ride out.

Willow and Crow Dress Woman rode up on either side of Mouse and gently turned her pony back the way they had come. The soldier had a grin on his face as though he had become part of their group; he saved his warmest smile for Mouse. She glared back at him.

White Rain remembered the white man's horse tied to her saddle; she pulled the pony to her on its headrope, leaned across and pulled out all the man's goods, including his powder flask, bag of lead ball and copper caps, from the leather saddle bag. She pushed the ammunition into her parfleche and let go of the headrope in front of the chief. She slapped the rump of the skinny pony and it walked towards him.

"Payment for your nose," she said coldly.

Buffalo Robe Woman and her husband rode past their daughter without speaking; she was a stranger to them now. White Rain looked at them with contempt - she should have left the old fools with the stupid Omissis. But, she reflected as she trotted after her ungrateful parents, her women warriors had achieved their mission - they had found the village and retrieved her mother and father. Her leadership, whilst slightly dented by Mouse's courageous actions and stout heart, remained intact; her three Forked Lightning soldiers drew their ponies aside to let her pass and she trotted after the swaying travois of her mother's pony. Her only cause for a troubled mind was the presence of the white soldier - if the Omissis did not want him killed in their camp then Bad Elk would probably feel the same way. Mouse would need to decide the man's fate but he couldn't be allowed to enter the Suhtai camp. He should be killed on the trail and left for the wolves.

Private Mulvenna was pleased; he was still alive and able to walk. Any deliverance from immediate death was an opportunity - it gave him time to escape. A plan slowly formed in his mind. A broad smile creased his face; an inner voice told him what to do: "Do what you do best Donal - charm them and then leave them…"

Of course, he would need a horse and food, so he may well have to kill one of the young women to get those things. He had never killed anyone before but it couldn't be too hard - his captors were, after all, just girls.

In front of him, the pony ridden by the young, stout-hearted woman, suddenly farted and staled; Mulvenna couldn't help but hope, as he stomped through the horse turds, that this wasn't an omen.

---- o o o ----

Chapter Twenty

See the Dark, Bad Elk and Viajero walked across to the pony herd admiring the collective wealth of their people. There were a lot of animals here now, the sun glancing off many sleek hides as they moved slowly, tearing at the grass. Soon the grazing would be used up and the People would have to move again. Some of Bad Elk's own ponies recognised him and sidled up – he patted them away, there was other work to be done.

Bad Elk looked at the grass and calculated two more feeding days at most. He would try and place the next camp close to a buffalo herd and call a general hunt to bring winter stocks back up to a level that would let them all survive. Buffalo were around but not in great numbers and the Cheyenne chief had been sent out scouts to look for them - they would report back soon.

Feathers on His Shield was one of the scouts Bad Elk had deployed, mainly to keep his temper in balance; the young man was becoming an annoyance - always asking where his new ponies were. Bad Elk had told him to be patient. He also cautioned him not to approach Viajero asking the same question - the matter would end badly.

The weather was sunny but the breeze had dropped and Yellow Bear, calling round to each lodge that morning, had declared that it was a good day for spells, especially when purification smoke was needed.

The skinny spirit diviner had spent three days looking for the correct herbs; it had taken longer than he had thought as none were to be found near their current campsite. So Yellow Bear had mounted his pony and ridden off to find them, scouring hills, patches of woodland and creek banks. The ride out from the village had pleased him - he couldn't remember the last time he had left the People and gone off by himself. He had enjoyed the time out alone in the wild country. In the bustling camp, it was easy to forget just what power Maheo, the Creator of All Things, had.

It was near the end of the growing season so he'd had to move quickly to make sure that the plants still had the right potency to remove any bad Ute spells. His hands were bleeding with thorn cuts and throbbed with pain from crushing various poisonous leaves as he'd dug and pulled at the chosen herbs. Yellow Bear didn't mind - he was at the service of his people and that was his task.

Riding back into camp, he kept the plants hidden from view; no-one could know his ingredients. Inside his lodge with the entrance cover closed and sealed from the inside with an arrow pinning the skins together, he had sung his purification songs and pounded the gatherings into a paste. He smeared this onto tapers of sage grass, dried them off over his tipi fire and carried them across to the horses.

Dark and Viajero had cut out the Ute ponies from the herd and tied by a linked headrope which Dark held tightly. They had corralled them into a small gully with a stream running through the bottom of it. Yellow Bear had asked that a fire be lit and Viajero was tending to the orange flames visible through the grey smoke. He coughed as spirals of smoke caught his throat and he stood up:

"Do *I* need to be here?" asked the Apache, voicing his doubts that a Cheyenne medicine man would have the power to purify the spirit of a warrior of the N'De.

"Of course," said Yellow Bear, "You and your family are part of this band and while you may pray to a different God, *here* Maheo is the one the People listen to."

Viajero sighed impatiently and sat down on the bank escarpment, re-tying his long moccasins; he would make his horned lizard spirit sign and talk to Usen later and see if there were any clearer instructions to cleanse him of any bad Ute spells that the old crone might have cast. He shuddered as he remembered the black snake emerging from her empty dress.

Dark was enjoying being part of the strange ceremony - he was simply dressed in elk skin leggings, his hair hung down his back, the lower ringlets tied and plaited with otter fur. He looked at his uncle and smiled. Bad Elk smiled back but did not say anything; in truth he was worried that the new ponies had indeed imported misfortune from the devilish Ute camp. Still, he trusted Yellow Bear to exert enough influence with Maheo to make everything right. He knew that Smoke on the Moon had paid Yellow Bear with good robes, food and a new knife to ensure the best outcome for his people.

Yellow Bear fussed around the fire, arranging the coated tapers onto a wolfskin, spread out on the stream bank. He lit a different taper, pulled a turtleshell rattle from his belt and with a cupped hand drove smoke across his forehead. He jiggled the rattle to scare off any unwanted demons, Ute or otherwise and then turned to Dark. He motioned the youth to come and stand beside him.

"Take one of the tapers laid out there and light it. When the sacred smoke comes, pass it over your body then over your three ponies."

While he did this, Yellow Bear chanted to Maheo, asking for his protection and the defeat of any Ute bad medicine. He shuffled round the fire, shaking his rattle and singing his cleansing songs. When Yellow Bear was satisfied, he told Dark to turn his ponies out of the gully; they were safe to re-join the herd.

Next it was Viajero's turn; he was reluctant to take part but knew it was the polite thing to do - especially as Bad Elk glared at him when he seemed to hesitate.

He took a taper and lit it. He felt vaguely guilty about washing himself in the Cheyenne sacred smoke but he would talk to

Usen later and see what he said. The Apache lined up the two sorrels and the mottled grey and started his ritual cleansing of them as he'd watched Dark do.

The sorrels behaved well but as Viajero brought the smoking taper round near the muzzle of the ugly horse, the creature snorted heavily and blew it out.

Yellow Bear was appalled. Bad Elk and See the Dark immediately climbed the bank and watched from the rim; warriors or not, bad medicine was bad medicine - it paid to be cautious.

Viajero recovered his composure, re-lit the taper and approached the grey; he was unnerved by its staring eyes but it needed to be dealt with - it was just a horse after all. The Apache had killed and eaten many of them in his raiding days down south. He grabbed the mane forelock and passed the taper over the animal's ears and down to its muzzle. This time the grey butted him with its bony head. Viajero dropped the taper in the stream and it fizzled out - he looked at Yellow Bear for guidance:

"Perhaps I should just kill the horse - it doesn't want to be purified."

"No," said Yellow Bear cautiously, "The sorrels are cleansed; you can let them go…"

Viajero slapped both fat sorrels on their rumps and they climbed up out of the gully and trotted off to join Dark's ponies.

The ugly grey strained up the slope after them but did not follow the sorrels to the herd. Instead, it just stood looking at the Apache, waiting.

"This horse is telling us something," said Yellow Bear, "I just can't understand what it is yet."

His purification ceremony not yet complete, the Cheyenne medicine man moved slowly up to the mottled grey. He patted and smoothed the strangely patterned hide - the animal was in good condition like the others. Its breathing was regular, it was not frightened. Yellow Bear couldn't see any injury or wound that might account for the animal's odd behaviour. It was puzzling; he walked round the animal inspecting shoulders, rump, tail and belly.

Watching him, Viajero called out:

"It's not important - this pony is for Feathers on His Shield - I don't care if it's strange."

Yellow Bear nodded and pulled up the hanks of hair on the horse's mane.

"Ah!" he said, as if discovering some deep secret. "I don't think you can ever give this horse away…"

Viajero looked puzzled, *of course* he could give the horse to Feathers - the grey was odd to be sure but it was sound and healthy - it would still count as part of the hurt price.

Yellow Bear called him over to look at the pony's neck; Viajero looked puzzled as the medicine man pointed to a pinkish mark.

"Isn't that your sign?" he said, smiling in triumph.

Viajero couldn't believe it - the pink mark was the in unmistakeable shape of a horned lizard. Usen had sent the pony!

"Your God has sent you your spirit horse," announced Yellow Bear.

"He could have sent me a better looking one," grumbled the ungrateful Apache.

---- o o o ----

Chapter Twenty One

Donal Mulvenna woke with a start - something was wrong. He was on his bed of stripped cedar branches beside the fire; red sparks still glowed in the pile of sticks through the ascending smoke. He sat bolt upright and looked around - he was alone. The four women had gone.

His pleasure at still being alive rapidly drained as he took in his plight - no food, no water, no boots or weapons. Just a ragged set of under drawers and his scalp still in place. He stood up and moved rapidly round the clearing where they had camped the previous night - there was a trail of four ponies but it petered out over some rocks. It also wound through some thorn thickets and he'd want to avoid those to keep his feet in one piece.

The old couple on the laden horses had not camped with them - Mulvenna wasn't sure why they had joined them from the other village but there seemed to be a tension between them and the girls - he couldn't spot the tracks of the travois pulled by the old couple's pony. It would be pointless to follow them anyway - there had to be a reason why they'd all stolen off like thieves in the night without killing him. Women, eh? He'd never figure them out.

The morning sun didn't give much heat but it did give him a general direction in which to travel - to the west lay mountains - those had to be the Rockies. And, in his untutored mind, California, and all its riches, was just beyond them.

The young Irishman's experience of mountains was limited - the Ballyhouras and Boggerahs had been in his backyard at home but he'd never set foot on them. They were a place to be avoided, full of blanket bogs, bandits and English patrols. The Rockies though had a romance about them - they were high, to be sure, but if wagons could cross them then so could a spirited young man like himself.

Donal cheered up a bit though his belly rumbled with hunger to remind him that he hadn't eaten for days - the women hadn't fed him anything and had only grudgingly allowed him to drink from a stream.

Stumbling head down, roped behind a horse had stopped Mulvenna taking an interest in the countryside he passed. He was sure that the last stream was miles back - he didn't want to go back over his own trail and perhaps run into those bloody Indians again. No Sir, better to push on into the mountains - there could be a trading post or trappers up there who could help him get to California. Optimism and some painful walking would see him through.

He scoured the trees and underbrush for anything that looked edible but didn't find a scrap. He shrugged; as a boy he'd endured far worse pangs of hunger than this - especially when the Potato Disease came when he'd been around twelve years old. Now, those really *were* hard times - evicted from their house to make way for cattle pasture, his parents had begged for coppers on the Grand Parade in Cork to put food into his mouth. They had often come up short.

A chill breeze pushed through the holes in his long johns so Mulvenna hunted for wood around the edges of the clearing - the fire was starting to fade back and he needed heat today before he set off into the grey fastness above him. Under a deadfall tree he found a bonus - a rotting skunk. It had already been mostly eaten by smaller critters but some shavings of flesh were still on the red-rimmed bones. He shouted in delight and pulled the suppurating mass across to the fire.

The flames began to lick higher with the extra wood so he skewered pieces of the foul-smelling meat onto green twigs and pushed them into the fire. The flesh sizzled and dripped an oily liquid into the embers. No matter, he thought, I've got food - it's a good sign, a promising omen for the journey.

Partially burnt, the meat tasted relatively good - it was a bit like pork or, as he remembered a less favourable meal in Liverpool, like rat. Donal Mulvenna smiled as he ate and chuckled to himself as he remembered his attempts to seduce his four young lady captors. It hadn't gone well…

The pretty one had seemed to be in charge - but she wouldn't even look at him so he'd turned his attention to the younger, plump one. He'd been tied to her saddle since he'd been captured and, though she'd clobbered him with her stone club, she seemed to be the most skittish and approachable. She had darted looks at him at the campfire though the looks didn't seem to involve any affection. That didn't matter; Mulvenna had wooed and won many more difficult specimens than her.

He'd decided to sing to them - adopting a theatrical pose on one knee he graced them with *Kathleen Mavourneen* as well as a few verses of *Skibbereen*. Cracked as it was, he let his voice soar, declaiming the point of the songs with exaggerated hand gestures and mime. The pretty one was unimpressed, the tall thin one stared at him as if he was mad, the one with teeth on her dress, though, clapped her hands in delight while the plump one giggled and hooted.

Next he tried some hymns, dimly remembered from enforced attendance at St Assumpta's hidden chapel in the hills. These went down less well, even the plump one turned to stoke the fire. If they were disinterested, he would be lost - he needed them to like him so he'd tried a jauntier tune and danced a jig as he sang the lurid *Naked Nell from Old Clonmel*. He'd only got as far as the second verse when the pretty one strode across the clearing and walloped him with a broken branch. He'd stayed down in the dirt and crawled off to lie by the fire.

He tore at the sizzling skunk and smiled ruefully - everyone was a bloody critic. He heaped some more wood into the flames and watched the smoke spiral into the sky, the top feathered by the breeze. It would soon be time to climb into those foothills.

He was too engrossed in eating and planning to hear them approach. He'd started *Naked Nell* again:

*...she had no clothes
She was poor, I suppose...*

...when he heard the twig snap. It wasn't an accident, either. A ragged squaw stood there with the two pieces of dry wood in her hands - she needed to get his attention.

Mulvenna stood up with the ribcage of the skunk in his hand and tried to smile. As he did this, a younger man limped heavily across the clearing from another direction, beckoned by the old woman. She said something to him and the man turned to face him; the older woman walked across and joined them.

Donal looked hard at the young cripple; the Indian was about his own age but he was a weird one all right. His left forearm ended in a red stump and his hair seemed to have grown cock-eyed. Even in his starving state, Donal reckoned he could whip him. Despite the threat he laughed:

"Is that a bloody wig, or what?" he hooted.

Still, smiling and more confident now, he turned to the old gal and realised then something serious was happening.

What he thought was a dark scarf around her neck suddenly moved and a snake's head curled over his shoulder, slithering to the back of his neck. Donal stepped to one side and tried to brush it off but the snake coiled around his head, lashed out and bit into his eyeball.

The snake venom paralysed Mulvenna's body but did not dull the pain as the first cold, searching thrust of the skinning knife cut into his back. California was suddenly far away.

---- o o o ----

Chapter Twenty Two

Henry Armstrong's lecture at West Point had gone well. The Cadets, sitting stiffly upright in their high-buttoned gray blousons, were interested to hear tales of hard soldiering on the Plains.

It had been Colonel Sumner's idea to let him speak to up-and-coming officers – and he had been looked after like royalty. It was a world away from the bare-plank realities of Leavenworth. Now he sat alone in a guest room overlooking the Hudson River drinking coffee from a porcelain cup. The young cadet assigned to look after him stood outside the open oak door.

Henry drank in silence and smoked a cheroot. His departure from Fort Leavenworth, once he had got over his disappointment at being shouldered out of the regiment, had been cheerful and full of goodwill. Colonel Sumner had organised a leaving party and, over drinks with his fellow officers in his quarters, he had paid tribute to Henry's skill in the saddle, courage on the battlefield and concern for the welfare of his soldiers. Sumner had stressed - his booming voice rattling the window sashes - that Henry was only leaving the 1st Cavalry because, politically he could not stay. Using an English officer to subdue potential American rebels in Kansas would not sit well in Washington. Many toasts were drunk and songs sung and Henry had departed the Commanding Officer's house on a cloud of happiness and brandy.

The regiment's NCO on duty had collected him at the steps of Sumner's house to escort him to the Mess Hall where the troopers waited. Again, with many sentiments expressed and whiskies drunk, Henry had been persuaded to stand and give a farewell speech:

"Gentlemen…" there was a roar of laughter and cheers, soldiers were not used to being addressed like the officers. Henry remembered swaying slightly as the drink unsteadied him.

"Gentlemen, it is time for me to unsaddle my American cavalry horse, groom it and take it to the stable…" Henry paused for effect.

"…of course, as an English gentleman I couldn't possibly do that myself - I always need Trooper Herschel to help me!"

Herschel had grinned broadly, pleased that his name had been mentioned. Henry had barged on:

"My fellow cavalrymen, as you can see I have dined and drunk unwisely…"

The duty NCO had steadied him as he climbed onto a table to see everyone:

"I hope you all enjoyed your dinner - Trooper Garber I trust that the chef found enough grasshoppers to make you feel at home!"

There were roars of shared laughter as everyone turned to look at the unfortunate Garber, trying to forget his wanderings away from the column, north of the Arkansas. Garber though took it in good part and bowed his head, gracefully accepting the banter. Henry had forced himself to say something meaningful:

"On a serious note though, it is always a great sadness to leave behind one's comrades from the field of battle - we have endured, fought and endured again. There is no closer bond between men…"

A round of appreciative applause had broken out. Now, the room had gone silent, all faces upturned to look at him. Henry prayed that he wouldn't vomit over those nearest to him.

"My time with this great regiment has been the highlight of my life - may success and good fortune follow each and every one of you against enemies present and future. Good Luck to the Fighting First!"

There had been a flood of genuine emotion from the assembled troopers. Henry found himself being carried aloft as the cheering men picked him off the table and transported him to the front of the room where Herschel had been waiting for him with a small, neatly wrapped parcel. The lanky Moravian drew himself to up attention, ramrod straight but, like Henry, swaying slightly:

"Sir, the men decided to give you a small token of our esteem - I hope you'll honour us by accepting it."

The trooper handed the parcel to Henry, who was too befuddled with whisky to open it. His fingers skittered over the paper covering and he failed to pull off the decorative string.

Herschel took the parcel back and opened it for him - he handed Henry the contents.

It was a steel pocket watch bought from the sutler with precious dimes and cents from the pockets of impoverished soldiers. Henry gulped and was speechless.

Herschel again came to his rescue:

"Sir, there's a sentiment from the men engraved on the inside cover. I'll read it to you..."

"To Lieutenant H.L Armstrong,
From the men of the 1st Regiment of Cavalry
1776 and 1812 are forgotten,
But you won't be."

Many of the men hadn't had time to see the inscription before it was presented. They had bellowed their approval of the engraving. They had often joshed Henry about the wars between America and England - Henry, in return, chaffing them that America only won the Revolutionary War because of help from the bloody French. The words would be a great reminder of comradeship shared.

Henry had held the watch high, shouted his appreciation again and then, in tears, fell down puking over the unfortunate Herschel.

Now in the quiet, well-furnished West Point ante-room he took out the watch again and flipped the cover. The sentiment always overwhelmed him and his eyes filled - he put it away hurriedly.

The Cadet escort strode into the room and looked into the coffee pot:

"Can I get you some more coffee, sir?" asked the pudgy-faced young man.

"Er, no thank you - It's almost time for my buggy back to the steamer…" Henry tailed off, lost for something better to say.

"We all enjoyed your talk on your battles with the savages up at Blue Water and on the Solomon. You're lucky to have seen so much action." said the Cadet.

"Thank you," said Henry "Are you destined for the cavalry too?"

"Well, this is just my first year so where I go in the Army will depend on my grades - they're not too good at the moment" grinned the Cadet.

The buggy crunched onto the gravel outside the window and Henry stood up, it was time to go. Despite the fact he was now in a civilian suit, he had retained his Hardee campaign hat, stripped of all its badges and regimental markings. He crammed this onto his head and walked down the corridor towards the door with the Cadet.

"Are you going home to England, sir?" asked his escort.

"God no!" said Henry. "I'm going to stay in America and head west to see the Indian country before it all disappears. We have nothing like this at home."

The Cadet put Henry's small case under the seat of the waiting buggy - it contained the arrow head and blood-stained journal that he'd produced as part of his talk; the Cadets had crowded round to examine them at the end - the Cadet stood back stiffly and saluted. Henry doffed his hat:

"Thank you for all your help and attention today. We were introduced in a hurry - did you say that we had the same name?"

Henry got into the buggy as the driver prepared to set the horse in motion. The Cadet threw a blanket over Henry's knees and said:

"Only my middle name is Armstrong sir. I'm George Custer - George Armstrong Custer."

"Perhaps we're related Mr Custer," shouted Henry as the buggy pulled out.

"I very much doubt it Sir!" yelled the young man, his voice just topping the noise of the wheels on gravel.

---- o o o ----

Chapter Twenty Three

Winter had come and gone and the spring grass was up. See the Dark always hated the cold season - the tedium of watching the immobile pony herd scratching for pasture under snow, the ugly greying ice on the rivers and the deadness of the encampment as people stayed in their tipis under buffalo robes and waited until the earth came back to life. And worse - it reminded him of his physical limitations; the wind brought unwanted tears to his eyes, even from the empty left socket. They would freeze on his stone eye and keep his eyelid open so he looked like some crazy man; children would point and shout before running off to hide behind their parents. It was depressing.

Bad Elk had moved the village away from their last winter camping place and the small band headed north towards the Red Shield River. He and Yellow Bear watched the winding procession of their kinfolk from a nearby hill.

Out in front rode Broken Knife's Thunder Bear soldiers, in an arrow formation as the People's first line of defence against enemies; off on each flank were warriors of Smoke on the Moon's Striking Snakes military society. All rode upright and alert, singing their warning songs - letting the breeze carry their voices to any waiting foes.

In the middle came the procession of families - ponies pulling fully laden travois, the weight of their possessions making a broad trail in the earth as the poles dug into the softening soil. Small children bounced on the willow baskets on the travois cross beam, hanging on to the packed lodge skins and food parfleches. Some older folk, like White Rain's father rode the ponies but many of the women just walked beside the horses and mules, chivvying them along with willow switches. Dogs raced up, through and round the column in yapping packs, dodging beneath the feet of the clusters of colts driven by the older children. There was much chatter and laughter - moving was always an exciting time - everyone hoping that the next place would be rich in game, grass and timber.

At the rear, was the pony herd - the horses' urge to run being controlled by the older men. It was important to push the ponies slowly, avoiding a stampede that could lose horses to injury or death. The herd was growing well - the new spring colts not roped to their owners in the family column came along under the protection of the mares in the herd. A docile mule with a cow bell on its neck plodded ahead.

Bad Elk nodded in satisfaction to Yellow Bear; both men took their responsibilities seriously - the lives of their small band depended on it:

"It's good to be at peace for a while," said Bad Elk.

Yellow Bear just grunted - peace was always fragile.

"We are forced to be at peace - our people couldn't go to war if they wanted to; they need all their arrows and bullets just to kill buffalo to re-house their families. It will take many hunts to replace the lost tipis of all our cousins..."

The defeat of the Cheyenne war bands at the hands of the white soldiers last summer still weighed heavily on the minds of the younger men. Broken Knife and Smoke on the Moon had both reported the dissatisfaction of their soldiers at the last council fire.

One of the hotheads was Feathers on His Shield of the Thunder Bears - he openly called for revenge raids on the whites to settle the score. There had been much shouting and Broken Knife and Smoke had only just managed to take the heat out of the situation by promising to find and attack the Pawnee in the summer and take their horses.

"We may have kept the younger ones calm but those women are creating difficulties…" Yellow Bear pointed to the far distance, beyond the pony herd guards. A single line of riders abreast rode slowly at the rear. It was the Forked Lightning Women.

Bad Elk sighed:

"They behave like men. I suggested rear-guard for the village for this move but they won't be satisfied with that next time."

Yellow Bear hissed through his teeth in frustration - those women should be married off and leave the war trail to the men - that was the traditional Cheyenne way. But he knew his influence was limited; even Bad Elk could not tell anyone what to do. He could encourage or warn but the final decision to do anything lay at the feet of each individual - man or woman.

"Will your nephew ever marry the leader?" asked Yellow Bear, hoping that there was some way to break up the group and lessen their influence.

"I don't know - the boy is still set on finding guns and more horses. I hear that White Rain is also being courted by another man so…." Bad Elk tailed off, shrugging.

Down below a covey of sand grouse clattered out of the sage and startled the pony herd into a short run. The outriders responded quickly and turned the massed animals in on each other until they quietened down and resumed their slow pace behind the mule.

See the Dark, as one of the pony herders, pushed the milling animals into a tight swirling group and helped calm them. He whirled a looped rawhide rope and touched the flanks or shoulders of any mounts that threatened to break loose. The task was mundane but he was grinning with his own secret glee.

Soon he and the Traveller would depart the village and set out on a proper war trail. Not against the whites or even another tribe - no, that would be asking for trouble; they would raid a people who mattered little to anyone on the great grasslands.

---- 0 0 0 ----

Chapter Twenty Four

The idea for the raid had come on a clear morning in the Moon of the New Grass. Dark and Viajero were testing their new war ponies at some distance from the camp; three pronghorn antelope bounded out of a creek bed and both warriors gave chase on their new mounts.

Viajero's ugly horse had become the subject of much laughter in the village but the Apache was secretly pleased - the pony had good wind and speed. It also had a regular pace so firing a rifle on the move would be much more accurate though, as he constantly reminded himself, he couldn't actually prove this until he'd got another gun.

For now, the Apache's spirit horse stuck to the fleeing pronghorn as they jinked and swerved across the flats, tiny explosions of dirt flying from beneath their feet, sharp little heads turning to see where their pursuers were. The antelope were just playing with the riders, both men could see that.

See the Dark's sorrel wasn't far behind but it wasn't nearly as fast as the Traveller's blotchy grey. Dark hadn't bothered to unsling his bow to chance a shot at the swiftly departing animals but he was happy to let the sorrel run and guide it towards the bounding white rumps of the antelope. The Ute horse was a good prize.

A lone stranger had been watering his horse in the creek when Viajero spotted him. He reined in his pony from the chase, turned its head then charged towards the man yelling his war cry; he didn't know if it was an enemy or not but it did no harm to be prepared.

The rider's head whipped round towards the direction of the noise and quickly kicked his skinny pony out of the gully and tried to bolt. Viajero's ugly horse caught up easily and the Apache, disdaining a weapon, just pushed the man out of the saddle with his foot. The foreigner landed in some cactus, his right foot still trapped in his stirrup and he lay staring at the sky, singing what Viajero assumed was his death song.

See the Dark heard the Traveller screech and spurred his own horse towards the fallen rider, unslinging his bow as he did so; it was a chance for a much-needed scalp or count of coup.

He was disappointed to find the man and Viajero talking in a language he didn't understand. The man had a poor horse though its saddle and bridle were strung with highly decorated bones; they might make a decent prize if his friend didn't want them.

The man still lay in the cactus and the Traveller stood over him, growling in some sing-song tongue.

"Which people is he from?" asked Dark.

"He's a Tonkawa, an enemy of the Comanche," answered the Apache without looking up.

"Then that makes him *our* enemy doesn't it? The Comanche have been friendly and fed our people when they fled the veho soldiers."

Viajero held up his hand and resumed his interrupted talk. With a mixture of hand sign, his own N'De tongue and broken Spanish, Viajero spoke to the badly frightened warrior.

The Apache bent down and pulled a long, iron knife from the man's belt. Then reaching across to the man's saddle, took a white cotton sack from the pommel and looked inside. He brandished both of these in front of the Tonkawa's face, his voice coming in small explosions of breath as he spoke the tongue of the N'De.

He questioned him for some time - Dark sitting impatiently on his sorrel waiting for the Apache to finish. Eventually the Traveller hauled the man upright and dismissed him with a wave of his hand. The Tonkawa was happy to be released and, leaping into his bone strewn saddle, galloped off on his worn-out pony. A necklet made out of the bones of a man's hand flew from beneath his long dark hair, clattering on his back with the motion of his horse.

Dark was downcast and his impatience burst out:

"Why did you let him go? We should have killed him and taken his scalp..."

The Apache stared at Dark for a long time, pondering on the Cheyenne youth's immaturity. The boy always thought in the short term and had not noticed anything interesting about the Tonkawa.

"I was going to kill him but decided that he had information we needed..."

He held up the knife and the cotton sack:

"These," he said flatly.

See the Dark looked puzzled - a knife and some flour in a bag?

Viajero explained patiently - it took a while as he now had to translate from his conversation with the Tonkawa, via his N'De tongue and into his version of the Cheyenne language. As usual, at the end of it, his head hurt.

"Mexicans make this flour and these knives for trade with the Snake People. The Tonkawa recently killed a Comanche and took these goods from him..."

Dark looked unimpressed.

"The Tonkawa saw where the trade was done. I know how to get there - I used the same trail when I was killing Texans."

Dark's interest suddenly perked up. Killing Texans sounded promising - whoever *they* were - Dark had never met one. Scalps and coups were honours to be sought - it didn't matter too much where a man got them providing the fight was honourable.

Dark had not seen the Traveller look so fiercely pleased for a long time. The traders, he told Dark, were mainly Mexicans - not from the south but off to the west. Viajero had always told him that one of the reasons that the N'de people were put on earth was to exterminate all Mexicans. But, he stressed, these were not the lowly chicken stealers and general traders who sometimes came into Cheyenne camps but a different breed.

"Some of these men are robbers and soldiers - they don't just barter blankets and bread but guns, powder, cattle…"

The Apache sought the Cheyenne word:

"…and captives," he added.

Viajero climbed back into the saddle and smiled as he saw the light of future battles spring into the eyes of the young Cheyenne. But he held up a warning hand:

"These traders are close allies of the Comanche but we can get our new guns from them."

Both men let their horses drink at the creek then, at a lazy trot, headed back towards the camp.

See the Dark, excited at the prospect of new guns, mulled over the prospect in his mind. Soon a difficulty suddenly emerged:

"We have nothing to trade for the guns - how will we get them?"

Viajero snorted impatiently - he obviously hadn't made himself clear:

"We'll kill the traders and take them."

The young Cheyenne brightened up immediately - guns *and* scalps! Dark noted that Viajero's tone when talking about these new people had not been as dismissive as he usually was when he talked about Mexicans. There was an element of respect in his voice. The scuttling southerners didn't die well but the westerners seemed to be a different folk.

"Do these Western Mexicans belong to a different people to the southern ones? What are they called?" he asked.

Viajero remained impassive but told him what the traders were known as. Dark tried the difficult Spanish word and laughed at his own poor efforts, mangling it badly. He tried it again:

"*Comancheros*"

Still, it didn't matter if he couldn't say their name; killing them didn't require any conversation.

---- 0 0 0 ----

Chapter Twenty Five

"That's the trouble with being dead..." said Pythagoras Carver.

"What?" said Henry Armstrong, not paying attention to the musings of the wolf skinner but looking at the parts of a freshly disinterred corpse scattered along the wagon road.

"...all the stuff that should be on the *inside* ends up being on the outside... Here, Lootenant. This woman's bones and guts are outside for all to see, lyin' in the dust. It just ain't right. No sense of decency in it."

"Perhaps you should speak to the wolves that dug her up and ate her. They *were* wolves, right? You showed me what their tracks looked like - they're all over here" said Henry, squatting on his haunches to inspect the paw prints.

"Yeah, Lootenant, you're learning fast. Game must've been hard to come by after a bad winter..." Carver trailed off and looked at the ragged torso; yellowing white ribs with attached gobbets of brown flesh stuck through the dead woman's shroud and flies had gathered to share in the bounty.

"...she was buried in a light blue dress, maybe late last year. Cold probably kept her fresh. Young too, I reckon; there's a corn doll under her hand here..." Carver pushed the remaining shreds of a white sheet aside with his hunting knife.

Henry looked around the clawed-out grave, looking for a marker to say who she was but there was none. He remembered Billy Cobb's grave down near the Arkansas; like this woman, he was just another pile of bones that future generations would ride over without a thought.

"We'll wait for the wagons to catch up and borrow a couple of shovels to rebury her. It's all we can do." Henry used his boot to assemble the scattered parts into some sort of order, kicking and scraping entrails and lower limbs into a pile. He stopped when slime from the decomposing tissue stuck to the leather.

Henry examined the skull as it lay on the ground. The woman's head was in two halves where a wolf or maybe a bear had cracked it open to gouge out the brains - she'd been blonde and fair skinned judging by the remaining side of her face. He looked up as shapes crossed the sun – a swirl of vultures and ravens flew above the carrion – it was their turn next. Whoever she was and wherever she was going, she was now just a pile of drying chunks of meat by the side of the Oregon Trail.

He looked back along the rutted road - the wagons were slow moving but white canopies were cresting a slope a couple of miles away; he reckoned that the oxen pulling them would take an hour to reach them. He snorted in frustration at the delay - moving west took time.

The sun clouded over and gave a welcome blanket of shade for a moment or two. He watched as his companion used a flat rock to scrape the body pieces into a decent pile ready for a new burial. At each movement of the rotting flesh, a buzzing cloud of black flies flew up, hovered for a second or two then settled back onto their feast. Pythagoras Carver held his nose as he dealt with the stink of putrefaction. Henry smiled:

"Odd to see, Mr Carver, how the stink of bad flesh affects you - considering your previous occupation and all…"

Carver looked up and tipped the broad brim of his hat back and looked at his new boss:

"Well, Lootenant, dead animals don't smell the same as dead people. This here girl still has the scent of civilisation on her …"

Carver tailed off, thinking about his dead Cheyenne wife - not that his wife ever had any scents of *white* civilisation on her skin. No, she'd smelled of wood smoke, bear grease and spruce boughs but they were comforting smells that made him easy by her side. He thought about her more now, especially as he'd signed up as a guide to the young Englishman to go back west into the Cheyenne Smoky Hill country where she had been born.

"...well, kings or cardsharps – we're all just walkin' worm food."

"More wisdom from Grandmaw?" ventured Henry

"Yup," said Carver and just squatted on his haunches and looked off into the distance.

As Carver drifted off into his own private thoughts Henry wondered for the hundredth time if seeking out the Cheyenne was a good idea. Taking the wolf-skinner with him seemed a practical use of Carver's talent with the Cheyenne tongue and his knowledge of the Smoky Hill would be useful but the nagging doubt that comes from overconfidence troubled him. What if they didn't find any Cheyenne...or worse, what if they *did*? The trouble was that Henry was in love and the sagging confidence in his brain was easily suppressed by the desires of his heart.

Of course, his love was not for a woman - he'd scarcely had time to meet any since leaving the cavalry. Even his brief stay in New York and at West Point had not thrown up any opportunity to meet suitable young women, apart from seeing some pale specimens at dreary recitals in overstuffed parlours in the city.

No, it wasn't romantic love that gripped him; Henry recognised the symptoms of the constant English affection for the wild lands - *any* wild lands - and those who lived there. He put this down to coming from a small island, buffeted by sea and bad weather. He thought that it probably explained why the English were an Imperial power - anywhere would seem more interesting or vibrant than a safe and secure rocky fastness protected by the Royal Navy. It was why the English roved across the globe, conquering, settling and bringing culture and civilisation to natives - whether the natives wanted it or not.

Now that he wasn't a soldier any longer, going to meet the Cheyenne seemed a natural thing to do; he had been much impressed with them at the Solomon skirmish and meeting the Suhtai youth later. Of course, as Henry reflected, perhaps it was only a natural thing for the *English* to do. While he had been in his US cavalry uniform, he had just been part of the Cheyennes' American enemy - now, as an English civilian, he came in peace. He just hoped that Carver would get a chance to explain the difference if they ever met any of the Medicine Arrow People.

Back in Independence, Henry had sold off one of his two saddle horses to help finance the trip, though he had wheedled some extra cash as a loan from his father's contacts in a New York bank. With it he'd bought gifts of cloth, iron knives and axes. For good measure he had added in some combs and mirrors and a couple of trade blankets as a way to appeal to tribal women. He'd convinced himself that all he had to do was to present the gifts and begin the exploration of the Cheyenne life and country from there. If the damn French could do it in the early days, so could he. Carver, for some reason, had seemed less positive.

He almost didn't recognise Carver when they met up in Independence - gone was his wild hair, beard and reeking wolf skins. The clean-shaven man in buckskin jacket, linsey shirt, leather pants and broad-brimmed hat was a much younger version of the grizzled wolf skinner than Henry had been expecting. He was still older than Henry by some eight or nine years but not the fifteen or twenty that Henry had assumed when they rode together down to the Arkansas. It seemed a good omen - fresh views on a fresh life.

Henry smiled as he remembered the awkward socialising that the two of them had done in the town; sitting drinking coffee in a draughty hotel foyer wasn't Carver's idea of amusement - it wasn't Henry's either but funds were low by this time.

While he waited for his captured Sharps rifle to be cleaned and serviced, Carver had gone out to find a two-dollar whore and returned disgusted when he found that the cheapest was three dollars and fifty cents. Henry's explanation that it showed the signs of a booming economy didn't sit well with the wolf skinner.

Henry leant back on the short prairie grass and put his hat over his eyes to keep the sun off. He was happy in the West, even though his rapid shipping off to America had been used to avoid a family scandal, he was a contented man. He had seen a book of George Catlin's pictures of the American Indians that his father had bought at the Indian Gallery exhibition in London.

The portraits of the warriors - Osage, Pawnees and Sioux - were impressive but Henry had been much taken by the paintings of the Comanche villages, hunts and battles and, just as hints in the background, the broad sweep of the land. Even Catlin seemed to have sensed, almost three decades earlier, that this way of life was doomed and he wanted to capture them in oils on canvas before it was too late.

Henry was of the same mind; seeing what the wild men saw, breathing the same air and living in their country, whatever the risk, was above any value of dying of old age on his father's estate surrounded by ledgers and ink pots. No, far better to meet sudden death whilst answering his restless nature was preferable to a rickety, unadventurous decline into the grave.

Carver stopped gathering body parts and came over to sit beside Henry; their horses, hobbled in case they got startled and tried to bolt, moved slowly across the poor grazing ripping at the dry grass.

"Them wagons'll take an age to git here," said the wolf skinner, "and that stink'll only git worse.

Henry didn't reply so a companionable silence settled between them. Some of the flies had followed Carver over to where the men were sitting and now buzzed around their heads.

"What do you think of this country, Mr Carver?" asked Henry suddenly.

He always called him 'Mr Carver' and never 'Pythagoras', mainly because Carver had never asked him to use his first name and because he would have found it constantly amusing to address his rough diamond companion by the name of a long dead Greek mathematician. Carver always called him 'Lootenant' - Henry was not sure if it was out of respect as he'd retired from the Army weeks ago or if the wolf skinner was making some sort of sly joke at Henry's unemployed status.

Carver looked at him with eyebrows raised:

"*This* country? Well Lootenant, this country is harsh, dry and goddamn dangerous. If it's not wolves, it's Indians or the goddamn weather…."

"No, no, Mr Carver - not what's *in* it but what it *looks* like? Don't you think it is beautiful?"

"Beautiful!?" snorted the wolf skinner and spat into the dust; the flies followed the spittle and drank.

"Hell, Lootenant, I've trapped from the Canada line damn near to Texas and I ain't seen anything I'd paint a picture of - the place is just hard goin' and hard times."

Henry smiled and shook his head:

"No, my friend, you aren't being honest with yourself. You wouldn't have spent all those years in such harsh country, as you call it, if something about the place didn't hold you here."

Carver kept silent but, in truth, he knew that Armstrong was right. He'd tried living in a town once but the free life of a trapper drew him back into the wilderness - back to the danger and the silence. Once he'd met and married his Cheyenne wife, he knew he'd never go back and live with whites again. Whites - and it was odd that he now thought of them as some race apart - were too damn keen on building things, smashing down the wild places - their civilisation wasn't for him. No, the free life was still in the desolate lands where there were no signposts or wagon roads. The birth of his daughter on the banks of the Musselshell seemed to confirm that he was where he should be. His eyes filled briefly with nostalgic tears and he hid them from Henry.

"You're lucky to have all this emptiness Mr Carver. My own country is too bloody civilised, too ordered - railways, towns, newspapers and the God-awful British public. I live on a small, damp island with very few empty places - I envy you this..." Henry gestured expansively at the rolling grasslands and at the far Rocky Mountains, dimly rising in the west.

Carver could see that the young Englishman meant what he said and, if he could but admit it to himself, some of the land up along the Yellowstone was the finest he'd ever seen. It was God's own country sure enough.

"Well, what's your own country like Lootenant? Ain't it beautiful too? I saw a paintin' once in a Scotchman's saloon of a place called the Tro-Sacks - it looked kinda like somewhere back east or in Canada maybe - woods and lakes and stuff."

Henry pondered on Carver's version of the Highlands and laughed:

"Well Mr Carver, the Trossachs are in Scotland and so don't count, though the Scotch are probably just as much barbarians as the Cheyenne. We English have similar lakes and mountains in my own county of Cumberland but where I live the earth is more gently rolling - green and boggy up to the Scottish border..."

"Good pasture then…" interjected Carver.

"Indeed - my poor old horse misses that."

Henry nodded at his mount's disdainful chewing of the dry prairie grazing. In fact, his big gelding had managed well in America though it had lost its glossy English sleekness and its raw-boned frame showed through its dusty coat. The animal eyed Henry with its usual gaze of moral superiority - as though a titled Earl had been forced to eat in a soldiers' chow house. The look reminded Henry of his mother.

A thudding of hooves brought both men alert - the wagon company boss rode into view and stopped near the pair. Chester Hood was a rangy Texan with a red forked beard, a brace of Colts and a bad temper:

"What the Hell are you boys doin'? Them wagons'll be up in a few minutes and I don't want them damn pioneers takin' an early noon break - we gotta keep movin'."

Carver shifted uncomfortably but said nothing. Henry looked coolly at Hood and said:

"Well, those 'damn pioneers' pay your wages Mr Hood and we're waiting for the wagons to arrive so we can bury her…" he pointed to the small mound of flesh and bones buried under a seething mass of flies.

Hood dismounted and inspected the pile and the despoiled grave.

"*Her*, you say? This is just a pile of damn wolf food - they'll be shitting *her* out in the woods right now. Git mounted boys, we got places to go."

"I don't think so," said Henry, surprised at his own boldness.

"No, we'll just wait, borrow a shovel and bury her in a proper Christian manner."

Hood's hand moved to the curved pistol grip on the left Colt but he didn't take it out of his belt:

"*Christian*? Listen mister, buryin' is a waste of time - them wolves'll be back for their picnic if they can't find nothin' else. All we get out of it is wasted time on the trail - we should be pushin' on to the fort."

Henry continued to stare at Hood. After an uncomfortable silence Henry said:

"Well, Mr Hood, you may instruct your wagons as you see fit but you will remember that Mr Carver and I are not part of your pioneer company and we can depart at any time. Our pack mule is tied to the tailboard of Mr Russell's wagon and we'll gather that up when he reaches us."

Hood snorted and rubbed his palms down his thighs. He hesitated to back-talk the Englishman as he was happy to have their guns along on the trail, especially if there was Indian trouble. Most pioneers were poor marksmen and would crumble under real pressure - an experienced Indian fighter like Armstrong and his trapper companion could make the difference in a tight spot. He would try to be more conciliatory, though it was against his nature as a Texan; back home he'd be more inclined to shoot dissidents out of the saddle than waste breath arguing:

"Well, Mr Armstrong, you got me there. I know you just agreed to accompany us to Fort Laramie and I'd hate to lose you boys too early. I'll halt the wagons here and we can bury this girl - perhaps Pastor McCormick could say the words…to make it right like?"

Henry nodded his agreement and Carver breathed more easily. That boy was hardening up but seeing off a Texas blowhard was easy compared with how the Englishman might deal with the wild Cheyenne.

---- O O O ----

BOOK TWO

Leave no tracks on the ground
Nor on my heart
Even if you learn to fly
I will find you

(Song of Pursuit - Mouse, of the Suhtai Cheyenne)

Chapter Twenty Six

The ride towards Texas was long and hard but Viajero and See the Dark rode at an easy pace to spare the horses. Each had brought an additional pony and their small food supply swayed on the backs of two protesting, pack-saddled mules. The food, dried buffalo meat and pemmican, was for the return journey - there would be no time to stop and hunt if they were fleeing pursuit.

Telling Bad Elk that they intended setting off on their own war trail against the Comancheros had not gone well. The chief had called in some of the elders including Dark's father as well as Yellow Bear and Broken Knife to try and reason with the youth and the Traveller:

"Raiding the Mexican traders for their guns will only bring revenge attacks on us from the Comanche - those two peoples have traded together for many summers - you will be taking *Comanche* weapons. They will not rest until we are all punished…" said Bad Elk.

"The Comanche treated us well after the fight with the soldiers - they fed our cousins and gave skins for lodges to the homeless ones," added Smoke on the Moon. "It would be impolite to steal from them…"

Unusually, Broken Knife interrupted the conversation:

"We are not afraid of the *Nerm-en-uh…*" he said, using the Comanches' own name for themselves, "…they rarely come north of the Flint Arrowpoint River now and probably couldn't find us if they did. Let the Traveller and the son of Smoke on the Moon go and get their guns - bring spare ones back if you can - we'll need all we can get if we are to fight the whites again."

Bad Elk and Smoke both snorted in exasperation; Broken Knife was a true warrior and rarely considered consequences. Dark smiled at the outburst but said nothing.

There was a lull in the arguments as Bad Elk considered a different approach. Turning to Yellow Bear he said:

"What are the signs saying? Will their raid succeed?"

Yellow Bear frowned at the unexpected question - he hadn't consulted Maheo about how the raid might play out. It seemed pointless anyway, the pair had determined to go and all the good advice in the world would not change their minds. He just shrugged and said he didn't know; Bad Elk looked sourly at him.

Dark had made his case for the raid:

"It is true that the Comancheros are allies of the Comanche - the Traveller explained this to me…" he looked around at Viajero who grunted in assent.

"…but our need for guns will increase if more whites come. It may be better to be enemies of the *Nerm-en-uh* but be well-armed…" Dark stressed the 'well-armed' phrase by holding an imaginary rifle across his chest, "… than to be paupers with only bows and arrows when even more veho soldiers arrive in our country."

Broken Knife nodded in agreement; the young warrior had put it well – upsetting the wild riders of the southern grasslands was secondary to the survival of their beloved Suhtai.

Smoke and Bad Elk though looked unconvinced. They could not stop the pair going on the war trail - that was a decision taken by individuals at their own risk but Smoke was not going to offer support from his Striking Snakes military society. And, even though Broken Knife approved of the mission, he would not let any of his soldiers go either and said so.

Yellow Bear, trying to gain some common ground said to Viajero:

"My friend, you have experience with these Comancheros - are they good fighters? Will your raid succeed and return you to your families?"

Viajero, gathering the Cheyenne words in his head, replied:

"The ones I raided many moons ago were easy to kill - they were just farmers out to trade…"

The Apache remembered the abject fear on the faces of the traders when he and his shrieking war band had attacked them just east of the Pecos River as they plodded their way to the *Comancheria*. The Mexicans had tried to flee but Viajero and the others had prised them out from their hiding places in the red mesa, staked them out on the ground and lit fires on their chests. Whooping, they had run off the mules, overturned and torched the wooden-wheeled *carettas* and taken a child as hostage. The plunder had been poor - no weapons, no ammunition and no whiskey; even the child was troublesome so Cruz, his war companion, had smashed its head against a rock and left it there as the vultures wheeled in the sky.

Yellow Bear and the others sat up and took an interest in the ease of the Apache's previous raid but Viajero was nothing if not truthful:

"…but that was a long time ago. I've heard that the Comancheros are now better mounted and armed. There are renegade Texans and Americans who ride with them and guard their goods."

None of the assembled Suhtai knew the difference between a Texan and an American and didn't ask. They were all white and therefore, enemies. Viajero spoke again:

"In Texas, the traders go to small houses that they have built in certain canyons so the Comanche can come to them. We will attack them, before they get there - they will be too far away from their own settlements to the west and still not close enough to allow the Comanche to come to their aid."

Exhausted, Viajero sat back, his head throbbing from the mental effort. Dark though was proud of him - a straightforward warrior's plan - it would work. He and the Traveller would need to select the Comanchero group carefully, ensure it was carrying guns and ammunition and then attack it. Dark harboured a faint doubt about the escort of renegades and how many guns they would have but he trusted the Apache to have a plan to overcome them. He sat back in contentment. There was a buzz of conversation between the tribal leaders but he ignored it - the war trail waited and he wanted to be on it.

Smoke looked up from the chatter and spoke directly to his son:

"I hear that White Rain Woman is courting under the blanket with another - won't you stay and court her yourself?"

Dark shook his head. White Rain had told him that Feathers on his Shield was now seeking her for his second wife, whether she'd said it to make Dark jealous, he didn't know or even care. He had tired of her constant indications towards marriage and now stayed away from her tipi. He still felt strongly for her but was now more worried by his lack of personal possessions, weapons and ponies - he was not a prime choice for a husband and, while White Rain insisted on her warlike ambitions, she was not a good choice for a wife either. Gloom had settled on him as he thought about it over the winter - only the cleansing breath of danger on the war trail could sweep his misery aside.

Now, out in the clear, sparkling air of the south west he felt alive. Even Viajero, normally cautious about expressing any happiness or contentment, was alert and upright in the saddle and sang a song in his own tongue, which once Dark had asked him, turned out to be about the red earth and horned lizards. The Apache had almost smiled.

Suddenly, the mules started braying and jerking on the head rope; the spare ponies cast anxious looks at them, wondering what had startled them. The lead mule suddenly stopped, bucked its rear end towards the sky and its pack saddle slopped to one side almost underneath its body.

"I told you a Cheyenne travois would have been better," said Dark conversationally.

Viajero dismounted and grunted:

"The travois is for women and families. These pack saddles will carry a lot of weight when we get the rifles - they just need to be balanced properly…"

He pulled the head rope tight into his saddle and tied the mule's head close. The mule still kicked and lurched as the willow boughs of the pack frame cut into the soft skin of its belly. Its front hoof landed on the Apache's foot making him grimace with pain.

Viajero punched the animal in the head - it bared its yellow teeth and tried to bite him. Dark rode round and picked up the bridle of his spare horse and took it out of the way. The Apache's ugly horse had refused to be tied to a saddle but seemed happy just to follow in Viajero's wake, untethered. It stood and watched Viajero deal with the mule.

"…and anyway, we'll have to go through narrow canyons, up steep hills and maybe run for our lives - travois are not good for that."

"True," said Dark, "If we don't find the Comancheros, we can always eat the mules."

"It would be a pleasure to eat these two, "muttered the Apache getting back into the saddle.

The pair rode on in silence for a while – a slow, unhurried pace over the flat scrubland.

"How far is it to Texas?" asked Dark eventually, childishly bored with the inactivity.

"Days yet," answered Viajero impatiently - he had already explained to the young Cheyenne that they were not going directly to Texas, merely in that direction. The plan was to find the Comancheros *before* they got to their trading posts; he blew through his teeth at the boy's inability to hold onto details.

"How will we know when we get to Texas," said Dark, looking away to hide his smile as he knowingly pushed at the Apache's limited patience.

"There will be a Texan tribal sign once we cross into their country," said the Traveller looking serious.

"Is that true?"

"Of course not! You're an idiot."

Dark cackled with laughter at the Traveller's unexpected humour; the outburst of noise spooked the ponies and he looked back to calm them.

It was then that he saw the dust - just a faint swirl, blown up by the wind but easily seen at great distances across the flatness of the southern Plains.

"You know we're being followed?" he said.

"For two days now," said the Apache.

Dark fell silent, chastened that he hadn't spotted the pursuers before and bitterly disappointed that the Traveller had failed to tell him. Battle may be closer to hand than even he had hoped.

---- o o o ----

Chapter Twenty Seven

Feathers on His Shield looked down into the still waters of a pool beyond the bend of the river and combed his hair with a bunch of porcupine quills. His long black locks draping over his shoulder framed a strong face. He nodded in satisfaction and began to plait the otter fur bands into each side - he was a handsome man and he knew it.

Tonight, was special; he had to look every inch a Cheyenne warrior and, even though he already had one wife, a suitable, prospective husband for another.

He had prepared well over the last few months; everyone knew he was wealthy - his personal string of ponies was some of the best in the herd and his current wife, Sweet Water, had a wide range of iron pots and skillets that helped her prepare the feasts that her husband had often laid on for the poor of the small band of Suhtai. There were widows and the infirm who couldn't hunt any more or who had no-one to hunt for them; Feathers had ensured they were fed and had also made sure that everyone *knew* of his generosity, mainly by proclaiming this regularly around the camp.

He didn't do this himself, of course, - no that would be boastful - instead he gave gifts to another man, Wolf Runs Him, to do this on his behalf. So, Wolf Runs Him had duly mounted his pony and ridden round the camp as a crier, declaring Feathers' greatness in battle and generosity in peace.

Inside the lodge of the Forked Lightning Women, White Rain Woman sat facing her soldiers. Wolf Runs Him passed by outside, calling all to yet another feast at the lodge of Feathers on His Shield. Mouse looked towards entrance flap:

"Perhaps we should go and eat?"

White Rain snorted in derision; all her soldiers were constantly hungry:

"Go if you want to - but remember what it would look like for the rest of us…"

"What do you mean?" rasped Willow in her strange Lakota accent.

An irritated White Rain pointed to their cooking pot:

"We have food. If we eat at that man's feast, the People will be convinced that we can't hunt for ourselves - we'll be like my father with his crippled leg; just another useless mouth to feed."

Mouse was about to speak but Crow Dress Woman got in first:

"We've had two rabbits in three days…" she said.

"And a fish," added Mouse, slightly ashamed as Cheyenne were not supposed to be fond of fish. It was not the true food of a warrior and hunter people.

"…and a fish," conceded Crow Dress. "Well, I'm hungry and if anyone is offering free food, as warriors, we should take advantage of it. My brother does and he's a Thunder Bear soldier, just like Feathers on His Shield."

"It can't do any harm," said Willow as the other two nodded their agreement. None of them mentioned that Sweet Water's cooking was better than White Rain's.

White Rain said nothing but let her three companions choose their own path, shuffling to one side as the young women opened the tipi flap and walked off into the darkness. Their chatter receded into the gloom as they made their way to the far side of the camp; a coyote yipped nearby and a skein of geese arrowed their way towards a small lake beyond the trees, honking loudly.

White Rain poked her head outside of the lodge flap to see if she could see where the geese had gone - they may have to shoot a couple of those tomorrow if they could get close enough.

She stepped outside; the light from her cooking fire flickered against the nearby trees and rocks. It was a peaceful, starlit night - she and Dark had often met and coupled under such a canopy. But he was gone now - two days on the trail towards Comanche country. Again, there had been no farewell though he had ridden past her lodge to let her know he was going. One look and a curt nod from astride his pony seemed cold and dismissive.

It was a mystifying time - Dark had never spoken of love, let alone marriage. The times when she had raised the matter had been met with silence or he had just walked off. Perhaps he was just immature. Her dead husband, Spotted Buffalo, had been nothing like Dark - he had been outgoing, a good provider and her best friend. Tears came and she pushed the ball of her hands into her eyes to wipe away the tell-tale tracks down her dusty face. She exhaled to calm herself and looked up at the stars.

A hand plucking at her sleeve made her jump:

"You see how stealthy I am - it is why I'm a great warrior and hunter," hissed Feathers on His Shield, putting his arm around her shoulders and covering their heads with a blanket.

White Rain pushed him away; she had previously been polite and had stood under his red trade blanket while Feathers had whispered his hopes and dreams for them both. She had not encouraged him and, as many Cheyenne girls did with men they didn't like, would wait and hope his ardour faded. Tonight though, politeness was absent - she was not in the mood and the heavy red material slid down to the ground. Angrily, Feathers picked up the blanket:

"I am a wealthy man - my dowry price for you as my wife would be great. Your father would be very pleased…six ponies would show him how much I look forward to our marriage…"

White Rain snorted with contempt:

"Is this why you have organised a feast? So you can get me alone while your real wife does the work at your campfire? My man will be interested to hear about this."

Calling Dark 'her man' seemed odd, even as the words came out of her mouth. She hoped Feathers would take it as a threat.

The warrior looked at her and laughed:

"The son of Smoke on the Moon is just a boy - off on some crazy war trail with that foreigner. He'll be killed soon enough and then you'll have no-one…"

Feathers grabbed at her sleeve again and tried once more to put the blanket over their heads. This time White Rain knew what to do.

Pulling the itchy red cloth violently down so she could see his face, she punched the persistent warrior in the mouth. She felt his teeth smack the inside of his lips and saw the blood spurt in a red spray. She hurt her hand, of course, as she'd forgotten Bright Antelope's instruction to clench her knuckles tight - but the pain was worth it.

Feathers staggered back with the shock and would have attacked her if the other three Forked Lightning Women had not returned from the feast early. Hearing their chatter coming from the darkness he gathered up the robe and, hissing promises of revenge, slunk off.

The three girls gathered round their leader, unaware of her eventful night. White Rain had been right, they told her - people had nudged each other and whispered - the Forked Lightning

Women were not *real* warriors or hunters - just girls unable to provide for themselves properly. Disgusted with their gossiping kinfolk, they flung themselves around the campfire and talked. They needed something brazen and warlike to do to prove their worth once again; to recapture the respect they had after the fight with the Pawnees. But what?

After rattling off suggestions to one another and a foolish song from Mouse about no glory for women, it was not White Rain that came up with the answer but Willow.

All four laughed at the boldness of her words and the sheer, almost impossible, scale of her plan. But the more they came up with practical problems to stop them even starting out on it, the more enthusiastic they all became. It would be their own quest with glory, respect and honour at the end of it - or, as Mouse pointed out, they could all be killed.

---- 0 0 0 ----

Chapter Twenty Eight

Henry Armstrong and Pythagoras Carver followed their guide to the crest of a small hill, leaving their horses and pack mule tethered at to an elder clump at the bottom of the slope.

Lucas Snyder spread his arms with evident pride and said:

"Gentlemen, my dwelling is less than twenty yards from here - can you see it?"

Henry and Carver were beginning to regret their decision to follow Snyder away from the wagon train; they were still a two-day ride from Fort Laramie and they had been looking forward to several beers from the post sutler. Still, Snyder seemed to offer a way to contact the Cheyenne that Henry couldn't ignore.

"No Mr Snyder - I can't see your house - show me if you will sir," said Henry, trying to sound interested.

Snyder whooped with delight - he didn't get many white visitors and he was anxious to make his point:

"Why Mr Armstrong you are standing right on it! It is right under your feet sir!"

Unashamedly unimpressed, Henry and Carver looked down at the ground and shrugged. At the urging of the small, stocky trader they then followed him back down the hill and around to the other side. Lucas Snyder gestured theatrically at the hill's unusual vertical side:

"Voilà!"

Carver didn't trust anyone white man who couldn't speak English and ground his teeth in disapproval - the word sounded something like a Goddamn Frenchy or Dutchman would say.

The sod house was hard to see, either from a distance or close up, and Lucas Snyder liked it that way. Digging the house into a low, curved hill had saved him the work of building three other walls so he was able to lavish care and attention onto his outer wall, cutting prairie sod into usable lengths and laying the earth clods into a bastion two feet thick. The door, a disused table top, had been tricky as there was nothing to hang it on. But his ingenuity had prevailed and he had shaped discarded planks from wagon beds as a frame, jammed it into the soil entrance hole and hung the door from leather hinges made from a discarded belt. Lucas Snyder's main considerations were to have a house that was wind and fireproof - prairie fires and the constant wind across the rolling grasslands were things to be avoided - and the soddy fitted that bill. Of course, it leaked when heavy rains came - the water seeped through the earth as a natural course and he shared the place with rodents and insects - only that morning a surprised prairie dog had fallen in from the roof during unwary excavations of its own burrow. But it was Snyder's home and he was proud of his handiwork.

True to his word, the house was not far from the wagon road or the river where, during the travelling season, Snyder would make his living, trading goods and services to passing pioneers and, as he had casually mentioned, Indians.

"You live in *this*, Mr Snyder?" said Henry as he poked his head through the doorway, scarcely containing his disdain for Snyder's choice of home; back in Cumberland, his father had hound kennels bigger than this The only light, other than from the open door, came from a rough window frame, again bounded by cut-down planks, covered by a piece of muslin waterproofed by deer tallow. The interior of the hole was dimly lit by the hazy yellow light from the cloth.

"Yes, sir I do," said Snyder firmly, sensing the young Englishman's disapproving tone.

"Forgive me Mr Snyder," said Henry, realising that if he wanted to make an ally of Snyder and use him to contact the Cheyenne he would have to tread more carefully. He tried a different tack:

"May I ask how you make your living along the trail sir?" he asked, sticking to his father's advice on how to make small talk by getting people to talk about their favourite topic - themselves.

Snyder was overjoyed that someone seemed to be taking an interest in what he did:

"I, sir, am a *refurbisher*."

Carver, now standing in the door way after tethering the animals, did not understand - 'refurbisher' was probably another foreign word:

"What the Hell's a refurbisher, Snyder?" he asked brusquely, lacking any similar parental guidance on polite conversation.

"Well, Mr Carver - you may have noticed all the dumped goods by the side of the trail on your journey out here...?"

Carver and Henry nodded. They had seen plenty - new pioneers always overloaded their wagons at the outset of their journey across the Plains, anxious to carry much of their eastern life with them. Then, as their ox or mule teams struggled with the distance, weather or harsh terrain, found that they were forced to abandon their heavier possessions - everything from brass bedsteads, carved wardrobes, grandfather clocks and iron ovens lay back along the Platte River road for miles. But a *refurbisher*...?

"...well, I collect all the cast-off goods that I can, make them into something useful - in other words, I refurbish - and then trade for the things I need."

Henry thought that the word 'refurbish' wasn't the correct one but chose not to point out their new host's inadequacies in the English language. Carver seemed unimpressed, right word or not.

"Like what?" he demanded.

"Look around you sir - the panelling you see on my walls…"

Snyder pointed to sections of wooden panelling around the bottom of each internal wall:

"These are from closets, wardrobes and so on - they stop the internal walls crumbling… my hanging lamps are made from metal bedframes, my work bench from a heavy table - *refurbishment*, gentlemen, it is the future of our wasteful race."

Now that Henry's eyes were becoming accustomed to the poor light, he had to concede that Snyder's hole in the ground was quite well appointed. He had chairs, an iron stove that appeared to be used for heating metal as well as cooking, a workbench with tools, an anvil and a willow basketwork chest that contained some bolts of cloth. Iron nails, ripped from disintegrating furniture had pride of place in a large glass jug and some sleek elk skins hung from a wooden frame jammed into the ceiling.

Even Carver was impressed as he picked up a roughly made baby's crib:

"Well, Mr Snyder, you must be real good with your hands - I couldn't make this stuff in a month of Sundays…"

Snyder smiled indulgently, absorbing the praise, as Henry wandered around, looking at the range of goods on the shelves.

Henry picked up a collection of slightly rusting wedges of plate iron and asked Snyder what they were for.

"Arrow heads, Mr Armstrong - for the Indians. I'll heat them, flatten them out and improve the point - they're very popular."

"I'm sure they are," murmured Henry, remembering the iron arrowhead that had gone through his journal and damn near killed him. He wondered if Snyder had traded it to the Cheyenne.

Suddenly, a bell clanged from somewhere close. Both Henry and Carver jumped at the alien sound. The bell, a souvenir of Snyder's past life on a Mississippi steamboat, hung from a tree leading to the soddy.

"Ah," said Snyder, "Customers!" and bustled outside; Henry could have sworn he was rubbing his hands.

Carver, nearest the door, looked outside and quickly ducked back in:

"Lootenant… them customers? They're Cheyenne."

---- o o o ----

Chapter Twenty Nine

They had called the child 'Flea' - a term of affection more than a formal name - though Smoke on the Moon had suggested that 'Fart' might be more appropriate, given the boy's propensity for expelling wind. Badlands Walking Woman held the boy close to her as she sat astride her pony. The animal was at an easy walking pace as it pulled a travois up to the earth house of the strange veho trader. Smoke rode alongside her with Bad Elk, her brother-in-law, slightly ahead carrying a white rag on the end of his rifle. All were dressed in their finest clothes and hoping that the white cloth sign of peace worked.

Flea was growing and now too heavy for his cradleboard but he still went with his mother when she was doing her chores. Badlands reflected on the long gap between the birth of her first and second sons – she had been surprised and a little alarmed to be pregnant when most other women of her age in the Suhtai band were considered to be past child bearing. Badlands put this down to her superior Kiowa Apache heritage though, diplomatically, she never said this in public.

She had given birth to Flea while the village was on the move; Smoke worriedly joking that it was typical of the contrary way that his wife did things. The contractions had come when she was walking past a stand of live oak so her friends in the column quickly gathered round to take her inside the screen of bushes; the women chattering excitedly as they pushed Smoke out of the way – he could not be present at the birth. She had dropped her second-born son onto a carpet of gathered leaves only a short time later.

She recalled her two failed births over the past years and knew the boy was a blessing – any male child was an asset – he would hunt, feed his people as well as take to the war trail to protect them when the time came.

The boy was becoming a definite character; he had developed a taste for the deer brains that she used for dressing skins so she constantly had to pull his chubby hands out of the gourd that held them, admonishing him gently in her own tongue. She smiled as she continued with her secret purpose of making Flea able to speak in two languages - Smoke, she hoped, would be impressed with her efforts in the boy's later years.

She was startled out of her thoughts by a loud clanging noise. Bad Elk had rung the metal bell hanging from the tree, its jarring tone making their ponies skitter sideways before being brought under control.

Bad Elk could see the familiar mule and cart of the veho trader standing in the shade off to the right; off to the left, however, just outside the flat earthen wall were two unfamiliar horses and a pack mule - the horses carried the saddles of white men. Bad Elk tensed and looked at Smoke on the Moon. His brother unslung his bow from across his back, drew an arrow from his quiver and held it in his hand along the bow stave.

The short white man hurried out to meet them, making the same strange hand sign of an open palm that most *vehoe* seemed to think meant 'peace'.

"I see you," said Snyder as the Indian with the white flag made the cut finger, Medicine Arrow sign of the Cheyenne.

"I remember you," Snyder continued, making a passable effort to speak the Cheyenne tongue.

Before Bad Elk could answer two more white men walked out of the earth house and looked at him and his party. Smoke rode up alongside him for moral support - if there was a fight, they would cut the travois loose and charge their way out.

Both warriors relaxed when they saw that, whilst the white men both carried pistols, their rifles were in the saddle buckets on their horses. The whites didn't seem alarmed - in fact, the younger one looked positively happy to see them.

"I have brought you one of your own people," said Bad Elk, "he is sick." He gestured with his chin towards the travois.

Snyder, Henry and Carver moved towards the litter, Carver translating what the Cheyenne had said for the young Englishman. Pulling aside a heavy buffalo robe, Snyder revealed an emaciated white man who, when he saw the white faces began to weep.

Carver looked up at Bad Elk and said:

"Who is he, where did he come from?"

All of the Cheyenne adults looked amazed that two white men out of three could speak the tongue of the Tsis-tsis-tas; Flea burped contentedly and watched the whites closely while his mother, her hand unseen under the chubby body of her son, loosened the knife in her rawhide belt.

Smoke butted in, forgetting his brother's role as chief and main spokesman:

"He was starving to death in one of our valleys; he had iron tools - I think he meant to dig out the yellow metal in the mountains."

Carver and Snyder continued the conversation while Henry looked at the small party. Both men looked like experienced warriors - the one with the white flag tied to his rifle looked calm and thoughtful; the Hawken rifle looked well kept - the red wooden stock and butt gleamed with protective beeswax and the brass scrollwork gave off a dull glow under the sun's rays. A white man would have given his eye teeth for a Hawken - he wondered how the Indian had got it.

Henry also noted the arrow in the hand of the other man and, in his own protective move, furtively unhooked the leather thong across the hammer of his holstered pistol. His Colt Dragoon was newly bought in New York; the rarity value and high price reflecting that only those going west carried heavy sidearms - city dwellers preferred lighter pistols that could be concealed in a coat pocket. He had only practised with it once as they rode with the wagon train from Independence; it was heavy and a brute to aim and fire but if one of the balls hit a man, he stayed hit.

He turned his attention to the woman - she seemed to have different facial features and skin colouring to the men. She was darker and, in her own way, looked fierce. The child was just a child - it was hard to tell if it was a girl or a boy. But, if what Carver had said was true, Henry was now in the presence of the Cheyenne; he could scarcely believe his luck and his brain raced for ways to capitalise on this early and unexpected boon.

After gesturing to the Cheyenne to dismount and relax, Snyder and Carver picked up the sick man from the travois and carried him into the soddy. Instinctively, Henry moved across to help the woman and baby dismount only to be met by an unfriendly hissing from her and a steel trade knife pointing at his throat.

"Whoa, steady Madam if you please - I was just trying to help."

The warrior with the bow said some apparently calming words and the woman walked over to a small clearing by the mule and cart and sat the child on the grass. She walked back to the travois, never taking her eyes off Henry, and took the discarded buffalo robe and spread it on the ground in the clearing, putting the baby on it. She sat down with a grunt and glared at Henry.

"Charmed to meet you, I'm sure," said Henry sarcastically and watched the two men.

"Do you think we'll get any presents for bringing the veho to his own kind?" asked Smoke of his brother as they sat down next to Badlands.

"I hope so," said Bad Elk, remembering the last time they had brought a sick white man to a passing wagon train. Then they had been shot at so they dumped the man on the ground and galloped off, shouting their indignation at the ungrateful whites.

Carver and Snyder came out of the soddy - the trader went to converse with the Cheyenne and Carver came over to Henry to report:

"The bag o'bones in there is a gold miner - or would have been if he'd reached Pikes Peak. Usual story - got lost, ran out of food and water. Cheyenne huntin' party found him a few days ago and brought him here to get him on the wagons to Laramie. He ain't the first either…"

But Henry wasn't listening - he had a plan. He held up his hand to interrupt the wolf skinner:

"Mr Carver, we have an opportunity here - let's deliver some of our gifts right now. It will show our gratitude to the Cheyenne for returning the miner to us…and, if we're lucky perhaps we can persuade them to let us visit their village…"

Carver looked dubious:

"Lootenant, it's a Hell of a long step from giving presents to visiting their camp. What reason will I give?"

Henry, though, was ahead of him; he pulled out his battered journal from his shirt, the deep indentation from the Cheyenne arrow still clearly visible:

"This," he said.

"A book?"

"Not just a book now, Mr Carver - it's my new sketch pad. We'll go and capture the Cheyenne and their way of life through the medium of art…"

Carver gaped. The Englishman was an idiot. He gave vent to his anger:

"Them Cheyenne aren't fools, Lootenant. Us wantin' to visit 'em? They'll just think it's a plot to find their families and send more soldiers to destroy them all. There'll be only one result here – our scalps are gonna be hangin' from Cheyenne lodge poles within hours of gittin' to any village; especially if they ever find out that you'd tried to kill 'em on the Solomon."

Carver, unused to long tirades, was spent.

Henry smiled reassuringly:

"Not so, Mr Carver. Don't forget George Catlin - he managed this sort of situation very well nearly quarter of a century ago…"

"Catlin?" exploded the wolf skinner, "Who in the name of Christ is he?"

Henry explained about the famous painter of wild Indians and how he survived travelling from tribe to tribe just to pursue his art. In fact, Henry had only a patchy knowledge of Catlin - he had seen his pictures in his father's book but had no idea how Catlin had managed to paint so many warlike tribes without getting his own scalp lifted. He tried to reassure Carver:

"We'll just tell 'em that I've come to capture their image for posterity - to ensure that the greatness of the Cheyenne will live for ever…"

Carver snorted in disbelief:

"Ain't no Cheyenne word for 'posterity' Lootenant. And I'm damn sure that the Cheyenne already think that they're God's greatest creatures - they don't need no damn scrawlin' to give them eternal life."

Henry was about to remind Carver that he was just an employee when he saw the Cheyenne group with Snyder preparing to leave:

"Just do your best Mr Carver - we'll need to be quick."

Carver strode across to the Cheyenne and asked them to stay; saying that the young white man had presents for them – to reward them for saving the miner's life. Henry walked over to the pack mule and lifted a canvas sack from the saddle cross trees and staggered across to Snyder's group now re-seated on the buffalo robe.

With expansive gestures and his most expressive Cheyenne words, Carver tried his best - the gifts were to recognise the Cheyenne's courage in bringing in their sick brother. The generosity of the gifts from the young veho was to demonstrate his admiration for them as a people. And - one more thing - the young man would like to draw pictures of them as a permanent reminder of their visit.

Bad Elk digested what the white man had said - his Cheyenne was poor but understandable - but it was a strange request. Still, the presents were generous and he, Smoke and Badlands were in no particular hurry:

"Brother, what do you think about this?"

Smoke considered his reply:

"I see no harm to it - the veho will just do what Yellow Bear does when he records our Cheyenne life on his buffalo skin…"

Bad Elk nodded - their medicine man's drawings on his specially prepared buffalo hide kept track of all the major events in the life of their small Suhtai band - fathers brought their sons to see it and explain the meaning of all the symbols. Obviously, the vehoe did the same thing - meeting the mighty

Cheyenne and *not* being killed would be a significant event in any white man's year.

He was about to consent when Badlands Walking Woman chipped in:

"The veho is *not* drawing me or my son…" she said, wrapping Flea closer into the folds of her shift. "It may be a plot to make us weaker - when he makes these marks, he will take away an image of us - part of us will be with our enemy. No."

Smoke on the Moon shrugged at Bad Elk - Badlands would not change her mind - but that was not a reason why two, well-dressed and handsome Cheyenne warriors should not show their enemies images of their power and presence.

Carver passed on the good news to Henry, scarcely believing that the Cheyenne had fallen for the enticements.

Henry's smiles, though, were short-lived - he remembered that his artistic skills had never been a strong point. Mr Fairbairn, his art tutor back at home had despaired of him - perspective, shading and depth of colour had been lost causes to Henry. His rendering of still life - a dead pheasant, some apples and a corn sheaf - had attracted much mirth; not just from Fairbairn but from his bloody patronising sisters. Even his mother could scarcely hide her laughter, reassuring him that his destined regiment, the Light Dragoons, needed dashing, sabre-wielding officers not soft-handed, sensitive artists.

Well, it was too late now - Henry took out his journal and a pencil and prepared to bluff three wild Indians.

---- o o o ----

Chapter Thirty

Viajero and See the Dark took their ponies and mules through a narrow defile in the caprock, making sure that their trail would be spotted by those coming on behind; if their pursuers kept on the same track, they would be forced to follow them through the steep, sandstone sides.

Once through the defile, both warriors dismounted and led their animals across a rocky, shallow escarpment that led up to overhanging bluffs; they would leave no tracks here. After a short walk, Viajero found a small box canyon; there they hobbled both their mounts and mules to stop them straying or being spooked by the scent of approaching strange horses.

The plan was simple - lure the followers through the narrow gap, let them be confused by the disappearance of the tracks and then kill them while they tried to find the trail again. Viajero and Dark strung their bows and each man nocked an arrow onto his bowstring - each man wishing that they had a gun instead.

The Apache unslung an elk skin robe from the rear of his saddle, threw it over his shoulders then climbed to a ledge that overlooked the entrance to the defile and Dark followed. Here the Traveller lay down on the sun-blasted rock and pulled the elk skin over him, the tan colour blending with the earth and stone. Unselfconsciously, Dark crept under the same robe and shared it with the Apache. Viajero squinted back along the trail; he was puzzled:

"Those riders have made no effort to catch up and kill us - they just seem to be trailing us, following our tracks. Perhaps they are just using the same trail to Texas…"

Dark, embarrassed that he had not spotted the riders himself and still put out that the Traveller had not mentioned that they were being followed, sniffed sarcastically:

"Well, if we can see their dust, they can see ours. Perhaps they are seeking the Comancheros too…perhaps we could help by leading them there…perhaps we could share the guns with them…"

Viajero snorted impatiently and pushed Dark out from under the robe. Dark rolled over onto a small cactus probing towards the sunlight from a dirt filled cleft. He yowled in pain and surprise and sat upright, trying to pluck the sharp spines from his shoulder. Viajero didn't offer to help him - the young Cheyenne could be a trying companion sometimes. Any of his White Mountain Apache brothers would have got a quirt across the face for such impertinence. He seethed but remained calm:

"We'll wait and see who follows our trail between the rocks. If there are a lot of them, just let them pass - we can't take on a large party. Not without guns anyway…"

See the Dark, immediately contrite and wishing he could control his tongue, agreed:

"If we see many riders from a distance, I'll unfasten the animals and take them out of the way - around that way…" he gestured with his free hand towards the back of the caprock.

Viajero grunted in agreement and looked more closely at the approaching dust cloud:

"I think that there are only a few riders - less than the fingers on one hand. They're not Comancheros - they have no carts; they don't ride like white men. Could be Comanche…or Kiowa perhaps."

See the Dark strained his one eye - for objects that were close his loss of sight had not proven to be a great disadvantage but at distances, especially over country that he was unfamiliar with, his shortcomings were brought home. He could see the dust cloud but those making it were lost in the distant, rising eddies of smoking earth. The riders would need to be a lot closer than that before he could be sure if they were foes. He was uneasy - while the Comanche and their close allies the Kiowa, were not enemies of his people, any war party would want to know what they were doing in their lands. For now, he flexed his bowstring and made sure that he could shoot down into the defile.

Both warriors kept their heads down, below the edge of the caprock. The riders got closer though the pursuers were still well out of accurate bow shot. The ponies were not being made to gallop or even trot - they came at a steady walk. Viajero, with the robe framing his face risked a quick peek over the cliff edge. He was quiet for a short time than spat out a disgusted:

"Hah!"

Dark, puzzled by his tone, was about to ask what he'd seen when he heard the object of the Apache's displeasure. A high, singing voice, croaking slightly from breathing in the dust, rose from the churned-up trail below:

I am like the scorpion
My gun gives me my sting
Tremble in fear
If you must face me

Dark breathed out in a defeated, irritated sigh - the singer was Mouse. The Forked Lightning Women were here.

---- 0 0 0 ----

Chapter Thirty One

Henry's sketches of the two Cheyenne warriors had gone well - both men had seemed satisfied with their images. Henry had torn the two pages out of his journal and presented a drawing to each of his sitters. He had a slight moment of anxiety when he saw that each page had the arrow hole through it and an edging of his blood; neither warrior mentioned it though.

One of the men took his portrait over to show the woman but she turned her head away and refused to look, shielding the child's eyes from the monstrosity. Henry was irritated but said nothing.

Smoke said: "See wife, the veho has given us our images, so they won't remain in the hands of an enemy. I may put this in our lodge…"

Henry's hands had been shaking during the actual drawing but a few lucky lines had enabled him to capture the essence of both men, even if their facial features had turned out to be decidedly similar. He was fortunate that each man had a distinctive hairstyle and had different markings on his skin shirt - the warriors had seemed to be more interested that he had caught the details of their adornments rather than what they actually looked like. Carver breathed a sigh of relief and told Henry that their conversations indicated approval.

Snyder came back out of the soddy - the miner had fallen asleep so the trader had reheated a large pot of stew and invited the Cheyenne party to eat. The warriors accepted but the woman, whilst she sat in the circle to eat, would not touch any of the food. Neither of the men would eat from a tin plate or use a metal spoon but Snyder, well versed in Cheyenne traditions brought out carved wooden bowls and spoons made from elk horn. After filling up each person's plate, Snyder lit a small campfire and hung the stewpot over it from a forked stick. After a stilted silence, Bad Elk asked Carver:

"Who is the young man who doesn't speak our tongue?"

Carver, cautiously avoiding all mention of the Army, said:

"He is my chief. He has heard of the mighty Tsis-tsis-tas and wished to meet you. I have come to show him the way to your country."

Bad Elk and Smoke nodded, expressing pleasure when Carver revealed that he had been married to an Omissis girl and sorrow when they were told she had died. The admission seemed to appeal to the woman too - she caught Carver's eye and nodded in sympathy.

"Why did the young man want to meet us, the Cheyenne? Why not the Lakota - there are many more of them than us? They are easier to find," said Bad Elk

Carver knew it was time to stretch the truth a little:

"He has heard of the Lakota of course but he says that many years ago - in the time of his grandfather's grandfather…"

Carver used the only way of depicting a long way back in time that he knew.

"…his own family were similar to the Cheyenne - they hunted, raided and fought; they were horsed warriors too."

Bad Elk and Smoke seemed impressed; even Badlands was surprised that a white man could have been part of a free, horsed tribe - even if it was a long time ago.

In truth, Carver was hazy on the details of Henry's border bandit family - or 'Reivers' as Henry used to remind him. The boy had tried to explain several times but Carver had often become numb with boredom, more interested in real things like a drink or a whore. Those long-ago wars between the English and the Scotch, now three centuries on, didn't hold much fascination for him.

Occasionally some fact about Henry's family past would stick and he racked his brain to recall one now. He knew Henry wore a red flannel strip around the top of his right arm, put there since his baptism to shield his arm from the holy water - it meant that all of the young Englishman was Christian except his right arm which was free to strike his enemies.

Carver considered telling this story to the Cheyenne but it was too complicated, especially as he didn't really understand it himself. Neither of the Indians would understand why, like them, his whole body and life was not devoted to slaughtering their foes. Instead Carver told a simpler tale:

"My young chief says that his family always raided at night carrying fire at the tip of their lances…"

Smoke looked astonished:

"Wouldn't their enemies know they were coming?"

"Of course. That was the point - to strike fear before they even got there."

Bad Elk and Smoke absorbed this fact. It was impressive - the young veho was obviously from a powerful tribe who feared nothing. The young man seemed unafraid in the presence of two powerful Cheyenne warriors. True, he had guns but he had chosen to draw pictures instead of fight. The veho had nerve.

Carver turned to Henry:

"Just been tellin' 'em about your warrior family Lootenant - they seem pleased…"

Henry smiled at the praise but was frustrated that he couldn't join in any conversation. Snyder seemed to be less fluent than the wolf skinner but could, at least, make himself understood.

Suddenly he had a thought and asked Carver to translate it for the Cheyenne. It was just a question - and a minor one at that - but it would show that he was still part of the gathering, that Henry was Carver's boss and that he had some experience with other Indians.

The wolf skinner sucked his teeth; he was surprised at the question as it bore no relation to getting them to visit a Cheyenne village. His question moved away from polite discourse to the realm of information gathering - something that would make the Cheyenne wary. He was uneasy as he remembered that the last time he had heard the question was when he and Henry were in the cavalry column on the way to the Arkansas. But, as a paid employee, he asked it anyway:

"My chief asks if you have heard of a warrior from a southern people called 'Makes the Rivers Red'."

Both Smoke and Bad Elk shrugged at the name - it seemed a deviation from the polite conversation they were having. They had not heard of this warrior - they were not sure if the young veho meant someone from the southern bands of the Cheyenne or from a completely different tribe like the Comanche or Kiowa. No, they confirmed, that name was not familiar to them. Carver breathed a sigh of relief - at least they had got through that. But, hidden from his sight behind one of the seated warriors, he had reckoned without the woman.

Badlands tensed when she heard the Cheyenne rendition of the name. Neither her husband nor her brother-in-law would have heard of it - but she had. The name had been mentioned to her when the Traveller and Bright Antelope had first come to stay with the People. Badlands as a Kiowa Apache had made the first efforts to communicate with them as they struggled to talk in their different Apache dialects. Makes the Rivers Red was the name of Viajero's father.

Her brain raced - where had these treacherous *vehoe* heard it? It was an easy puzzle to solve - they could only have heard it from the lips of the Apache himself.

---- o o o ----

Chapter Thirty Two

The Forked Lightning Women were not welcome - Viajero and See the Dark made that very plain. Mouse and Crow Dress Woman were surprised and chastened by the outburst. White Rain though, along with Willow remained haughtily aloof from the recriminations.

There was much shouting in the small, narrow canyon, loud enough to spook the horses and unsettle both men and women. Mouse and Crow Dress took the bridles of the four ponies and held them quietly in the lengthening purple shadows of the caprock.

Viajero's objections faded first as he found it hard to put the extent of his anger into Cheyenne words. Instead, he stalked back to the mesa rim and sat facing their back trail, refusing to take part any further as he watched the sun take its daily slide towards the horizon. The arguing was too loud for the Apache - passing enemies would be drawn to the noise. See the Dark though continued the verbal assault below, in the gathering gloom of twilight. He reserved all his scorn for White Rain, rudely pointing at her:

"You should know better! I thought you had the wisdom to lead but it seems that isn't so. You and your stupid girls will get us all killed…"

Willow interrupted:

"You didn't say that when we helped you defeat the Pawnee…"

Dark shouted again:

"Pawnee, Pawnee - that's all you ever say! Things were different then - we men needed all the help we could get. Most of our warriors were dead. We even took ten-year old boys along with us. You women were nothing special…"

Even as he said it, Dark knew he was being unfair about the women's role up on the Loup River. If the women had not run off the entire Pawnee horse herd, their enemies would have pursued them home with disastrous results. And even he had to concede that, here on a dangerous trail to Texas, the women were just doing what any war trail novices would do - they could join any war party provided that the pipeholder or leader agreed.

White Rain decided to let the insult to her soldiers pass and tried to calm Dark down:

"We know that this is a war quest for you and the Traveller - we just offer help...."

"Help that you didn't get from the Striking Snakes or Thunder Bears," interrupted Willow.

White Rain motioned for Willow to be silent and continued:

"We are all armed and can use our weapons; who knows how many of these Mexican traders you will find..."

Viajero, hearing the conversation take a calmer turn, scrambled back down the rock to the canyon floor. He stood behind Dark and listened.

"...we may be women but we are still warriors - proven in battle..."

Dark opened his mouth to speak but White Rain, rudely as he thought, placed her fingers over his lips. He dashed her hand away but it was too late to stop the determined Cheyenne woman:

"...Who leads your war party? Is it you or the Traveller?"

Dark looked at her in confusion - he had not thought of themselves as a war party - there had been no rituals or spiritual blessings, he had not prayed to Maheo for success and they were not heading for Texas with any real encouragement from their Suhtai band. It was a good and direct question from White Rain though and he considered it carefully before answering:

"We are here as two war companions only - we have not elected a leader, there is no pipeholder…"

Sensing an opening and opportunity for harmony, Viajero placed a quietening hand on Dark's shoulder and interrupted:

"My war brother speaks the truth. We have no leader but only I know the trail to find the traders and their guns - so I act as leader on this part of the war trail…"

White Rain came back quickly. She looked directly at Viajero:

"As is Cheyenne custom, if you as leader send us back - we will obey and go…"

The other three women gasped in surprise; Mouse, about to object, was held back by Crow Dress Woman who struggled to hold the small, plump girl.

"…but we are not novices - there may be a need to steal more horses, get food, scout ahead, guard our back trail on the ride home - my soldiers can do all that. We can fight too. Any wise pipeholder should be glad of more warriors."

White Rain nodded her head once sharply in defiance; her speech was ended. Willow barked something in her own Lakota tongue - none of them knew what it meant but it sounded like a shout of approval.

Viajero, feeling odd in his role as peacemaker, stepped between Dark and White Rain and put a hand on each of their shoulders:

"Your woman speaks wisely - we can manage against the Comancheros with just the two of us - but with four more warriors we can be more …" the Apache sought the right word "…ambitious."

White Rain glowed at the Traveller's mention of her as Dark's woman; even See the Dark smiled at the odd use of the affectionate term in the middle of an unseemly bout of shouting. All the women nodded in approval at being referred to as 'warriors' - the Traveller had wisdom.

In the gathering dusk, Viajero smiled to himself; he was experienced in these things, after all he was a man who had married twice - it was sometimes important to use the right words to take the sting out of a quarrel. That, or just let the women believe that they had been right all along.

See the Dark, knowing he and Viajero had somehow been outmanoeuvred, shook his head in silent disbelief that women could so easily manipulate things to their own advantage. But he was gracious in defeat:

"Now we are a true war party!" he yelled, brandishing his bow.

He looked at White Rain, and remembered that this was no ordinary woman. She smiled back at him. For now, she mused, they would go into battle together - if they both survived and returned safely to the Suhtai, then things would need to change.

Smiles and acceptance had replaced shouts and tensions and the falling darkness required practical measures. Viajero decided that the canyon, even though it was without water, would be a good place to camp - it was easily defended and had good spots to place their new companions as sentries.

He was about to move off with Dark to collect the horses and mules from the box canyon when Mouse and Crow Dress led their horses forward. Mouse gave her pair of reins to Crow Dress and stepped back to open up the rolled robe at the rear of her saddle. She held up the carbine and pistol that she had taken from the white soldier:

"I have the power of many warriors in these. I have brought all my bullets and powder - those Mexicans will be no match for us…" she said laughing, her face and bright eyes showing just how young she was.

Both Viajero and Dark had forgotten Mouse's guns - the power of both would allow seven bullets to be fired in a very short time - it may come in useful when they met the Comancheros.

"I can compose a song if you like," she said.

"No song!" the rest said in unison as they prepared their night's camp.

---- 0 0 0 ----

Chapter Thirty Three

Juan Castillo de Coronado smiled as he reached down from the saddle to shake eager hands, reassuring his cheering investors as his trading column rode out of Santa Fe and headed towards the Pecos River.

A small brass band was playing rousing tunes on the steps of the Mayor's house but they spluttered to a stop when the choking dust of the passing column blew into their instruments. Juan lifted his sombrero and saluted them for their efforts - the bandsmen dashed the dust from their blue uniforms and waved back. The bandmaster bowed and beamed at the recognition.

Castillo was content - the people were noisy and happy and he was their champion. Though he had an overblown, false name, his reputation was real enough. The townsfolk idolised him for his exploits as a Comanchero and because he made them rich.

His father waved an enthusiastic farewell from the front porch of his dry goods store; his mother, as usual, stayed inside - she was a Pueblo Indian woman so Juan and his father kept her hidden as much as possible. The fake aristocratic lineage of his surname overshadowed the fact that he was of mixed blood; many believed his mother was merely a servant or housekeeper. Neither of the Castillo de Coronado men did anything to dissuade them from that train of thought.

Juan removed his hat and, with a dignified sweep of his arm, saluted his father and bowed his head slightly. The crowd clapped at the loving and respectful gesture - such aristocratic behaviour was entirely expected from one whose surname was linked to the famous Spanish Conquistador. Though the original de Coronado had sought elusive profits in the Americas for the Spanish Crown, Juan Castillo amassed real profits for his Santa Fe investors by trading with the Comanches in Texas.

Emilio Montoya, his boyhood friend and one of the few who knew that Juan's father had bribed the *Alcalde* of Santa Fe to falsify their names, rode up alongside him and gave him a mock military salute:

"All is well with the wagons, *Jefe* - no animals or men sick. The special goods are all loaded in the last wagon ready for when we meet up with Alvarez…"

Juan nodded and looked back over his column – ten laden wagons pulled by oxen or mules - it was a satisfying sight. White canvas covers swayed in time to the pace of the draught animals, whips cracked and axles creaked as they cleared the town limits.

There was a scuttling through the cholla cactus as a small family of wild pigs raced off to safety, squeaking loudly. Juan's horse stepped sideways in alarm, barging into Montoya's pony:

"Your horse needs some courage, Coronado…"

Montoya often called Juan this, usually after his friend became too insufferable on the trail - a subtle hint that *he* knew the truth about his non-existent ancestor:

"If it's scared of a few *javelinas*, God knows what it will be like if it sees a buffalo…"

Juan looked at Montoya coldly - friend or not, he, Juan Castillo, was his employer and was due some respect and deference. It was true that his horse was newly acquired from a gentleman's blood stock ranch in Kentucky but it was not Montoya's place to question his choice of horseflesh. Emilio's place was to obey:

"Where is the Taos column?" he asked, a chill edge to his voice.

Montoya, recognising the rebuke, said:

"A few miles ahead, the Texan is making them move as fast as those damned *carretas* will go. Do you want me to ride ahead and check on them?"

"No…" answered Castillo, still irritated by Montoya's insolence:

"…stay with the column and I'll do it."

He spurred his horse and trotted over a low rise and out of sight of the wagon train. Being alone was better than having to deal with irritating subordinates and he relaxed slightly, enjoying the smooth pace of his new, expensive, horse. Money that bought luxury, he thought, was money well spent and, as his opulent lifestyle in Santa Fe expanded, he always needed more of it.

He went over the business plan in his head. Being a successful Comanchero leader depended on agile thought - dealing with volatile and untrustworthy Indians required cunning and courage. His relatives had traded with the Comanche for over sixty years but – and there was always a 'but' to this business – they always said that it never paid a man to forget that he was dealing with people from the Stone Age. The Comanche only tolerated the trade when it suited them, when he had something they wanted. And, back in the column, he did.

His 'special' goods, as Montoya called them, had only recently arrived from factories back east – two boxes of new Sharps carbines and two crates of Colt repeating rifles – these were for his best customer, Iron Hat, the wily chief of the *Nokoni* band of the Comanche.

Juan patted the cigar case in his breast pocket; talks between himself and the Comanche chief needed plenty of cheroots and whiskey. He and Iron Hat had a special relationship - neither of them trusted the other. It worked well.

The Comanche warrior would always attend their meetings wearing his prized iron military helmet - and, to emphasise his greatness, would say that he had personally taken it from a Spanish soldier. Juan would then congratulate him on his great age for, to have done so, would mean that Iron Hat was over three hundred years old. The wizened old fool would cackle with laughter, take a handful of Juan's cheroots and they would discuss what each of them wanted over rotgut liquor and a smoke.

Now, as the edge of the Staked Plains caprock came into view in the far distance, Juan had got what Iron Hat wanted; he just hoped that Iron Hat had done the same.

---- o o o ----

The rolling dust cloud spread for a long way across the *Llano Estacado*. Riding in front, Iron Hat looked back at the cloud with satisfaction; the Comanche nation, or at least the part he could muster, was on the move.

The Comanche rode upright on a fine Appaloosa pony and searched the horizon for landmarks to indicate that they were near the trade rendezvous. His array of warriors, families and stock stretched as far as the eye could see across the flat and featureless Plains. He had not only brought his Nokoni people but other bands of Comanches – *Penatekas* and *Kotsotekas,* their numbers lessened by diseases from the white man, had also tagged onto the retinue. Even some Kiowas, long-time allies of his people, rode on the far flank, smothered in the rising dust from the baking plains.

He slowed his pony down and shouted:

"Water!"

At the signal, one of his wives, riding just behind him brought him the skin water pouch. He rode with his long, flexible war lance planted in his left stirrup and now steadied it in the crook of his arm as he swigged water and wiped his hands down his grimy deerskin shirt. He handed the pouch back:

"Where is my son?" he asked his wife without looking at her.

"He has ridden off as you instructed," she said, "he left at daybreak."

Iron Hat just grunted and waved his wife back into her place. Red Bark Tree was still young but was barren – he would need to take another wife to keep his line going. His son's mother, Black Shawl Woman, somewhere in the dust cloud, was ageing badly; there would be no more children from her. Perhaps she would die on this trip and leave a welcome space in his lodge.

Yes, he thought, being a leader brought many responsibilities to ensure his people thrived. Before they got to the rendezvous, he decided, he would look over the captives and see if there were any worth breeding with.

---- o o o ----

Chapter Thirty Four

The small Crow war party reacted quickly. They were on their way back north after a successful attack on an Arapaho village - three scalps and ten ponies had been a successful raid. Black Bull Shirt, their leader, saw the Cheyennes first as they emerged from the treeline - four men, a woman and a child would be an easy victory.

"Friend, herd the spare ponies in that gully over there!" he shouted to one of his warriors, pointing to a small hollow some way off. The man looked crestfallen - he didn't want to miss the fight - but he did what his war leader ordered.

With the pony herd headed for safety, Black Bull Shirt rode his warriors to the crest of the hill. He was a quick thinker and had suffered losses at the hands of the Cheyenne before:

"Wolf Ear, ride with Bear Tooth into those woods down there - attack them from the right side…"

"There are two white men with them, they have guns…" cautioned Wolf Ear.

"I see that," snapped Black Bull Shirt, "…the guns will make good prizes."

The mixed Cheyenne party appeared not to have heard or seen them and still plodded on, deep in conversation. The Crow leader steadied his other six warriors:

"Be brave - we're just flesh and blood. Only the land will remain and this is *Absaroka* land, *our* land - those filthy Cheyenne are defiling it - let your bullets and arrows give us more scalps!"

Waving his rifle above his head, Black Bull Shirt yelled his war cry and thundered over the crest of the hill towards the enemy. His pony still had war ribbons woven into its mane and these streamed out from its neck in the wind; Black Bull Shirt's own feathers flattened against the top of his head with the force of his charge.

The rest were close behind him, bringing rifles up to a shooting position or nocking arrows onto bows. The earth shuddered under the hooves of their ponies and clods of dirt flew all around as the warriors closed in. Ducks from a nearby lake rose squawking into the sky as the trembling earth carried the shockwaves across the water.

Bad Elk and Smoke had been in a conversation with the dark haired veho who spoke their language; the younger, fair-skinned one rode behind in frustrated silence whilst Badlands Walking Woman brought up the rear, seething with anger at being silenced by her husband when she had tried to bring up her doubts about the two white men.

She though, was first to hear the Crow coming and screeched her warnings. Jerking her pony's head round quickly, she rode back into the trees and dismounted, bundling her son deeper into his robes as she sought protection in the timber. She held onto the bridle of her horse in case she had to remount and escape - she had not seen the attackers and didn't know how many they were. Badlands took out her butchering knife and pushed the blade in the dirt - it was the only weapon she had. She peered through the leaf cover to see where her husband had got to...

Smoke and Bad Elk, startled by the yelling, dismounted and ran behind some deadfall logs for cover, checking where Badlands had gone. Bad Elk pulled a small copper percussion cap from a deerskin pouch, put it onto his rifle and cocked the hammer back fully; Smoke strung his bow and took a handful of arrows from his quiver. A surprise attack like this meant that neither man had time to go through his war rituals - neither had spoken to Maheo - both hoped that the Life Giver would understand their discourtesy. They shouted to the white men to take cover.

Instead, Henry Armstrong and Pythagoras Carver stayed mounted and turned their horses face onto the attack, making smaller targets. Henry stayed in the saddle because of his cavalry training while Carver did it out of self-preservation - being astride a horse could save your life if things went bad.

Lead balls whined past their heads from the Crow rifles and an arrow thumped, quivering, in Carver's saddle pommel. Other arrows flashed past, whirring and slamming into tree trunks. The Crow riders charged fearlessly into the fight, screeching with the wild joy of battle. To Henry it sounded much like the Cheyenne war cries on the banks of the Solomon Fork. These people would always fight for their land.

With the first round of shooting from the Indian single shot rifles over, Henry brought up his Sharps carbine and fired - the boom of the discharge brought a flash of flame and gout of smoke from the barrel - the bullet hit the closest Crow warrior in the chest, toppling him backwards out of the saddle. The dead man lay face down in the dust, two protruding shards of his collar bone stuck out through his skin.

Henry quickly chambered another linen cartridge and sought a fresh target; this was the first kill he had made with the Sharps that he'd taken off the Apache - he was impressed with its stopping power and accuracy. He was pleased he had kept it as a trophy and had let the gunsmith in Independence strip it down and clean it.

Carver, steadying his pony with his heels, fired his long rifle at what he presumed was the leader. Black Bull Shirt slumped in the saddle with his lower jaw shot away - blood and teeth spilled into his porcupine quill chest plate. But he wasn't dead - in gurgling, wordless fury he dismounted and ran at Bad Elk, his war axe held high. Bad Elk shot him again in the midriff, the shock of the heavy calibre round doubling the Crow warrior up and he sank backwards into a sitting position, head flopping forward with blood and spittle streaming into the dust.

Yelling wildly, Smoke dashed over to the wounded man and buried his hatchet in his head, blood and brains spattering over the Crow's feathered headdress.

With the loss of their leader, the remainder of the Crow pulled back to regroup, riding off to a rocky outcrop next to the lake, out of range of the Cheyenne rifles.

"No shot for me there, Lootenant - too far away but your carbine might manage it," shouted Carver. Henry nodded and brought up the weapon into the aim.

Another booming from his barrel brought a Crow pony down - the animal reared and threshed in its death throes, hooves churning dust as the other warriors moved to one side leaving their comrade to be crushed to death under it. The Crows, astonished at the reach of the rifle, quickly kicked their heels into their ponies' flanks and moved behind the rocks.

"Are they finished, Mr Carver?" shouted Henry.

"Nah, Lootenant. They're Crow - they don't give up easy. Just keep loadin' and firin' when you see 'em."

A shriek from Badlands, hidden in the woods, signalled that the Crow were trying to attack from her side. Smoke raced back into the timber with his hatchet at the ready. He was just in time to slash at a plump young Crow warrior creeping up through the brush. The Crow tried to duck back into the undergrowth but Smoke hauled him out by his hair and drove his axe vertically into the youth's face, smashing the bone from hairline to chin and cleaving an eyeball.

Badlands hastily pushed Flea under a log, scraping some skin off the boy's face and ran forward to scalp the dead Crow. The boy cried a little, distracting them both for a short time. Shots outside the treeline showed that the white men and Bad Elk were still fighting.

Smoke was admonishing her for deserting their son when a second Crow warrior ran down a trail towards them. This one was bigger, well-made and still painted in the black and white striped war face that he'd used against the Arapaho.

The Crow's yells numbed Smoke for a second - he had been in the act of shaking Badlands by the shoulders and hadn't nocked another arrow onto his bowstring. Smoke's brain seemed unable to stir - his wife and son were in danger; he could see the Crow was carrying a heavy axe from a white trader, shield and bow slung across his shoulder. Why couldn't he move?

He was surprised when the warrior's hate-filled face exploded into fragments after an explosion behind him. Looking round, he saw the young fair-skinned veho, still mounted, reloading his rifle and charging back into the clearing.

The Crow were now leaderless and able to see that they had taken severe losses in such a short battle. They again rode off, back to the outcrop - this time making sure they stayed out of range of the white man's rifle.

"What do you think Mr Carver?"

"I think they're done Lootenant but stay low until we're sure."

Carver, still in the saddle, reloaded his long rifle, tipping an extra measure of powder down the barrel from his flask; the gun was a smallish calibre but good enough against wolves. It needed more heft to kill men.

Behind his logs, Bad Elk did the same; he was more sparing with his powder - he had to be as he relied on trading with white men to get it. But the heavy weapon had performed well and he had lost none of his skills - he rammed the large ball down the barrel and pushed it home with the ramrod. Smoke stayed in the timber and was ready with his bow. He was shaken that he had paused in battle - it had been an unusual experience for him, perhaps he was getting old.

There was some yelling from the attackers as the remaining Crows danced their ponies on the skyline, gathered their stolen pony herd and rode off, still shouting insults at the Cheyenne.

Carver nodded in satisfaction:

"I reckon that's it Lootenant - them Crows have had enough."

Henry paused, elated at the successful outcome of the fight:

"Nice shooting there Mr Carver - that rifle of yours is a tad ancient though!"

"It does the job Lootenant!" Carver yelled back, though secretly admitting that the long-barrelled Pennsylvania rifle was difficult to handle in the saddle. It was his father's gun and at least fifty years old - he now admired the Sharps carbine of his boss; he should get one - if he ever came out of the Cheyenne camp alive.

Smoke and Bad Elk counted coup on the dead bodies; Smoke touching them with his bow and Bad Elk with his rifle barrel, then they scalped them. Holding up the hanks of dark hair, dripping with fresh blood, both men yelled their triumph at surviving the attack. Remembering their good manners, they came over and spoke to Henry who still sat astride his horse, rifle resting on his thigh, bemused by the words of the smiling Cheyenne.

"They're saying thanks, Lootenant - especially for saving that one's wife and son." He pointed to Smoke on the Moon.

Badlands though, clutching her son to her chest, was less gracious and not inclined to gratitude. She had worried how the whites had known the name of Viajero's father and now she had more proof of their treachery. She pulled roughly at her husband's shirt and hissed:

"I tried to tell you before. The young veho is carrying the Traveller's rifle!"

---- 0 0 0 ----

Chapter Thirty Five

Alicia Gadd and her daughter Rebecca stumbled over the vast shale plain, wincing at the heat from the rocks as it burnt their unshod feet. Small cactus and agave plants, barely visible in dirt clefts, added to their pain. They were tied to a mule which, like them, was near death.

Alicia took a quick look around her; they were not alone. Over twenty women and children were being herded - and 'herded' was the only term she could think of - prodded onwards like so many beasts of burden by Comanche women with sharpened sticks. All the captives were bound to mules or slow-moving cattle - many of them, humans and animals, were close to collapse.

Alicia did not recognise all of the captives; she reasoned that they may have been held by different groups of savages and just brought together now for some reason. She could see though that all were in the same condition of ragged desperation. Some still wore the remnants of their calico or linen dresses but others - probably those who'd been in captivity longer - wore the same filthy deerskin shifts as the Comanche women. All of them bore the scars of captivity.

The urge to keep upright and moving was great. She remembered that Mrs Richardson, one of her West Texas neighbours, had fallen behind in the early part of the march and had been speared to death with the fire-hardened points by those damn squaws. Likewise, the Hoggert boy, who had been awoken every morning with a burning twig pushed into his nose, had looked at himself once in a pool of water, caught sight of his scabbed half-face and thrown himself off a mesa cliff. Only the iron-willed survived as Comanche captives.

The Gadds' mule began to plod even more slowly and then stopped, its breathing laboured and final. In the dust cloud, the Comanche women didn't seem to notice and drove the rest of their charges onward. The animal keeled over onto the red earth, hooves flickering feebly in its death throes as it wheezed its farewell to the world, its open eyeball not flinching from the settling layer of dust.

Alicia and Rebecca stood next to it, unsure of what to do next. Alicia found her uncertainty odd - she was an intelligent and practical woman, a school teacher from a good family, but captivity had changed her. Many rapes and beatings at the hands of the Comanches had taught her not to use her own initiative - a supine acceptance seemed to be the best way to survive. She had no idea how long she and her daughter had been in this miserable slavery nor where she was now, or where they were going. She was sure of one thing though - and she whispered this to Rebecca this every morning - she would make sure that they both lived - and lived long enough to kill every Comanche that she could find, especially those cruel, stick-wielding squaws.

 She could see no-one in the dust cloud and, as the air cleared around them, she began to untie her daughter from the rawhide ropes. The child had long since ceased to cry but, once freed, hugged her mother - a luxury not permitted when they were in camp:

"Why Becky Gadd, we're both just bags o'bones."

She looked ahead at the disappearing dust haze; no-one was coming to get them back - now there was a slim chance to get out of this Hell Hole….

---- 0 0 0 ----

Juan Castillo sighed at the growing noise and spurred his horse forward. Up ahead, a jarring, screeching howl announced the presence of the Taos column - rickety, home-made carretas with just two solid wooden wheels on ungreased axles were urged on by chattering crowds of farmers and their families.

A tall man rode at the head of the column, apparently oblivious to the noise and Juan rode forward. The Texan was new to the Comachero business, on just his second season, but he was an Army deserter from Fort Mason and needed a job that kept him out of the way of patrols. Juan was able to reassure him that where his Comancheros went, no soldier would ever follow.

The Texan tilted his hat back and reassured Juan:

"Yessir, Alvarez passed through a coupla days ago. We lost two broke carts just out of Taos so they turned back early and ol' Hector back there will keep me on the right trail to Las Lenguas - nothin' to worry about here, boss."

"Good," said Juan and reined his horse back towards the Santa Fe column, retracing his own dusty hoofprints. The report on Alvarez was comforting - Alvarez would play a leading role in the coming trade. He and his crew would dig deep caches well away from the rendezvous point at Las Lenguas Creek and store the 'special' goods there - cases of rifles, ammunition and whiskey - until the Comanches paid up. Only then would Juan tell Iron Hat where to get his special goods.

Juan congratulated himself on keeping Alavarez's role secret from the Texan - the *gringo* had been a steady presence so far but he didn't need to know *too* much just yet. Juan also hadn't told the tall man that the Comanches always demanded a hostage until they had found their stashed goods. It needed someone of courage and dependability - the Texan would probably fit the bill. If not, he was expendable.

---- o o o ----

Red Bark Tree Woman brought the bad news to her husband - two of the captives had escaped. Iron Hat reacted badly, bringing his long war lance up and slashing the woman across the face with the shaft:

"Then find them! Those whites are valuable to Castillo - he will only trade good rifles and ammunition for *them*..." he shouted.

Red Bark Tree had fallen from her pony under the weight of the blow but she had wisely retained the bridle in her hand. Equally as wisely, she kept silent - her husband was still shouting:

"...I don't know why I favoured you with marriage - you are useless to me! Find them before nightfall or I will stake you out on the *Llano* and let the wolves find you."

The woman kept her head held low in submission as she remounted and galloped back across the empty plains. That woman and girl had nowhere to hide; she would soon track them down.

---- 0 0 0 ----

Chapter Thirty Six

The two things had happened almost simultaneously - Mouse realised that her pony had gone lame and, after dismounting to check its hooves, had heard the sound of digging. It wasn't the soft thud of deer antler picks tearing the earth for root vegetables; it was the sound of metal on rocks - a noise only a white man would make.

She backed up her pony into a dry stream bed and tied a cloth over its head to keep it quiet. Pulling back the hammer of the soldier rifle, as the Traveller had shown her, she placed a copper cap over the small tower that took the spark to the powder in the barrel. She smiled at her own confidence and knowledge in these things.

Mouse now knew about guns and it was all down to the Apache. She was grateful to Viajero for the advice; no other man, including her own father, had ever complimented her on her capture of the soldier guns or had bothered to explain how they worked. Well, that was the problem for the Cheyenne menfolk in the future, she would gain glory and reputation from this war trail and intended to make sure that all her Suhtai kinfolk would see her arrive back with many scalps, guns and ponies. And, though she may consider a suitable marriage sometime in the future - she wouldn't be looting any cooking pots from *her* battlefields. Her new place was in the war saddle and not at the campfire.

After blowing her breath into the pony's nostrils, she patted its neck then climbed cautiously to the top of a nearby boulder, peering carefully over the rim and looked out into a narrow valley.

Two creekbeds, long without water, merged into one at this point and at the junction Mouse could see four men digging holes with iron shovels; a fifth man, mounted but unmoving, sat in the saddle of his horse and gazed out across the mesa.

The young Cheyenne woman almost gasped when she saw them - the enemy! And, she - Mouse of the Suhtai Forked Lightning Women - had found them first.

Ducking back below the rim, she forced herself to breathe easily and keep her nerve. The men were only a bow shot away and she could hear them talk in their strange language. There was too many for her to fight alone of course, she would need the help of all of her war companions. Carefully easing the rifle hammer down onto the cap, she walked back to her pony and led it, limping on a rear hoof, behind a screen of rocks and went to find the Traveller.

---- 0 0 0 ----

Chapter Thirty Seven

Henry and the wolf skinner were nervous – dismounted, they stood alone at the edge of the Cheyenne village. The two warriors and the woman accompanying them had entered the village first, proclaiming their visitors.

There had been a slight pause as people digested the fact that white men were present and then, as if at a pre-ordained signal, the entire population came boiling out of the tipis to see the strangers.

Women waved knives and antler picks, men raced up with hastily grabbed lances and bows, children hid behind their mothers' skirts and even the elders limped over to take part. It was pure unadulterated noise - screeching, yelling and banging of drums, dogs barking and ponies whinnying. And worse, the two warriors had now disappeared into the circle of lodges.

Carver tried to calm things down by talking in their own tongue but this just seemed to annoy them; the younger ones rushed at him and knocked him over, beating him with clubs and lance shafts. When Henry tried to intervene, he got the same treatment. The screeching got louder as both men went down under the blows and soon Henry and Carver found it impossible to stand up, surrounded by a press of nervous Cheyenne.

Henry managed to unholster his Colt and, sticking it through the sea of faces above him, shot into the air. The crash of the explosion made the Cheyenne step back and the yelling tailed off to a frightened muttering. Smoke on the Moon came hurrying out of his lodge with Bad Elk running up behind him:

"Leave them, they are friends!" shouted Smoke.

"They are white enemies!" yelled Feathers on His Shield and ran towards Henry with his hatchet raised. Henry raised his Colt Dragoon and pointed it at the charging man.

He didn't need to fire though. Bad Elk rarely moved quickly these days but now darted forward, grabbed Feathers by his hair and yanked him off his feet. The crowd gasped at this insulting behaviour.

"These vehoe are guests of the Suhtai - we bring them in honour after they helped us defeat a Crow war party. The young one saved the lives of Smoke on the Moon's wife and son," said Bad Elk, his usual loud tone rising above the murmuring of the suspicious crowd.

"That is true…" said Smoke "…see the Crow scalps." He held up the thick hanks of black hair, each with its own circle of dried, bloody skin attached. As an afterthought, he held up the trade gun he had also captured:

"These white men helped us kill at least five Crow; they seek none of the battle trophies - they come in peace, just to visit us for a while."

Bad Elk let go of Feathers on His Shield's hair and the young Thunder Bear soldier stood up, his eyes still blazing with anger and embarrassment at being denied his prey. His hair now hung loosely, sticking to his face with the sweat of his exertions. This would not do - his brave charge had been challenged in public, brought low by a move that little girls used when they played. Bad Elk and the two whites would pay for this at a time of his choosing.

The anger in the crowd seemed to subside and now all looked at the white men with a mix of anxiety and curiosity - for many of the younger ones, this was a first sighting of the pale monsters.

Some of the elders merely turned on their heel and walked away, feigning disinterest. Children were the first to make a move, reaching out to touch the veho clothes and skin, fascinated by the blonde hair on Henry's arms. Small, curious hands explored the butt of his holstered pistol and the decorated sheath of his hunting knife, Henry gently pushed them off.

Carver took the percussion cap off the rifle and let the young ones hold the long weapon; there was laughter as toddlers tried to heft it into the aim, the heavy iron barrel wobbling from side to side:

"Well, that was exciting Mr Carver," said Henry at last, recovering some of his spirit. He had been unsure about drawing and firing his pistol but, on balance, it seemed like a good idea. Better to die on your feet than on your knees.

"Huh!" snorted Carver, now even more convinced that they would die there.

"Those two Cheyenne we rode in with won't always be here - that young 'un they stopped still wants to kill us both…"

Henry was disappointed at Carver's attitude:

"Oh come on Mr Carver, you've been in Cheyenne villages before. I'm sure it was all just a show of bravado."

Carver snorted again:

"There was more than just goddamn bravado in that buck's eyes - it was pure, plain dealin' hate. We'll have to make sure that we don't turn our backs on *him*."

He pointed in the direction of the lodge where Smoke and Badlands had gone:

"That squaw don't like us neither. You may have saved their lives but she's got something against you, me or both of us."

Both men unsaddled their ponies and unloaded the mule. The mule seemed especially pleased to be relieved of its burden and brayed noisily.

Still surrounded by children and some of the younger women, Henry and Carver pitched their tent by the treeline of a stand of live oak and slung their bedrolls inside. Carver went into the woods and brought out some kindling and thicker boughs for a cooking fire while Henry rinsed out the stew pot in the river, scouring the remnants of previous meals off with wet sand.

Dusk was falling and the moon came up as the spectators drifted away. Guests of the Cheyenne they may be but both men kept their weapons close to hand.

Bad Elk loomed out of the purpling sky and strode up to the white men:

"We will celebrate our victory against the Crows with a feast and a Scalp Dance. You will eat with us."

Carver translated for Henry who smiled, walked up to the Cheyenne chief and rattled him slightly by grasping his hand and shaking it. Henry had asked Carver to teach him a few words of Cheyenne on the trail and now he put them to use:

"I see you - I am a pony's arse" he said proudly.

---- **0 0 0** ----

Chapter Thirty Eight

The drink in the muddy creek had refreshed them and made Alicia think straight; mother and daughter now walked only at night. They had no food or any chance of catching any edible prey but slashed cactus with sharp rocks and sucked on the soft, fleshy interior. Alicia tried to keep them on hard ground to avoid leaving tell-tale tracks; she had long ago stopped using the churned trail of the Comanche horde to hide their foot prints as it could only lead them back to the *Comancheria* and captivity. She decided to use the North Star to guide them and hoped it would bring them to safety, even if that safety wasn't in Texas.

Now they waited for night to fall again, crouched in the poor shelter of a clump of waist-high, prickly agave plants. Alicia knelt behind her daughter, keeping much of the harsh sun off her.

She looked at Rebecca and smiled:

"We'll try and find some more water tomorrow darlin' - that last drink perked us up some. Just wish we had our old buttermilk jug to carry some of that creek water in."

"It's fine Momma," replied the girl, "If I think real hard about something else, I don't feel thirsty."

"Oh really, Missy? What do you think about to take your mind off it?"

"Well… buttermilk mostly," said the girl and laughed. Her mother chuckled with her and beamed with pride at her stoical child. But their laughter hid the approach of the pony.

Red Bark Tree Woman found them in the twilight; ears attuned for any abnormal noise - and, out here in her harsh homeland on the Llano, laughter was abnormal. Spurring her horse forward with a whoop, she crashed her pony into the cactus and leapt onto Alicia, rope in hand. The pudgy Comanche forced Alicia's face into the dirt - it wasn't hard to do as the Texan was already starved and exhausted. She pulled her captive up to a sitting position and yelled her triumph as she knotted the rope around Alicia's neck.

But the white woman wasn't done yet. Waiting until the squaw had hauled her to her feet, Alicia leant her head right back and headbutted the Comanche in the face, her forehead connecting with the bridge of the Indian's nose.

Her Scotttish Grandafther, who had taught her the blow, had called it a 'Glasgow Kiss' and she, as a lady, had never expected to have to use it. But the thought of Comanche captivity took away any of Alicia's guilt about bad behaviour as the squaw sat down on her haunches in surprise, dabbing at the blood seeping from her nose. If the headbutt was good enough for a drunken brawl outside a Glasgow pub, then Alicia felt more than happy to use it on wild Indians.

Alicia was also surprised - amazed that she had fought back and now seemed to have an advantage. But she would have to be quick, the Comanche woman was trying to struggle to her feet but her moccasins caught in the fringes of her shift and kept her legs bent, knees on the ground. The squaw shrieked in anger and Alicia quailed a little as the woman ripped her troublesome moccasins off her feet and finally stood up. She leapt on Alicia again, taking advantage of her weaker opponent and slapping her repeatedly as the Texan went down onto her back and wriggled ineffectively under the weight of the heavier woman.

Red Bark Tree Woman had found her second wind and strength as she prepared to beat the pale foreigner into submission. Her husband would be pleased; she yelled her victory song as her opponent became limp. She had, though, forgotten about the daughter.

While the squaw's anger was directed at her mother, Rebecca Gadd had slipped along to the pony and taken the pointed stick out from the pad saddle. Using all her strength she swung the heavy pole in a wide arc and thumped the Comanche woman on the side of the head with it.

Red Bark Tree felt the blow, shook her head and looked around:

"My husband hits me harder than that - you'll need to do better to defeat me."

Of course, neither Alicia nor Rebecca understood the Comanche words but they didn't need to. Alicia used the pause to grab handfuls of dust and shale and ram them straight into the squaw's eyes. The Comanche stood up and rubbed at her inflamed eyes, shaking her head from side to side and screaming in pain and surprise.

Alicia scrambled up and, though shaky, took the sharp-edged piece of shale that had slashed several tough cactus skins and stabbed the Comanche in the throat with it. Even Alicia knew that it wasn't a killer blow but was too exhausted to try anything else. The squaw gurgled and sat down heavily.

Rebecca though had thought of something else. She threw the sharpened stick to her mother and ran around to the back of the Comanche woman's head, wrapped the Indian's long braids of hair around both arms and dived into the dirt. The squaw fell backwards, her neck resting on Rebecca's arms and she yelled in pain and anger. The woman tried to grab Rebecca and throw her off but the girl avoided the flailing hands and wrapped the greasy braids closer to her skinny forearms.

While she was still yelling Alicia Gadd rammed the pointed stick into the woman's open mouth and rammed it down into the Indian's throat. Rebecca, instinctively knowing that more force was needed, wriggled out of the confused lump of bodies, came to her mother's side and helped her push the stick deeper into the gullet of the Comanche.

The screaming was now replaced by sharp gagging breaths, deep retching sounds and frantic scrabbling at the pole to dislodge the whites who were killing her.

Both Texans put their full weight onto the shaft and felt tissue rip in the squaw's throat. Blood bubbled up in the woman's mouth, a flood of dark red that rose between her teeth and she stopped thrashing. But Alicia dare not let the Comanche rise again.

With renewed vigour, Alicia now screwed the point deeper into the throat, feeling it crunch against the Comanche's spine. She freed her daughter from the task:

"Get her shoes and the pony darlin' - we'll ask forgiveness later!"

---- 0 0 0 ----

Chapter Thirty Nine

Mouse tried to remount and ride her pony but the split hoof made it stand still and refuse to move. She quirted it for a while but the horse would not go forward; it just stood and whickered at the pain of the beating. It would only walk with Mouse leading it by the bridle and then only at a pace that allowed it to take the weight off its injured foot. It would take a long time for her to get back to the Traveller and report her findings.

Back at the waiting place, White Rain and her remaining warriors had been anxious about their youngest war sister; Mouse was undoubtedly brave but she was untested as a lone scout and fighter. Hidden out of sight in a rocky gully, she spoke in low tones to Willow and Crow Dress Woman, out of earshot of the Traveller and See the Dark:

"She's been gone a long time - I hope nothing has happened to her," she said, glancing across at the two men who were pointedly looking at the sun's place in the sky, silently calculating how much longer they could wait for Mouse's return.

Viajero blamed himself for sending Mouse - it was a gesture to appease the women; give them some responsibility and see what they made of it. The small girl had courage and spirit; he had explained to her where to search and what to look for but he knew, in his heart, he should have gone himself. They were deep in Comancheria and it was no place for an inexperienced warrior, man or woman.

White Rain's concern was not just for Mouse's safety; she did not share this with the others but Crow Dress Woman did:

"If Mouse messes up this scout, the men will never forgive us…"

Willow cut her short:

"She has her guns - she would have fired shots if she was in trouble. She was told not to go too far ahead."

White Rain was about to reply when See the Dark suddenly stood up:

"Ah, she's coming!" he said with some relief and hurried out to meet her, followed by the others.

Viajero was about to rebuke Mouse for lateness when he noticed the ungainly pace of her horse and went to inspect its foot.

Mouse was excited; clasping the hands of the chattering, happy women, as she proudly reported to Viajero that she had found the enemy:

"It was just as you said - they were digging holes but put nothing in them. The holes remain open to the sky."

"Good," said Viajero, "you will lead us there tomorrow but you can't ride on that."

The Apache pointed to Mouse's pony, now trembling with the effort of walking on its bad leg. She would have to kill her horse - it couldn't be left to wander and betray the presence of the Cheyenne in strange country. She would do it tomorrow - a knife in the neck would the quietest way - she had ridden it since it was a colt and it seemed only right that she should be there at its end. She did not have a spare pony - she would have to ride double with one of her friends.

The young Cheyenne woman, however, was not one for lingering on sad thoughts - she beamed with pleasure at being given the honour of leading the war party to their target. She was about to break into song when she noticed her surroundings:

"This is not your campground - others have been here," she said, pointing at the outlines where two lodges had stood not long before. A cold cooking fire, probably abandoned in haste, with a roasted joint of meat on a charred skewer lying in the blackened ashes was between the shelter shapes.

"I'm hungry," said the young woman and moved towards the meat. The others said nothing but moved aside, Mouse did not see their smiles.

Mouse picked up the haunch of meat and sniffed it - it was hard to identify what it was - not buffalo, nor antelope or bear. Perhaps it was an animal that only lived out here in this strange, flat wilderness? Still, on the war trail, food was welcome – whatever it was. She was about to taste it when Viajero spoke:

"You are right about this place - it is a Tonkawa camp."

Mouse nodded; she had heard the name of the Tonkawa people but knew little else:

"So?" she said, wondering why the entire group was now grinning broadly at her, anticipating her next move. The young Cheyenne woman was hungry - she brushed the ash off the surface of the meat and bit into it impatiently. She was puzzled and slightly upset when all her companions roared with laughter as she chewed the stringy mouthful.

The Traveller came forward and gently took the roasted joint from her:

"The Tonkawa eat the flesh of men - this is a Comanche leg bone," said the Apache, neatly ducking out of the way as Mouse spat out the gobbet of flesh and wailed in disgust.

"Welcome to the war trail, little sister," said Dark, smirking.

---- 0 0 0 ----

Chapter Forty

Pedro Alavarez blushed at the praise; his boss was impressed:

"Excellent Pedro - they are easy enough for the Comanches to find - but not *too* easy..." Castillo laughed. The caches and their contents would be his leverage point with Iron Hat - no white captives - no good rifles for the old savage.

Juan Castillo strode around the four well-dug holes, testing their depth with a shovel handle. He nodded with satisfaction:

"...so, unload the wagon now..."

Juan pointed to each hole in turn:

"...put the cases of rifles in these two but ..."

Castillo tapped each rifle crate with his boot,

"...open that one and the smaller one first- I'll take a sample of each type to show the heathens how to use them."

Alavarez, warmed by the words of his boss, brushed the two men aside who were starting on the task and prised open the wooden slats of the arms cases himself and, beaming with pleasure, handed one of the guns to Castillo.

"No better guns than these in Texas, *Jefe* - the Sharps carbine, you already know about. Remember this new one shoots quicker 'cos of these..."

Alvarez took the Sharps back and showed Castillo the loop of copper caps inside the gun:

"...No need to put a fresh cap on after you've fired the cartridge, the gun does it for you."

Alvarez grinned and laid the rifle on a piece of canvas on the ground. Juan, bristling slightly at being told what he already knew, nodded curtly. Alavarez, not noticing the chilling in the atmosphere, went on:

"But if you show the Comanche how to fire this one…"

He took the Colt rifle and held it as if aiming it:

"…Make sure both hands are behind the trigger when you pull it."

"Alvarez! This is just a Colt pistol with a longer barrel and a shoulder stock - what could be simpler?"

Pedro Alvarez stopped smiling, sensing that he had overstepped some invisible mark. He would have to overcome Castillo's obvious ignorance on the shortcomings of the Colt; some judicious grovelling seemed to be the best way:

"Forgive me *Jefe* - I am entirely to blame. I neglected to tell you this but, when we collected these Colt rifles from our agent, he said that there was a minor fault in this model. It is rare that it happens but…." he shrugged.

Pedro took the rifle and explained the fault to him. Eventually, Juan nodded and, to lighten the mood and settle the watching men, smiled:

"Oh, *that* fault! Well, do not worry my friend; I already knew that these Colts can misfire…"

Alvarez smiled worriedly back; perhaps his boss *hadn't* understood his explanation. The fault was not a misfire but a possibility that all the six chambers of the loaded rifle would fire *at once*. The spark from one shot could ignite powder remnants in the mechanism. If you held it like a rifle, supporting the barrel with your left hand, the damn thing could 'chain fire', as the *gringos* called it, and shoot most of your fingers off. He just hoped that he wasn't around when Castillo demonstrated the Colt rifle to the Comanche. The gun was a menace.

Juan, silent for a while, now decided it was time for leadership:

"Alvarez, load the Colt and we'll see what it does!"

Pedro shook his head sorrowfully; he really didn't want to touch the damn rifle. Still, he inserted the paper cartridges and a copper cap on each of the six nipples. He was about to shoot it, carefully keeping his hands behind the trigger guard, when Castillo took the gun from him.

"No, my friend - I'll do it…"

Nothing that Juan Castillo did was ever by chance. He was certain that the gun would *not* misbehave as it was still smeared in its packing grease. It would only have been test fired once - if at all - at the factory and then cleaned before packing so there was little chance of any powder remnants lurking in the working parts of the gun. Of course, Juan relied on his men being too ignorant to know this. His act would look decisive and heroic - the boss taking the risks instead of them.

He held it, as Colonel Colt had intended, like a rifle and aimed at a rock wall some fifty yards away. Six perfect single shots cracked and splatted lead balls against the surface; making greyish white roundels against the red rock. Castillo laughed and held up his left hand:

"See Pedro, I still have all my fingers!"

The men clapped and cheered their leader - Juan Castillo de Coronado was indeed a hero worthy of their loyalty and service.

Castillo smiled to himself at the applause. The truth was he had already paid for the Colt rifles *before* he'd heard about the chain fire problem. But he was a businessman and he had to make his investment work for him. He reasoned that with some guile, good timing and thorough cleaning before the weapon was test fired by the Comanches - he could probably get away with it. He just needed a stooge to do it when he was well clear of the Indian camp. The Texan seemed to be the ideal candidate.

The sun was setting behind the rock wall and the lead splashes from the bullets faded from view. Behind the mesa wall, unseen onlookers had also witnessed his shooting - they were impressed too but for different reasons.

---- o o o ----

See the Dark thumped Viajero on the shoulder when the Mexican had fired the rifle - six shots without reloading. That was the gun for him! The Apache brushed him away and continued to look through a gap in the rocks at the movements of the Mexicans.

Though he did not show it, Viajero was pleased too - even at this distance, he had recognised the first gun. It looked exactly like the precious carbine that the veho soldier chief had taken from him when he and Dark had been captured by the Army column. He would be happy to get another one of those.

After the man with the big horse had finished shooting, the remaining Mexicans seemed happy. The Apache watched them as they unloaded the wagon and put rifle boxes into two of the holes, ammunition into another and earthen ware jugs into the last one.

There was a wriggling beside him as Mouse pushed Dark aside from the concealed place where they could spy on the Mexicans; he hissed in protest but to no avail. The determined girl had some nerve:

"What is in the pots?" she whispered.

Viajero sighed with exasperation - these women were just not disciplined enough for the war trail. Brave, yes but they acted like novices.

"Whiskey" he muttered, before clamping his hand over her mouth to stop further dangerous conversation.

Viajero only assumed that the jugs contained whiskey - but long experience told him that no Indian deal with Mexicans or whites would be complete without it. He had tasted the stuff before in his past life and it had tasted like liquid fire. Worse, the drink had taken his legs away. He had staggered like a child and puked outside his *wickiup* on the Gila. Usen, the One God, had deserted him during that time. He would not touch it again and would try to make sure that See the Dark didn't either. Whiskey made warriors weak.

The Apache settled back under the ledge and saw that the Mexicans had finished filling the holes with stores and now began to pile earth back on top as concealment. When they had finished, each man stuck the shovel at one end of each hole, its white wood shaft upright and clearly visible.

"What's happening?" hissed See the Dark, anxious in case he missed some vital point when Mouse had pushed in.

Viajero, blowing frustration and irritation through his teeth, turned around, sat up and put one hand fully over the faces of both Dark and Mouse. He spoke in his battle whisper - a sound that matched the breeze blowing or leaves rustling; a sound that would not alert enemies, even when they were close. Both Mouse and Dark noticed the urgent change in tone:

"They have cached their trade goods and marked the site - they'll leave now."

Viajero glanced down at the base of the sloping mesa wall; See the Dark's woman held the reins of three ponies that they had ridden up on - she, at least, was silent and reliable. White Rain had covered their muzzles with a length of deerskin to keep out the scent of the Mexican horses. Mouse and White Rain had ridden double on the elder woman's pony to reach the mesa wall but he knew that this couldn't be the case when they rode back to the Suhtai country. He sulked slightly as he realised that Mouse would have to use one of the spare ponies that he and Dark had had the wisdom to bring. Those Forked Lightning Women may be warriors but their planning and preparation for the war trail was poor - it would take all of his patience and cunning to get them home alive.

"They're going…" whispered Mouse, peering between a rocky overhang at the Mexicans.

Viajero wriggled back into his viewing point but grunted in annoyance. Only the wagon and the leader on the big horse were going - the other five men brought out their horses from a hidden *arroyo* and started to unsaddle them. Coffee pots and skillets were pulled out of saddlebags and mesquite brush collected to start a fire.

The Apache's plan - to wait until the site was deserted then dig up the rifles and vanish north with them - had just unravelled. They would have to take the rifles and ammunition by force. And they would have to do it before the Comanches arrived.

---- 0 0 0 ----

The Hunkpapa girl sang a low song in her own tongue as she carved slices of meat from the rump of the dead pony. She and Crow Dress Woman would have preferred to be with the others to spy on the enemy but the Traveller was wise in his preparations for battle and flight back to their own country.

They would need food and Mouse's slaughtered pony would provide it. She stopped singing and looked up as a trampling of hooves on rock and a loud braying showed that Crow Dress was not coping well with the mules.

"Sister! Do you need help?"

Crow Dress merely grunted in reply and continued to struggle with re-saddling the stubborn animals. Horses she could deal with but mules needed more effort.

The spare ponies, hobbled to prevent them running off, shuffled sideways putting space between them and the struggling woman. Replacing pack saddles on obstinate mules was a new experience for her; it took at least two attempts before she realised that the saddles were on the wrong way round. Snarling with frustration, she hoisted the wooden frames as high as she could and thumped them against the flanks of the nearest mule; it brayed and kicked back at her.

Willow walked over, smiling, and took the head of each mule in her hands. She breathed into their muzzles and sang a soft song to calm them. Crow Dress was a brave young woman but lacked patience with chores:

"Here, come and hold the mules and I'll saddle them," Willow said.

Crow Dress looked downcast, as though her inability to saddle a couple of mules made her less of a warrior. She held both animals by their rope bridles and tried to avoid their eyes - she was sure they were laughing at her. Worse, they made no complaint when Willow quickly and effortlessly, saddled them both and then patted her on the shoulder. But Crow Dress was at least gracious:

"Thank you, sister. I'll help you take the meat from the pony - we'll need to be quick though…" Crow Dress pointed to the sky; vultures were circling on swirls of warm air and showing their position.

"You are right - let's hope the Traveller and the others get back soon."

Both women got to work with their butcher knives and stripped flank and backstrap from the pony, their hands now black with dried blood. The earth beneath the dead animal was a scuffed red mud as they toiled to turn the corpse over to get at the choice cuts; dust clung to the pieces of meat that they piled onto a deerskin and flies gathered. The pile of greenish yellow guts shone in the sunlight.

Crow Dress had regained her sense of humour and both women chattered as they took the pony down to its bones:

"Who is the man that courts you under the blanket? Will you marry him?" asked the younger Cheyenne woman. Willow snorted in a derisory fashion:

"Hardly – I call him my 'Too Man',"

"What's a 'Too Man'?" asked the younger woman.

"Too old, too short and two wives!" hooted the Lakota girl, laughing at her own joke. Crow Dress cackled; Willow was very forthright.

"What did he think of you coming south to find the Traveller?" asked Crow Dress.

"I have no idea," retorted the Hunkpapa girl, "I didn't ask him."

She peeled away a long piece of pony hide and inserted her butcher knife under the bloody twist of muscle. She looked up at Crow Dress:

"And what about your young man? Was he pleased to be less important than your war trail?"

Crow Dress kept her head down to her task:

"He does not come to see me any more - we parted before the last full moon. He wasn't happy that I was a warrior…"

She stopped, sensing a change in the behaviour of the tethered animals. Both mules had raised their heads in unison - someone was coming.

Willow stood up and looked out from their rocky enclosure at the lone, approaching horse:

"Is it the Traveller?" asked Crow Dress

"No…" said the Hunkpapa girl uncertainly as she shielded her eyes from the glare of the setting sun and peered more closely at the shadowy figures. She quickly knelt back down again and hissed to Crow Dress:

"It's a woman and a child - I think they are both white."

---- o o o ----

Chapter Forty One

Henry was flicking through his journal when Smoke on the Moon walked up. He was carrying the old rusty trade rifle that he had captured during their fight with the Crows - he had tucked it under his arm so that it would not appear threatening to the white men. Carver, squatting in front of the fire roasting some sage hens on greenwood skewers, greeted him and motioned him to sit down.

Henry smiled and tried out his Cheyenne:

"White leaves nearly gone," he said, showing Smoke the leather backed journal with its full complement of sketches.

The war leader of the Striking Snakes took the book and went carefully through it. He was too polite to ask about the arrow mark and dried blood that spoiled every page; the young veho would mention it if the time was ever appropriate. Smoke liked the young man and was honour-bound to recognise the family debt that he owed him.

Henry reckoned that the drawing was going well. He didn't put any price for putting pencil to paper for anyone in the encampment; people now trusted them more and showed up outside his tent flap and ask to be sketched. Some wanted to take the finished drawing with them but Henry tried to explain that the renderings would be his memories of the Cheyenne when he left the village. Sometimes they brought gifts of food as payment to try and persuade him to part with a sketch; he wondered if Leonardo Da Vinci had got the same treatment in Italy.

Whatever the outcome of the sketching, it had been a good idea and Henry was pleased; even Carver, over coffee at night, admitted that the scheme had worked. What he hadn't mentioned to Carver or the Cheyenne was that soon he would need to go back to the wagon road and barter with passing pioneers for more paper.

"Your Cheyenne is improving..." Smoke said to Henry. Carver chuckled and pitched in:

"Yellow Bear is a good teacher..."

"He's not..." said Henry, pointing at the wolf skinner

Smoke smiled and nodded in agreement - Bad Elk had told him of the language trick that the wolf skinner had played on the young, fair-skinned veho. Indeed, Bad Elk had told several other people about it and now children shouted the rude words at Henry. Yellow Bear, appalled at this treatment of their guests, had taken Henry under his wing and had decided that the beauty of the language of the People should not be despoiled by childish insults; so, each day he had visited the white men and tried to improve their knowledge of the Cheyenne tongue.

Yellow Bear, walking both men round camp pointing out objects and giving the Cheyenne words, had shown them his buffalo hide pictograph and, as part of the lessons, explained some of the incidents that they showed. In turn, Henry had shown him the sketches he had made – Yellow Bear had looked politely through the book, impressed by its etched leather cover and the fine surface of the paper, running his fingertips over it lightly – though politely did not mention that the sketched faces of people he knew in the village now all looked alike. One thing had interested him though, on the very first white leaf:

"What are these lines?" he had asked, pointing to Henry's handwritten scrawl of two limited sentences made during the Sumner expedition. Henry had been baffled as to what to say but Carver had stepped in:

"We use these lines to send messages to one another – like the Cheyenne leave behind stone and skull signals for friends to find the right trail or to warn enemies."

Yellow Bear looked sceptical:

"But how does your friend know what you want to say if the lines stay in your …." He had no word for book so held up the journal.

Carver racked his brain to explain:

"The vehoe do not move around like the People – so we make the lines on a white leaf and send the leaf to our friends."

Yellow Bear had just shrugged – it seemed a pointless waste of time. He had more questions but, for now, continued his tour of the camp and language lessons.

Now at the campfire, as the sage hens started to sizzle, Henry and Carver both watched Smoke carefully - the impressive war leader did not appear to be one who just passed by for a casual chat. He seemed to have something on his mind but was finding it difficult to put it into words.

Smoke, after some strained talk about horses and the next village move, handed his captured rifle to Henry:

"Is this a good gun?"

Henry understood the question but knew that his grasp of the Cheyenne language couldn't cope with a full answer so he passed the weapon to Carver.

The wolf skinner, turned the rifle around in his hands, cocked the hammer and poked the ramrod down the barrel - the brass tip scraped the inside surface and he could feel the build-up of burnt powder - the thing hadn't been cleaned in years. He tried to unscrew the percussion cap nipple with his fingers but it was rusted in tightly. He held the gun at the point of balance in his palm and looked at Smoke:

"Well, we know it will fire - those Crows shot at us with it…"

It was meant as a light remark but Smoke just nodded gravely.

"Guns always need to be cleaned. This one needs to be cleared of dead powder so that you can trust it in future."

Again, Smoke nodded without smiling and took the gun back - Carver guessed that he already knew about cleaning rifles. After all, his brother, the chief had a handsome and well-kept Hawken gun - he would be the best person to go to for advice. No, Smoke on the Moon had other things on his mind - even Henry sensed it.

"Is he actually asking your advice on gun care, Mr Carver?"

"Sorta, I guess. I reckon he's got something else to say or prove"

Smoke was uncomfortable and he sensed the white men knew it. He was a man unused to deception - it was not the way of a Cheyenne warrior to conceal what he felt or what his intentions were but the nagging instructions of his wife were forcing him to be diplomatic - an act that he considered cowardly. Pretence was for women and girls, not for men. But Badlands Walking Woman was not to be denied her opportunity to find out about the young veho's rifle:

"Could I look at your gun?" he asked the wolf-skinner. Carver nodded and, with only a moment's hesitation, passed him the long rifle.

Carver was puzzled at the request but happy to comply knowing his gun was unloaded. Despite now being much more relaxed in the Cheyenne village, his instinct for survival would never allow him to hand a loaded weapon to an Indian. He watched as Smoke held the unwieldy rifle, feeling its weight and balance, lining up the sights, stroking the polished woodwork and looking down the barrel. It was an exaggerated performance and all three men knew it.

"Good," said Smoke approvingly and handed the long rifle back to its owner. Then, turning to Henry he said:

"Your gun is different to his, can I see that?"

Carver had to intervene to translate some of the words but Henry was happy to oblige:

"Yes, here…"

Unlike the wolf skinner, his Sharps carbine was already loaded so as Henry leaned across to pick up his rifle, he cocked the hammer and removed the percussion cap and put it in his shirt pocket. He hoped the Cheyenne war leader would not see this as a sign of mistrust. Smoke noticed the precaution and smiled:

"A good idea - children are playing here."

Smoke then went through the same elaborate ritual with the Sharps - caressing the woodwork, testing the sights and hefting the weapon in his hands. The Cheyenne examined the wooden stock closely, smoothing over the polished wood with his fingers and making sounds of approval. He seemed to be inspecting the grain of the wood. He handed it back to Henry; his mood seemed lighter and friendlier:

"That is a good gun too. I see that you load it from the other end of the barrel…"

Carver translated and Henry, glad to help, showed him one of the paper cartridges:

"Shoots quicker," said Henry and Smoke laughed.

"Where did you get this gun?" asked the Cheyenne warrior in an unexpected turn in the conversation. Henry and Carver both tensed up inside - was this what the examination of the guns was about? Henry pointed to Carver who gave the explanation:

"My chief bought it from a gun seller, many days ride away on the banks of the Big Muddy River."

"Ah…" said Smoke, "…then I'm pleased you bought it - it helped save my family." The Cheyenne war leader seemed genuinely grateful and, resting his own rifle butt on the ground, used it to pull himself to his feet. He smiled, bade both white men farewell and strode off back to his own lodge.

Badlands Walking Woman was waiting for him; she had ensured that she passed by the meeting place with the vehoe and had seen her husband handle both guns:

"Well?" she demanded, "Did you see the Traveller's spirit sign on the young veho's rifle?"

Viajero's horned lizard sign was distinctive; she had watched the Apache while he had spent several days carefully driving the decorative copper nails into the woodwork to make sure that the shape was recognisable by Usen, the Apache's god. She could not stop and stare, of course, as the process had been accompanied by many prayers.

Unfortunately, she could not remember exactly where the nails had been. Even consulting Bright Antelope had not been useful - the Mescalero woman could not remember which side of the shoulder piece the nails had been on or how big the lizard shape was. Viajero kept his beloved rifle in a soft deerskin case to protect it - she had never been allowed to handle it and so could only speak from indistinct pieces of memory. The gun belonged to her husband - she rarely saw it.

Even Badlands knew that the chance of the copper nails still being in the rifle stock was slim but the holes could still be there. This was her last hope of catching the veho out in a lie.

She was disturbed that the two whites were becoming popular in the small Suhtai encampment; young women giggled foolishly in their presence and had taken to sitting around their tent flap at night. In fact, women at the washing place in the river had hinted that both white men had bedded some of the Cheyenne girls. The foreigners were becoming part of the village. Badlands Walking Woman though never gave in to doubt - the vehoe were a bad influence and, in her heart, she knew that they had had some form of contact with the Traveller. How else would they know his father's name?

Smoke, however, was not prepared to spare her foolish fears. He would often go to great lengths to avoid an argument with his wife - her formidable temper was something to avoid and he would sometimes leave the lodge to get away from it. But now she had driven him to a despicable act of betrayal with the men who had saved this ungrateful woman and their son. She had forced him to act like a skulking coyote instead of a man of the Tsis-tsis-tas. He looked coldly into her eyes:

"There is no mark of the Traveller on the rifle," he said.

---- o o o ----

Chapter Forty Two

It had been a while since See the Dark had had a good idea – but he had one now. It was an idea worthy of telling the Traveller – an idea for a plan that could help against the Comancheros. He hoped it would help redress some of the more immature thinking that he had been doing recently. He felt proud and excited as the plan had crawled into his head.

His last good idea had formed the seed of the battle plan the Suhtai used when they rode in revenge against the Pawnee up on the Loup River some two winters ago. Then, he had been idly running his fingers through a spooked column of ants, dividing their forces with ridges of dust, when the notion of attacking the Pawnee when they were in separate hunting camps came to him. It had worked too - his mother had told him afterwards that he was destined for great things and he had believed her. Of course, it took him a while to realise that *all* mothers probably said the same thing to their sons no matter how dumb they actually were.

He was back on the mesa rim where the Mexican leader had fired his repeating gun. He had ridden far that day - a long, looping ride to see if he could see the Comanche trading camp but hadn't found it. He had ridden out before dawn broke to look for the first tell-tale smoke of the morning cooking fires as the sun came up that would point to a large gathering of the Comanche; there was none. At least he could report to Viajero that the Comanches were probably more than a day's ride away. The Apache would be pleased - they would need all the extra time they could get.

The arrival of the white woman and the girl had thrown them into confusion. It had forced them to think again about their quick plan for attacking the Mexicans and digging up the rifles.

See the Dark had wanted to kill the white woman and child and said so - he had no idea where they had come from; they seemed to be a warning sign from Maheo that all was not well with their planned attack on the Mexicans. How had she managed to find their small war camp in all of this vast space? Perhaps she had been watching them and was a diversion for an attack? And why was she riding a pony with a Comanche saddle on it? On reflection, he had been over-excited.

The woman herself had seemed brave - she kept threatening them all with a pointed stick; the girl child, wearing Comanche moccasins that were far too big for her, seemed equally undaunted. The woman gibbered away in a foreign tongue – even White Rain and Willow thought she would have to be silenced.

The Apache, however, had stopped any killings and remained stubborn - Dark had thought that perhaps Viajero was getting soft, now that he had a wife and daughter of his own. But Mouse and Crow Dress Woman, at least, were relieved that two innocents would not be slaughtered.

Mouse's admiration for the Apache's wisdom - already high after his teachings on the rifle and scouting –had grown rapidly. Crow Dress noticed her friend's blushes whenever the Apache praised Mouse and nudged her knowingly, giggling as she did so.

The Apache's orders to the rest of the war party had shown his experience in dealing with unexpected incidents on the war trail and making the best of them – to Viajero, the two extra people meant that they now had two white captives who could prove useful later.

See the Dark always felt like an inexperienced boy when the Traveller did this. Dark knew he was still just an instinctive and basic fighter compared to his mature and thoughtful friend.

Now he watched the Mexicans as they idled their time away guarding the buried rifles; the four white wood tool handles still stuck in the earth. He assumed they had horses but he couldn't see where they were being kept.

Two men slumbered in the harsh afternoon sun, stretched out with heads on saddles, faces covered by their broad-brimmed hats. Two more sat in the shade smoking tobacco and talking drowsily. The fifth man though was mounted - he seemed alert and vigilant and rode a lazy loop around the small encampment always looking to the south and east. No – the Mexicans were watchful - it would be difficult for their war party to get close to them and kill them all without a risky battle.

As instructed by the Traveller, he counted their guns and assessed their condition as enemies. These Mexicans were not weak; they were well-fed and seemed to have plenty of water. They also had one of the earthen jars of whiskey with them and they passed this round but did not seem to be drunk - See the Dark had seen drunks before when some Minniconjou Lakota braves had ridden loudly into their camp last summer and demanded food; Smoke and Broken Knife had called out their soldier societies to take the whiskey bottles from the Sioux. Whiskey made men crazy.

Suddenly, the mounted sentry called out to his companions and Dark instinctively ducked down behind the rimrock. Surely it couldn't be the Comanche? He would have seen them coming - the Nerm-en-uh always rode wildly to show off their fine horses and so people could see their excellent riding. No, he reassured himself - there would have been a dust cloud and a lot more noise.

He peeked cautiously over the rock again and almost laughed out loud. No Comanche horde was coming, just an elderly man carrying a long pole with a short cross-piece at the top and leading a single donkey; the animal brayed enthusiastically at the scent of the unseen Mexican horses and nodded its head up and down, a brass bell clanked on a leather thong around its neck.

Dark watched as the elderly man spoke a few words to the assembling Mexicans; they seemed glad to see him. Dark was puzzled by the man's clothing - all the Mexicans he had been watching wore pants, shirts, boots and gun belts but the newcomer wore only a rough gown of black cloth and some sort of thin leather strips on his feet.

All the Mexicans gathered round him as the old man jammed the long stick into the earth. Dark was astonished when all the gunmen shook out into a line, knelt in front of the pole and bowed their heads – what magic was this?

It was obviously some sort of ceremony, perhaps sacred to the Mexicans. The old man seemed to give out some sort of food to each gunman who took it in cupped hands; this was followed by a drink from a small silver cup, just a sip for each one. It didn't seem like a proper meal - Dark's belly rumbled, he hadn't eaten in a while.

Dark's good idea came as he patted his gurgling stomach. The ceremony didn't interest him even though it seemed to involve food. No, the exciting thing took him a while to realise.

The old man in the black robe, even if his presence was unexpected, had been welcomed by the gunmen – no warning shots had been fired and he had not been challenged on the way into their camp by the outrider sentry. It was a peaceful approach to the armed and vigilant Mexicans.

Whatever or whoever the old man was, Dark's companions would need to make use of it to get to those rifles.

---- o o o ----

Chapter Forty Three

The Comanchero camp was a tense and dangerous place. Juan Castillo kept his pistols fully loaded in his gunbelt as he watched the noisy and argumentative trading between his people and the Comanches. Even the Taos farmers, often poorly armed compared to the Indians, were confident enough of the value of the trade to strike hard bargains – a few pounds of flour would fetch one good pony from a horse-rich Comanche who wanted a change of diet.

Castillo's talks with Iron Hat had followed the usual pattern, sitting on the earth floor of the trading shanty out of the harsh sunlight and trading stories, whiskey and cheroots. He thought of the *Nokoni* chief as an old man but, Juan concluded, that was probably just how he looked - especially when he was wearing his iron helmet. The chief's face was as lined and cracked as a drying turd and of a similar colour. Deceit and spite shone out of his eyes – there was nothing good in the man. Though both men had a common purpose, Castillo despised the Indian and would have gladly shot him to avoid any future meetings. Profit, however, was a strong calmer of queasy stomachs and Castillo grinned falsely at the Comanche's tales of his warrior's life, his expertise at torture and his career of raping women.

During his bragging sessions, Iron Hat watched the Mexican's reactions closely and noted the air of disdain that Castillo tried to conceal. The Comanche snorted inwardly - the Mexican was just a soft-handed trader who carried a lot of guns. He would love to rip Castillo's scalp from his head to see how loud he yelled but – guns were guns and he still needed the arrogant one to produce them.

He motioned for the Mexican to follow him outside to get some air. Castillo hauled himself up and joined the Indian on the stoop and sat down again using the front wall as a backrest.

"See my friend," said Iron Hat in passable Spanish, "our two people trade well together…" He gestured at the large camp.

Castillo nodded as he looked across the broad plain filled with animals, people, carts and noise.

He peered through the rising dust from the constant wind. Comanche lodges had been erected, though not in circles – for this camp they were in straight lines with roped off divides to separate their trade animals and goods from others. Off to one side was a makeshift race track where Kiowas, Comanches, Mexicans and some whites pitted their horses against one another, betting heavily on the outcome. Old women took the bets and lashed anyone with rawhide quirts who disagreed with their verdicts. Even experienced warriors backed away from the ruthless crones. Shots echoed from far away – shooting contests were popular for those who had guns but many of the poorer men simply shot arrows or threw knives or axes at wooden targets, betting their trade goods on the outcome. Juan knew that some of his Comancheros would go home broke.

The *carretas* of the Taos column had quickly been emptied of trade goods - corn, pinole, bread, onions and beans had found eager customers amongst the Comanche women - and Castillo watched the unmistakeable figure of the tall Texan getting the Taos families organised for the long trail back to their homes.

Juan reckoned they had done well – the carretas were now filled with buffalo meat and hides. Trade horses, only recently stolen from Texan and Mexican ranchers, were now proudly tied to the carts – small, separate *remudas* that would bring riches when sold back in Santa Fe. Stolen cattle, marked with coloured paint, would be moved in one solid herd across the Llano and fattened up before being sold to the US Army. Castillo allowed himself a smile of pleasure at his achievements – he would now be welcomed in both Taos and Santa Fe as a man who kept his word and increased investments.

"You are right, Jefe – our trade is ancient and long-lasting. Long may it continue."

He raised a whiskey bottle to his lips and pretended to drink a slug of the cheap liquor, letting the whiskey wash against his teeth before spitting it back into the bottle. It didn't pay to be drunk and insensible when surrounded by Comanches.

Though it always took a few days, Iron Hat was now impatient for the main trade to begin. He had tired of the company of the fastidious Mexican:

"Where are my guns and whiskey?" he said bluntly.

"Safe," answered Castillo, allowing himself a faint smile as he recognised the usual turn in negotiations – he had bet Montoya a silver dollar that it would take less than a week before Iron Hat wanted his 'special' goods.

Iron Hat was irritated by the Mexican's impudent smirk – it was the smile of someone who knew a secret and would only disclose it when he was ready. Still, whilst Castillo was in a strong position, so was he – those white captives had not yet been seen by Castillo's crew. The Comancheros did not know how many they were or what condition they were in. This was just as well – many were in poor shape after the journey. Two had died on the march, two had escaped and those still alive needed cleaning up to get the best deal in guns.

"Safe?" queried the *Nokoni*.

"You know our terms, Great Chief. I see the captives and you get the guns – and no trash like last time. I trade for white folk only – if any of my people want to take a black or a Mexican, they can do their own deals with you."

Iron Hat was nodding slowly – a sign he knew that the Mexican would interpret as absorbing wisdom and advice – when the Texan rode up to the stoop.

"Taos column's ready to move out at sunrise, boss – they'll be pleased to leave. Some of their women are havin' to fight off this old bastard's warriors."

Iron Hat couldn't understand English but he noted Castillo suddenly seemed to get sober and took command. The Mexican turned and spoke to him:

"Our trading is almost done this season, Jefe; show me the captives and we will arrange the handover of the guns and powder."

Iron Hat nodded curtly; he shouted out to a group of warriors who brought him his pony, his long lance tied to the saddle. Juan noted the practised swing into the decorated hide cantle and concluded that he hadn't been the only one to pretend to drink the rotgut. The Nokoni needed a close eye kept on him if they were ever to make a profit or even get out alive.

Juan unhitched his horse and told the Texan to follow them; the three men rode through the busy camp, out towards a large buffalo skin shelter on the southern edge of the village.

Children, showing a wide variety of skin colours, dashed up to their stirrups and begged for tobacco or food. Iron Hat ignored them and rode through the cluster of thin, outstretched arms; Castillo looked at them coldly – they were the very proof that the Comanches couldn't survive without taking others into their people from other tribes or cultures – he quirted them away.

The Texan though, leant down from his tall horse and gave them the corn biscuits that he had saved from his breakfast. The bigger children took them from the small ones and crammed the food into their mouths, slapping the others as a sign of their prowess. The Texan sighed:

"These are hard folk, Boss," he said in English.

"Yes – I'm glad that you realise that. We must make our bargains with them but never trust anyone who has never planted a seed or built a house. These people lack any hint of civilisation."

Juan remembered that he too had never done either of those things but the Texan seemed to understand. He kicked his horse in the side and outpaced the squalid youngsters. The riders continued on in a plodding line.

Castillo saw that there was a small thorn bush close to the shelter, with a woman apparently tied to it with some sort of shiny rope. She raised her head to look at the approaching riders. Black Shawl Woman weakly put up a hand in salute. She was a Comanche woman and would not show weakness.

"Isn't that your wife?" asked Castillo.

"One of them," replied the Comanche

Iron Hat did not look at her but rode past with his head held high, as if he held her in contempt.

He had sent her out to track down his other wife, Red Bark Tree Woman, but she had failed to find her. At least, that was what she had said. He suspected that Red Bark Tree had run off after her beating or that both women had conspired to cheat him out of his escaped white captives. So, on Black Shawl's return his warriors held her down while he had made a small cut into her belly and pulled out a length of her gut, wrapping it round the lower branches of a thorn bush. It looked like a silver and blue snake coiling through the sharp branches. She would die soon.

"What has she done?" Castillo asked looking back from the saddle as they rode past.

"She was careless," said the Comanche.

---- 0 0 0 ----

Chapter Forty Four

Feathers on His Shield had found the buffalo; it was only a small herd compared to the vast, meandering herds that he had seen as a boy - herds that, if you rode carefully enough not to spook them, took from sunrise to sunset to guide a pony through. No matter, food was food and the Falling Leaf Moon was getting closer - this herd was more than enough to provide meat for the entire village.

He dismounted and looked into the valley; even here, high on the ridge, he could hear the great beasts grunting and calling as they tore and chewed on the dry grass. The valley floor was covered with a moving brown mass of animals – dust rose in layers and settled onto the broad backs of bulls and cows alike.

Feathers was a happy man – back in the village his persistence and determination as a buffalo scout would be highly praised.

Many of the others would have returned to camp by now, disappointed and dejected. Feathers on His Shield would, once again, be singled out as a fine example of a Cheyenne hunter. This was important if he wanted to be chief – a man who can find buffalo would be highly respected, followers would sing of his great deeds and, when he eventually wrested power from Bad Elk, Feathers would be the natural choice as leader of the Suhtai. When that happened, he would take the Suhtai to great glory – he would seek out the hated vehoe and sweep them from the sacred country of the Tsis-tsis-tas. But first he had to get back to the village and report his success – he remounted and reined the horse's head round, ready to ride off, when he heard the noise.

A faint explosion rose from the valley floor brought him trotting back to the ridge. A buffalo at the edge of the herd lay crumpled in a heap; others in the herd, curious rather than frightened, walked cautiously forward and sniffed at the fallen animal. Another buffalo soon fell over, the report of the explosion echoing up the rock face.

Feathers was incensed – someone was in the valley and shooting the buffalo that *he* had found! Though, of course, he didn't own the buffalo – no-one but Maheo did – Feathers took all slights personally that rendered him less in the eyes of men.

He nocked an arrow onto his bowstring in case the shooters were enemies and rode down into the valley to chastise those who had stolen his moment of glory.

---- o o o ----

Henry couldn't believe that the buffalo he had shot from cover would go down so quickly with his Sharps carbine:

"Excellent shot, even though I say so myself Mr Carver – what say you?"

The young Englishman was even more amazed that the animals had not stampeded and run off.

During their time with the Cheyenne they had hunted buffalo before, chasing a few isolated cows from horseback – then the animals jinked and charged their ponies, trying to unseat and trample the yelling hunters. It was different firing into a running, woolly hump from close range – almost unfair with the Sharps. The dying animals would cartwheel in the dust and slide to an ugly stop, blood gushing from their nostrils in their death throes.

But hunting afoot, firing from a distance – although as Carver had reminded him, not *much* of a distance – the animals crumpled with hardly a cry, just a grunt, expelling air as they toppled over.

Carver didn't answer but took aim with his long rifle and pulled the trigger. The weapon boomed – a more delicate note, Henry thought, than the Sharps, probably because of the weapon's smaller calibre – and again a buffalo fell to its knees, chin resting in the dust and flanks quivering from the shock.

"Nicely done, Mr Carver!" shouted Henry, loading another cartridge and cap. Carver, pleased at his own shot, grinned:

"Easy enough Lootenant, when we're close enough to shoot 'em with a garter pistol."

Carver had been introduced to the garter pistol when a whore had lifted up her skirts and pulled one on him back in Independence when he was a dollar short in their transaction. The pistol looked like a toy but Carver, not wishing to die on the tent floor of a soiled dove, had paid up and backed cautiously out.

"Oh, come on Mr Carver we must be a hundred yards away."

"Eighty– maybe," said the wolf skinner. They were about to fire again when they heard a horse, pushing through the box elder on the hill slope.

"Rider comin'" said Carver and rested his rifle on his hip; Henry followed suit and, hand shielding his eyes, looked up into the sun at the approaching silhouette as the unknown horseman came towards them.

"Damn!" said Henry, "It's that bastard who doesn't like us."

"Which bastard is that? There's a whole bunch of them Indians don't like us." Carver squinted again at the rider and saw him more clearly:

"Oh, *that* one. You're right, he don't look too pleased Lootenant."

Feathers reined in his horse as he recognised the white men he loathed; his brain churned – was cheating him out of the buffalo discovery a good enough excuse to kill them? Possibly not, but then there were the rumours - rumours about the young fair-haired veho were all over camp – the young white man had been rutting with Sweet Water. She, of course, had denied it – even after a severe beating - but jealousy and hurt pride was now a wall between him and the white interlopers. He had wanted to kill them when they first entered camp, just because they were enemies. Now, the insult to his reputation as a husband joined in the mix of hostility.

Clarity borne on hatred entered his brain. If he fought well now, he could kill them both and hide their bodies so that the rest of the village wouldn't find them. He would decry them back in camp, saying they had left without thanking the Cheyenne for their hospitality – just another sign of the greedy invaders.

"What's he up to, Mr Carver?" said Henry, moving a short distance to stand under a leafy tree as a light rain began to fall, all thoughts of butchering their kills now cast aside.

Carver, still standing in the rain, covered the mouth of the rifle barrel with his hand. Something was wrong with this buck and it wasn't anything good.

"God knows Lootenant. Could be he's pissed off at us shooting these buffs afore a proper hunt with the rituals and all. But you can be damned sure that he's heard about you givin' the glad-eye to his missus…"

"Nonsense, Mr Carver – she's the one who's been batting her eyelashes at *me*."

Henry was uneasy – Sweet Water had indeed spent some nights with a group of other young women as they clustered around his tent flap. For want of better entertainment, Henry would often sing to them – 'Amazing Grace' being a particular favourite. What induced these wilderness savages into liking John Newton's greatest hymn, he never knew but afterwards Sweet Water would often fix him with her wide brown eyes and stare at him until, unnerved, he would crawl back into the tent.

Carver later told him that she was there as chaperone for her sister, New Grass, one of the young women that the wolf-skinner had taken a fancy to.

Though both white men had been watching Feathers on His Shield closely, they were unprepared for what happened.

Just as quickly as it had begun, the rain stopped, clouds parted and a beam of yellow sunlight shone directly onto the mounted Cheyenne warrior. This seemed like a signal and, to Feathers, a favourable omen - he jolted awake from his thoughts, raised his bow in the air and shrieked his war cry. He kicked his pony into a charge from a standing start – a move designed to throw enemies off balance – and it worked.

"Jesus!" shouted Carver to no-one in particular and brought his rifle up into the aim. The Cheyenne pony thudded across the short space between them, its rider already loosing off one arrow. The arrowhead went into Carver's left forearm as he was holding the rifle, punched through the flesh between the bones and pinned into his bicep, locking his arm in a vee-shape. He pulled the trigger as the barrel was opposite the charging warrior's chest but the empty snap of the hammer onto a percussion cap told him that the rifle had misfired. No time to reload now, he threw the useless weapon to one side and ducked.

Feathers was shrieking his victory song. Carver, with one arm disabled and in searing pain, turned to face his enemy, clawing at his holster to retrieve his pistol.

Feathers had wheeled his pony round to charge the fair-haired one. Now he would die for coupling with his wife. Another kick into the pony's flanks and he thundered towards the young white man.

The final sight for his eyes in this life was the blue gout of smoke from the veho's rifle and his last sensation was the heavy punch through his porcupine quill breast plate as the lead bullet tore through his chest. His brain registered sharp shock – shock at being defeated, shock at a vanished chance to be chief and shock that this was all there was to life – a hole through his heart and blackness.

His spirit had already fled his body as he fell backwards over the pony's rump and finished up face down in the damp earth, smoke from his burning wound seeping out from under him and bone fragments protruding from his back.

"Nice shot, Lootenant," said Carver slumping into a sitting position, his arm still pinned through by the arrow.

Henry watched as an unconcerned spider walked across Feathers' open eyeball.

"Now we're in trouble Mr Carver…we'll have some explaining to do." But the wolf-skinner didn't hear him – he had fainted.

Up in the box elder, a wolf howled. Henry smiled grimly at the irony.

---- 0 0 0 ----

Chapter Forty Five

The plan was taking shape – and See the Dark was glad. At last he was contributing to the war trail on an equal footing with the Traveller. Like the last time against the Pawnee, it was only the seed of an idea – but the others smiled and nodded enthusiastically when he'd explained it. Even White Rain patted him affectionately on the back for his good thinking; they would all make it work.

Out on the edge of the Llano, Willow and Crow Dress, their horses better rested than the others, scouted out in a wide loop to the south and east. Excited by their important task, they had tried to look serious as the Traveller had given them their instructions - their job was to look for any Comanches approaching the cache of rifles and ride back to warn the others. Both women knew that their smiles of pride had unnerved the dark southerner but, shaking his head in amused disbelief, he had patted them both on the shoulder in a fatherly way as he sent them off – they could see why Mouse liked him.

As instructed, both women kept off the skyline while they were mounted but would seek what little high ground there was on the Llano, tether their ponies out of sight then creep to the ridgeline to scan the country is all directions.

"Sister, this is much better than butchering a horse," said Crow Dress as she lay on a small hill of grey shale. She was happy to be on the war trail with her friend; their bond of friendship, close even before they had joined the Forked Lightning Women, had become closer when they had entered the wild country. They braided each other's hair, exchanged gossip and jokes about the village menfolk and looked out for each other. Neither of them had a sister – until now. They would die together if they had to.

Willow, too busy watching the possible approach of wandering Comanches, answered first in Lakota – then remembering, laughed:

"That is true – if only our mothers could see us now…"

Crow Dress looked at her friend with a twinge of sadness – she wasn't sure if Willow meant her Hunkpapa Lakota mother or the Cheyenne one that had brought her up after she had been captured.

"They would all be very proud," she said diplomatically.

---- o o o ----

White Rain Woman gave a mouthful of water to each of the captives; both said something in a foreign tongue and tried to smile. White Rain looked at them with impatience – she would have preferred to plunge a hatchet into their heads rather than make them part of the plan but she had, like the others, to follow the war leader's instructions. She turned her head as a burst of unseemly laughter erupted from across the camp ground.

"Steady little sister," said Dark grinning as Mouse jigged in excitement, "this will be a dangerous thing to do."

"I know!" she yelled in triumph and clapped her pudgy hands.

"All your thoughts should shine only on your task – no distractions," said Viajero trying to look serious. But even the impassive warrior was tempted to smile at Mouse's enthusiasm – this young woman would make a good Apache or, as he acknowledged a recent guilty thought over the past chill nights, a good second wife.

The young Cheyenne woman nodded her head at the Traveller's advice but was irrepressible at the importance of her role:

"I know, I know. Thank you for letting me do this."

Even White Rain seemed caught up in Mouse's eagerness and a tight smile briefly crossed her lips. She felt a stab of jealousy as she watched Dark good-naturedly banter with Mouse – they hadn't shared those moments for a while now and she missed them. They had lain together but once in the past few days and that, at first, seemed to promise better times but the planning and preparation for the attack took a lot of time and Dark then seemed as distant as ever. She sighed – it would be good to settle marriage matters before the coming battle but it would be unfair to distract him from his own task. White Rain swallowed her annoyance and went across to prepare the mules.

"Why is that girl laughing Momma?" whispered Becky Gadd.

"Not sure honey but they seem to be getting ready to move out,"

"Will they take us with them?"

"Hard to tell but my bet is we'll be too much bother and they'll just let us go…" Alicia Gadd hid her face from her daughter as she said this; the girl just looked at her and shook her head:

"No Momma – I reckon they'll just cut our throats."

Alicia put her arm around Becky's shoulder and tutted about foolish talk but, in her despairing heart, she knew that her daughter was probably right.

---- o o o ----

Chapter Forty Six

The smell from the skin shelter made the horses of the Texan and Castillo rear and plunge; even their riders gagged. Iron Hat sat on his steady Appaloosa and just watched – white captives were always ripe, especially the women. Still, his warriors had told him that they were ready for display to the Mexican. Water had been too precious to use for cleaning them so milk from the mares in foal and a stringy cow had been applied with deerskin scrubbers; the milk had soured in the noon heat and worsened the stench.

The three men dismounted and handed their reins to a Comanche sentry – a young boy who carried a flintlock pistol and a lace parasol.

"Señor Van Horn," said Castillo in English "No emotions please, remember this is just business."

"I know Boss," replied the Texan. Lyle Van Horn set his mouth in a determined attempt to remain unmoved – in truth, he had not set eyes on white captives before and he was not sure how he'd react. The previous time the captives had all been Mexicans, Pueblos or *mestizos* and of no value to Castillo – on those occasions the viewing process hadn't taken long and Castillo had stormed out.

Castillo, first to duck under the overhang, held a silk handkerchief to his nose. Though the skin shelter gave protection from the sun, it offered none from the Comanche squaws who beat the women with mesquite boughs and dragged their charges into sitting positions so the Mexican could see the colour of their hair and skin.

"Great Chief, please stop the beatings – they need to be in good condition if I am to sell them back to their families in Texas," said Castillo, a false smile of comradeship appearing on his lips.

Iron Hat stared hard at him, scarcely containing his mounting irritation, but barked an order and the squaws stopped. Castillo muttered his thanks and set off down the rows of squalid women to try and assess his coming profit.

He looked closely at the first two – they were badly emaciated but plainly white and seemed to understand some Spanish. One wore the remnants of a pink gingham dress, the other a typical brown working frock and a ragged apron. They had been badly abused but they were not unintelligent; they saw that the Mexican seemed to be a way out of this Hell Hole – they pleaded with him to take them. Castillo did not seem to be interested and walked away. Lyle Van Horn moved alongside his boss and tried to intercede:

"These gals are white Boss; it's what we come for…"

Castillo looked at him coldly:

"Silence, *Tejano*! These women are no good to me – look at them. They are too weak and would die on the trail – that's wasted money to me. Look at their hands, they are both farmer's wives – their families won't be able to afford my asking price – they stay."

The women heard the English conversation and now pleaded directly with Van Horn but Castillo dragged him away, hissing in his ear:

"Don't let the Comanches see that you are weak – be strong or I'll sell you back to your Army at Fort Mason…"

Van Horn's bile rose; he glanced at Iron Hat – the old fool was just grinning at the sharp exchange of words though he didn't understand what had been said. The Texan swallowed hard and continued down the line of frightened women. The first woman that they had looked at now shouted out in English:

"They're here to trade for *us*, girls! The ones that git out, send our menfolk back to kill these red bastards!"

A Comanche squaw stepped out and hit the white woman hard, smashing her jawbone and silencing her.

A gust of warmer air swept into the pen of captives as the flap of the shelter raised; Castillo looked back over his shoulder - another Comanche warrior came in and stood behind Iron Hat, he carried a well-kept Colt and two war axes in his belt. Iron Hat looked pleased and said:

"This is my son, Toad. He is a great warrior and understands the words of the *Americanos*."

Toad whispered in his father's ear:

"We could not find the hiding place of the rifles and whiskey; the Comancheros are cunning – I think they are further away this time. We'll have to go through with the trade."

Iron Hat looked impassive but nodded slightly; it was a pity, he was hoping to kill Castillo *and* find the rifles as well, dispensing with the tedium of trading with the arrogant Mexican. But the new guns had now become even more important – word had reached them from the eastern *Comancheria* that Texas Rangers had attacked the villages of their *Kwahadi* band and killed many of their kinfolk not long ago.

Castillo and Van Horn just looked at Toad, then at each other – it was a silent pact to keep their talk to a minimum and they continued down the line of moaning prisoners.

Striding quickly past several mixed bloods and other poor-quality whites, their status meriting only a cursory glance, Juan stopped opposite one woman and pulled her to her feet, looking her up and down. She had once been beautiful but her hair was matted and crawled with lice. Her skin though was smooth and, under the shade of the canopy, looked white:

"This one," he said to the Texan.

"Nope Boss, she's a high yaller – looks white but ain't. Look at her nose."

Castillo, disgruntled at his elementary mistake, threw the woman back down. Toad had now joined their search and led them down through the ranks of tethered women and children, offering what he thought were suitable candidates:

"Here - my own prisoners, Mr Castillo – I took them from rich men in West Texas." He had a hissing, sibilant tone and, close to, was extremely ugly – he was well named.

Castillo chose three women and one boy child who looked to have fine features and may have good breeding; these things meant profit from Texans who would *appear* glad to have their women back at any price. But Juan knew that, even if the women were actually accepted back into households, there would be a lifelong gulf of silence between many men and their wives about being raped by Comanches.

Van Horn stood behind his boss's shoulder as he completed the search; two more children, a boy and a girl, were added to the list. Both children bore scars on their faces and it worried Castillo, not out of concern for their welfare but because the scars could affect his profit.

He remembered the early days when he traded at Las Lenguas Creek, Comanches would deliberately disfigure white children to increase Texan anxiety and speed with which ransoms were paid. He had asked Iron Hat to stop the bad treatment but could see that his words had little effect. Badly marked children struggled to adapt back to the life of whites; every glance in a mirror would remind them of their captivity. Acceptance back into family folds by parents, siblings and school friends was not guaranteed. He seethed at the Nokoni's casual disregard of his instructions.

Juan struggled with the financial risk and calculated the exchange terms and how much ransom he would get from Texans – it needed to cover his outlay for the rifles and bring a handsome profit. He was absentmindedly looking at an older woman – too old, he thought, to have any value – when she spoke:

"Lyle?"

The voice was croaking and weak and he hadn't heard it for nigh on four years but Lyle Van Horn recognised it – it was his mother.

There was a moment of silence in the shelter as the outer skin flapped idly in a sudden breeze, the lowing of stolen cattle in the camp could clearly be heard - as could the high voice of the boy sentry, singing his own song outside. Iron Hat sensed the tightening of tension when the old woman spoke to the white man, Toad was still trying to understand what had been said and Castillo was turning his head to the Texan in disbelief.

The pause was only a heartbeat and was followed by a blur of action. Van Horn, who had been a good cavalry soldier and had trained hard with the pistol both before and after he had deserted, reacted first.

Toad was still digesting what was taking place when Van Horn shot him through the head, the bullet travelling through bone and brain and out again, hitting Iron Hat. The lead ball was spent though and merely slammed into the old man's shoulder, knocking him over.

The captive women cheered, thinking that they were about to be released. Castillo, his rising panic bringing forth only a stream of incomprehensible Spanish, tried to grab the pistol away from the Texan but was too slow – Van Horn shot him through the cheek, fragments of teeth exploding out of the other side; the Mexican staggered back and collapsed onto some of the tethered women. One of the newer captives, a Pueblo woman, dragged Castillo's Colt from his holster and, with great effort, thumbed back the hammer and shot one of the Comanche women dead as she leapt towards Van Horn with an upraised club. The rest of the squaws sliced through the shelter skin, dived out and, shrieking in anger, ran to raise the alarm.

The Texan now had his arm around his mother and tried to get her out of the shelter; he snapped off another shot at Iron Hat as he ducked out under the covering but only hit the young sentry who screamed with pain and dropped to his knees, still holding the parasol aloft. The Comanche chief joined the yelling women outside.

The wounded boy dropped the reins he had been holding and the three visitors' horses scattered. Many more warriors, now horsed, came charging out of the camp towards the shouting melee of the shelter. Some of the white captives who were still able to run tried to escape but were cut down by arrows or war hatchets, the Comanches yelling anger and vengeance. The trading was over – this was what they did best.

One warrior, seeing his chief afoot, charged his pony at him and, holding onto his saddle pommel formed a loop with his bent arm. With clods of earth flying from the pony's hooves, Iron Hat grabbed the arm and swung into the saddle behind the rescuing rider, yelling into his ear:

"Take the Mexican alive, we need to find those rifles!"

Lyle Van Horn was now outside, arm still around his mother and trying to keep her on her feet. A Comanche buck, his face painted black and wearing a wolf robe, drew alongside and tried to axe the Texan; Van Horn shot him and grabbed the pony.

He pulled the dead warrior to the ground and quickly mounted the strange high-pommelled saddle, dragging his screaming mother up over the cantle like a sack of grain; he noticed how light she was - bony and fragile - she had soiled herself:

"Easy Ma, easy," he said, patting her back as she lay across the horse, "We're goin' home…"

He swung the horse around and was about to head away from the camp when the first arrow struck him in the back and a second went through his thigh, pinning him to the saddle cinch. The animal reared, hooves flailing and the arrow head was wrenched out as Van Horn and his mother slumped off its back into the dust.

Deserter or not, like all good cavalrymen his pistol was still in his hand as the clarity of peril swept over him; the Texan smiled at his clear thoughts at such a dangerous time.

Prone in the swirling dust and cradling his mother in his left arm, he rested the pistol on her bony chest and smoothed her hair with his right hand; the strands were harsh, matted and broken by the poor diet. Her face seemed much older now – lined and wrinkled, she moaned a little but it wasn't a complaint, she was just happy to see him again. He kissed her on the cheek and tilted her face so she could see him.

Oddly comforted by her presence, Lyle Van Horn took up his pistol and shot his mother through the head. A lance thrust from a mounted Comanche now tore through the back of his rib cage and into his heart; mother and son, clinging together, pitched into the perpetual blackness.

---- 0 0 0 ----

Chapter Forty Seven

"Pedro, Father Ignacio is coming back…"

"Surely to God, it's not Sunday again so soon?" said Pedro Alvarez, struggling back from sleep; he had been happy to receive the Sacrament from the little priest a couple of days past, but this?

Montoya, up on the rocky lookout, shaded his eyes from the sun. It was difficult in the heat haze to work out what was in the small column coming towards them:

"He's leading his own *burro* and two mules with full pack saddles – someone else is walking with him…My God, they're women!"

"It must be a reward from Our Lady for all my good works!" yelled Herrera, as he hastily cleared the untidy camp site, stuffing dirty skillets into saddlebags. The horses tethered in the arroyo snickered as they caught the scent of the mules.

The slow file of people and animals came closer and Montoya scrambled down the rock face. Two women, tied to each other by a neck halter, trudged alongside the mules – a girl child led both animals by their headropes. The packsaddles each contained a long canvas roll. Montoya, Herrera and Alvarez stood in a puzzled line and watched respectfully as the man approached. Each had removed his hat and stood waiting for the priest to explain and see if they could help.

Suddenly, Father Ignacio crumpled onto his knees, his cowled head on his chest, hands clutching his belly. His burro, dozing under its fringed eye strap, walked into him and pushed him forward. The priest still knelt there, a hooded pile of black cloth. Alvarez was about to rush out when one of the women called out in poor Spanish:

"Sir! Careful, we have sickness!"

The woman was white; she motioned for the girl leading the mules to take them off to one side, behind a rock pinnacle and away from the priest:

She kept repeating:

"La Peste, la peste..." and held up her hand to stop them coming any closer. The other woman, who looked like an Indian, now untied her neck halter but went behind the rock to join the child with the mules.

Montoya looked anxious; they had not been told that the priest would return –the old man had not mentioned it at Communion. Their peaceful, somnolent camp was unravelling fast:

"Where have you come from? What is the matter with Father Ignacio?"

The woman looked blank and shrugged so Montoya and Herrera went forward to help up the priest while Alvarez kept a safe distance from either – plague was nothing to be trifled with:

"Father, are you sick too?"

They took him by his arms, stood him upright and steadied him – the priest, still with his head down, swayed slightly. It was stiflingly hot so Herrera pulled back the priest's black hood.

Both Mexicans were surprised to see that Father Ignacio's gaunt and weather-beaten face had been replaced by that of a chubby Indian girl with a fork of yellow lightning painted across her face. The girl grinned and, oddly, both men broke into smiles.

There was a moment of puzzled silence while the girl opened the robe at the front – both men were interested, it had been a while since they had seen a woman undress. Their smiles faded - the open robe revealed a cocked Colt pistol in the girl's hand - this sobered them, but not quickly enough. At point blank range she shot Montoya in the stomach and, her small thumb struggling to re-cock the hammer, shot Herrera behind the ear as he instinctively ducked.

Alavarez, though shocked and bewildered by the noise, pulled his revolver quickly and snapped off three shots at the robed girl. They all missed but he saw she was battling with cocking the weapon for the third time, her thumb sliding sweatily off the hammer. He ran towards her pointing his pistol and firing again; the girl dived to one side but, encumbered by the robe, could not move quickly. One bullet hit her and she squealed and went down.

Pedro Alvarez, pulling out a loaded cylinder from a leather pouch, reloaded his pistol in an almost leisurely fashion as he strolled over to the fallen girl. It would not do for this heathen to impersonate a Man of God; she would have to pay. He smiled as he prepared to dispense heavenly justice – his mother would be proud.

Pedro Alvarez died with that smile on his face; a heavy calibre carbine bullet smashed into his back and he slumped forward spouting blood from his mouth.

The two other Mexicans who had been tending to the horses and on their way to see the priest again, stopped in their tracks as the shooting started. When they saw Alavarez go down, they ran back down into the dry gully. Manuel and Jorge Jimenez were not gunfighters – if a *pistolero* like Pedro Alvarez had been overcome by some unseen enemy, they wanted no part of it. The brothers carried the revolvers merely to impress the women in Santa Fe; fighting someone with handguns was not for them.

Viajero, with Mouse's soldier gun still in his hand, ran from behind the rock pinnacle towards where the young Forked Lightning Woman had fallen and shouted to Dark:

"Brother, you and your woman take the two men in the arroyo – try and get their horses!"

He gestured to the white woman to help Mouse then ran into the arroyo. A drumming of hooves from close by made him turn his head – it was the other two Forked Lightning Women bringing all the rest of their horses, both women yelling their war cries. Gunfire had been their signal; Dark's plan was working.

See the Dark, like the Traveller, had been released from his canvas roll on the packsaddle by White Rain as soon as the mules were hidden behind the rock, out of sight of the Mexicans. It had been hot in there and his war paint had smeared with his sweat; the Apache was the same – his distinct red and yellow lines that crossed his face now blurred into each other. But it was not a time for beauty or ritual. White Rain sent the girl back out to her mother who was kneeling to tend to Mouse; she was worried about her young war sister but there was a battle to be won.

Dark was already heading into the arroyo, cautiously probing the rocky riverbed looking for his prey when White Rain joined him. Both carried their war bows and, despite the tension of tracking the Mexicans, White Rain was amused at their situation:

"This could be harder than we thought," she said, gesturing at the bows. "I've never used mine in battle and you are a poor shot."

"Thank you for reminding me," said Dark through gritted teeth.

"Where are they?" she whispered.

Dark just pointed to a rocky outcrop where grey boulders jutted up from red sand. He made the sign for silence as he and White Rain listened then closed in.

Behind the outcrop, the Jimenez brothers struggled to saddle their spooked horses; their mounts plunged and reared, cinching the saddles was hard and sweaty work and both of them had been kicked by flailing hooves. Panic now swept over them. Manuel was first in the saddle:

"For God's sake Jorge, get mounted…!"

Jorge's horse though kept turning around in a tight circle as soon as he'd put a foot in the stirrups - he couldn't get a hand grip on the pommel to heave himself up. Manuel rode close to his brother's horse and took its head rein in his hand and tried to quiet it and stop it circling. It was the delay that their pursuers needed.

On a rock overlooking the chaos below, Dark was finding it difficult to aim with his bow and three arrows had flown wide of the mark. But the calming of the circling horse gave him a chance and he shot off another. White Rain's arrow followed his at the same moment.

Both struck flesh but, wastefully, both went into the same target and Jorge Jimenez toppled from his saddle with one arrow pinning his arm to his rib cage and one through his neck.

Manuel, on the point of fleeing and abandoning his brother, now got angry but a lot calmer. Dismounting and seeing two Indians scrabbling down the shale slope towards him, he remembered his holstered pistol. It was odd, he thought, that shooting back hadn't occurred to him during the melee. He took out the Remington and strode, firing, towards the Indians. One of them seemed to be a woman so he discounted her as a threat and concentrated his fire on the male warrior.

Dark leapt to one side and yelped as a bullet grazed his ribs – he had been impressed by the Mexican's courage in coming back for his fallen friend; it was the sort of thing that a Cheyenne would do. But he had now dropped his bow and tripped up over it, tumbling down the slope. The Mexican's remaining bullets flew over his head.

Manuel seemed surprised when his pistol clicked uselessly – far too late, he dimly remembered a harsh instruction from Alavarez that it was important to count the number of bullets he had fired. It would cost him.

White Rain's next arrow thudded into his chest; at such close range it penetrated as far as the feathered flights and stuck out of his back. Bubbles of bright blood from his mouth showed the devastation of his lungs. The man staggered back, fell over the prostrate body of the first Mexican and lay still. White Rain whooped her triumph and ran forward to grab the spooked horses.

The horses were big, much bigger than their own mustangs, and took some calming. Dark, clutching his side, hobbled over to help her:

"That was a great fight, sister. You fought well."

White Rain was annoyed at the lack of affection in his tone – Dark also called all her other warriors 'sister'. She looked at his wound and sniffed:

"You stay here and tend to your scratch, I'm off to get those other horses."

With some difficulty she climbed up into the unfamiliar saddle, contemptuously shrugging off a helping hand from Dark, and cantered off to gather in the other three Mexican horses that had wandered down the arroyo.

Over in the clearing, Crow Dress and Willow eventually corralled the spare horses and brought them under control; the animals had been spooked by the shooting and the smell of blood. Both women rode quietly round them and turned the ponies' heads inwards; gradually the small remuda settled into a tense circle whickering softly to one another. Even Viajero's ugly grey had caught the panic.

Crow Dress gestured to Willow, pointing back along their trail; in the near distance was a circling stream of vultures - some rising, some falling - as they fed upon the small, Mexican spirit caller they had killed two days earlier. Willow had not taken the old man's scalp – mainly as he had little hair – but had kept a small black ornament on a silver chain that she had taken from him as a war trophy. She wore it round her neck and held it up proudly to Crow Dress.

Her friend smiled and nodded; she too had taken a war prize – a set of shiny beads each encased in fine silverwork that the old man had had in his hand when Willow had knifed him. Crow Dress, at the same time, had driven her hatchet into the back of the man's head. It had been a good killing; the war sisters had been properly blooded and they were glad for each other.

Dragged from his shallow rocky grave by the vultures, beyond any help from his crucifix or rosary, Father Ignacio Morales, the Wandering Priest of the Pecos, said nothing.

---- o o o ----

Chapter Forty Eight

Iron Hat watched as the arrogant Mexican screamed and begged for death; putting fire to men's feet had always proved successful in making them talk and Castillo had caved in quickly. The Mexican had told them where the rifle caches were – though it hard been hard to make out what he was saying because of the holes in Castillo's face - but Iron Hat needed proof. The Mexican could be lying just to make the pain stop. The loss of his son and the other fallen warriors would be grieved for in true Comanche fashion – but it would have to be later, after his People got the guns.

Juan Castillo de Coronado was surprised to be hauled to his feet and his horse brought to him:

"Mexican! Mount up and take us to the rifles or I will burn all your farmers and their families."

In too much pain to answer or even stand, Castillo nodded but slumped to the ground again, shuddering with agony as the burnt stumps of his feet failed to bear his weight. Mounted Comanches surrounded him and hauled him into the saddle, Castillo screamed again as his smouldering flesh came into contact with the stirrup irons.

A great cry went up as he struggled into the saddle; turning around he saw the entire Taos column and his own Santa Fe wagons were now surrounded by a ring of howling Comanche warriors. Over by the trading shack, staked out in a row were the surviving gunmen and soldiers of fortune who had tagged along in Santa Fe. With their eyelids cut off and their outstretched hands and feet alight, they shrieked in agony as they awaited the advance of the Comanche women.

---- o o o ----

Chapter Forty Nine

They saw the lodge poles first, just visible in the grey dawn above the treeline in the valley; Bad Elk's new camp had been easy to find and Henry Armstrong was glad of it. He and Carver were days overdue, though they brought much needed buffalo meat to the village on a hastily made travois pulled by Carver's pony.

Henry looked across at his friend who, though sallow and sickly with his arrow wound, rode upright in the saddle, reins held lightly in his right hand while his injured arm now rested against his chest in a sling made out of buffalo skin.

"You'll be able to rest properly now, Mr Carver," said Henry pulling down on the brim of his hat to keep it in place as a squall of light snow flew around him.

Carver did not answer but just nodded wearily; getting to the village had been simple but covering up the death of Feathers on His Shield would be more difficult. They had agreed the story they would tell but the young Englishman was coaching him one last time before they arrived with the Cheyenne:

"Remember Mr Carver – we found a few buffalo and killed a couple…" That much at least was true, though with Carver disabled, Henry had to butcher his first animal alone; it had been hard and bloody work. His clothes were soaked with the dark stains of his amateur knife work.

"…then we were attacked by the Crow, that will account for the arrow wound in your arm…" The arrow had been difficult to get out – it had to be completely removed as Feathers' distinct tribal markings were all over it; none of it could be left in Carver's arm or brought back into camp.

"…and your recovery from the wound is the reason we are late." This too was partially true – Henry sought comfort from the small percentages of truth that he could wring from his lies.

But the real time, he knew, had been taken by burying Feathers, deep in a stand of live oak, shooting his pony and, at Carver's insistence, driving the buffalo from the small valley in case other Cheyenne scouts found the herd and chanced upon signs of their fight with the Thunder Bear soldier.

Carver just grunted:

"Lootenant, I just want to git off this damn horse and crawl into bed."

"Not long now, Mr Carver, "said Henry brightly masking his own guilt and feeling of disgrace; God may well forgive him for his lies but if the truth of Feathers' death ever came out, the Cheyenne wouldn't be so merciful.

---- 0 0 0 ----

Chapter Fifty

Viajero looked back at his small column – he had never been happy travelling in groups, even in war parties of his own Apache people. There would always be one weak link; it might be an inexperienced warrior or even a badly-behaved horse that threatened the discipline of the trail and increased the chance of enemies spotting them. No, he reflected, being alone was always better but his responsibilities in getting the young Cheyennes back to their people bore heavily on him – he and Bright Antelope would be eternally grateful to the Cheyenne in giving them a home; now it was time to repay them.

He knew he was pushing them all hard on the long trail back to the Smoky Hill country but with the loaded mules and Dark and Mouse both wounded, he also knew they were travelling far too slowly. His N'De people had been at war with the Comanches for a long time – he knew that when in pursuit, the Nerm-en-uh would not rest until they had all been made to pay.

A nudge on his leg made him look down. He was still riding his sorrel, not wishing to saddle his ugly horse unless it became urgent to get away quickly. The soft tap had been from the muzzle of his spirit horse as it trotted, untethered, alongside him. The blotchy pony had been unhappy to travel with the others and had now taken to keeping pace with him, content just to be at his side. Usen, the One God, had given him many gifts in life but none stranger than this horse.

He wheeled his pony and trotted back towards the rear of the slow-moving column – it seemed to be spreading out, dangerous gaps appearing that could lead to disaster if pursuit by Comanches or Comancheros struck them. He rode back through the rising dust, the ugly horse at his side, shaking its head and snorting.

The girl with the elk-tooth dress – Viajero had not bothered to ask her name – rode one of the fresh Mexican horses and led the others in her own little remuda. He looked over the ponies with a practised eye - all the roped horses carried some of the large amounts of powder and ammunition they had plundered from the Comancheros. The guns and the ammunition would be welcome in the Suhtai camp. The young woman was doing well handling the Mexican mounts:

"Sister, trot your horses more – we can't rest yet." Viajero knew that the Comanches would not be sparing their own horses to catch up once they had arrived at the empty holes and found they had been robbed.

The girl nodded. Like all the others, she carried one of the six-shot rifles that they had taken from the gun boxes. Viajero wanted none of them – he patted the bright new carbine in his saddle bucket – this was his prize; he had taken no scalps at the cache fight but had immediately taken one of the new guns from its crate, worked out how to use the looped caps and grabbed handfuls of the linen cartridges for his shoulder pouch. Now he was complete as a warrior.

The Apache reined his horse aside and let the girl pass, the canvas bags on the captured horses slapping against saddle leather as they picked up speed.

He rode down from a small ledge and met White Rain Woman; she had taken charge of keeping the mules moving steadily from dawn till dusk. Each animal now had two heavy boxes of rifles on the cross trees of its pack saddle.

"How are the mules behaving?" he asked Dark's woman.

"They are getting used to the weight …" said White Rain, grateful that someone had spoken to her;

"…they are learning to walk in a different way; it's smoother now."

Viajero nodded: "Make them go faster – keep up with the ponies."

White Rain opened her mouth to keep the conversation going but the Apache trotted further to the rear. She kicked her pony in the flanks and broke into a trot; the mules brayed at the change of pace.

The Apache reined in his horse and waited for the next riders to come out of the dust. Impatient when no-one appeared, he pushed into the swirling powdered earth and found Mouse and Dark chatting to each other on sauntering ponies. Slightly to the rear of them, astride the Comanche horse and leading the priest's plodding burro, was the white woman and the girl child.

Back at the rifle cache, the child had refused to let Viajero kill the *burro,* standing between the animal and Viajero's knife. She wanted to keep it. The others had found the girl's display of courage funny – a small piece of humour as the ecstasy of killing subsided. Dark had led the jeers but Mouse had ended the chatter by saying the girl had earned her war honours too – she should keep the burro. Though he couldn't remember why, Viajero had relented and let the animal live – his explanations about the need for a fast ride home falling on deaf ears. His explanations that the Comanche, once in pursuit, would cover a normal three-day ride in a single stretch from dawn to dusk, was met with disbelief. But Viajero had seen it many years ago – he knew what the Nerm-en-uh were capable of.

He grabbed the reins of the white woman's horse and cantered with it towards the front of the column, the burro protesting loudly. The white pair were now strangely clad in cut down clothes from the dead Mexicans – he couldn't afford to let them fall behind in any pursuit; not only would he lose their value as hostages with any whites they might encounter but they had too much information about the Cheyenne war party to allow them to fall into the hands of the Comanche. Still, they had each played their part in deceiving the Mexicans and had earned the clothes and food they had scavenged from the saddlebags. Hard as it was to like the *indaa,* he admired their bravery.

Viajero looked round in the saddle and shouted at See the Dark:

"Brother! Move up, you are going too slow."

Dark, sighing at the reprimand and wincing slightly from the wound to his ribcage, trotted alongside Mouse who had only managed to sit back in the saddle two days ago.

"How's the wound, little sister?" he asked, grinning.

"Shut up," she said rudely "Being shot in the backside is still painful."

"Well, it was a big target," joked the young Cheyenne warrior.

"How's your 'scratch'?" countered the girl "White Rain told me she'd seen bigger wounds on old women sewing buffalo robes…"

Dark snorted, annoyed that White Rain had mentioned it to others. He knew it really *was* a small injury – the pistol ball had only punctured skin and thin flesh before bouncing off one of his ribs – it still hurt though, especially when he was having to ride all day. At least he and Mouse had survived their wounds:

"I see that you have scalps now," he said, nodding towards the bloodstained locks strung onto her belt

"Yes – two…" she replied, grinning; Mouse was not one to bear grudges "…I was lucky to be able to shoot those Mexicans quickly."

"You did well," said Dark "You were more than just lucky – you are a true warrior; the Traveller is very proud of you." He watched Mouse's face to see if she blushed when he mentioned the Apache's praise and then smiled when she did.

"I see that you got a scalp too," said the girl, though she had heard of the spat between White Rain and See the Dark to get it.

"Yes, White Rain was about to take the scalp that belonged to me from the rider we both shot first – I had to stop her…"

Dark was ashamed - it had been an unseemly argument, solved only by examining both arrows from the body of the Mexican.

"…My arrow was the one that went through his neck, so my shot had killed him; hers only went into his arm…"

Mouse was silent.

"…White Rain got a scalp though from the other Mexican she killed."

Mouse just grunted; it didn't sound like approval.

Far to the rear of Viajero's column, Willow climbed her pony to the top of a small hill and watched the back trail. There was no sign of any dust but she knew it wouldn't be long before the Comanches discovered the empty cache - then a storm of vengeance would descend on them all.

---- 0 0 0 ----

BOOK THREE

You cannot hide
I can see where ghosts have walked
Don't sleep
I am near

(Song of pursuit, Medicine Wolf, spirit tracker of the Nokoni Comanche)

Chapter Fifty One

Iron Hat watched his friend anxiously. For many years, they had called the boy 'Chuco' – a derisory name given by a passing Comanchero when he saw how dirty he was. His real Comanche childhood name had long been forgotten and the boy had been happy with the Spanish name – even though it translated out as 'filthy' – as it seemed to symbolise his life of closeness to the surface of the land.

And it was true, Medicine Wolf had spent his childhood lying on the bare earth – whether it was shale, sand, rock or just plain mud – closely observing the marks made by any living creature. Small indentations in the ground, insect trails over faint hoofprints, bent grass, dried-up patches of horse piss, even a sweat stain on a rock – invisible to most – all painted a picture in his mind; anything that moved on land, he could follow its trail by sight, smell or sound.

Now he was at the empty rifle cache, three of the holes stood open to the sky and young men used abandoned shovels to open the last one while Iron Hat, squatting by the fetlocks of his Appaloosa, watched as Medicine Wolf went through his rituals to make the earth talk to him.

They had been joined by more warriors from the trading camp who had stayed behind to paint their faces black and don their buffalo-horned war helmets. They rode up in noisy groups, shouting and yelling only to be silenced by their war leader as he let Medicine Wolf harness his magic. Iron Hat looked on as the sullen half circle of riders, irritated at being stopped on their vengeance trail, watched the tracker in frustrated silence. The exit trail of the cache robbers was easy to see, and they wanted to be on it, but Iron Hat, always cautious in these things, wanted to know who they were and how strong an enemy they might face.

Iron Hat wasn't scared of any living man but he was always wary around Medicine Wolf; they had grown up together but the boy had always seemed more interested in tracking than fighting. While Iron Hat had practised with bow and lance on his pony, Medicine Wolf had preferred to see what marks small rodents or even insects made as they passed over the ground. Chuco could tell how old the trail was by the dryness of the droppings – animal or human – and spot any weakness in gait by looking at how a print embedded into the earth. The boy learned to harness lingering scents in rock clefts and sheltered places to help his magic – he had once trailed two white men over trackless rocks by sniffing their tobacco and sweat smells that lay, days old, under rimrock overhangs. Iron Hat considered himself an expert tracker but even he knew that Medicine Wolf was better than him and any other warrior in his Nokoni band.

A sizzling sound made him look up and Iron Hat turned his head to look at the nearby boulder– a long, rattling sigh marked the death of the Mexican, now scalped and disembowelled – his entrails slid into the hot ashes. Castillo had been foolish and arrogant – torture and death were justified punishments for him. He had led them to the place where the rifles had been; his usefulness was over.

More riders now came up, a regular drumbeat of hooves towards the cache site and pushed in behind the Nokoni war party. Iron Hat couldn't control these young men, they were not from his war band – they were Penatekas with their own views on what should be done.

Many of them were clothed in items traded with white men. Iron Hat remembered that such contact with the despised *taibos* came at a cost. The Penatekas had been swept by white men's diseases and decimated – the remainder had been taken to a reservation up near the Brazos; now a few had ridden out to reclaim their old way of life. They were boisterous, nervous and unsure but Iron Hat tried to calm them anyway:

"Enough noise brothers! Let our spirit tracker do his work…"

"Huh!" snorted one – a young Penateka called Tree in the River, "...spirit tracker? Does he track ghosts?"

Iron Hat was about to answer, to caution the young man about his careless, insulting tongue, when Medicine Wolf wearily rose to his feet and walked over to the Penateka's pony, taking hold of the twisted rope bridle. He looked up at Tree in the River and growled:

"I am a *Puhakut*; my medicine gives me the power to follow spirits – so, yes, I can track ghosts."

The young man looked dubious and tried to wrench the bridle out of Medicine Wolf's hands but the tracker held on. A young Nokoni, one of Iron Hat's nephews, called out:

"It is true – Medicine Wolf once followed a ghost to find the body of a dead warrior. He had been killed during a battle and we couldn't find him afterwards - his spirit wanted him buried in the Comanche way. Medicine Wolf's *puha* gave him the magic to track the ghost."

The Penateka warrior looked nervously around him, looking for support from his tribal brothers but none came – no man should dispute the magic of another. His pony, seeming to recognise something disturbing about the tracker, tried to edge away. Medicine Wolf bared his teeth, sharpened to points like his namesake, and hissed:

"Your ghost sits in the saddle behind you, boy – I can summon him if you wish?"

The Penateka's jaw dropped but not in disbelief. Tree in the River, his flesh crawling in fear at the obvious magic, merely shook his head vigorously and turned his pony back towards the trading camp, kicking his horse into a gallop – he wanted nothing to do with any Puhakut who was against him, he would never survive the war trail. He hoped his ghost wouldn't stay on his pony.

Medicine Wolf watched him ride off, nodded with satisfaction and then walked over to report to Iron Hat. The two men walked over the ground together, as the spirit tracker pointed to his findings.

They would pursue a very strange enemy indeed. The Cheyenne tracks seemed out of place – four out of five of them belonging to women. It seemed almost treacherous – his cousins in the *Yamparika* Comanche bands had fed and helped the defeated Medicine Arrow people after the attack by the pony soldiers last summer. So, stealing rifles was a strange way to repay hospitality.

In truth, the Nokoni chief was happy that no sign found by Medicine Wolf showed a large force was involved – perhaps just some renegades, including an Apache and two whites. But Iron Hat's greatest reassurance was the short, jerked stride and deeply indented prints of two heavily-laden mules - the thieves' greed and the slow-moving mules would be the death of them.

A whooping from the younger diggers at the fourth hole signalled the finding of the whiskey; Iron Hat let them uncork the stubby flasks and drink.

"Silence!"

This time the order came from the spirit tracker; something on the trail had called to him and Iron Hat recognised when the *puha* had spoken.

He looked over at Medicine Wolf who had suddenly lain down on the ground again, cheek in the dirt as when he was a boy. He appeared to be in deep thought and had started to chant his pursuit song. The tracker held his downturned palm over one set of pony tracks and as though absorbing some unseen energy from the hoof prints. He walked around the tracks to the other side, carefully avoiding stepping on them and lay down again. This time he pulled out his amulets from his medicine pouch and scattered them on the ground. Sitting up and covering his rituals from onlookers, Medicine Wolf absorbed the spirit.

Iron Hat was starting to get worried – Medicine Wolf's magic could foretell good or bad things. He could only watch and wait.

Eventually Medicine Wolf picked up his amulets and put them back into his pouch and walked back over to his chief:

"We will never lose them now – they have a spirit horse with them."

---- o o o ----

Chapter Fifty Two

Bad Elk was glad that the two white men were back. Even as he walked towards the wolf skinner, he could see the younger fair-haired veho walking off hunting, rifle over his shoulder and followed by a chattering group of older children:

"I see you Kah-vuh," said Bad Elk; he had asked the wolf skinner his name so he could distinguish between the two in the many conversations that he had with his people about the presence of the whites.

"I see you, brother," replied Carver, once again pleased that he hadn't burdened Bad Elk with his Christian name. He winced as New Grass applied a fresh poultice of mustard root and some other goddamned thing that hurt like Hell. The girl smiled shyly and tutted at his poor resistance to pain.

"How is your wound?" asked the chief.

"It closes up well. New Grass is a good healer," said Carver. He resisted the urge to ask if there was any sign of Feathers on His Shield.

Bad Elk nodded and looked at Carver knowingly:

"Good healers make good wives so I hear" he said.

Carver just grinned. At New Grass' instruction, he clamped a leaf across the wound on the lower part of his forearm and crushed a poultice between the other two wounds in the crook of his arm. New Grass bound his arm in that position with a strip of soft deer hide.

"Are your brother and Broken Knife back yet?" asked the wolf skinner, trying to keep any anxiety out of his voice.

Bad Elk had pushed out search parties to look for Feathers on His Shield but no trace had yet been found. Two small parties were still scouring the grasslands and valleys within a three-day ride of their previous camping ground; Smoke on the Moon was out with a soldier from his Striking Snakes and Broken Knife, as usual for the aloof warrior, was riding out alone.

Though Bad Elk would never mention it to anyone else, in his heart he knew that Feathers' absence had quietened the camp and balance had been restored. The man's constant state of hatred for their two white guests, his boastful feasting and sense of permanent injustice made him a difficult companion. Even Sweet Water seemed to be more pleasant to her neighbours. While the chief knew that the absence of a warrior was always serious for his small band of Suhtai, Feathers' presence had been like poison in a wound – now he was gone, even if only for a short time, they could recover.

"Not yet. Broken Knife scouts to the north while my brother and his soldier went to the south. The soldier returned this morning to say they had found no sign."

"Why didn't your brother come back with his soldier?" asked Carver; slightly nervous that the Striking Snakes leader was staying out longer. Had he found something?

"He looks for his son."

"Your brother has *another* son? We've only seen the baby."

"Yes, his son is on a raid against the Comanche for guns and horses."

"Then he must be a great warrior – the Comanche are much feared – even up here."

Bad Elk was about to rebuke the wolf skinner for suggesting that the Cheyenne were afraid of any living thing but thought better of it.

"Has the young man taken a lot of warriors with him?" asked Carver.

"He has with him those who wanted to go – it will be enough for the Comanche," said Bad Elk diplomatically, avoiding the mention of the Forked Lightning Women.

"My brother knows the trail that they took to the Flint Arrowpoint River and will scout south of there for a while."

Carver was intrigued; so, they hadn't met the entire village yet – the young Englishman would be interested when he got back. He would need more paper to sketch on.

---- 0 0 0 ----

Chapter Fifty Three

Viajero waded his ugly horse into the Pecos River and beckoned the others to follow. The mules with the heavy pack saddles were nervous of the rushing sound of the swift water and needed much pulling to get them into mid-stream. His spare sorrel, like Dark's, was now attached to a mule saddle and the rest of the horses and riders entered the river without mishap, though the Comanche pony ridden by the white woman plunged and reared a little, she controlled it well.

Once in the middle of the river, it was time for Viajero's part of the plan. All the riders, except the white woman and child, dismounted and started on the preparations, though when she realised what was going on, the white woman got out of the saddle and helped.

Alicia Gadd knew that their lives were still in the hands of these Indians but acceptance and some Texan fatalism had gone a long way to ease her mind; her daughter's stoical attitude had also helped – Becky was not a whining child – they could have been killed at any stage back on the Llano but here they were, still upright and above ground. It was a miracle.

The preparations took half a day of walking in the cold water; moccasins and leggings clung to skin and they all shivered. A swirl of early light snow showed that the Tree Popping Moon was close

"My brother…" said Mouse to Viajero, limping as she helped, "…why do this in the river?"

The Apache noticed how sickly she looked and was about to reply when White Rain butted in:

"Because, little sister, Comanche trackers could work out what we were doing if we did this on land."

Mouse blushed, embarrassed that she had not worked this out for herself but Viajero came to her aid:

"It's a good question but White Rain is right – we'll be splitting up here to fool the Comanches."

Mouse was appalled – no-one had mentioned splitting up; she hoped that she would be with the Apache's group.

Once Viajero was satisfied with the preparations, he left the white woman holding the bridles of all the mules and horses while he took his raiders back to the muddy bank. Smoothing out a surface to draw on, he took a stick and drew some rough lines in the mud:

"This river leads to a Mexican settlement and your soldiers…." pointing the stick at White Rain "…leave the river on the east bank and head north and north east until you find the Flint Arrowpoint River. Let the whites go towards the settlement - they will only slow us down…"

Alicia Gadd knew that their fate was being decided as the dark-skinned warrior was pointing at them. She whispered to her daughter:

"Becky darlin', we may need to cut loose in a hurry so you'll need to leave Johnson behind if I say so." The girl nodded her assent though leaving Johnson, the burro, would be hard. He was reliable and steady and, because of his willing nature, she had named him after one of their slaves back in Texas.

"…Then," continued the Apache, "…you must ride long and hard to find our village. Don't stop, no fires, no sleep – you must ride like…." the Traveller paused as he thought of a suitable word; he could only think of one:

"…like Comanches!" There was burst of laughter from the others – it wasn't often that Viajero made a joke.

"And where will you go, brother?" asked Mouse, tentatively, as the others grinned at her forwardness; the girl was becoming fonder of the Traveller every day.

"Dark and I will take the pack mules and head to the badlands north west of here..." He made a puncture mark in the wet sand showing the approximate place where the badlands were.

"...we must go where the Comanches cannot use their horses and we can slow them down."

See the Dark caught White Rain's eye and he could see that, despite all the coolness and distance between them, she was concerned – everyone knew that the Comanches would follow the laden mules. It was going to be dangerous work. He checked his rifle and the extra ammunition they had offloaded – he would need to keep it dry if the Comanches attacked.

Viajero now scrubbed out the markings in the mud and led them all back to their ponies still shivering in the river. Once mounted, they all set off, still in midstream and headed north.

Now released from the chore of chivvying the mules along, White Rain rode alongside Dark for a while, offering advice on the best way to make the mules work better. He accepted this with good grace – after all, she had been doing this longer than him. He thought that he should say something but no words came. She though, spoke her mind:

"You'll need to be careful in the badlands – I don't want another dead husband…"

Dark's brain reeled – husband? Would this woman never stop? White Rain would never make a traditional wife – her new-found urge to be a warrior seemed to overrule any sense of wifely duty, yet she still talked of marriage as something to achieve in life. He had no cravings to be a husband – he liked children, provided they belonged to someone else – but worried about his skill to feed any of his own and the responsibility that would confine him to a life in his own tipi. He was irritated and on the verge of pushing her away when he saw The Tree.

There were many trees along the river and many were far better shape than this one - the top leaves and branches had been flattened by the constant wind and it stood gaunt, misshapen and alone. It didn't seem to fit with the rest of the cottonwoods along the same bank and stood apart – it had grown in the wrong place to ever reach its full height. The tree seemed to call to him and he shifted uneasily in his saddle. The tree was symbolic of…. something.

Dark, never one for deep thought, had avoided going on a vision quest, where young men went off into the wild places, fasted and looked into the sun to ensure that their life's vision would come. He had been pretty sure that Maheo would not waste time on a one-eyed youth. His long dead friend Shining Horse had once said that Dark should try the quest - even if with a single eye he could only see *half* a vision. But now, without the sun and the strict fasting, the oddly shaped tree seemed to speak to him and made him shiver. Now he knew why – the tree looked exactly like a Cheyenne funeral scaffold.

He fell silent as their two ponies splashed along side by side. Although White Rain was still speaking, he paid her no heed but absorbed the importance of the symbol as he rode by.

At this strange time and in this desperate moment, Maheo, the One God of his people had spoken to him – the Life Giver had chosen this time to bring him a seed of maturity, even though it was stunted and undernourished, just like the tree. War and danger were his favourite states of being and he gave little thought to the consequences – it was how a Cheyenne warrior was supposed to be - unthinkingly brave and, as he'd previously admitted to himself, only interested in his own deeds and glory.

Now, as he rode into danger, he felt that the tree was a sign of his life – and death – to come if he didn't grow up. He would live in loneliness and die the same way if he didn't change. He still didn't have any wealth but when he got home – if he and the Traveller *ever* got home – success in bringing back the guns should assure him of a respected place in the Suhtai camp. It would be a great achievement and a good start for the new life that he knew he must lead. So, he was as surprised as White Rain when he spoke to her again:

"When the Comanche find our trail, they will split up and follow you too – so obey the Traveller and keep moving. When you find our village, send help towards the badlands - we may need it…"

He was about to continue when Viajero called to him to ride towards the west bank – it was time to part. White Rain dutifully led her own group towards the eastern shoreline but knew that the conversation wasn't over:

"Yes?" she asked, twisting back in the saddle and reining in her mount.

"…and we'll need our own lodge!" he shouted. It was not a traditional proposal of marriage but the closest White Rain would ever get.

Dark pulled the mule across to the riverbank and led it up the muddy slope and out of the water. Viajero watched in puzzlement as the Cheyenne youth went over to a poor specimen of cottonwood tree, pulled off a leaf and put it into his medicine bundle that he wore round his neck.

See the Dark and White Rain Woman, both smiling, turned to their separate and dangerous trails as the cold waters of the Pecos River flowed between them.

---- o o o ----

Iron Hat swayed slightly in the saddle – he had taken some of the whiskey with the young men and now his head hurt. He had been trying to figure out why the Cheyenne had brought their women with them on the raid – though Comanche women sometimes rode along with their husbands, their real place was with the children and to get camp fires and food ready. It was puzzling. He was glad Medicine Wolf was doing the tracking though he wasn't really needed, the *Puhakut* stayed in the saddle, just glancing at the ground occasionally; the trail was so clear that a child could follow it. Indeed, some of the young Penatekas had ridden ahead to see if they could spot the thieves.

A wind was getting up when they returned – the warriors were impatient, quarrelsome and still slightly drunk – the wind blew the ponies' manes out sideways and made riders hunch up in their robes and blankets:

"You Nokoni ride like old women!" one warrior yelled at Iron Hat. The chief looked up with bloodshot eyes but chose not to answer; he would quirt the boy later if he didn't fall silent.

Medicine Wolf had responded to the taunt by deliberately dismounting and walking his pony. An outspoken Penateka called Spotted Hand, drunker than the rest, rode up alongside him:

"Puhakut, we should pursue the enemy quicker – we don't need you to find their trail…" He pointed to the deep prints in the soft, dry earth. Medicine Wolf just glared at him with glittering black eyes and as he did so, the wind gusted heavily – a sharp, bitter squall - raising dust and swirling pieces of dried plants, wiping out the tracks in front of their eyes:

"How about now?" he growled.

---- 0 0 0 ----

Chapter Fifty Four

Alicia Gadd sipped heavily sugared black coffee from a porcelain cup and leant back into the cowhide armchair; she was bone weary. The *Alcalde* of Santa Fe had been very kind and solicitous when she and Becky had been led up to his house on the Comanche pony. A local cattle herder had seen them approach the town and brought them straight to him.

The Comanche horse and Johnson the burro had been put into his stables and fed, both animals enjoying the rich supply of food and ready water in the trough. Her daughter now sat out on the stoop of the house drinking lemonade from a crystal glass and trying to talk to one of the servants. The change from a barbaric to a civilised existence, from imminent death to sudden life had caught Alicia by surprise when she had arrived the previous afternoon and she had burst into tears. But now she had recovered her composure and, after the *Alcalde* had sought her agreement, was expecting visitors.

Their release by the Indians had been swift and unexpected. To Alicia's surprise, the occasion had been tinged with some regret on her part. The taller of the women had pointed west from the river and said some words she didn't understand. The woman then flapped the back of her hands at them - just as Becky used to do to keep her geese off the back porch - and when that had no effect, pulled the head of her pony round to face the right way then slapped its rump to get it moving. Before mounting, Becky had hugged the young plump girl, who just looked embarrassed. Her daughter had shouted farewell but the Indians were already riding north. No-one looked back.

"Momma, some soldiers are here…" Rebecca, still clutching her glass of lemonade, came into the room looking behind her. There were voices outside, some orders given and a rattling of harness. Alicia looked out of the window and saw four horses with their riders dismounted – a small, stocky man in a faded green uniform coat walked up the steps and spoke briefly to the *Alcalde*.

"Señora, may I introduce Captain Ernesto Ruiz? He is our local militia commander and is anxious to talk to you about the Indians that held you captive." The Captain removed his hat and bowed.

"I'm not sure I can tell you much Captain…" she said, "…we were held by a small group and travelled through country that I hadn't seen before."

Alicia motioned for Ruiz to sit down and shooed Becky back out to the stoop – this talk would be for adults. Ruiz's English was fair; he traded with Government officials and often had to talk to American soldiers when he sold them horses or cattle. After some questions about their health and if she had been abused – or as Ruiz genteelly put it 'did they cause you or your daughter any distress' – he moved on:

"Señora, do you know who the Indians were – which people they came from?"

"No," she replied truthfully.

"How many Indians were in your party, were they armed, in which direction did they travel?" The questions came rapidly, Ruiz was remorseless and - for some inexplicable reason - Alicia Gadd got defensive.

She fanned her face with her hand and sought time to think:

"Why do you want to know all this Captain?"

"Well Señora, if they are a small party, my men…" he pointed outside to the small patrol, "…will pursue them and kill them."

Alicia pretended to faint slightly but recovered enough to say:

"Captain Ruiz, may we talk a walk around the Alcalde's house – the fresh air will do me good…"

Ruiz stood up and offered his arm:

"Of course, Madame, please forgive me for my lack of manners – the directness of a soldier I'm afraid."

Alicia smiled forgivingly and went out onto the stoop, telling her daughter to stay there. Holding onto Ruiz's arm they walked up to the corral fence where some fine chestnut mares trotted around the dusty paddock. She stopped by the feed box and held out a handful of oats, three of the mares walked over to her and ate from her hand.

"Well, Madame – can you remember anything else about those savages? You say you were a captive twice but escaped the first time?"

"Yes, my daughter and I were taken by Comanches from our ranch – the Bar G – earlier this year, I can't remember when…"

For Alicia, time had stopped whilst she had been in Comanche hands – no matter how much she racked her brain, she couldn't remember the month or day she had been wrenched from her vegetable patch at the side of her barn. She had been thrown across a Comanche saddle and the shrieking war party galloped off, followed by their stock of horses stolen while they had been grazing on the lower forty. As she was thrown around across the galloping horse, she saw that her house had been set ablaze and her husband, Valentine, lay spread-eagled by the front porch, pinned to the ground by a Comanche lance.

"But you escaped? Was it the Comanches who recaptured you?"

Alicia still had no clear idea whose tribe she had stumbled on out on the Llano; the older dark-skinned one had possibly been an Apache – she had seen Lipans before, begging for food at her door one harsh winter – but something cautioned her against telling Ruiz. Those people, whoever, they were, had not harmed her or Becky. No, they had brought them along, helped them to escape the pursuing Comanche and then released them near Santa Fe. She had already decided to lie to Ruiz when one of the three chestnuts turned its flank to her. She went silent as she absorbed what she saw. That settled it. Theatrically, she shook her head and announced:

"Captain Ruiz, the fresh air has certainly helped and I'm sorry for my confusion but I'm only a woman and my grasp of such important details is poor. But I remember the second group now – they were indeed Comanche and I think they were heading south."

Ruiz smiled triumphantly, bade farewell and strode off to join his patrol; he was pleased that the Texan woman had said they were Comanches – it meant less work. His patrol could ride out, looking determined and important but he would never attack Comanches – their trade made Santa Fe, and him, rich. No, he would put up a show, return in a couple of days and say he lost the trail – the woman and child could go back to Texas and balance would be restored.

As Alicia stared back at the chestnut in the corral, she knew that Ruiz and the Alcalde were only making empty promises; there on the flank of the horse was the brand of the Bar G ranch; this was her own stock – these bastards were in league with the damned Comanche.

---- 0 0 0 ----

Chapter Fifty Five

Medicine Wolf now led the Comanche war party as the wind shrieked around them and buffeted them in their saddles. All rode hunched in robes; the wind had a bitter edge to it as the Starving Moon came closer. The trail of the thieves was now long gone except in rock overhangs or the rare stand of stunted trees where it was shielded from its force.

Iron Hat sat grim faced on his pony as it plodded on through the howling wind. He had been foolish to allow the young men to drink so much whiskey and delay the pursuit of the Cheyenne gun robbers. At one place where the tracks were still in evidence, Medicine Wolf came to report:

"They are four or five days ahead – we are going too slow."

"Will this wind wipe out the trail of the spirit horse?" Iron Hat asked, holding the hood of his robe with his hand to allow him to speak above the norther.

Medicine Wolf grinned his humourless smile, Iron Hat was always slightly daunted by the sharpened teeth:

"The wind can only take away the shape of its hooves on the earth – it can't take away the track of its spirit."

"Can your puha work in the dark?" asked the war leader.

"Of course," said Medicine Wolf "When I found our dead Nokoni brother all those years ago, I tracked his ghost at night."

Iron Hat nodded, remembering the ripple of fear that raised the hairs on the back of his neck when Medicine Wolf had found the corpse during a black, moonless night.

There was a noise at the rear of his group – the Nokoni youths that he had sent back to camp for supplies had returned. Iron

Hat had realised his poor judgement and now wanted to provision his war party for a much longer trail.

There was much hooting and yipping – the young men had brought much needed food, water and spare ponies. Several other warriors had also joined them, one a very old man called Rides His Pony in the South – he was anxious to be back on the war trail, tired of making arrows for younger men he wanted to recapture his past glory. Many of the younger ones had never seen him in his full war regalia – Rides His Pony had left the war trail long before they had been born – and were shocked by his adornments. His robe was not a buffalo skin nor any animal that they could recognise – his scrawny body was fully encased in the fur of a huge spotted cat, much larger than any puma. His war helmet was not the traditional buffalo horns but a leather skull cap embedded with bright red, blue and green feathers – he had told campfire tales of these birds with the cruel beaks and their unsettling cries when he had raided far to the south. Rides his Pony was always keen to stress that the raids were not just in Mexico, but far, far to the south - where open country ran out and the tall, green, dank forests began – where tiny, hairy and agile people lived in trees and screeched instead of talking any known language. He had only been on the one long raid when he had been very young but its success had made him famous amongst all the Comanche bands. It had also made him arrogant.

Rides His Pony walked his horse up to Iron Hat and Medicine Wolf:

"You are going too slow," he announced to the war leader and the Puhakut. Neither man said anything in reply but seethed at the intrusion of the ancient one, telling them things they already knew.

"This wouldn't have happened in my day," sneered the old warrior.

Iron Hat paused only for a moment, revenge on the old man would be needed as he had been insulted in the hearing of other warriors. He could not kill Rides His Pony – that would bring a bad puha to their war trail - but he could make life uncomfortable for the old fool and so he called out to his cluster of warriors:

"No more overnight camps! We ride day and night and change horses once a day; we'll eat in the saddle."

All the war party yelled their approval, waving weapons in the air, robes billowing in the constantly howling squall; this what their people did – track, pursue and kill. Those Cheyenne thieves were doomed.

Medicine Wolf kicked his pony and headed to the front of the war band. He had tied his puha amulets to the neck of his pony and felt the familiar tingle through his body as he connected to that other, faraway place where the ghosts and spirits lived. He could never describe his powers to any other living man – he didn't need to because no-one now questioned it – so he settled into the saddle and followed the gift of his magic as it homed in on the spirit horse.

---- 0 0 0 ----

Mouse was getting weaker. Willow and Crow Dress inspected her wound. Though the pistol ball had gone right through her buttocks, the place where the bullet had burst out was an ugly mound of purple skin and exploded flesh the size of a child's fist. The dark red hole in the fleshy pulp continued to bleed even though White Rain had applied all the remedies she knew to stop it.

Crow Dress Woman and Willow, despite the Traveller's instructions not to rest, had insisted that Mouse dismount and lie down while they gathered spiders' webs from between the agave leaves on the dry southern flatlands. They had drinking water but none to spare for bathing wounds so they bound the webs with the fleshy marrow from a cactus and used their own spit to shape the mixture into balls. They pushed the ball into the entry wound and a larger one into the exit hole. None of them had dealt with a bullet wound before and they discussed what they should do next. Unless they could relieve the pressure on the exit hole, Mouse would be unable to ride. The women looked to White Rain as their leader:

"Shall we cut the lump off?" said Willow, pointing to the exit wound. "It is this that stops our sister from riding properly – without it she may be able to stay in the saddle until we get home."

Mouse wailed her disapproval:

"There will be no carving lumps off me! The wound isn't that bad."

Even White Rain looked doubtful:

"That will just make her bleed more and she will get even weaker…"

Mouse lay on her side on the bare earth, her shift around her waist and probed the lump gingerly with a grubby finger, wincing in pain as she did so.

"Why not just slice into the lump, lay the parts flat against her skin and bind that tight with a strip of hide?" said Crow Dress.

"…then when we get to where moss grows on the trees, we can gather that and soak up the blood with it."

The women nodded – it seemed like a good idea. Even Mouse thought it was a better plan than just hacking off her disfigured flesh. Crow Dress was not just a good warrior, she was a turning into a thinker and a healer. White Rain lodged that thought in her memory; it would be useful when they went on the war trail again.

Willow sharpened her knife on a rock and walked towards Mouse; the girl went pale but gritted her teeth – she was a Cheyenne woman and would not cry out.

Crow Dress grinned at Mouse:

"I don't think you'll have a song for this," she said.

---- o o o ----

It took Viajero and See the Dark a long time to reach the badlands. The Apache had been there before and was pleased that he had found them again:

"When the horned lizard sent me north all those moons ago – before I came to live with you and the Tsis-tsis-tas – I rode past here…"

"I can see why you call them badlands…" interrupted Dark as he gazed at the strange, bare rocks doubtfully. "…we'll never get the horses through here let alone the mules."

Viajero nodded – the rocks had been twisted and shaped into towering pillars and short, deep canyons; stray rocks sat on top of some of the towers, some piled in untidy heaps as though placed there by a child's hand. The surface of all the land that could be seen from the backs of their ponies had changed from bare earth to smooth, red brown rock that bulged and folded out in layers as though molten mud had frozen as it came out of the ground – it was a hostile onward trail of uncertainty and, possibly, magic. Even the Apache thought that spirits could live here but he kept his thoughts to himself.

"We have to get to the middle of all this," said Viajero, "…but it will be hard to get to…"

"Then why go there?" demanded Dark, tired and dispirited – the rocky wastelands depressed him and he failed to see why they had come here, "…our horses are almost given out and the mules are done."

"I know," said the Traveller," …but we must make one last effort to draw the Comanches to us …"

Dark was about to whine and again ask why but stopped himself in time; the Apache, remembering the times when his N'De people had fought the Nerm-en-uh, they had discovered a weakness. Viajero supplied the answer unasked:

"…because Comanches are predictable."

---- 0 0 0 ----

Iron Hat's war party was closing in – Medicine Wolf had followed the invisible trail of the spirit horse to the Pecos River and the young men now whooped in triumph as they, at last, rediscovered a trail *they* could follow. Two trails – one leaving the river to the east and one to the west - were in mud and unaffected by the wind. They had completed the ride in just over one day and night, shortening the gap between the Cheyenne robbers and Comanche revenge.

Spotted Hand, now sober, had found the eastern exit from the river and splashed back into the river to report to Iron Hat:

"The main group left the river here and have gone north – it may be a false trail though. The pack mules and four horses aren't with them."

"I know," replied the chief, waving towards the opposite bank, "that group has left over there and headed north west…"

Iron Hat stared at the young man; the Penateka's insolence had abated as the whiskey had worn off. He issued orders:

"My Nokonis will follow the mules and the other two riders leading them – you take your Penatekas and follow the main group…"

Spotted Hand reined his pony's neck round and splashed past the immobile, Nokoni group back to his comrades. Rides His Pony in the South could not resist a parting, scornful shot:

"You Penatekas will be following women, so try to be brave – and be careful they don't defeat you!"

Gripping his reins tightly to prevent him killing the old fool, Spotted Hand pushed through the swirling water back to his own war band – they didn't need any Nokoni spirit tracker now - they could count horse tracks just as well as anyone else. They would have their enemies in sight soon.

---- 0 0 0 ----

Chapter Fifty Six

Smoke on the Moon was thin and hungry by the time he found Bad Elk's camp again. Badlands Walking Woman bustled around him bringing soup and meat until his strength returned. She sat next to him as he lay against his spruce backrest, smoking a pipe and looking out of the tipi onto the snowy ground. His pony was hobbled and picketed outside and brushed the thin coating of snow off the poor grass with its muzzle – the People were settling in for the winter.

Bad Elk came into the lodge to check on his brother's health:

"I chose to come back to this place so your son and the Traveller can find us again…"

Smoke nodded, puffing at his field tobacco. It was a good and familiar campsite – plenty of timber for fires, pasture for their pony herd – at least for a time - and near a clear stream. See the Dark and the Traveller had been to this place before and the Suhtai could stay here for a while. The buffalo hunts had gone well – their white guests were still in camp but now helping more with routine camp duties - and the food supply was good. Smoke knew that bitter weather would come but the stripped bark of the cottonwoods would provide extra feed for their horses and the people would be warm and well-fed.

"Did you see your son's trail?" asked Bad Elk. Smoke nodded:

"Only in the early part of my scout – the wind and rain took most of it away later on. I followed it down to the Flint Arrowpoint River then across and south west during the good weather. It was a long ride.…"

There was a pause and Smoke continued:

"…the Forked Lightning Women went the same way."

"I know," said Bad Elk and stared into the cooking fire.

Flea crawled over the buffalo robes on the tipi floor and onto his father's lap; Smoke held him in a distracted way and continued to puff at his pipe:

"They have all gone deep into Comanche country – we may never see them again...."

"Nonsense!" barked Badlands, taking the child from his father and holding him close: "They are all experienced warriors and more than a match for any Comanche."

Smoke was about to answer when there was a sound of yelling at the southern edge of the camp; it was impossible to hear what was being said as so many voices were shouting at once.

The Striking Snakes leader grabbed his rifle and ran outside; Bad Elk went back to his own lodge to get his gun – neither was sure if it was a true alarm meaning that enemies had been sighted or just general excitement. The brothers ran down towards the commotion together.

Smoke pounded past the older folk who got in his way, pushing them rudely aside – he would apologise later. Bad Elk paused to fit a percussion cap onto his rifle then continued running.

There at the edge of the village was a dying horse, silver steam rising from its flanks with the exertions it had made and, surrounded by a crowd of children and women, was a lone figure on the ground. Burnt Hair, Bad Elk's wife had got there before him:

"It's the Lakota girl, Willow – she's alone!"

---- o o o ----

Chapter Fifty Seven

Spotted Hand's legs were aching; he and his Penatekas had ridden hard and now their reward was in sight. He reined in his pony on a rocky crest overlooking a narrow valley; there below were the tiny figures of their prey driving a small remuda of horses relentlessly northwards. He could hear their yipping and shouting even up here.

The young Penateka was excited. Almost by accident, he had found himself leading a war party for the first time. If this pursuit was successful, it would mean great personal honour but, for now, he was anxious - anxious about his abilities and his lack of experience. War leader or not, he had been confused when one of the unshod ponies and the burro had left the women's group on the outskirts of Santa Fe; he was unable to work out why. His boyhood friend though had the answer:

"The Cheyennes have released them – the burro was slowing them down…"

Spotted Hand had nodded sagely as though he had known it all along; Coyote, his friend, had smirked at him – a knowing smile of unspoken superiority. Coyote liked to go on raids but didn't want any responsibility – happy, as some men are, merely to criticise or undermine. He would have to be watched.

Spotted Hand decided he would have to be at the forefront in the coming fight. Even as he thought about it, his anxiety returned – he was brave, of course, as befitted a Comanche warrior but his Penateka people had been herded onto a reservation up on the Brazos for almost ten years and his battle experience was thin. He and his friends had sneaked off to join Iron Hat's trade with the Comancheros as it promised guns and whiskey but the actual amount of fighting that he had previously done had been confined to white women and children, mainly when they had been running away. Of course, the Cheyenne that they had now found were only women too but he would still need to show courage and set an example, especially to the insolent Coyote.

He looked round at his warriors:

"There are only three riders now – perhaps the one who was wounded has died…"

They had found the discarded pieces of bloody deerskin amongst a whirl of tracks of shod and unshod horses. It was a rare pause for the Cheyenne – they were avoiding resting at night and fleeing for their lives.

"We have them now – it's time to show them how the Comanches punish thieves."

His dozen warriors rode into a circle and faced their ponies' heads inward. Taking their battle paint and headdresses from their saddle bags, they made their preparations and summoned their magic. Anxious to lead, Spotted Hand wrenched the head of his bay towards the trail down from the crest. Kicking into the pony's flanks he galloped, shrieking and shaking his war lance, into his first real fight.

---- o o o ----

Viajero stroked the mane of the ugly horse and then plunged his hunting knife into its neck. Its misshapen head jerked upwards and its eyes rolled back into the skull, whites showing. Blood spurted out of the puncture wound over the handle of the knife and onto Viajero's moccasins; the Apache avoided the rest of the flow by stepping round to the other side of his pony's head. The spirit horse fell onto its front knees and swayed sideways onto the red earth, its blotchy grey body crumpling into the dust, legs thrashing feebly as life left it.

For the first time in his life, Viajero was unsure about what to do; normally he just killed lame horses, sometimes he ate them if there was nothing else. But *this* one was a link to Usen, his god. Still, the horse had a split hoof and its working life was over.

Unusually for Viajero, he held the horse's head on his knees until its spirit had departed, cupping his hand over the animal's eyeball so the settling dust wouldn't get into it. Still kneeling, he sang of his thanks to the Life Giver – a high, toneless and repetitive heartsong that Dark had never heard before. The Apache was solemn as he laid the horse's head gently onto the earth.

Dark sat quietly on a rock mound in the badlands and watched his friend. He knew the lizard spirit sign on the ugly horse's neck made the mount special to the Traveller – he was glad he didn't have the same problem.

From his high perch, Dark checked their back trail and now he saw what they had been waiting for:

"They're coming," he said and scrambled down, crumbling rock following him in a small, skittering cascade.

The Apache nodded and rose to his feet. Both men now led their two fresh sorrels up onto the rock plateau by a narrow track and jammed their bridles into a rock crevice to hold them there. Then they descended the track again, back to where the ugly horse lay, all twitching ceased. Dark's used sorrel and the two laden mules, still encumbered by full pack saddles, swayed from exhaustion.

The two warriors now knifed the remaining animals. When the killing was done, Dark wiped the blood from his knife. Their fight with the pursuing Comanches would be made here.

"I hope you are right about them being predictable," he said as he checked the loads in his repeating rifle.

---- 0 0 0 ----

Chapter Fifty Eight

Iron Hat had been here before – he had trailed and fought Apaches around these badlands and he smiled as he recognised the twisted pillars of rock:

"They are leading us into the rocks that hold our magic – this is Comanche land from our grandfathers' times. Those thieves will die here!" he shouted back to his column of warriors.

The men dutifully yipped and yelled their approval. There were only around twenty men now; Iron Hat had sent many back to camp as there wasn't enough food to sustain the entire war party on its march. There had been some disappointed faces amongst his fighters but many were secretly relieved to go home and, hopefully, help plunder the Taos column of all its goods or even take a woman or two. Many of them had considered that it was bad judgement by Iron Hat to keep them all on the trail - such a large force was not needed to track and kill just two enemies.

The Nokoni leader still sat on his pony – a spare mount now – and didn't bother to get off to look at the trail; it was as clear as could be. Two deep sets of mule tracks, the depth of the prints showing that they were still fully loaded, now bore signs of staggering or hesitation. The animals were tired and almost played out. The two ridden horses bore the same signs. Medicine Wolf had pointed out the signs of impatience that the fresher, riderless ponies showed at the slow pace and their annoyance at being tied to the plodding mules. The end of the chase was near.

Medicine Wolf knew it too because he had *felt* it first. The tingling effect from the invisible trail of the spirit horse that had been his constant guide through wild weather and over trackless country had briefly crackled into fiercer life then ebbed and faded. He saw Iron Hat watching him anxiously as he halted the column and took his amulet necklace from around the neck of his pony. The tracker squatted on the ground, scattered his magic bringers onto the tracks of the spirit horse and ran the downward palm of his hand over the dirt. The spirit essence was fading. He stood up and walked over to Iron Hat:

"It's just as well we can see the tracks now – that spirit horse is dead."

---- o o o ----

Chapter Fifty Nine

Burnt Hair and a throng of women laid Willow on a buffalo pelt; eager hands grabbed at the edge of the fur robe and carried her into her mother's tipi. They chattered excitedly amongst themselves – where were the rest of the women warriors – and the men too?

The Lakota girl was pale but she was young and already recovering her senses. Her Cheyenne mother, who had taken her in after Willow had been captured, did the only thing she could think of to help – she put a kettle of soup onto the cooking fire to heat up; her girl needed hot food.

Willow tried to stand and Burnt Hair steadied her as she rocked uncertainly on her feet:

"Sister, I need to talk to your husband…" she croaked.

Burnt Hair gave her a drink of water from a skin pouch as Willow put a hand on her shoulder to catch her breath and then talked a little more. The girl was babbling slightly from lack of food and sleep but her point was clear - Burnt Hair ducked outside the tipi flap to find Bad Elk.

Her husband and his brother, like all the men, were standing outside, talking and scuffing their moccasins over the hardening earth as they waited to see if the girl had brought any news. Healing a woman was not what they did and they had few concerns about her condition – she was, after all, a strange speaker of their tongue and a member of a troublesome and assertive group of women - but they were impatient to know the whereabouts of the rest of the war party. Some in the group of men openly admitted to Bad Elk that it wasn't the women they were worried about but the Traveller and See the Dark.

Burnt Hair overheard the mutterings and snorted scornfully:

"Husband…" she began.

Though she was addressing Bad Elk she made sure that the others heard what she had to say.

"...that girl has had a long hard ride; all alone for many days. She brings news of her Forked Lightning Women – and she brings word from the Traveller and the son of Smoke on the Moon."

At the mention of Dark's name both Bad Elk and Smoke on the Moon strode towards the lodge. Burnt Hair was about to step aside and let them in when Willow staggered out of the tipi and leant against a lodge pole to help her stand up:

"Brothers! The Comanche are gaining fast on my war sisters and their lives are in peril..."

Many of the assembled warriors had never heard Willow speak more than a few sentences and had to struggle to understand her strange, accented way with their language. Some understood quicker and shrugged – if those women called themselves warriors then they should just fight the Comanches. How hard could it be?

"...one of my sisters was wounded after the fight with the Comancheros but we got away with many guns. The Nerm-en-uh followed us closely and now they are in danger."

The injury to a young, irresponsible woman was of little concern; Bad Elk himself had predicted a bad outcome to the raid. But the mention of precious guns made many of the warriors pay closer attention.

Broken Knife had wandered down to see what all the commotion was about and had heard the girl speak:

"Where is the Traveller and See the Dark – and when will they bring the guns?" he said.

"On the Traveller's instructions, we split up so we don't know where they are now but I can lead you to the women…"

Willow's mother looked aghast and was about to forbid it but Broken Knife butted in again:

"No, we must find the men and the rifles! Your women must do their best to escape the Comanches and join us back here…"

At this point, Willow knew that she hadn't explained herself well:

"The Traveller's instructions were clear – he insisted that you must go to the aid of my war sisters. That is the reason we split up."

Broken Knife and Smoke listened in disbelief as the Lakota girl explained why an experienced warrior like the Traveller had divided their forces on such a dangerous trail. But both soldier society leaders were practical men – there was only one thing to do:

"Striking Snakes – get mounted! Bring rations and weapons – it will be a long ride and then battle," yelled Smoke.

Without waiting to see if they were included, Henry and Carver did the same.

Broken Knife followed with the same orders to his Thunder Bears before stalking off to his lodge to make his own preparations; it was a hard decision for him – unique in his life – the Suhtai band would go onto a war footing to save some over-ambitious women. He hoped they would be worth it.

---- o o o ----

Chapter Sixty

Alerted by the high-pitched barks and yells of their enemies, White Rain, Crow Dress Woman and Mouse saw the Comanche war party come streaming off a nearby ridge and loop out towards them, reining in their ponies when they saw the women. Their slow but deliberate advance made the sounds match the sight of the Comanche line – they sounded and looked like a hungry wolf pack that had spotted its prey.

White Rain issued calm orders and her Forked Lightning Women led their captured Mexican horses into a tight circle, roped heads all facing inwards. The ponies jostled and whinnied in this unfamiliar formation and all three women had difficulty in getting them to stand still.

All the unridden horses now carried packs– some were just blankets taken from the Mexicans and used as coverings, others were stretches of canvas taken from the rifle cache. All the packs were bound with rawhide strips and either tied to the Mexican saddles or lashed directly onto the horses' bodies; pack grated against pack as the animals moved uneasily. But White Rain made sure that they could not run off when the fighting started. Then, with their new repeating Colt rifles in hand, the three women reined their ponies into an arrowhead shape to face their enemies.

White Rain shouted to them:

"Remember what the Traveller told us! Stay mounted and keep together; try to spot the leader and kill him!"

The new guns were heavy but Mouse was relaxed as she looked at the reassuring presence of the four guns she now had – two pistols, the soldier's carbine – already looking cumbersome and old-fashioned - and the new rifle. She felt that she could take on the Comanche war party by herself. She shifted uncomfortably in the saddle, the pistol in the holster would sometimes rub up against her wound and bring on the pain again. But, no matter -

she smiled her young smile at her sisters and didn't want to be anywhere else.

Crow Dress grinned back and hoped that Willow would bring help soon. She was happy enough to fight but would have been more at ease if the Lakota girl had been with her. She looked down at her decorated shift with its elk teeth adornments, sniffed it and decided that she would wash it at the next opportunity. The dress, taken as a prize from the Crow people by her father many years before, had given the young Cheyenne woman her name; she would be happy to die in it.

White Rain saw Mouse smile and, despite wondering where See the Dark was and the uncertainty about the coming battle, smiled back. She had been happy about Dark's promise of a shared lodge when they had split trail; she just hoped she would live long enough to see it. But dwelling on dreams did not win battles, leadership and fighting spirit needed to be summoned; she yelled above the shrieking of the advancing Comanches:

"Sisters, our time in this life is short! We are but dust – only the earth shall last!"

Her women responded by ululating their Cheyenne cries and brandishing their rifles. Mouse sang her song that told all that she was a timid creature in name only – she was a panther inside.

Spotted Hand and his advancing warriors were in no hurry – they rode into extended line, each fearsome in their black and red face paint and waving the powerful totems of their sacred shields and lances as they gave throat to their war song.

The young Penateka smiled at the comforting words that reminded him and his warriors of the courage of their warlike people, the magic of the summer raiding moon and the death and destruction that they would wreak on any enemy –white, Mexican or red.

The Comanche ponies, even though they were the spare mounts ordered by Iron Hat, were thin and weary. But the sudden alertness of their riders, the strange smell from the foreign animals to their front and the noise meant only one thing – they had work to do. Their ears pricked up and each shivered with excitement as they prepared to charge.

White Rain just grunted as she saw the extended line – the Comanche leader must be inexperienced – she had been able to count his warriors and there were a lot less of them than she had thought when they charged down from the ridge. She sat quietly and cocked her rifle, listening for the clicks that her warriors had done the same. It was her pony facing the line, Mouse and Crow Dress would guard the sides of their small, restless remuda.

There was a sudden shot from behind her and her pony, unnerved by the sound, jumped forward and she instinctively ducked. The Comanche line halted and one of the warriors clutched the side of his head and yelled. She looked round – Mouse had tried a lucky shot with the soldier's carbine and shot the man's ear off. The young woman, as ever on their sisterly adventures had taken the initiative against an enemy. Mouse was smiling broadly and whooped her triumph.

White Rain had expected that the shot would goad the Comanches into a charge but no – a slim young warrior, almost indistinguishable from the rest in his battlepaint, shouted some instructions and the Comanches spurred forward into two circles – an inner and an outer - and rode round in two different directions, now out of rifle range.

White Rain recognised battle discipline when she saw it – the Cheyennes never did anything as complicated as this; it was unnerving to see the six inner riders and the six ponies in the outer circle pass by each other in mesmerising displays of calm riding. But she had spotted who was in charge of the Nerm-en-uh:

"Their chief is riding the bay!" she shouted to the others.

"I see him!" yelled Mouse and pulled out a revolver and fired at him. The ball struck harmlessly into the dust, well short of the chief's pony; the Comanches did not even break step. In fact, they laughed at the woman's ineptitude. White Rain watched them closely – the circles were getting closer to them.

"Save your bullets, little sister," said Crow Dress "they'll come soon."

Spotted Hand was nervous; he was pleased that the two circles battle ride was going well and that they had gradually closed the distance between them and the Cheyenne women but the reckoning time was near. Soon he would be within range of the Cheyenne guns. Only two of his impoverished warriors had guns – each one an ancient flintlock pistol with little powder and few bullets to reload. It was time for the arrows.

Yelling instructions, he turned the head of his bay towards the Cheyenne, took his bow from round his neck and loosed off three arrows at the women. His warriors did the same – one Penateka, even more inexperienced than his friends, shot too high and saw one of his arrows bury itself deep into the chest of another Comanche warrior on the far side of the circle. The man toppled from his horse and lay still. The pony, uncertain at losing its rider so suddenly, reared up and cantered away. There was an exhalation of collective breath from the Comanches – a sigh of irritation and fury that their battle had not started well.

Spotted Hand heard a shout from the Cheyenne women – he couldn't see which one – and three plumes of gunsmoke issued from the Cheyenne rifles. None of the bullets hit, though one did whine past his knee, and this braced his courage for the charge.

He did what his people had always done against guns – endure and evade the first bullets then charge before the firers had chance to reload. Now he stood up in his stirrups, bow back across his body, and waved his lance as a signal for the charge.

Despite a limited life as a warrior, Spotted Hand knew that this was the Comanche way – stay mounted and get in close as the enemy struggled with powder and ball. He saw one of the women riders was doubled up in the saddle – someone's arrow had been successful and two horses, heavily loaded, had fallen onto their sides, bodies bristling with arrows. Spotted Hand's spirits soared – he had found his puha. There was no stopping him now as his pony's hooves tore clods of earth from the ground and he closed with the Cheyenne thieves.

Coyote was the first to realise that something was wrong – the women were not reloading their rifles. None of the three was pouring powder down barrels or spitting lead balls into the muzzles. They merely raised their guns and fired again. One girl was aiming at him! He quickly slipped out of the side of his saddle on the safe side of his horse, knee across his mount's back and veered his pony away from the gunfire. A lead ball hummed close to his horse's neck.

Crow Dress was disgusted that her rifle ball had only shot empty air – these Comanches could ride well. She winced in pain as a long Comanche lance speared into her calf from a warrior who had approached in the dusty melee.

The Comanches were now all around them, shrieking and howling like wolves; the loaded horses in the remuda were only stopped from stampeding by the headrope that lashed them together; their rear legs kicked out in terror.

Crow Dress re-cocked the hammer and fired at her attacker who looked surprised as he toppled out of the saddle. More shots came from White Rain and even Mouse, with an arrow deep in her side, had pulled her pistol and shot rapidly into the throng of enemy bodies.

The sharp cracks of the rifles gave way to the flatter explosions of the pistols. The breeze had died down and now blue gun smoke hung in the air and ringed the small battle field. The Forked Lightning Women found it difficult to tell what was going on until there was a yell and the Comanches pulled back.

The shout had come from Coyote. He knew about repeating pistols of course, many of Iron Hat's Nokonis carried them, but his Penatekas, isolated up on the Brazos reservation, were poor in firearms and had not experienced the repeating rifles.

"They have guns that shoot many times! Stay back…"

Coyote expected a rebuke from Spotted Hand but his friend was too busy counting away the ebbing moments of his life in front of the Cheyenne woman who had shot him. His face had been smashed by the heavy calibre bullet and it had blown out the back of his neck. His brains stained his spine as he lay face down; some blood dribbled down his ribs and pooled quickly in the cool air. He twitched as though he was about to stand up but it was just his last, involuntary shudder as his puha faded. His pony nudged the prone body with its muzzle and then wandered off.

The surviving riders gathered around Coyote; it had been a disaster – six warriors lay dead in front of the triumphantly yelling Cheyenne women and three more, though still in the saddle, were wounded. Struggling to assert some sort of leadership, Coyote tried neatly to avoid any blame:

"Spotted Hand's puha and judgement was bad – the Cheyenne guns were powerful. We should go home, gather more warriors and then ride the revenge trail when we are ready…"

The exhausted warriors looked at him dully. Coyote had given them the chance to ride away and salve their consciences. No-one spoke but all felt it; they had been defeated by women – heavily armed to be sure – but women nonetheless. They would be in disgrace.

White Rain watched them carefully in case of another charge but the Comanches appeared to be leaving. She sighed with relief – her rifle and pistol were empty and they would all need to reload. The rifles had worked well and she had been impressed by the usefulness of a pistol – she could see why the Mexicans carried them. All her women warriors would now carry them to mark them out as different to their bow wielding men.

She turned around in the saddle and was just about to give instructions to unload the dead horses and transfer their packs to the captured Comanche mounts when Mouse fell sideways from her saddle and lay still.

---- o O o ----

Chapter Sixty One

Iron Hat saw the two dead pack mules and his heart soared:

"Quickly! Unpack those rifle boxes – those robbers are near!"

Four of his Nokonis dismounted and ran wearily forward; they had been in the saddle for days.

Vultures, busy feasting on the carcasses, rose on heavy wings and bellies into the sky, squawking indignantly. The warriors slashed the heavy wooden boxes from the pack saddle frames and the boxes slid onto the hard ground. All the war party were now excited and more dismounted to help the others– it had been a long hard ride but now it had all been worth it. Going home, triumphant with the new guns would bring great honour.

Medicine Wolf rode up but stayed quiet – he seemed more thoughtful than the others but Iron Hat didn't notice his silence. He did notice though that the spirit tracker had stayed behind to paint himself yellow – his battle colour to protect himself from bullets.

Medicine Wolf dismounted and walked over to the body of a blotchy grey pony that had obviously been killed by its owner. He knelt and stroked its mane – a vulture watched him, talons clinging to the whitened branch of a dead tree.

"This is the spirit horse," he said to Iron Hat.

"Well, it's a dead spirit horse now," replied his war leader without looking at him.

Iron Hat never took his eyes off his warriors, prising the wooden lids off the boxes with their hunting knives. Then, overcome with impatience, he too dismounted and strode over to the noisy group of young men and shoved them aside – this was his moment.

It was also the moment when Rides his Pony in the South, still mounted, rasped scathingly:

"A proper war leader would have noticed the change in the trail made by the thieves."

Iron Hat looked up angrily; what was the old fool talking about? He looked at Medicine Wolf questioningly; the spirit tracker just shrugged and said nothing.

Deep down though the Puhakut was uneasy – he too had seen the change in tracks when they left the river but was so busy following the essence of the spirit horse that it seemed insignificant; a hesitant wavering from the mule prints as they adjusted their footing coming out of the water. It could have been caused by tiredness of the pack animals, or the cold or, as Rides His Pony seemed to imply, a shift in pace due to carrying different weights on their backs. Medicine Wolf had not told Iron Hat this – they were closing on the enemy, that was the main thing.

Iron Hat seethed at the old warrior's impertinence but there were more important matters to hand. At last, he managed to rip one of the wooden slats from a rifle box and stared down dumbly at the contents.

The Nokoni chief shrieked his fury and then redoubled his efforts with the other three boxes, ripping away at the wood until his hands bled. There was not a single rifle in any box, just rocks. Iron Hat kicked the worthless boxes to one side, his face darkening with boiling anger.

Rides his Pony kicked his horse forward and looked into the boxes:

"I could have told you that…" the smug old Comanche said as he shrugged deeper into his spotted pelt cape.

Iron Hat felt the red mist of rage clamp down over his head; he had felt it many times in the past when he had killed Texans and Mexicans. The inside of his skull became hot and his sight blurred – it was a time when his courage surged but his judgement receded. Fellow Comanche or not, respected raider or not, the old fool had said too much, too often.

Iron Hat pulled out his revolver and shot Rides his Pony out of the saddle – the bullet travelled upwards through the old man's chin and blew off his leather cap with the gaudy feathers, a spray of blood, bone fragments and brains close behind it. The explosion of the shot reverberated off the rocky buttes of the Badlands.

And then something odd happened – so quick that Iron Hat, in his rage didn't spot it – only his warriors saw it. More blood appeared on Rides his Pony's chest at the same time that the Nokoni war leader had shot him through the head. Someone else was shooting!

At the sound of the pistol shot, Iron Hat's warriors had gasped at the murder of one of their own and dived beneath the rocky outcrops. He now remonstrated with them:

"What are you? Women!?"

The men stayed where they were. One of them was shouting out that they had heard another shot when his warning was drowned out by a loud clang and Iron Hat fell over.

Up on the grey mesa, another puff of smoke drove a second bullet into the Comanche chief's inert body:

"These rifles fire well," said See the Dark casually as he adjusted his Colt's aim and fired at a foot sticking out from the cover of the rocks; he missed.

"Don't waste your bullets," growled Viajero as he fired at a fleeing Comanche who was trying to mount his pony. The man flung up his arms and cartwheeled under the impact of the heavy bullet from the Sharps.

Dark fired once more then paused, none of the Comanches in cover were moving:

"Do you think we've killed the chief?" he said.

"Perhaps – the old man with the feathers and spotted cloak may have been one. The one with the metal helmet could have been a chief too. It's hard to tell, all Comanches look the same to me."

Despite the tension of the fight, Dark smiled at the Traveller's light remark but he still had questions:

"You said the Comanches would break off if we killed their leader but they are still there; perhaps he is still alive?"

Viajero shook his head and silently wished that he had never mentioned about the predictability of Comanches; the boy always took him at his word. Sometimes in the past, when his people had fought Comanches, the killing of a Nerm-en-uh chief had signalled that their magic was not working that day and they had gone home to mourn. It was too early to say if this was going to be one of those days. He contented himself with a harsh look at the young Cheyenne who now fell silent.

Down in the mesa gully, Medicine Wolf ran over to Iron Hat's body. It was a brave thing to do and inspired confidence in the younger warriors in the cover of the rocks. Whoever was shooting had good guns – the bullet had passed through one side of the iron helmet, through the chief's head and out of the other side – a circular hole with iron shards protruding from the other side of the Nokoni's metal hat showed the power of the rifle.

Medicine Wolf looked down at his boyhood friend sprawled in the dust; Iron Hat seemed to have shrunk in size and looked more like an old woman than a dead warrior.

The crouching Nokonis now shot back – only a few had guns and those were ancient and badly-kept but they provided covering fire as the spirit tracker examined the body of their chief. Two crawled under the low rock overhang to where their ponies had been tethered and got their bows; when they completed this without falling victim to the bullets, more warriors tried it.

Viajero ducked as a poorly aimed lead ball smacked into the rock well above his head and whined off into the air. The Apache now saw wriggling figures under a rock overhang and fired at any exposed flesh; there was a satisfying scream of pain after a good shot.

But now the Comanches were getting more confident. One of them had found the nerve to run to the dead body of the Comanche with the metal hat. Viajero steadied his aim and pulled the trigger. The Apache grunted with frustration when the shot missed. The man, who wore strange yellow paint that set him apart from the other Comanches, merely stood up and walked back under the shelter of the mesa.

"The Nerm-en-uh are getting their courage back," he said to Dark. "We'll move up there…" he pointed to a higher ledge of rock, "…so we can hit them even when they are hiding."

Both men scrambled up the rock face and out onto the barren plateau; Dark collected the horses and, sweating with the effort, pulled the unwilling animals up over the slippery rock face to the mesa top. Their hooves clacked on the rocky surface and they danced with nerves, spooked by the shooting and poor footing.

Glancing behind him the young Cheyenne saw the Comanches start to climb up after them, the yellow-painted man leading his warriors, darting cautiously from outcrop to outcrop, staying out of the way of the powerful rifles. Those Comanches weren't retreating.

Dark hefted the base of each of the deerskin bags criss-crossed over his shoulders to feel the weight of the remainder of his ammunition; he knew he had a little extra in a small cloth sack across the cantle of his saddle; it was enough for now but not if the Comanches kept coming. Sighing with the inevitability of using it, he took his bow and arrows from his saddle and just hoped that the fight could be decided with guns.

Viajero's rifle boomed off to Dark's left, the noise echoing around the standing rock pinnacles:

"That yellow man may have some power – he's evaded all three of my bullets," he called.

Dark just grunted and stood behind his pony, resting his rifle on the saddle seat while he aimed. Out of the corner of his eye he could see some of the Comanches make skittering runs, bent over and ducking off out of sight:

"They're trying to surround us," he shouted.

"I see them," said the Traveller calmly and shot one of them down; the rest froze but only for a moment before continuing to encircle the pair.

Dark sighted along his rifle and waited for movement back along the way they had just climbed.

Suddenly, the yellow man appeared only a bowshot away; he walked out from behind a stone pillar and stood still. Dark yipped in pleasure – the man was obviously crazy; he was daring him to shoot! He squeezed the trigger and the rifle cracked; the grey smoke hung in a circle in the air but there, unharmed in the centre of it, was the silent Comanche – and he was closer now.

Some of the other Comanches saw the powerlessness of the thieves' rifles against Medicine Wolf and one of them, an older warrior called Long Shadow called out:

"See brothers, the spirit tracker has the puha here!"

Other warriors had noticed the same thing and yelled their encouragement and sang their war songs. Long Shadow was glad – they had ridden far from their people and when Iron Hat had been shot, they had been on the edge of retreat. But now, Medicine Wolf was showing that he had a chief's greatness and courage; the Comanches would win.

Viajero cocked his head to one side and listened to the singing, not because he like the songs but it betrayed where his enemies were.

He moved across to where Dark had led the ponies into a shallow cleft of rock, out of harm's way. Confident Comanche arrows now sang in the air and while they splintered on the rocks around and above them, Viajero knew what it meant. Kneeling down above a flat piece of sandy earth, he sketched the enemy positions based on what he had heard from the Comanche voices:

"They have almost circled around us – they are closing in for the kill."

---- o o o ----

Chapter Sixty Two

Comanches are small," said Dark conversationally as he fired at one getting too close to the rock cleft. He'd said it to try and remain calm as the Nerm-en-uh closed in, yipping and screeching to keep up their courage. The arrows had stopped coming now but there was still the occasional pistol shot that smacked against the hard rock before whining off into the sky.

Viajero just grunted; small or not, it didn't affect their fighting spirit. Killing the warrior in the metal hat as well as the one in the spotted cape had made no difference – the Comanches had regained their confidence and united around the yellow painted man; so, *he* must be the chief.

The Apache was pleased that the Comanches were afoot – once out of the saddle they seemed stunted, bow-legged and not well fed. One of the reasons for luring them to the badlands was to prevent the Comanches from riding them down –Viajero knew that it was next to impossible to defeat horsed Comanches. He had seen their battle tactic of surrounding and closing with their foes while still in the saddle.

But now, even though the Nerm-en-uh were not mounted, they were still a vexing enemy. The pillars of rock that provided shelter and safety for himself and Dark also provided cover for the Comanches to move closer. Only their guns prevented an all-out attack.

"Can you see the yellow man?" he said to Dark.

"Not now," replied the young Cheyenne, "He keeps moving around." He shot at two sprinting shadows that raced from one rock to another but hit nothing.

"Well, night is coming on – we need to find him and kill him."

Dusk was settling over the small battleground; the towering rock pillars looked like heavy black stumps of strange trees set against the streaked orange of the evening sky; bats streamed out of caves to form a squeaking throng that undulated towards the horizon and wolves started to howl.

Viajero was surprised by Dark's hand on his shoulder:

"You watch the horses and I'll go and find him," he said as he slung his rifle over his shoulder, drew his war hatchet and slipped out into the hostile night.

---- o 0 o ----

Chapter Sixty Three

"Stay in sight in case you are attacked!" shouted Smoke on the Moon. But it was wasted breath, Willow just spurred her pony onwards - well ahead of the main war party whose exhausted mounts were now at a walk. He knew the girl had been upset at leaving her war sisters behind to face the Comanches alone but galloping off into the unknown was dangerous; even experienced warriors would think a bit more before they did that. Still, the pipe holder admired the girl's courage and she was free to make her own decisions.

"She'll kill her horse if she keeps that up," grumbled Broken Knife as he reined in his pony and rode alongside Smoke. He shook his head – these women were not mature enough for the war trail. Smoke saw the gesture and spoke out:

"If the Forked Lightning Women have the guns, then they will have done us a great service."

"True…" admitted Broken Knife "…but I wonder what they will want as a reward?"

"Perhaps just recognition," said Smoke.

"I already recognise women as our life givers – just not as warriors," said Broken Knife.

"If they have the guns, you may have to change your mind," said Smoke as he kicked his heels into his pony's flanks to close the gap with Willow. The other Striking Snakes noticed the change in pace and drove their ponies on faster. Broken Knife and his Thunder Bears followed on behind.

Henry spurred his pony on and caught up with Carver:

"Well, this is better than just hunting – what say you Mr Carver?"

"Well Lootenant, jest pickin' the corn don't make any biscuits…"

"Granmaw?" said Henry.

"Yup," said Carver.

Henry looked puzzled;

"What does it mean?"

"No idea – Granmaw was kinda lackin' in the makin'-any-sense department."

Henry snorted with laughter and Carver chuckled at his own admittance. They rode on through the war party, still laughing.

The Cheyenne now rode up a long but shallow escarpment that Willow had just crested in front of them; she had disappeared from view and Smoke was nervous. He was even more nervous when he heard the shots beyond the ridge. He halted the war party and spoke to Broken Knife.

Henry and Carver both heard the shots:

"What d'ye think Mr Carver? An attack?"

Both men pulled out their rifles and warriors unslung their bows. Carver stroked his beard:

"Nah, too few shots Lootenant; too well-spaced – a signal maybe."

They were about to speak to Smoke on the Moon when a rider appeared on the distant ridgeline – it was Willow. She was carrying a rolled-up robe that she threw up in the air once.

"What does that mean, Mr Carver?" asked Henry.

"One dead," answered the wolf skinner.

---- o o o ----

Later in her life, Crow Dress Woman would often remember that Maheo had not been merciful to Mouse in her final hours – the Comanche arrow in the girl's side had punctured most of her vital organs but the relief of death to escape the pain had eluded her for a whole day.

Crow Dress Woman had tended to her young war sister as best she could to ease her way into the next life but she had seen animals with similar wounds before and they, like the young Cheyenne woman, had thrashed around for a long time before death eased the earthly pain:

"Lie easy, little sister," she'd said, giving Mouse sips of water from a horn spoon, then tightened up the canvas strip that she had bound around the girl's body to stop the blood flow.

Mouse, though in severe pain, had refused to cry out; she knew that death was close but she would face it like any Cheyenne warrior. White Rain knelt beside Mouse's head and stroked her hair:

"We beat off those Comanches, thanks to you little sister…"

"Did we get all their scalps?" croaked Mouse, ever the practical bloodletter.

"We did," replied White Rain "Two each."

"Tie mine to my rifle and give it to Willow…" instructed Mouse weakly, "…so I'm not forgotten."

"Stop ordering us around," smiled Crow Dress and smoothed Mouse's forehead with her fingers. The girl coughed up some blood, spitting it out of her mouth leaving red tendrils on her lips and chin. She arched her body as a spasm of pain took her but she clenched her teeth and said nothing.

White Rain and Crow Dress felt helpless; their war sister's agony was unsettling.

During one of Mouse's worst moments, she had tried to sit up and begged one of them to kill her – to use her rifle and put her out of her earthly misery. Both women had blanched at the thought but White Rain put it into words that Mouse, despite her pain, could understand:

"Hush sister. You will not die by the hand of a Cheyenne."

Mouse had fallen back, exhausted but understanding the mood of her sisters.

At that moment, there was a fluttering in the air above where Mouse lay. It could have been a breeze – the hair of White Rain and Crow Dress lifted in wisps and curled round their cheeks – but the breeze seemed to blow just in that one place. It was like a small, invisible twist of disturbed air that reached down to the wounded woman warrior. Mouse's hair blew out too; she knew what it was:

"It is the *Maheyuno* - they are here!" she gasped as she reached out into the air above her.

White Rain looked at Crow Dress calmly:

"Yellow Bear told me that no-one got to see the Maheyuno except at special times."

"Well," said Crow Dress "this *is* a special time. Maheo has sent his helpers to collect our little sister – and not before time either."

White Rain was slightly shocked at Crow Dress's criticism of the Life Giver but she too was anxious that Mouse should suffer no more. They lay down on either side of wounded girl and held her in their arms, wrapping her shivering body and giving their warmth to her.

They felt her chest heave and listened to her crackling breath struggle to leave her mouth.

After a while, both women realised that Mouse's breathing, whilst ragged and signalling her end of life, was rhythmic and had meaning. Though it was probably the wrong time, they grinned at one another; the indomitable girl was singing her death song.

Don't let me lie
In the cold lands
Where my heart
Will never rest...

Then the croaking rhythm tailed off and they felt her heart flutter for the last time. Unshackled from earthly cares and free from bodily pain, her spirit took flight. Mouse, the small but fierce Suhtai warrior had sung her last song.

Tears streamed down the cheeks of Crow Dress and White Rain as grief overtook them. White Rain, though wracked with the depth of the loss, recovered first and cupped Mouse's pale face in her hands and looked into the brown, unseeing eyes:

"Farewell, dear Panther," she said.

Both women took out their hunting knives and hacked their hair short and gashed their arms and legs; they fashioned a travois from branches and tied it to Mouse's pony, covering their friend's body with a robe. They sang a warriors' song of mourning as they rode north.

---- o o o ----

Chapter Sixty Five

Long Shadow was surprised when, out of the darkness, a firm hand clamped over his mouth. He had thought that the silencing hand belonged to one of his Comanche brothers – maybe moving between positions and not wanting to alarm him – and so hadn't struggled and merely waited for the hand's owner to identify himself.

There was no further identification for Long Shadow; immediately after the hand came the sharp, life-ending blow of an iron point into the back of his skull. The Comanche's shriek of pain was muffled into an anonymous grunt as he slid to the ground, his bow clattering on the surface of the hard rock mesa.

See the Dark knelt in the blackness, his hand still pressed against the Comanche's mouth; he didn't want to release him in case the man was not yet dead. Soon though, perhaps two or three heartbeats later, came the familiar rasp of death as the last air escaped between Dark's fingers and he let the head fall. Now he knelt in silence – listening for other Comanches in the deep darkness. It wasn't long in coming.

"Brother?" came an urgent whisper off to Dark's left; he couldn't understand the word of course, but the Comanche breaking the silence had revealed the direction and distance of Dark's next target.

Dark moved towards the sound, grinning as he did so; he remembered that Viajero had always said that whites and Mexicans constantly talked during battles and that had always got them killed; he had thought that the fierce Comanches might be better than that.

The Apache was forever boasting about the discipline of silence that his N'De people observed when pursuing enemies. Dark had argued that he would prefer his enemies to know that they were being hunted by the mighty Cheyenne and, on some occasions, a war song or two would be the right thing to do.

Still, on this occasion, the wise Apache was right and See the Dark took extreme care with each foot fall – toes probing for a hard, unyielding surface before his full body weight was placed onto it. He also controlled his breathing, drawing and expelling breath silently through his nose as he felt his way round a rock buttress towards his prey. Like many other warriors had told him when he was younger, his heart was pounding so fiercely that it would seem that the enemy could actually hear it. He crept forward slowly, occasionally stopping to listen to new sounds.

"Brother? Did you drop your bow?"

Dark had been padding forward again but stopped at the whispered sentence - the words coming from just two or three paces in front of him; he couldn't be sure but the Comanche seemed to be facing away from him as the words seemed to float away into the night air.

He knelt down again and looked up – trying to silhouette the warrior against the sky and work out an angle of attack. But it was no use – he couldn't see him against the cloudy, moonless expanse – the Comanche could also be kneeling or lying down. There would be no gagging hand or silent death this time even though the Comanche was obviously close by and still seemed unaware of his presence. Dark couldn't risk his attack failing at this stage so he silently unslung his rifle and calmly shot at where the words had come from.

The explosion of the shot echoed from rock butte to shallow canyon rims and rattled off mesa walls. It was followed by Dark's war shout and an outcry from the Comanches who, still wary of the guns, nonetheless moved towards the sound of their enemies.

The wounded man screeched in pain as the random bullet tore into his lungs and burst out of his armpit; gurgling and spitting his own blood he lay on his back and sang his death song. The Comanches homed in on the chanting – even as he lay dying their friend was calling them to him, signalling where he was – there was a scuttling and scraping over loose shale as they moved closer.

Dark knew that the high-pitched chanting was giving away his position and his first thought was to finish the wounded man off but, in a moment of maturity that Viajero would have admired, he let the dying warrior sing on. He reasoned that more Comanches would come and he could kill them too, even if he still couldn't see anyone in the blackness. Dark moved back around the rock buttress, re-cocked his rifle and waited.

A black cloud moved away from the moon, exposing a silver rim that threw some light downwards; Dark could now see the wounded man with two others round him; the wounded man was pointing to where he thought Dark was, though he was actually pointing in the wrong direction. From the cover of his rock, Dark waited until one Comanche seemed to be standing in front of the other then fired again.

Bad Elk had always told him that trying to hit two men with one bullet is always a risky tactic but it seemed to work, especially at this close range; one man went down quickly with a hole in his side and the other jerked upwards and sat down in a heap, his back against a rock face. He probably wasn't dead but he was down.

The first dying warrior now screeched a warning to the others and they answered in kind – an ululating wail now echoed among the rocks, as the advancing Comanches, able to see in the shafts of moonlight, moved more confidently and called each other onto the target.

Dark peered out from behind his rock column; none of the men he had hit with gunfire was the yellow man. The first man he had tomahawked *could* have been him but it had been too dark to see anything then and the young Cheyenne couldn't now see the dead man from his new position.

He was pondering his next move when he sensed that something - a threat - had moved closer to him.

It was the smell came to him first and so he sniffed. Dark was always attuned to different smells – he remembered the rank smell of the soldiers when he had been caught by the Army column; a white man's scent that was a mixture of urine, tobacco, leather and horses. Now came this different scent – it was the smell of a man who lived in wild places, whose sweat contained traces of his poor diet and devotion to horses. It was the smell of a Comanche - and it came from behind him.

Dark whirled around, bringing up his rifle with his right hand and steadying himself against the rock with his left. There in the broadening moonlight, sharpened teeth bared in a snarl of hate, was the yellow man.

Medicine Wolf had leapt forward at the young Cheyenne thief, his war cry echoing between the rocks. He was about to tomahawk him when the boy's rifle fired.

The spirit tracker-turned-war chief was stopped in mid-air by the shots. The Puhakut was dead before he hit the rock floor. The other Comanches heard Medicine Wolf's cry of pain and paused.

Dark shook his hand free of the faulty rifle; the force of the three chambers exploding at once had jarred his wrist but at least he had been sure of killing the Comanche chief whose chest now leaked blood from three holes. He was yelling his victory song when Viajero slipped round the pinnacle and found him.

"You are lucky little brother, the Comanches have fled back to the base of the slope."

"Good…" said Dark as he knelt down beside the dead Comanche. The moon rose brighter and higher and they could see the Comanche down in the floor of the rimrock, tightening the cinches on the saddles of their ponies.

At the base of the mesa slope, the remaining Nokoni warriors looked round as a soft, repetitive thud came towards them, the sounds getting louder and louder.

The men were fretful and spooked; they were anxious to go home, no-one wanted to investigate; Half Moon Face was not yet mounted but he went towards the sound. His pony reared up suddenly and he had to grip the bridle tightly to stop it running off. Then he saw the reason for his horse's panic – there, lying on the grey rock, resting against a greasewood plant and silvered by moonlight was the head of Medicine Wolf.

An owl glided by on silent wings and a horned lizard scuttled out from the base of the shrub, disturbed by the bloody intrusion; Half Moon Face gritted his teeth and mounted up. Medicine Wolf would track no more ghosts.

---- o o o ----

Chapter Sixty Six

Carver strolled down to the river and cracked the surface ice until he could dip a tin mug into the sluggish flow beneath. He sipped a little, shuddering as the cold spike of liquid went down his gullet. Then, turning to the steaming basin of heated water by his side, he poured in a little from the cup to cool it down.

Squatting on his haunches, he dipped his shaving brush into the hot water, scraped it around the remnants of the soap tin and lathered his face. Soap was a luxury for Carver but Armstrong had given the remnants to him; the Englishman was getting used to his own red beard and had stopped shaving, not least as the unusual colour attracted some female admirers in the Cheyenne camp.

The wolf skinner had no mirror but he'd chosen a spot beside a still pool where he could lean over and see what he was doing. As he pushed the suds into the thick black hair, he heard the rattle of footfall on rocks behind him:

"What are you doing? "said New Grass.

"Getting rid of the hair from my face, like you asked," he said.

"Thank you," she said "It burned my face when you rubbed it on me."

Carver opened his folding razor and tested the edge of the blade. He had never owned a razor before coming west with the Englishman – he'd previously avoided shaving until he'd hit town with enough money to afford a barber. The edge was still sharp but spots of rust were appearing on the metal, he'd have to take better care of it. He took a look at his reflection in the river, then carefully angled the blade against his skin and drew it downwards over his beard:

"Did the young woman warrior have a proper funeral?" he asked.

"Yes," said New Grass, "Her name was Mouse – she was very brave..."

Carver nodded thoughtfully. In all his dealings with the Cheyenne, past or present, the presence of an all-woman warrior society was new to him.

He and Henry were keeping away from the Cheyenne mourning time for Mouse; it would have seemed intrusive and disrespectful if they had been there. Earlier that day, the Englishman had set out with his rifle on a hunt that would keep him out of the village for a while. Neither man had met the young woman but, from New Grass's tales about her, both men wished they had.

"...I'm happy for her that she now rests in our own country. She will be long remembered for bringing those guns back to our people."

New Grass and her sister Sweet Water had ridden out to see the cottonwood funeral scaffold standing on a lone hill overlooking the great grasslands. Mouse's share of the ponies had, in keeping with Cheyenne custom, been killed alongside her and she had been wrapped in her bear robe with her weapons – except for her rifle that had been her legacy to Willow - held close to her heart.

Both New Grass and Sweet Water were impressed with the attention and recognition that the Forked Lightning Women had brought to the camp. The war trail could be a noble calling, perhaps better than marriage.

Carver finished shaving and stood up to let New Grass see the result. The young woman walked over and ran her fingers down his jawline:

"That's better, husband," she said, smiling. She walked back towards her mother's lodge but turned around and said:

"Oh, did you hear the good news today?"

Carver, wiping his face with a dirty piece of sheeting, looked up:

"No. What was the news?"

"The son of Smoke on the Moon and his war brother are back with us. They too escaped the Comanche and have great tales to tell."

"Good," said Carver, genuinely pleased for the leader of the Striking Snakes; he knew that Smoke had been worried about his son's safety when he and Henry had joined the war party on the trail south.

"Tell me, were these men not part of Smoke's soldier group?"

"Oh no," said New Grass, "His son – See the Dark – has never been a member of the Striking Snakes because he lost an eye when he was young. And his friend could never be; he's not even Cheyenne."

"What is the name of the friend and to what people does he belong?" asked Carver, suddenly bitten by suspicion.

New Grass looked nonplussed:

"I don't know his real name but we call him The Traveller – he calls his people the N'De."

Carver stood open-mouthed - a one-eyed youth and an Apache?

A small worm of fear squirmed in his heart.

---- o o o ----

Chapter Sixty Seven

"Veho!"

Carver looked round and stared into the face of the stone-eyed youth. The young Cheyenne looked much the same as when he had questioned him on the way to the Arkansas – a bit leaner maybe, but the black slash of the obsidian globe in his head made Carver shiver. Now the young man was on his own turf – not tied up and sitting on the ground - he looked like a true killer.

His worst fears had come true – now they would be found out and killed. Carver's brain whirred in confusion and the blood pounded in his ears…

Badlands Walking Woman had been overjoyed to see her son return safely but had lost no time in alerting him to her suspicions about the white men in camp. Dark had yawned and remembered what his father had said:

"Mother, the vehoe in our camp saved your life and that of Flea – you should be more grateful."

"Yes, yes," she said, irritated by her son's lack of interest, "…but the fair-haired one has the Traveller's rifle and the dark one spoke of the Traveller's father…"

Dark snorted in exasperation:

"I've told you this before – we only met two white men up close when we were captured – even then it was at night and we weren't in their camp for long. The young soldier chief who took the Traveller's rifle was killed when we escaped and the other one was very hairy and smelled bad..."

Badlands gritted her teeth and was about to explode when Dark said:

"…and I've just seen the dark one walking round in camp – he is nothing like the man we spoke to."

Dark though, like his father, recognised the danger signals when his mother was pushed too far so, trying to lessen the tension, added:

"I'll go and see him up close and be sure."

See the Dark had waited until the next morning to find and talk to the white men. He walked across to the tent the vehoe shared, now just outside the centre of the lodge circle, closer to the tipi of New Grass's mother. The fair haired one was not around but the other one was walking back from the pony herd when Dark called out to him.

…The wolf-skinner's survival instinct kicked in and he assessed his odds of success in a fight with the young Cheyenne. His chances weren't good - his rifle was twenty paces away, lying beside the tent wall as was his pistol. All he had was a skinning knife in his belt and a cup of coffee in his hand. Even if he had managed to best the Indian, the Englishman still wasn't back from hunting - even urgent self-preservation wouldn't let him desert Armstrong - and attacking the youth would have got him killed before he'd cleared the village…

Though only a heartbeat later, Carver's fevered mind registered that the Cheyenne youth was smiling:

"Thank you for saving my family…" the young man said and put his hands, palms down, on Carver's shoulders, patting them in a comradely way.

Carver gulped in relief and remembered to smile back:

"It was a pleasure to be of service to the Suhtai people."

"You speak good Cheyenne," said Dark, remembering the poor version that the veho in the soldier column had spoken.

"Well, I am married to a Suhtai woman now, so I still learn every day."

Dark smiled at the smooth faced man – he seemed much younger than the one in the soldier column and smelled much better:

"Perhaps we can hunt together soon?" said Dark

"Yes," said Carver, lost for the next move. Feeling ungainly carrying the coffee cup, he clasped Dark's upper arm in friendship with his free hand and walked unsteadily towards his tent.

Still shaking, he sat down and sipped his coffee, staring into the rippling black pool inside his cup to gather his thoughts. Why hadn't the boy betrayed him to the Suhtai; why hadn't he yelled out that the veho in the camp had been part of the Army column that had held him captive?

When the image of himself steadied inside the coffee mug, his face creased into a broad smile as the answer dawned – the boy simply hadn't recognised him. He had been bearded when they had met last; shaving had saved his life.

---- o o o ----

Henry Armstrong remained calm as he rode back into camp and saw the Apache sitting at the campfire outside the tent, chatting to Carver. The Apache was in Cheyenne clothing but Henry recognised him immediately:

"No time to warn ye, Lootentant," the wolf-skinner said evenly, trying to make it sound like a greeting, as Henry took the haunches of elk from his saddle.

"That's fine Mr Carver – this was always a possibility, however remote. Have you seen the boy as well?"

"Yep, he didn't recognise me without my beard and with you lookin' like a Missouri hog farmer, maybe we'll git away with it."

"Hmmm…" said Henry doubtfully, rubbing his beard as he walked across to the fire and sat down:

"Greetings friend," he said to Viajero in Cheyenne, "Will you eat?" He motioned to the stew in the cookpot.

The Apache shook his head, surprised that another white man could speak the tongue of the Tsis-tsis-tas, even if his efforts were as bad as his own:

"No. I'm here because the wife of Smoke on the Moon has said some disturbing things."

"What were they?" said Henry. Badlands Walking Woman had never openly accused them of anything while they had been with the Suhtai but they sensed her strong distrust of them both.

"She says that you know the name of my father. No-one in camp knew it but you, as strangers, said it to her when you first met."

Henry shrugged:

"What is the name of your father?" he asked.

"It *was* Makes the Rivers Red; he is dead now."

Henry paused for only a heartbeat and nodded sagely:

"It is true, we have heard of that name. We heard it from soldiers up north in the fort. We passed through to get supplies before we came to visit the Cheyenne..."

Viajero nodded – it was possible, he supposed. Indaa soldiers would be much like any other – exchanging stories about their war deeds with others.

"…the soldier we heard it from may have met your father."

"Any white man who met my father wouldn't be alive now," said Viajero.

"Ah…" said Henry, his mind churning as he thought of ways to distract the Apache:

"…I don't know why the wife of Smoke on the Moon would worry that white men knew your father's name. Was your father a great warrior? If he fought against the whites then they would know and fear his name."

Viajero nodded and stared at the indaa; in truth, he couldn't tell if either one had been in the Army column when he had been captured – it had been dark and all white men looked alike to him. They *seemed* familiar but he couldn't be sure. The red bearded one seemed too well-fed and muscular for the skinny soldier chief that he remembered and the dark-haired one now smelled better and was dressed differently. He hadn't seen the young veho chief lying with Smoke's arrow in him but Dark had – this couldn't be the same man. Time had passed since his capture by the soldiers and he had largely dismissed the incident from his mind – he and See the Dark had escaped with their lives and that was sufficient. He shifted uncomfortably on the ground but put his final point:

"My war brother and I were captured some time ago by an Army column – a young white soldier chief took my rifle. We both escaped but I had to leave the gun behind. That…" he said, pointing at Henry's carbine, "…looks like it."

Henry breathed out to calm himself but Carver now pitched in:

"It can't be your gun – I bought that for him from a white trader many days ride from here."

Henry nodded in assent then, with a silent prayer about the quality of gunsmithing in Independence, handed the rifle to the Apache for him to inspect.

Viajero handled the weapon, hefting it in his hands. It seemed the same but many white guns were alike; even the new one he had captured from the Mexicans looked and felt the same as his old one. This one was clean, polished wood with a lighter tint to it – though it had caked mud on it where the indaa had obviously held it in wet hands.

He examined where his horned lizard sign would have been but the holes where he had driven the nails seemed absent though some pock marks on the wood, now polished over, *could* have been them. Turning the rifle upside down he looked at the iron butt plate; he had scratched this on rocks during various hunting trips and actions with the rifle. The plate was now smooth metal though the indaa had marked it with some sort of tribal sign. He pointed out the marking and handed it back:

"What is this marking?"

Henry scraped the mud out of the stamped lettering 'HLA' that marked his initials:

"It is my name."

"Does your God allow you to tell me your name," asked the Apache politely. The indaa was a guest in camp and some tribes were unwilling to tell strangers their name – as were many bands of his own N'De people. It could be injurious to their spirit if their name was released; he would not press the indaa on it.

Henry digested the question – he certainly wouldn't be telling the Apache his surname; he remembered Carver's botched job of translating it into sign language.

"My name is Henry," he said.

"Hen-ree, Hen-ree," said Viajero, nodding, rolling the words in his mouth as though tasting to see if water was fresh.

He was just being polite – indaa names meant nothing to him, the words of their names had no power. Once he had conversed with a wounded white man in broken Spanish and Viajero had asked him his name. The indaa had told him – though he now couldn't now recall what it was. Viajero had then asked him what his name had meant – the white man had looked blank and said: 'It doesn't mean anything.' Viajero had shaken his head in disbelief – what was the point of a name with no meaning or power? So, he'd killed the man and stolen his mules.

Henry watched the mature warrior closely - the Apache seemed more relaxed; he hoped that this was a good sign.

"Well?" said Henry, clutching the carbine.

"The woman was wrong – that is not my rifle."

---- 0 0 0 ----

Chapter Sixty Eight

Bad Elk watched as Burnt Hair put the finishing touches to their lodge in the village circle. He was happy with the new campsite – an area of good pasture and, though a light fall of snow that morning had covered the shorter grass, it would still sustain the growing pony herd; the lodges were protected from the wind by hills to the west and north and, at ground level, by a good stand of timber. Water was close by in a fast-flowing stream that hadn't yet iced up and the late year buffalo hunt had given a supply of food that would, at least, take the Suhtai through until the snow broke.

Sitting on a bear robe and leaning against his wooden backrest, the chief sighed contentedly and puffed on his pipe as Burnt Hair drove the last of the tipi pins into the hardening ground:

"Wife! Make sure those are secure – I don't want any cold air blowing in…"

Burnt Hair looked up quickly, rock in hand, and a hard look on her face:

"If my strong and brave husband can do any better, then let him come and do so!"

Bad Elk was taken aback – he was only trying to help. Yellow Bear had heard the exchange and walked over to his chief:

"This talking back to menfolk is getting to be commonplace in the camp – some men have sought me out to make potions to keep the women quiet."

"Did they work?" asked Bad Elk as the spirit diviner sat down next to him.

"Too early to tell," said Yellow Bear cautiously.

The two men sat together and watched as Burnt Hair dragged two heavy parfleches through the tipi door and inside the lodge. The rawhide containers were elaborately decorated with quillwork and paint and Bad Elk recognised the one that contained the cooking pots:

"Will there be food soon?" he shouted to his wife. In reply, an iron trade pot came flying out of the lodge entrance, clanging as it hit the ground.

"Perhaps not…" he muttered under his breath.

Yellow Bear looked at him:

"This is the fault of those women…"

---- o o o ----

White Rain and the others could now relax; they had supervised Mouse's funeral and led the mourning for their dead war sister – now the girl rested on a faraway hill for eternity and they could do no more. They would not even think of celebrating their many successes until Bad Elk had found a new camping ground; boasting and feasting would not have been a worthy accompaniment to Mouse's burial.

The Forked Lightning Women now sat in their original warriors' lodge and smiled at the newcomers who sat around their fire:

"Welcome sisters," said White Rain. She held up an arrow so all could see it:

"Usually – when the earth is warmer – we stab this into the ground and each sister can only speak when they touch the arrow. But these days, the ground is too hard…"

The others smiled and nodded – the Tree Popping Moon would soon be here and the earth would harden even more.

"For now, if you want to speak - take the arrow and we will all listen."

Sweet Water and two younger women – Blue Wing and Looks Above – murmured their approval; discipline on when to speak would be a good thing.

White Rain leaned across Crow Dress and gave the arrow to Sweet Water:

"Sister, you are the eldest of our new friends – tell us what you have to say."

Sweet Water handled the arrow cautiously, undecided whether to put it on the ground in front of her or just hold it; eventually she held the shaft with both hands and spoke:

"I tried to join your warrior society before – when our People were going to ride against the Pawnee some winters ago…"

White Rain nodded but stayed silent; Sweet Water had been arrogant and gossipy then – Mouse hadn't liked her.

"…back then though I was young and callow – I spoke out of turn too often and was untrustworthy. I have changed now." Sweet Water's eyes shone with a liquid film – she was close to tears:

"My husband is gone – probably killed by the Crow and I don't want to marry again – not soon anyway."

Willow nodded in sympathy – no-one had heard from Feathers on His Shield since he had gone after the buffalo, moons ago. She urged Sweet Water to continue. The girl nodded and spoke again:

"I think I am now a better person and ready for the war trail – if the Forked Lightning Women will have me?"

Taking the arrow, White Rain said:

"Sister, you are brave to admit all that. It shows a mature spirit. We have no tests of acceptance as Forked Lightning Women. Men train from boyhood to be warriors. But we women don't. We must fight well immediately, so our guns will make that difference. All we expect is that you bring your own pony."

Sweet Water nodded; her husband had left his horses in the herd when he disappeared. Looks Above and Blue Wing nodded too – they had a pony each. Looks Above had a twinge of anxiety as she realised that riding high and slow on a horse laden with parfleches when the village moved would be different to charging into battle on a stripped-down war horse. She hoped there would be time to practise.

Crow Dress took the arrow from her and pointed it at the other two women:

"And you two – do you wish to become warriors too?"

The younger ones nodded but stayed quiet – Blue Wing wanted to speak but didn't have the confidence to reach for the arrow yet. Instead she sang her own song, rocking her head back and forth as she sat in the firelight. She started in a soft voice then got louder as her confidence grew and no-one silenced her:

Fear the blue flash
In the sunlight
My feathers
Are tipped with iron

Blue Wing looked up to see that the three older women warriors had burst into tears – she reminded them of Mouse.

---- 0 0 0 ----

"That was a good feast," said Yellow Bear belching slightly as he, Smoke and Bad Elk lay against their backrests around the dying cookfire; all three men smoked their pipes and nodded companionably. After a pause, Smoke said:

"The Forked Lightning Women have been wise in sharing out their guns and bullets with the Striking Snakes and Thunder Bears – we can defeat any enemies now."

Yellow Bear, always suspicious of the women's motives, said:

"Perhaps. They have earned their war honours, of course, but giving away their wealth in guns will come at a price."

"What price?" asked Bad Elk.

"They'll want to be recognised as warriors – not just in the occasional fight, but forever - as a true part of the fighting power of our People."

"Well..." said Bad Elk "...they've earned it. They did whip those Comanches..." He paused; then, in embarrassment, added:

"...with the help of my nephew and the Traveller, of course!"

Smoke laughed and patted his brother on the arm.

There was an uncomfortable silence – change was happening in their small band and people dealt with it in their own ways. For some it was too fast and would never be acceptable – they wished to return to the old ways – no women warriors and no whites in camp. Smoke threw a bough onto the fire and it crackled back into life – he decided to change the topic:

"Kah-vuh tells me that the fair haired veho will leave us in the spring – I'll be sad to see him go. He has been a good friend to the Tsis-tsis-tas."

"That is true," said Yellow Bear "Hen-ree has appeared in my dreams recently…"

At the sound of the young veho's name, both Smoke and Bad Elk looked impressed; their spirit diviner could speak the white man's tongue!

"Does his name mean anything?" asked Bad Elk anxious to collect any facts about the young man before he parted trail with the Suhtai and headed towards his own country.

"I did ask him that," mused Yellow Bear, slightly irritated that he hadn't been allowed to explain his dreams. "He said his name was the same as some of their great chieftains and warriors from the olden times."

Smoke and Bad Elk nodded wisely – that would make sense, Hen-ree himself was a fearless warrior. He had saved Smoke's family in the fight with the Crow, had ridden south with the war party when it could have meant battle with the Comanche and, with Kah-vuh, had helped feed the people during the year.

"In my dreams," continued Yellow Bear, "Hen-ree got further away from the village but stayed facing me, even as he disappeared over a far hill."

"What does that mean?" asked Bad Elk.

Yellow Bear dashed the ashes from his pipe bowl:

"It means he'll come back."

---- o o o ----

Chapter Sixty Nine

Sweet Water smiled at the song; Hen-ree had a good voice though she didn't know what he was singing about. When he had stopped, she said:

"Where is Kah-vuh?"

Henry took a sip of water from a wooden bowl; *'What shall we do with a drunken sailor'* always made Sweet Water clap her hands and laugh:

"He's with his wife; they've ridden out to look for lodgepoles with See the Dark and White Rain. Both will be building lodges when the snow breaks."

She nodded sagely:

"Those lodges will only be for short time; they won't get the proper skins until the buffalo are fatter – later in the year."

"Yes, Mr Carver - er, Kah-vuh - told me. They need the skins of three-year cows – and a lot of them, too."

"Well, they both have guns and will manage it well." The Cheyenne woman stopped and stared at Henry with her unsettling brown eyes; she was very pretty and smelled of pine cones. She had seen him sitting alone at his tent and asked him to eat at her lodge and sing to her and Henry, laden with guilt, had followed her. Several older folk saw them go inside and tutted their disapproval.

"My husband killed all the buffalo for this lodge – he was a very good hunter…" she said, waving her hands above her head to show the well-stitched skins.

Henry shifted uncomfortably on the floor of Sweet Water's lodge and remembered scraping at the hardening ground with a flat rock to bury Feathers on His Shield; it had taken a long time. He nodded as if in condolence.

"Kah-vuh says you will leave us soon, when the snow breaks."

"Yes," said Henry, "I will go back to my own country and see if my parents are still alive."

The young woman nodded:

"Where is your country?" she said.

Henry grinned, mainly at the difficulty of explaining to a woman who'd never seen or heard of an ocean, where England was:

"I live many moons travel to the east – across land then across a great lake…"

"How will you get across the lake," she interrupted; "Can you build a boat?"

She knew it took great skill to build a boat; the Cheyenne and Lakota did it sometimes to cross flooded rivers. Hides of buffalo bulls were required and shaped by wooden boughs; they floated, but only just.

"Other men have built the boat; I pay them to travel in it."

He watched her face as she absorbed these facts; Sweet Water was not unintelligent and seemed genuinely interested in him; he hoped she was. He hadn't lain with a woman since he came west and, up to now, had been too absorbed in his new life to let it worry him. He'd left the whoring to Carver in Independence and, now that the wolf skinner was married, suddenly felt left out and, sometimes, alone.

"Will the buffalo skins on the boat hold out to take you to the other side?" she asked.

Henry looked baffled by her question, then understood:

"Our boats are made of iron," he said laughing.

Now it was her turn to laugh. She hooted in disbelief:

"Iron sinks, you will drown!"

Henry threw up his hands in mock defeat; he knew he could never explain the mathematics and science behind ships' tonnages and water displacement to this young woman, even if she'd spoken English – mainly because he had no idea himself:

"Let's just say, we vehoe have magic that will make it float."

"Then I hope your magic works; I don't want you drowning," she said, moving closer to him and putting her hand over his.

---- 0 0 0 ----

Chapter Seventy

Henry saddled his tall, grey horse and strung a flat food pouch over the cantle. The snow had ceased several days before but he had lingered with Sweet Water, suddenly wishing that he could ignore the call of the trail home. She was round the other side of the horse, adjusting the cinch and tying the rawhide strings around his rolled-up bear robe. She stood on tiptoe to reach.

"Did you tell our chief that you were leaving?" she said, her eyes and forehead appearing over the saddle seat.

"Yes - and Smoke on the Moon and Yellow Bear too."

All three men had received the news gravely and asked him questions about when he would get home and how he would travel. Henry had answered in much the same way as he'd done to Sweet Water, though hadn't mentioned any iron boats.

Sweet Water pulled and tested the saddle's seat on the grey's back and walked around to the other side. Henry held her close, cupping her face in his hands and rested their foreheads together. Neither of them spoke – nothing about the future was certain and their intimacy too recent to have any firm foundations.

Sweet Water was stoic and kept back the tears; Henry was determined to do the same. He breathed her in for the final time and swung into the saddle. He was about to swing the horse's head to the east when he heard the noise.

It was hard to pick out at first, just a low but insistent murmur; it was coming from the far side of the encampment. Henry stood up in his stirrups and looked – there, walking through the lodges like a human tide towards him, was the entire Suhtai people. Ahead on ponies, Carver, See the Dark and Viajero, led the chanting:

"Hen-ree, Hen-ree!"

Henry looked down at Sweet Water, who now held onto the reins of his horse:

"What is this?" he said.

"The People want to say goodbye," she said, smiling.

Carver trotted up, followed closely by Dark and the Traveller. They stayed mounted, nodding companionably at Henry.

As the throng surrounded the horses, a figure pushed rudely through the crowd – it was Badlands Walking Woman. She hoisted a small deerskin sack of food up to the pommel on Henry's saddle and patted him affectionately on the back of his hand. Henry looked at Carver questioningly; the wolf skinner shrugged:

"Just accept it for what it is, Lootenant."

Bad Elk now spoke, his loud voice carrying over those who were engaged in their own chatter. He spoke of Henry's courage and generosity, his prowess with a rifle and…

"That's enough…" said Burnt Hair rudely silencing her husband; "…he'll die of old age before he leaves the village." She smiled sweetly at Henry who laughed out loud.

Smoke on the Moon and Yellow Bear also said their public farewells; Henry merely bowed his head at the praise. Yellow Bear, ever practical as well as spiritual, gave Henry a small skin pouch on a sinew thread to hang round his neck:

"This is your medicine bundle. It is empty now but no man can know what other men carry – when you decide what your medicine is – fill the bundle and carry it always."

Henry thanked him, overwhelmed by the significance of such a gift from the spirit diviner.

Finally, See the Dark, impatient as ever to address a crowd, pushed his pony towards Henry's. From his Mexican saddle bucket, he pulled out one of the new Sharps carbines, captured from the Comanche and waved it in front of the crowd:

"This is my gift to Hen-ree for saving my family! It is from one warrior to another!"

"See!" said Dark "Our tribal signs from all his friends in the Suhtai band are on the wooden part…"

He twirled the gun round so that his kinfolk could see the signs of Smoke, See the Dark, Bad Elk and even Viajero, etched in black on the red wood. Dark also handed over a generous supply of ammunition for the carbine.

"Hen-ree is now one of the Medicine Arrow people - one of us! He will always be welcome here."

The Cheyenne yelled their approval. Tears hit Henry's eyes for the first time and he was speechless; he looked round for Sweet Water and spotted her, standing off to one side alongside the Forked Lightning Women. Catching her eye, he nodded in understanding; her plans for the future were set. He put the rifle across his pommel and shook Dark by the hand, though the young man seemed confused by the gesture.

Viajero now kicked his pony's flanks to move forward until he and Henry were knee to knee. There would be no public speech from the Apache, just a handshake and a curt nod from the dark-skinned warrior.

Gathering his thoughts, Henry spoke at last:

"People of the Suhtai! It was a lucky trail that led me and Kah-vuh to your camp. I carry pictures of you on my white leaves to show my own father and mother. But the most important picture that I have is in my heart – there the memory of you all will never fade. I bid you farewell."

With many affectionate slaps on his legs, Henry eased his horse out of the crush of excited bodies and trotted off down the trail.

He was surprised to hear hooves behind him as Carver caught up and rode alongside. Henry reined in and Carver reached across to shake his hand:

"Henry, I'm proud we rode together." he said and grimaced at his first use of the Englishman's Christian name.

"Me too – Pythagoras," said Henry laughing.

"That don't sound right, Lootenant!"

"No sir, it doesn't" said Henry; then, remembering something, pulled out his old Sharps carbine from his own saddle bucket:

"I've got two of these now. You take this old one and put that long rifle of yours in a museum where it belongs."

Carver thanked him and held the carbine butt first on his thigh.

The wolf skinner and the English officer looked at each other for a few seconds – no words were needed. Then Henry Armstrong, late of Her Majesty's Light Dragoons and the United States First Regiment of Cavalry swung his horse out onto the beckoning Plains.

---- 0 0 0 ----

Printed in Great Britain
by Amazon